ALL
ADULTS
HERE

ALL ADULTS HERE

Emma Straub

RANDOM HOUSE
LARGE PRINT

Copyright © 2020 by Emma Straub

All rights reserved.

Published in the United States of America by Random House Large Print in association with Riverhead Books, an imprint of Penguin Random House LLC.

"No One's Easy to Love" written by Sharon Van Etten.

Excerpt from EVERY TIME THE SUN COMES UP
Written by Sharon Van Etten
© 2014 Big Deal Beats (BMI), Paperweight Music (BMI)
All rights on behalf of Big Deal Beats and Paperweight
Music administered by Words & Music,
a division of Big Deal Music Group.
All Rights Reserved. Used by Permission.
International Copyright Secured.

The author gratefully acknowledges permission to quote lyrics from "You Love to Fail" written by Stephin Merritt. Published by Gay and Loud Music. Lyrics reprinted with permission of Stephin Merritt.

Cover art: Tatjana Prenzel

The Library of Congress has established a
Cataloging-in-Publication record for this title.

ISBN: 978-0-593-17180-6

www.penguinrandomhouse.com/large-print-format-books

FIRST LARGE PRINT EDITION

Printed in the United States of America

10 9 8 7 6 5 4 3

This Large Print edition published in accord with
the standards of the N.A.V.H.

For my parents, who did their best,
and for my children,
for whom I am doing mine

Every feeling you're showing
Is a boomerang you're throwing
—ABBA

———

No one's easy to love,
Don't look back, my dear, just say you tried
—Sharon Van Etten

———

You love to fail, that's all you love.
—The Magnetic Fields

Chapter 1

The Quick Death

Astrid Strick had never liked Barbara Baker, not for a single day of their forty-year acquaintance, but when Barbara was hit and killed by the empty, speeding school bus at the intersection of Main and Morrison streets on the eastern side of the town roundabout, Astrid knew that her life had changed, the shock of which was indistinguishable from relief. It was already a busy day—she'd spent the morning in the garden, she had a haircut appointment at 11:30, and then her granddaughter, Cecelia, was arriving by train with two suitcases and zero parents (no school bus accidents there—just a needed escape hatch), and Astrid was to meet her at the Clapham station to bring her back to the Big House.

The bus hit Barbara just after eleven. Astrid was sitting in her parked car on the inner lane of the roundabout, the verdant circle at the center of town, adjusting her hair in the mirror. It was always the way, wasn't it, that one's hair always looked best on the day of a scheduled trim. She didn't wash her hair at home unless they'd gone to the beach, or she had been swimming in chlorinated water, or some foreign substance (paint, glue) was accidentally lobbed in her direction. No, Birdie Gonzalez washed Astrid's hair every Monday and had done so for five years, before which it had been washed by Nancy, at the same salon, Shear Beauty, which was located on the southeastern side of the round-about, in the quarter circle between the Clapham Credit Union and Susan's Bookshop, kitty-corner from Spiro's Pancake House, if you peered through the open sides of the white wooden gazebo at the grassy island's center. The professional hair wash-ing was a relic from her mother's generation, and an affectation that her own mother had not pos-sessed, and yet, there it was. It was not a pricey indulgence, if weighed against the cost of proper conditioner. On every eighth Monday, Birdie also gave Astrid a trim. Nancy had given slightly better haircuts, but Birdie was better with the shampoo, and Astrid had never been vain, only practical. Anyway, Nancy had retired and Astrid hadn't missed her. Birdie was from Texas, and her parents were from Mexico, and Astrid thought of her as human sunshine: bright, warm, sometimes harsh, but always good for one's mood.

It was the end of the summer, which meant that soon, from Monday to Friday, Clapham would belong to the year-rounders again. Kids would go back to school, and the summer inhabitants would go back to being weekend inhabitants, and life would return to its quieter pace. Astrid inspected her skin for spots. Ticks and skin cancer were the twin fears of anyone who spent time outdoors in the Hudson Valley, certainly for those over the age of twenty-five. In the rearview mirror, Astrid watched Clapham go about its morning routines: Women with rolled-up yoga mats plodded slowly out of the municipal hall, well-off summer residents strolled the sidewalks, looking for something to buy that they had somehow missed during the last three months, locals sat drinking coffee at the counter at Spiro's and at Croissant City, where every sixty-five-year-old man in Clapham could be found with a newspaper at 7:30 A.M., seven days a week. Frank, who owned the hardware store, which sold everything from window fans and fresh eggs to batteries and a small collection of DVDs, was standing beneath his awning as his teenage son pulled up the iron gate. The small shops that sold T-shirts and sweatshirts that read CLAPHAM in large block letters didn't open until noon. The fanciest clothing store on Main Street, Boutique Etc?, whose name Astrid had always found both grammatically and philosophically irritating, opened at noon, too, which Astrid knew because she begrudgingly bought most of her clothing there.

Astrid let her eyes wander to the eyesore, the bête noire of every Clapham resident, both year-round and summer interloper—the unwieldy, trapezoidal building that had been empty for a year, the large space inside totally bare except for things abandoned by the most recent tenant: a ladder, two cans of paint, and three overstuffed garbage bags. There was a Sold sign in the window, with a telephone number, but the telephone number had long since been disconnected. The county records, which were available to anyone who cared to look—and Astrid had—said that the building had indeed been sold a year ago, but no one knew to whom, and whoever it was, they'd done nothing but let the dust bunnies proliferate. What went in was important: If it was some big-box store, or a national chain, it would be war. A death knell for the town as the residents knew it. When Rite Aid came in, not even to Clapham proper but to the outskirts of town, which did need a pharmacy, people lost their minds. Astrid still had a KEEP LOCAL, SHOP SMALL sign in the dirt next to her mailbox. She'd spent her own money making the signs and distributing them. And if that had been in the village itself? Astrid couldn't imagine. If the person who bought the building didn't know or didn't care, there would be riots in the street, and Astrid would carry the biggest pitchfork.

Because the storefront was on the eastern tip of the roundabout, the direction from which most cars entered Clapham, the large empty windows were what welcomed people to town, a very sorry state of affairs. At least Sal's Pizzeria, directly next door, was charming, with its red-and-white-tiled walls and its boxes printed with a portrait of its mustachioed proprietor.

Barbara was standing on the sidewalk, just beside the mailbox in front of Shear Beauty. Her car, a green Subaru hatchback with a "My Other Car Is a Cat" bumper sticker, was parked in front of the municipal building, which held the mayor's office, a co-op preschool, yoga classes, and the winter farmers' market, among other things. Was she getting back into her car after mailing a letter? Was she looking across the street, squinting at the Sold sign, as if it would offer any new information? Astrid would never know. She watched as Barbara stepped around the front bumper of her car and into the street, and then Astrid continued to watch as the yellow sixty-four-seat Clapham Junior High School bus came barreling down the street, knocking Barbara down as neatly and quietly as her grandsons' toy soldiers. Astrid snapped the visor closed and leapt out of the car. By the time she'd crossed the street, half a dozen people had already gathered. There was blood, but nothing gorier than a twelve-year-old could see on network television. Astrid had seen death up close before, but not like this, not on the street like a raccoon.

"It was empty," Randall said. He owned the gas station, which made him an easy authority on vehicles. "Except for the driver. No kids."

"Should I cover her up? I shouldn't cover her up, should I? Should I?" said Louise, who taught the yoga class, a rather dim, sweet girl who couldn't remember her lefts and rights.

"I've got the police," said a nervous-looking man, which was, of course, the right thing to do, even though the police station was two blocks away, and clearly there was nothing for the police to do, at least not for Barbara. "Hello," he said, into the phone, turning away, as if to shield the other bystanders from what was still on the pavement. "There's been an accident."

"Oh, for Chrissakes," Birdie said, coming out of her shop. She saw Astrid and pulled her aside. They clutched each other's elbows and stood there in silence until the police arrived, at which point Astrid offered Barbara's husband's phone number and address. She'd always kept an organized address book, and this was why, just in case. The EMTs scooped Barbara's body up and put her on the stretcher, an unflippable pancake. When the ambulance had gone, Birdie pushed Astrid gently toward the salon's door.

Shear Beauty had made some improvements over the years, some attempts at modernization. The mirrors were frameless, and the wallpaper was silver with a gray geometric pattern, all of it meant to make the place seem sophisticated, which it wasn't particularly. Birdie never could let go of the bowls of dusty potpourri in the bathroom or the embroidered pillows on the bench at the entrance. If someone wanted a fancier place, they were welcome to find one.

"I can't believe it," Astrid said. She set her purse down on the bench. The salon was empty, as it always was on Mondays, when Shear Beauty was closed to the public. "I can't believe it. I'm in shock, I'm definitely in shock. Listen to me! My brain is nonfunctional." She stopped. "Am I having an aneurysm?"

"You're not having an aneurysm. Those people just drop dead." Birdie gently guided Astrid by the elbow and sat her down at the sink. "Just try to relax." Birdie also cut hair at Heron Meadows, the assisted living facility on the edge of the Clapham border, and she had a certain sangfroid approach to the mortal coil. Everyone shuffled, in the end. Astrid sat and leaned back until her neck touched the cold porcelain of the sink. She closed her eyes and listened to Birdie turn on the warm water, testing its temperature against her hand.

If Randall was right and the bus had been empty—that was important. Astrid had three children and three grandchildren, and even if she hadn't, the loss of a child was the most acute tragedy, followed closely by a young parent, followed by cancer researchers, sitting presidents, movie stars, and everybody else. People their age—Astrid's and Barbara's—were too old for it to be outright tragedy, and seeing as Barbara had no children of her own, people were bound to call it a blessing, that is to say, a blessing that the school bus hadn't run down someone else. But that didn't seem fair to Barbara. She'd had a husband, and cats. She'd been a crossing guard at the elementary school decades earlier—oh, the irony! **At least it wasn't her corner**, Astrid thought, exhaling while Birdie scratched her scalp with her short nails.

What was Barbara thinking about, when the bus was careering toward her? Why had she parked there and not across the street? What was on her list to do that day? Astrid sat up, her hair dripping on her neck and her blouse.

"Are you all right?" Birdie asked, moving a towel onto Astrid's shoulders.

"No," Astrid said, "I don't think so. I didn't even—you know this—I didn't even like Barbara. I just feel a little, well, shaken."

"Well, in that case," Birdie said, walking around to the front of the chair, crouching down so that she and Astrid were at eye level, "let's go into the back." Birdie's mouth was a straight line, as steady as a Catholic schoolteacher. She always had a solution.

Astrid nodded slowly and offered Birdie her hand. They walked around the half wall behind the sink, into the room where an eyebrow-less young woman named Jessica waxed off other people's body hair three days a week, and lay down next to each other on the twin-size mattress, Astrid on her back and Birdie propped up on an elbow. Astrid closed her eyes, suddenly exhausted. As usual, because after so long, there was a certain rhythm and sequence to what would unfold, Birdie started softly kissing Astrid's cheeks and ears and neck, everything but her mouth, but today was different, and Astrid reached up and pulled Birdie's mouth straight to her own. There was no time to waste, not in this life. There were always more school buses—how many times did a person have to be reminded? This time, it was clear. She was a sixty-eight-year-old widow. Better late than never.

Chapter 2

Taxi TV

Cecelia sat between her parents in the back seat of a taxi that smelled like body odor soup. Amtrak required unaccompanied riders between the ages of thirteen and fifteen to jump through a series of hoops, one of which was being escorted onto the train by an adult. The arrangement was supposed to be fun, but Cecelia could call a spade a spade. She was thirteen and had access to the internet. It was witness protection, more or less. Her school hadn't expelled her, not officially. It was more an agreement to take a break, the way people's parents did on television, right before their inevitable divorce. It was something Cecelia had said almost in passing when she and her parents were talking about what to do, how to solve the problem with her school. It was a joke, really—**maybe I should just go move in with Gammy for the year**. But the next morning, her parents were sitting at the tiny kitchen table, eyes bloodshot, as if they hadn't moved since dinner the night before, and they said that they'd written to her school and spoken to Astrid and that, yes, that was the plan. Cecelia was hard-pressed to decide whom she was angriest at—her parents, for yanking her, or at her school, for letting her be yanked. It wasn't close to fair. In fact, it was the opposite of fair. It was a Sucky Situation, even if it meant moving from a small apartment to a huge house. Any perks were vastly outweighed by the crushing feeling of apocalyptic failure and profound injustice. But Cecelia had tried to explain everything already a thousand times, and this was still where she ended up, so the idea of justice didn't really matter anymore. It was done.

"The Big House is really best in the late summer, the whole valley, really." Cecelia's father, Nicholas Strick, Nicky Stricky, was the baby of his family, and had run away from his parents' house before his eighteenth birthday and returned only for holidays and special occasions that had been guilt-tripped for months in advance. He was not a reliable source. The taxi turned onto Flatbush Avenue and headed toward the Manhattan Bridge. Cecelia thought her father could be the most handsome father in the world if he shaved his beard or cut the short, messy ponytail that he usually wore at the nape of his neck, or bought clothes that weren't made for ranchers and cowboys. Instead her father always looked like someone who could be handsome if he wanted to be, but the beard and the clothes and the hair were effective deterrents.

"She really does have great taste, and she knows everybody," Juliette said. Cecelia's mom was French and knew about good taste, everyone said so. Juliette liked Astrid better than her husband did. She may have liked Astrid better than her husband, period. "There are big, clean public swimming pools, and you only ever have to wait because someone is slow, not because there are a hundred people ahead of you. Clapham is great, **chérie,** you know that. You always liked going there, even when that house was like a toddler disaster, and I was always afraid you were about to kill yourself on the edge of something. And anyway, it's better to be in the countryside, it gives the blood more oxygen."

That didn't sound true, but Cecelia didn't bother to argue. And if it was, what the hell had her parents been doing, depriving her blood of maximum oxygen for the past thirteen years? "I already agreed to this plan. It's fine, really." Cecelia's suitcases were in the trunk. Together, the three of them—Cecelia and her parents—took up every inch of space in the car, like commuters on a rush-hour F train.

"D'accord," Juliette said, patting Cecelia's

thigh. Her chin wobbled, and she turned her face toward the window. "Okay."

"Are you sure you want to go by yourself? We could take the train up with you, get you settled." Nicky had never volunteered to go to Clapham before—maybe this was already progress. He rubbed his hands on his beard.

"Dad, it's fine. I'm just going to read the **Deathly Hallows** again. It's only two hours."

"Can you manage the two bags, you think? There are escalators." Juliette was a dancer, both strong and practical about bodies. It was a good quality in a mother. Whenever Cecelia had fallen down or injured herself as a child, Juliette would whip up a pant leg to show her daughter a scar. Cecelia was trying to remind herself of these things in order to decrease the life-size piñata of her parents that she was building in her mind at all times. It wasn't their fault, but it also wasn't **her** fault, and parents were supposed to be the ones who swooped in and fixed things. But her parents had never been the kind to make a fuss. Her mother was a dancer who pretended not to smoke cigarettes. Her father was a hippie who sold bundles of sticks and crystals to younger hippies on the internet. His claim to fame, outside of their family, where he was famous for his quinoa salads, trumpeting farts, and humorous, improvised songs, was playing a handsome high school student in one movie, **The Life and Times of Jake**

George, filmed when he himself was a handsome high school senior. He'd found the experience of teenage girl fandom so appalling that he'd become a Buddhist and spent the next year in a monastery in Tibet. They weren't the types to yell and scream on anyone's behalf, even hers.

"It'll be fine, Mom." There was a tree-shaped air freshener hanging from the rearview mirror, and Cecelia watched it swing back and forth as they drove over the bridge. Taxi TV blared, and Juliette silenced it with her thumb. It was a beautiful day—blue sky, no clouds, no traffic. It almost made Cecelia sad to leave the city, but then she thought about going back to school in September and having her best friend not speak to her and having everyone else assume, because she was leaving, that she was the guilty party—shaming her! Cecelia Raskin-Strick, who had slept with her American Girl dolls until she was twelve, just last year! And they weren't even soft plastic! And then she wasn't sad, at least not about leaving. For the rest of the ride, her parents stared out their respective windows and Cecelia looked over the driver's shoulder, trusting that he was going the right way.

Chapter 3

Eau de Goat

Porter's bathroom smelled like goats because Porter smelled like goats. She couldn't always smell it herself, certainly not when she was with the animals, but once she came home and got into the shower, the steam opened up her pores and the whole room bloomed into a barnyard. It was worse when she smelled like cheese, mostly because other people tended to be more likely to attribute the cheese smell to her own body, whereas when she smelled like the goats, the animals were clearly to blame.

After graduating from Hampshire College, Porter had moved back to Clapham fast, like a rubber band pinged across a room. Her father had been dead for two and a half years, and being at school in Massachusetts had felt so absolutely dumb, but her mother had insisted she stay. What was the point? her mother had asked. What would she do in Clapham but sit around and mope? Porter thought that if she was going to find her father anywhere, in whatever form, it would be at home. And so she came back, reverting quickly to her teenage habits, but with part of her family cleaved off, as if her father had been a dream. It had been like learning to walk with a limp—tough at first, but then she got so used to it that she couldn't remember what life had felt like on two solid feet.

She'd worked as a substitute teacher at the high school, then at the Clay Depot, a high-end pottery store on Main Street. When she was nearing thirty, Porter's childhood friend Harriet converted her parents' land into an organic farm, and then they bought some goats and read some books on fermentation, and now, almost eight years later, Clap Happy Goat Cheese was available in shops in New York City and at every restaurant in Clapham and at specialty cheese shops around the country. Harriet had sold Porter the land and her share of the goats (there were two dozen altogether) and moved to Oregon with her husband, and so now the dairy was Porter's alone.

It was maybe because of the goats that the idea of getting pregnant on her own didn't seem all that scary. She was used to assisting reproduction, to having a hand in creating life, even if it was goats. Sperm banks were stud farms, and she'd grown up around enough farmers to know how biology worked. Really, it was mainstream, heteronormative couples who were doing the crazy thing, picking a partner based on what, a sense of humor? Where they went to college? What they did with their tongue when they kissed? And then having a baby. Why didn't everyone pick one person to marry and then pick the sperm they wanted separately? Also, fathers died, anyone could die, didn't people understand that? You couldn't ask one person to be your everything, because that person could be taken away. **Would** be taken away, eventually. Obviously it would be ideal to have a partner to help with the child once he or she was born—she wasn't a fool, she knew she had only two hands—but she didn't want to wait until she was forty. Maybe if she lived in a bigger place, where the dating pool was larger, she wouldn't have felt in such a rush. But Porter knew everyone in Clapham who she could possibly have sex with, and there were no golden tickets on that list.

There were romantic partners Porter could have had babies with: Jeremy, her high school boyfriend and first love, who had wanted to marry her at eighteen and now lived across town with his perky wife and their two school-age kids; Jonah, her college boyfriend, who smoked weed more often than he ate food, and who had moved to Vermont and seemed to be a professional Bernie Bro Facebook ranter; Hiro—the boy she'd slept with once during the relationship with the pot smoker—a Japanese student who had no social media and an ungoogleable name, so she'd lost track of him. The sex hadn't been good, but what was good sex? He could have been a good husband, a good father, who knew? And he probably was, with someone else. Then there were the guys Porter had slept with after college: Chad, the lawyer, whom she'd found both sexy and boring, like a human baseball game; Matthew, the underemployed waiter she'd dated for a few months, who had another girlfriend but sometimes still texted late at night, little empty speech bubbles forever appearing and disappearing after **Hey, thinking about you;** Billy, the guy she'd met on vacation in Puerto Rico, who was on his own vacation from Wisconsin, and whom Porter was fairly sure had a wedding ring tan line; and then Ryan, her most recent boyfriend, the only one since college whom she'd actually introduced to her family, who probably didn't love her, and most definitely didn't want kids. Accidents happened, but Porter had been on the pill since she was a junior in high school, and since then they hadn't happened to her. All the while, her friends had endless engagement parties, weddings, baby showers, births, like so many rocket ships zooming away from her. Both of her brothers had children, and at least one of them, her niece, Cecelia, was the greatest child to ever be born. Porter was ready to zoom, too, and so she stopped waiting for a pilot to appear.

Choosing sperm was the ultimate online dating—you had all the information you needed on paper. Porter also wasn't sure she trusted what were essentially résumés—everyone stretched the truth on résumés—and so she focused on the facts. Porter was tall herself and didn't need tall genes; she wasn't Jewish and therefore it was fine if the donor was, in terms of Tay-Sachs and other diseases on the "Jewish panel," so said her reproductive endocrinologist. Porter wanted to make up for things she lacked—physical coordination, the ability to carry a tune. It was best not to think about these men masturbating into a cup. It was hard to decide which was more off-putting: a man donating sperm just to make some cash or a man donating sperm because he liked the idea of having lots of children borne by strange women. Porter put it out of her mind. The sperm was an ingredient, and this way, she got to choose what kind of cake she wanted to make. The child would be hers alone, and that cupful of swimmers was a means to that end. And now she was pregnant with a girl. Science worked, and miracles happened. The two were not mutually exclusive.

Porter turned off the showerhead and watched the soapy water pool around her feet. Her breasts had always been modest and small, even when the rest of her body had widened with age. Now they were full and hard, more than a palmful of stretching tissue. Her hips and tummy kept the secret with their soft width, a professional hazard. Porter didn't trust anyone skinny who worked in cheese. You met them from time to time, mostly on the retail side, and Porter always kept her distance. Enjoying the product was important. Thank god her cheese was pasteurized.

Now that she was halfway and starting to show in earnest, Porter knew she was going to have to start telling people. And before she told people, she would have to tell her brothers. And before she told her brothers, she would have to tell her mother. She knew that it would be unimaginable to most women not to tell their mothers that they were embarking on such an experience—she'd seen scores of adult women clutching their mothers' hands in the waiting room at her reproductive endocrinologist's office. But Astrid Strick wasn't like that. She knew how to get stains out of white shirts. She could name all the plants in her garden and identify trees and birds. She could bake everything from scratch. But she did not invite intimacy the way that Porter had observed in other mothers, the kind who would let their children sleep in their bed after a bad dream or get their hair wet in a swimming pool. Astrid had always existed—both before and after her husband died—in an orderly way. She had rules, and the proper clothing for any weather, unlike Porter, who had neither. That was part of it, of course. Porter was going to let her daughter sleep in her bed every night if she wanted to. She'd chew her food and spit it into her mouth, if that was what the baby wanted. Porter was going to be as warm as an oven. That's what she was going to tell her mother.

Russell Strick had loved **The Twilight Zone,** and Porter thought that that was how she might have told her father—she would have asked him to imagine an episode where a baby was made in a lab and put into her body. It wasn't fair, the way most people just got to keep both their parents, and have grandparents for their children, and cutesy nicknames. Porter was used to that unfairness—her college graduation, her brothers' weddings, her mother's fiftieth birthday, sixtieth birthday, all the big fucking days—but somehow that part didn't get easier. He was still gone, and he would miss her big days, too, in addition to her brothers'. He would have been happy that she was having a baby, maybe (in some weird way, a way that they wouldn't ever talk about out loud) even a little bit happy that he would be the primary male figure, apart from her brothers, that he, Grampa, would loom large. Gramps. Gamps. Pops. Popsy. Porter didn't know which he would have been, which silly nickname he would have been granted by Cecelia and then called by all his grandchildren in turn. Porter had had a dream that somehow her father was also the father of her baby, through some mix of time travel and magic but with none of the troubling connotations that such a thing would have in real life—in her dream, it was like her father was somehow her grandfather and her father and her child's father all at once, an age-less ghost, and the women in the family did all the work. It was like a Brad Pitt movie that would make you cry even though it got terrible reviews.

Porter stepped over the lip of the bathtub and wrapped herself in a towel. She wiped at the mir-ror with her hand, clearing a space large enough to see her reflection.

"You're a grown-up," she said to herself. "You're a grown-ass woman, with a growing-ass baby inside her. You are an adult. It's your life." Porter turned to the side and cupped her hand beneath her belly. "Hey, you. I'm your mom, and I swear to god, ev-erything is going to be okay. I am ninety-five per-cent sure that everything is going to be okay. At least seventy percent. I swear. Fuck."

She would tell her mother today. Or tomorrow. At the very latest, she would tell her mother to-morrow.

Chapter 4

Unaccompanied Minor

It was only four stops on the train—Yonkers, Croton, Poughkeepsie, Clapham. Cecelia had a window seat but kept her nose in her book. The conductor had given her a special bracelet that read UNACCOMPANIED but might as well have read ABANDONED FOUNDLING, PLEASE TAKE ME HOME AND MAKE ME A SANDWICH. All the mothers on the train—Cecelia could tell which ones they were, even though only a few of them actually had children with them—gave her pitying looks and asked her pointless questions, like "Sure is pretty out there, isn't it?" to which she would smile and offer an affirmative nod. Fathers either knew better than to speak to an adolescent girl they didn't know or were better able to shut off the part of their brain that noticed children not their own.

———

Other girls—the girls she had been friends with until very recently, the ones who drank the cold coffee from their parents' abandoned mugs on the kitchen table and sometimes even an inch of vodka pilfered from the freezer—might have hidden in the bathroom at the opportune moment and then leapt off in a place that sounded more exciting, like Rome (even if it was Rome, New York) or Niagara Falls (even though she didn't have a raincoat and was too young to gamble), but Cecelia didn't want her parents to worry. Especially now. What would happen if she didn't get off the train? Cecelia couldn't quite picture it—Astrid would no doubt know just what to do, how to stop the train, how to scour the platforms for the next dozen stops. She probably had a walkie-talkie in her junk drawer that could reach the conductor personally. And then Cecelia would be in trouble, and her parents would have to jump on the next train together and they would fight and then they'd be at the Big House and fight some more about whose fault the whole thing was, without ever figuring out that it was actually **their** fault, if you got down to it. Regardless, she had only forty dollars and a credit card that went straight to her parents' bank account, and so even if she didn't mind the idea of stressing everybody out, it wouldn't last long. She wasn't built for life on the lam.

The Clapham station was just a long platform with tracks on either side, a mouth with braces. The Hudson River moved swiftly alongside. Cecelia humped her enormous suitcases onto the platform with the conductor's help and tried not to die of embarrassment as he called her grand-mother's name, his booming voice carrying over the hum of the train and the sounds of passing cars and birds twittering overhead. The station was up a long, precarious flight of stairs, that's where the waiting room was, with benches made of wood slats. That was probably where Astrid was right now. There was no one else in sight. Some people found cities scary, Cecelia knew, but those people had been swayed by misleading statistics and **Batman** movies. There was nothing frighten-ing about being in a place where you were always surrounded by hundreds of people—there was al-ways someone nearby who could hear you scream. Cecelia knew, because she was a modern girl, that her race and economic status meant that not only could someone hear her scream, but that someone would also be likely to help. It was also true that, because she was a girl, her parents had taught her to carry her house keys in between her fingers like Wolverine, just in case.

The conductor called her gammy's name again— "Ast-rid Stri-ick!" as though her gammy were the only contestant on the game show **Who Wants to Take Care of This Minor?** Cecelia laughed nervously, knowing full well that her grandmother had never been late for anything in her entire life.

"I'm sure she's upstairs; she must just be in the bathroom." Cecelia crossed her arms over her chest. Everyone else had already disembarked and trotted happily up the stairs into their loved ones' waiting arms, or their cars, or Spiro's, which was one block farther from the water.

The conductor did not smile. Instead, he checked his watch. "We're now holding up the train, ma'am."

Cecelia was just about to ask him why on earth he would call a thirteen-year-old "ma'am" when she saw her grandmother running down the stairs, her purse flapping behind her like a taupe leather cape.

"There she is, she's right there," Cecelia said, so relieved that she thought she might cry. Once Astrid got to the platform, she waved with both arms until the second she was close enough to touch her granddaughter, whom she then gripped on the biceps and kissed on the forehead. They were more or less the same height now, with the balance tipped slightly in favor of youth.

"You may release her now, sir," Astrid said. "Mission accomplished."

The conductor turned on his heel with a small nod, and a moment later, the train pulled out of the station, as if in a huff.

"Hi, Gammy," Cecelia said.

"Hi, sweetheart," Astrid said. "I saw someone get hit by a bus today."

Cecelia's eyes widened. "Like, a person?"

"A person. A woman my age. I've known her for most of my life. So I'm feeling a little bit scrambled. Do you know how to drive, by any chance?" Astrid pushed her sunglasses up so they sat on the top of her head. Her eyes did look a bit swimmy, and for a moment, Cecelia wished herself on the other side of the platform, heading back in the opposite direction.

"I'm thirteen."

"I know how old you are. I taught your father how to drive manual when he was eleven." Astrid pointed. "We did parallel parking right over there, on the next street, next to the river." She mimed a car driving down the embankment and falling into the water. "Ha! Splash!" Nicky was the youngest of his siblings and had done everything early. The family lore was that if Elliot, the eldest, did something at six, Nicky would do it at three, with Porter doing it somewhere in the middle. Being in the middle meant no one remembered anything except as a foggy mist, just the most general idea that Porter had been there. That was sometimes how Cecelia felt about her parents, too, though of course she was an only child and they had no one else to pay attention to, other than themselves.

Cecelia cringed. "I don't have a car. Obviously.

I mean, even my parents don't have a car." It was warm, too warm to be standing in the full sun. It hadn't seemed so hot in Brooklyn. Cecelia was wearing a sweater and she wanted to take it off, but she already had the two suitcases plus her backpack and she didn't want more to carry. "Who got hit? Did they die?"

"Barbara Baker, a total pain, and, yes, she died. From where I was sitting, it looked instantaneous, which is what we all want, god knows. It's okay, I can drive. But let's make that one of our little projects, mmm? Every woman should know how to drive. You never know when you'll need it. Come along, I'll get one, you get the other." Astrid reached for the handle on the small suitcase and tugged it along behind her, bumping it up one step at a time. Cecelia grabbed the handle of the larger suitcase and followed in Astrid's wake.

It should have been a five-minute drive to the Big House, but the roundabout was closed, so it took eight. Astrid drove with her hands on ten and two when she wasn't using the gearshift. Cecelia held her backpack on her lap, hugging it close, a health-class flour-sack baby. Astrid clicked on the radio, which was set, as always, to WCLP, Clapham's local NPR station, the local news with Wesley Drewes, whom Cecelia had always pictured like a cloud with eyeballs, looking over the whole town, zooming in and out wherever necessary.

"When is your father going back to New Mexico?" Astrid didn't mask her distaste for the plan.

"I'm not sure. In a couple of days, I think."

"He sure likes it out there. How one could enjoy yurts and scorpions is beyond me, but that's Nicky. You know he never liked peanut butter, just because everyone else did? He pretended he was allergic. How about your beautiful mother?" This was said without sarcasm or rancor. Juliette had become a fashion model in her teens after a talent scout had stopped her and her mother on the sidewalk in front of her dance studio in Clignancourt. Her whole life had been like that—someone happening along with an idea, opening a door. Juliette would then walk through the door, whether or not it led to a laundry chute. Cecelia looked more like her father, with a wavy nose and soft brown hair that looked blondish if you weren't standing anywhere near an actual blond person.

"You know, the same. Eating radishes with butter, that sort of thing." The streets of Clapham were wide and leaf-dappled, at least in high summer. It was where Cecelia had learned how to ride a bike, how to swim, how to play catch with an actual baseball mitt, all the things that were harder to do in New York City, at least with parents like hers. She'd been forced into dance class with her mother, but through a combination of clumsiness and mutual embarrassment, Cecelia had been permitted to quit fairly early. "But mostly I think she's sad."

"No one wants to send their child away," Astrid said. "Well, no, I suppose some people do. Some people send their children to boarding school as soon as they can! But your mother is allowed to be sad. It's going to be just fine."

"Okay." Cecelia wasn't sure how much her parents had told her grandmother about what had happened in Brooklyn.

"You know, we thought about sending Elliot to boarding school in New Hampshire when he got to high school, somewhere he'd rub shoulders with future captains of industry. But Russell—your grandfather—was never going to let that happen. People move to Clapham for the schools, he'd say! Why would we send our son away? What's the point of having children if you get rid of them before they even have anything interesting to say?" Cecelia stared at the side of her grandmother's face. Astrid was often chatty, but the chatting didn't usually tend toward the personal. Cecelia made sure that her seatbelt was buckled, just in case. "How many interesting things does a teenage boy say, really? Though your father was interesting, he really was. All our conferences with his teachers were mortifying gush-fests, just fountains of compliments, as if they'd never met a charming person before." Astrid reached over and lightly patted Cecelia's backpack. "Becoming a widow is like having someone rip off the Band-Aid while you're in the middle of a totally separate conversation. When you're a widow, you don't get to choose. We were married for twenty-five years. A good run, but not if you take the long view. Not like Barbara and Bob." Astrid slowed to a stop at a red light— one of two in town—and leaned forward, resting her head against the steering wheel. "I should call him." The light turned green, but Astrid didn't move, and therefore didn't notice. Cecelia swiveled in her seat to see if there were any cars behind them, and there were.

"Gammy," Cecelia said. "Green light."

"Oh," Astrid said, sitting up. "Of course." She rolled down her window, stuck out a hand, and waved the cars to go around. "I just need to sit for a moment, if that's all right with you. And your mother mentioned something about some trouble with your friends?"

"Yeah." Cecelia's bag buzzed in her lap, and she dug out her phone. Her mother had texted: **Hi hon just checking to make sure Gammy picked u up + all is well. Luv u. Call when you get to the Big House. <3** Cecelia shoved the phone back into her backpack and shifted it down between her feet. "We can sit here all day, if you want to." There had been trouble with her friends, in a way, though the trouble was really just that some of her friends were under the impression that they lived in a video game and that they were adults whose actions had no consequences, not children whose judgment-making skills were not yet fully formed. The trouble was that people always told Cecelia things, and that she wasn't a lawyer or a therapist. She was just a kid and so were her friends, but she seemed to be the only one who knew it. The trouble was that her parents had given up at the first sign of trouble, like a disgruntled child's first game of Monopoly. They'd folded. Folded on **her**.

Astrid reached over and took Cecelia's hand. "Thank you, dear. I appreciate that. Most people are in such a hurry."

"Not me," Cecelia said. "Absolutely no hurry whatsoever." She closed her eyes and listened to Wesley Drewes describe the weather.

Chapter 5

Spiro's Pancake House

Elliot heard about Barbara Baker from Olympia, who ran Spiro's Pancake House. She hadn't seen it happen, but she had heard the ambulance and the commotion, and she had taken out the binoculars from under the cash register. She'd seen Astrid cross the street, and thank god, Olympia said to Elliot, thank god, your mother is the perfect person for that type of thing. Everyone knew that Astrid was capable in trying circumstances. Then Olympia had watched the EMTs lift Barbara's body onto the gurney. Elliot stared out the window as Olympia spoke, imagining the scene.

"And my mother was right there?" He pointed with his fork. "Right there?"

Olympia nodded. She was Spiro's granddaughter

and had babysat for the Strick children, which meant that she always asked personal questions and lingered too long after pouring coffee, but Elliot liked the food at Spiro's better than anywhere else in town and so he came anyway. Why were there binoculars under the cash register? Elliot wasn't surprised—Clapham was that sort of place, entirely too small for even the semblance of privacy. "Right there. She probably felt the breeze, you know, of the bus going so fast. You know that feeling? When you're sitting there, and a truck goes by, and the whole street rumbles?"

Elliot felt his body give an involuntary shake. "God," he said. "It could have been her. It could have been my mother."

Olympia tucked her lips into her mouth and bowed her head. "It's a tragedy."

"I would be an orphan," Elliot said.

Olympia put her free hand on his shoulder and left it there for a few seconds before turning her attention to her other customers.

At least twice a week, Elliot pretended to have early-morning site meetings so that he could leave home sooner and eat breakfast on his own. Meals at home were often a disaster, with chunks of oatmeal on surfaces that weren't even remotely close to where the oatmeal had been ingested, and wet bits of scrambled egg floating in his coffee. And that was on days when the twins were more or less well behaved. He had never screamed the way

Aidan and Zachary screamed, never—if he had, Astrid would have put him out on the front step. Elliot and Wendy were clearly doing things wrong, but he didn't know how to fix it. Wendy had the patience in the family. It wasn't sexist to say that. Surely the boys would grow out of their insanity eventually, and Elliot would again be in awe of them, as he was when they were first born and he was sure that their birth was the crowning achievement of his life, having had a part in their creation, even if it had taken a few doctors' assistance and, of course, Wendy's body to hold and carry and deliver. Maybe it was a blessing of childhood that most people couldn't remember much before they were five—what good would it do to remember life as a savage toddler, totally divorced from societal norms? It was as if each human evolved from being a chimpanzee in a single lifetime. No one wanted to remember the jungle.

Even when he came for lunch, like today, Elliot always sat at the counter and he always ordered the same thing—eggs over easy, extra bacon, wheat toast, no potatoes. Olympia filled and refilled his water glass every time he took a sip, the cold silver pitcher sweating drops onto the stack of paper napkins next to him. WCLP was playing over the diner's radio, as always, and had just switched from **Local News with Wesley Drewes** to **Clap**

If You've Heard This One, the trivia show hosted by Jenna Johansson, one of his younger brother Nicky's former girlfriends. Clapham was like that—everyone was someone's high school love, or someone else's mother, or your cousin's best friend from camp. Elliot liked where he was from, and **being** where he was from, almost always, but he did occasionally have daydreams that were just like his own life only with no wife or kids and he went through an entire day without bumping into six people he'd known since childhood, without knowing exactly where and when he would run into them. In general, though, he thought that the longer he'd known someone, and whether they knew his family, increased the chances of people hiring him and so Clapham seemed like the best place to be.

"Large hazelnut coffee, four sugars, lot of cream," Olympia said. "That was Barbara. For a little while, maybe ten years ago, she was into the egg whites, but not anymore. My brother said they stopped the bus just past the country fairgrounds. They set up two cop cars, and he could have crashed right through them, but he didn't. He just slowed right down."

"It was the actual bus driver? The school bus driver?" Elliot dragged some bacon through the yolk on his plate. He was still thinking about how many times he and his mother and his wife and his sister parked on the roundabout every week, how easily it could have been his mother, just now, flattened into oblivion. When his father died, Elliot had been too young to have accomplished anything—he'd been a larva, still full of limitless potential. That had been the tragedy, all the things that his father wouldn't see. But if his mother died, now, today, it would be a tragedy of another kind. What more had he become? Sure, he had a wife, he had children, he had a business, a house, but Elliot thought that by the time he was in his forties he would have **more**. The cruelest part of becoming middle-aged was that it came on the heels of one's own youth, not some other, better youth, and that it was too late to start over.

"Who else would it have been?" Olympia's grandfather had come from Greece, but she was born in Clapham. She was older than Elliot by ten years and had children of her own, one of whom had just graduated from high school, which Elliot only knew because her cap-and-gown photo was thumbtacked just behind Olympia's head. At least he thought it was Olympia's daughter. They were a huge family, and Olympia had a couple of sisters, Elliot knew—the graduate could belong to any of them. He should know, but he didn't.

"I thought it was someone who just wanted to take a joyride, you know, a kid. A drug addict, I don't know! I didn't think it would be the actual bus driver." Elliot shoveled half a piece of toast into his mouth. "That's fucking scary, excuse my

French. My niece is going to be on that bus in a few weeks, my kids are going to take that bus someday. I took that bus."

Olympia crossed herself airily and then kissed her fingers. "They'll have a different driver by then," she said. Someone shouted from the kitchen, and Olympia looked at Elliot's plate. "Want more toast?" He nodded, and she pushed through the swinging door back into the kitchen.

Spiro's was fifty years old, maybe more. Some years ago, after her grandfather died, Olympia had replaced some of the booths in the back, and a few years after that, she'd replaced the stools at the counter and the counter itself. The jukebox was the same one that had been there since Elliot's childhood, as was the ancient silver milkshake machine, which looked like a giant metal toilet plunger but made the town's best shakes and floats, hands down. Wendy, Elliot's wife, had never particularly taken to Spiro's, because she thought it was grungy, but most people acknowledged it as one of the main centers of town life, and it was where Elliot often met clients, to prove that he was Clapham through and through.

Some people wanted to get out of their hometowns, in order to prove themselves. That was the old-fashioned way, to set out for the big city on foot and drive home in a Rolls-Royce. Elliot felt exactly the opposite. What would success matter, if it happened somewhere else? He wanted witnesses. That was why, when the building on the corner came up for sale again, he'd bought it. Him, Elliot Strick. He'd bought it with every penny of his money and he'd routed it through a corporation and an address that belonged to Wendy's parents in California. It was his to figure out, his to build. And when he did, everyone would know it. It made his stomach hurt to think about it.

Elliot swiveled around on his stool, the same way he had as a kid. Unlike some of the other babysitters, who had been inattentive and careless, more interested in the snacks in the pantry and the cable TV, Olympia had been tough. In some ways, it was a relief, knowing that she had boundaries, and rules, just like their mother. Some of Elliot's friends had had mothers who went barefoot, mothers whose silky bras were slung over the shower rod, mothers who left candles burning after they went up to bed, and they made Elliot so nervous that he couldn't go to their houses anymore.

His phone buzzed on the counter, and Elliot flipped it over. His sister, Porter. **Just checking in, are you coming to see Cece today? Also hi you smell like poop.** Elliot rolled his eyes and chuckled, despite himself. He typed back: **Are we required to go to the Big House to welcome her? I have a meeting, boys have jujitsu. Wendy is bugging me.**

Elliot watched the three little dots appear and disappear, as if his sister was starting and restarting whatever she had to say. They weren't particularly nice to each other; were any adult siblings? They saw each other when their mother told them to. Elliot didn't care, it was fine. Finally Porter wrote back: **She's a teenage girl and I promise does not give a shit if you show up. This weekend is fine. If you wait longer than that, Astrid will murder you in your sleep.**

Elliot didn't respond. Olympia pushed back through the swinging door and slid another neat pile of buttered toast beside his mostly empty plate. Once, when he was probably seven or eight, Olympia had caught Elliot cheating at Monopoly, and she had banished him to the backyard like a dog with fleas. He'd had a bit of a crush, then.

"I heard that the building on the corner got sold again, did you hear that?" Olympia craned her neck to look over her patrons' heads, out the window, and across the roundabout. "I wish whoever it was would just get it over with. What's the point, you know? Buy it, turn it into a bank, whatever, just do it, you know?" She shook her head.

"You don't want it to be a bank. What do you think it should be?" Elliot asked.

"I'd like a really good Mexican restaurant, I guess. Or Japanese. But I'd settle for anything, as long as it wasn't another diner."

"We don't need another diner," Elliot said.

"We sure don't," Olympia said, and winked.

Elliot finished his coffee and sat. His meeting

didn't start for another half hour, and Wendy was in charge of getting the boys where they needed to go that afternoon. Traffic was moving normally outside. It was only hours ago, Barbara and the bus. Elliot watched the cars go around and around, himself with no particular place to go.

Chapter 6

The Big House

The Big House sounded impressive if you hadn't seen it, but once you had, you understood that the name was a cutesy diminutive, like calling a house a pile of bricks, or a love shack. It was a three-story stone mansion built in 1890, one of dozens like it dotting the Hudson Valley from their perches high above the river. Because there were others like it, and they'd had the money, the house didn't even seem so extraordinary when Astrid and Russell bought it in 1975. It was big enough for them, baby Elliot, and the siblings they imagined he would have. The acres-wide yard sloped all the way to the water, although the slope was only walkable for about a hundred feet, before the drop became precipitous. They had lost a lot of woebegone toys that way, seeing how far one could chuck a G.I. Joe, whether they could hear a splash. (They could never hear a splash.)

Astrid helped Cecelia to her room and then gave the girl some privacy, to settle in. Maybe that was part of the problem, how little space Cecelia had at home, how the three of them were always on top of one another like Charlie Bucket's grandparents, all in one bed. Astrid padded back down to the kitchen and opened the refrigerator. It had been so long since there was a child in the house, she had spent days shopping and baking and cooking. Cecelia's nutrition was at stake, her energy. Astrid had baked zucchini muffins with walnuts, an enormous casserole of macaroni and cheese, turkey meatballs, chocolate chip cookies, granola bars studded with plump raisins. She'd bought eight bananas. There were enough tomatoes to can and freeze soup and pasta sauce for a whole winter. Peanut butter, almond butter, three kinds of jam. If Cecelia was anything like her father had been, or her aunt and uncle, she would somehow still open the fridge and the pantry doors and moan that there was nothing to eat. But Astrid had done her duty. The blessing of being a grandparent was knowing all the things that had to be done and having the time to do them. Some of her friends thought that extra patience came with age, but that wasn't it, of course. Their calendars just weren't as full. Astrid was clear-eyed about her position. Nicky hadn't said, Oh, Mom, please talk to

Cecelia about everything, please help. He'd said, Can she come? And the answer was yes. Astrid was an able body; she was a safe house. He was complimenting her ability to keep children alive, not her parenting skills. Astrid knew that out of all her children, Nicky trusted her decisions the least. She was not his first choice, and the situation had to be fairly dire for him to even have considered the notion.

Astrid wanted to call Bob Baker. She'd been there, after all, and had seen it happen. Wouldn't he want to hear from her? Astrid hadn't ever called him in her life. She should write a note, she should take a platter of baked chicken to his door. She would do that too. But while she was standing there, somehow no longer alone in her big house, all she could think of was Bob, newly alone in his. Astrid walked over to the telephone on the wall—oh, how Elliot mocked her for her rotary phone, cream-colored and heavy as a brick—and dialed. Bob answered right away, and when he did, she realized that she hadn't imagined a scenario in which he would actually answer. It was today, after all, somehow still just **today** that it had happened, and Astrid knew from her own widowhood how many things would be on Bob's immediate list, things he likely had never thought about: hospitals, morgues, funeral parlors, calling the rest of their family with the news. Astrid knew some people (organized women, all) with terminal cancer who had set up elaborate phone trees, exactly the way they'd done for unplanned school snow days before email, to tell everyone about their deaths when the time came. Bob didn't have a phone tree. Somehow, he was at home. For a split second, Astrid worried that Bob didn't know, and that she'd have to be the one to tell him.

"Hi there, Bob, it's Astrid Strick." She tried to remember the last time they'd actually exchanged anything more than a cursory nod. Maybe when she'd been behind him in line at Clapham Organic, or standing at neighboring pumps at the gas station? But even that was just polite small talk, no more than you'd have with an actual stranger. It had probably been thirty years since they'd really spoken, back in the time of dinosaurs, when she was still young enough to imagine age was a basis for a friendship.

"Hi there." Bob waited. He didn't sound surprised to hear from her. Of course. "I understand you were there when it happened."

"I was, Bob." Astrid wound the cord around her finger, watching her flesh pinken and bulge. "It was the damnedest thing, and I am so sorry. Barbara deserved better."

"She did." Bob was not a garrulous man.

"I've got my granddaughter here now, Bob, but I'd like to bring over some food in the next day or so, would that be all right? I'd drop off a dish, you know, something easy to warm up. Just to cross one thing off the list, is that all right?"

"Sure, Astrid." Bob paused so long that Astrid thought he might have hung up. Then he inhaled long and hard, almost a snore. "Well, she was living over at her mother's, these last few months. At Heron Meadows. So I've gotten pretty good at feeding myself. I'd still be happy for a dish, though, don't get me wrong; I just wanted you to know."

Astrid tilted her head to the left. "You don't say. Well, a man's got to eat. I'll stop by. Thanks, Bob. So sorry, again. I've been there. It's a horrible thing to have to go through, and I'm sorry." Astrid hung up the phone with a decisive **clunk** and immediately doubled over with laughter, the source of which she was not quite sure. It bubbled up from her toes and roiled through her belly and came out her mouth like a gassy belch, and for a full few minutes, Astrid found that she couldn't stop. Her eyes watered and then they, too, sprung leaks, and the world turned blurry, and Astrid made her way into the bathroom and shut the door behind herself, just in case Cecelia came down the stairs and happened upon her. Her own children had never seen her cry. She sat on the closed toilet lid and tried to take deep breaths. When Russell died, she followed his body to the funeral parlor and then picked up his shirts at the dry cleaner on her way home. Astrid's greatest strength, as a person, had always been her iron tear ducts. When Russell died, she had reigned like a queen, or the dictator of a very small country. Everything was done on time, everything was handled. What happened to Barbara seemed too cruel to imagine: a woman who had finally decided to handle things on her own, as she wanted to. It could have been her, Astrid, who'd been caught by the bus's bumper, or it could have been Birdie, and then what? They would have each mourned a friend. Astrid's children would have limped on without her help. That pierced her too—the thought of her children, alone, none of the three of them quite adults, still, even now! When she was their age, she'd been ancient. It wasn't funny, none of it was funny. Astrid felt like she had food poisoning, like whatever she had ingested was foul and bad and needed to get out of her body one way or the other. Astrid breathed in through her nose and out through her mouth, the way she did when there was turbulence on airplanes. When she was finally calm again, Astrid picked up the phone and called Birdie's cellphone, not even giving her a chance to say hello.

"Birdie bird, you little snake, you didn't tell me," she said, and repeated what Bob had told her.

"You never asked! It was none of my business!" Birdie said. She wasn't a gossip, Astrid knew. Birdie probably saw all sorts of things at Heron Meadows, the many humiliations of age, and she never said a thing. Astrid was pierced with a sharp pang of desire—she wanted Birdie to come over, right now; she wanted to put her head in Birdie's lap and cry or laugh or both. Was that romance or codependence, the overwhelming need for another person in order to properly function? Birdie was doing her weekly reorders at the salon and had offered to go with Astrid to the train station and then home, whatever she wanted, but Astrid had refused. They were still careful in public, but truly, not more careful than Astrid would have been with a man. She wasn't into public displays of anything except irritation at those who didn't follow rules, like drivers who made rolling stops or those who didn't pick up their dogs' mess. It was hard to keep a secret in a small town, but as Astrid had learned, everything was easier when you were a woman over fifty. That's what made Astrid cry, she realized—Barbara had known that too.

Chapter 7

August in Purgatory

August sat in the back of his parents' car. Like everything else they owned, it was purposefully old, as if existing for long enough gave things extra value instead of the opposite. They owned a vintage clothing and furniture store, Secondhand News, and so he supposed it was true, that they literally sold things for more money than they'd been worth, but it still seemed sort of like an outlandish idea. The car was special, though, the kind of thing that young people with beards and tinted sunglasses oohed and aahed over when it was parked on the street in Clapham. It was enormous, the size of an ocean liner, and as square as a pretend car made out of a cardboard box. They called it Harold. The air-conditioning was broken, and so August's window was rolled all the way down, and the wind blew his hair around his face like a washing machine.

"Honey?" his mom said, turning her face toward the back seat. Her voice was barely audible over the wind, a signal through static.

"Mmm," August said, keeping his eyes on the trees whipping by. They were halfway home, and soon they would stop for lunch in Great Barrington, as they always did on the way home from camp.

There was a week left before school started. The eighth grade. If camp had lasted until five minutes before school started, that's what August would have wanted. School was full of people August spent every summer forgetting entirely, sometimes so well that he was surprised to see them in the fall, as if they'd died and come back from the dead. Not because they were all terrible people—only some of them were terrible, like the girls who always rode in the annual Harvest Parade, a new crop every year, girls who waved from elbow to wrist like Miss-Americas-in-training—they just weren't his people, and it was nice not to have to take up space with things you didn't need.

His parents didn't see things that way. They were menders by nature, fixers, and thought that anything could be solved by talking it into the ground.

"Honey?" August's mom said again. She motioned for him to roll up his window, which he reluctantly did, cutting off the noise of the road with a **thunk**.

"Yeah?" Now he could hear the music they were listening to in the front seat, Paul Simon, official soundtrack of liberal parents everywhere. Sometimes August wondered if there was a handbook that came with being a parent, full of the music and books and movies you were supposed to like (Aretha, Chabon, documentaries), and what kind of food to insist was delicious when clearly it was not (homemade hummus, lentil soup).

"Do you want to talk about it?" His dad swiveled around and cupped his hands around the headrest.

"Talk about what?" August tucked his hair behind his ears.

"You haven't stopped crying since we picked you up." His dad's voice was soft. He meant well— they both did. It wasn't their fault.

"I hadn't noticed," August said, which was true. Adults—even nice ones, like his parents, who understand that their children are autonomous human people and not robots created just to please them—couldn't remember what it was like. Here is a brief list of what it (being alive) was like: Being a naked person in the middle of Times Square. Being a naked person in the middle of the cafeteria. Being a hermit crab scurrying along the ocean floor in search of a new shell. Being a baby turtle in the middle of a six-lane highway. That didn't begin to cover all the ways August felt weird and strange and wrong every day.

"Oh," said his mother. She reached back and put her hand on his knee. "Love you, sweetie." Then August rolled his window down again and they left him alone until lunch.

If camp was heaven and home was hell, then Great Barrington was purgatory, a good place to stop to go to the bathroom. There were good sand- wiches and a spot around the corner with better- than-good ice cream. August reluctantly ordered a waffle cone with mint chocolate chip and rainbow sprinkles, because no amount of sweetness could make him less sad, which was what he wanted, to stay sad for a while longer. They sat inside at a small square table, all six of their knees touching.

"You can still go back next year," his mom said. There was an internal countdown. August had one more summer before aging out. Like a stuffed ani- mal on a teenager's bed, his days were numbered. They all tried not to talk about it, and this early mention of the ticking down of the clock from his mother felt like a breach of etiquette—he must have been crying a lot for her to resort to the prom- ise of next summer already, before they were even two hours gone.

August's mother, Ruth, had long brown hair and blunt bangs, like a 1970s teenager. She wore tight jeans and had charmingly unorthodontia'd teeth and had always, always been popular. August often watched her interact with people—ice-cream shop employees, friends, random strangers at the grocery store—and wondered what life would be like if he could be like her. Every year, she told him that it would be the year that he would finally find his people at school, not just at camp. He didn't have the heart to tell her that it was about as likely as being struck by lightning while juggling bowling pins. There were people at school whom he could tolerate, people whom he could call for the homework assignments if he'd been out sick, but they weren't friends. They were colleagues in the business of surviving junior high. In August's best and dearest fantasies, he would get his GED by age fifteen and go straight to college in New York City or San Francisco and be a camp counselor in the summers and only come back to Clapham on holidays. But he couldn't tell his mother that. She was under the mistaken impression that he was still a child.

"I know," August said. His dad rubbed his beard.

The ice-cream parlor was packed, and their table sat right underneath a large community board covered with tacked-up homemade signs about dog-walking services and guitar lessons, photographs of cats that had gone missing.

"Ooh," Ruth said, pointing to one about an

estate sale. This was August's whole childhood, trailing his parents around dank old houses filled with a dead person's belongings.

"Absolutely," John said. He'd fallen in love with Ruth first, then old things. When he'd gone to Clapham High, he'd been the captain of the tennis team, as preppy as they come, with hair that swooped like a cresting wave. Slowly, his mom had transformed his father's closet of pastel staples into earlier versions of the same, and now he was just as bad as she was, in short-shorts that dads would have worn to pick up their children from camp in 1980. Somehow, even when his parents bought new clothing, it still looked old.

"Do you mind, honey?" Ruth asked. But she wasn't really asking. This was what the Sullivans did. They bought old things by the bushel and, through their touch, transformed them into something desirable, something new. August wished that his parents could work their magic on him too.

The house was small, a sun-bleached blue, like a boat that had been sitting in salt water for decades. A few lookie-loos were standing outside the garage, but it wasn't crazy the way it sometimes was, in fancier neighborhoods, with lots of pickers like his parents craning their necks to find expensive things to put in their shop windows. This was just a little house in a small town that had to empty itself out, one way or another. August followed his parents through the front door. He knew the drill.

They looked for furniture first, because it was worth the most, and something valuable (a mid-century credenza, antique mirrors, milk glass light fixtures) would sell fast. Then they looked for objects and clothes and art, in that order. You wouldn't believe how much someone would pay for a hand-carved wooden duck. His parents split up, one upstairs, one down, their eyes trained at knee level. August followed his dad upstairs and ambled into one of the bedrooms.

August had described this process to his friends at camp, and they had unanimously pronounced it creepy AF. They loved to talk about it on the nights when bunks took camping trips, sitting around the fire, marshmallows on sticks.

"So, like, the people are **dead,** right?" his best friend, Emily, had asked.

"Super dead. At least I assume so. I mean, otherwise it would just be a garage sale, and they'd be sitting there with a fanny pack, telling you how much their juicer costs."

"Why don't their husbands or wives or kids do something with all their stuff? It just seems so sad, to open your doors and be, like, have at it." Quinn shook her head.

"I think that is how they deal with it. And some

people don't have husbands or wives or kids, you know? Or maybe they live far away?" That settled everyone into a shared silent paralysis.

"Damn," Emily said, finally.

"But they find cool stuff?" Quinn asked.

"Sometimes. Sometimes weird dolls with one eye. My mom loves those, actually."

Emily smacked him and then buried her head in his stomach. "Oh my god, you're going to give me nightmares!"

The bedroom that August had wandered into was mostly empty, with washed-out pale pink flowery wallpaper. There was a small bed with musty piles of quilts stacked on top—his mom would want those. There was a large homemade dollhouse on a ledge beside the window, and August knelt down next to it. His mom would want this too—it had a miniature roll of toilet paper in the miniature bathroom. She loved that kind of thing, something that someone's grandmother had made. The small people had vanished, but that didn't matter. Small people were easy to come by. He pressed a finger against a tiny swinging door and watched it flap back and forth. August rocked back up to standing.

There was boarding school, but those places were worse. August had read books: drugs, eating disorders, murder. There was home school, but neither of his parents could do math. And high school was bound to be better, right? Teenage

rebellion had to help, right? And there were a few
more artsy places in the Hudson Valley, private
schools that his parents could afford if they sold a
thousand dollhouses a day. One girl whose blog he
liked had somehow convinced her parents to buy
a Winnebago and spend her junior year of high
school driving across Mexico. His mother poked
her head into the room and squealed with excite-
ment. His parents only drove around looking for
more stuff to anchor them down. August pulled
the dusty curtain back and looked out the window.
At camp, he could be himself, and people loved
him for it. At school, costumes were required.

His mother started riffling through the quilts
on the bed, separating them out in piles based on
the colors and patterns she liked and then unfold-
ing them to look for stains. She was engrossed, petting the stiff cotton squares, clearly thinking about
how much she'd pay, and how much she'd charge
for them in the store once she brought them home.
August turned toward the closet, which was open,
as if the girl who'd lived in the room was in the
process of getting dressed and had just been rap-
tured away.

The closet wasn't full; there were only a dozen
or so things on hangers, waving slightly with the
movement of August's hand. He brushed his fingers across them, just feeling the fabric. It was easy
to tell when something was well made, if it was
worth money, and that had little to do with the

label inside. He stopped on a white eyelet dress and swiveled the skirt out so that he could see the whole thing.

"Pretty," his mom said, looking over her shoulder. "Last days of summer? We can sell that. Even after Labor Day." She straightened her back and hugged a small stack of quilts against her chest.

"I thought you meant me," August said, and fluttered his eyelashes.

"Always," his mom said, blowing a kiss into the air. August looked more like his mother than his father, a fact that always made him happy. August blew a kiss back, making his face her mirror, and she smiled at him before turning to the dollhouse and making a fuss, just as he knew she would.

Chapter 8

A Funny Story

Porter had a key to the Big House, though she had to riffle through her pockets several times to remember if she had it on her—she was finding pregnancy to be something of a fugue state, where she often couldn't remember whether she'd already brushed her teeth or washed her hair and would end up doing something two or three times, just to make sure, or realizing at noon that she'd done neither. Porter kicked off her shoes at the door and walked in.

"Mom? Cecelia? Anybody home?" Porter knew that some of her friends from growing up, the ones who'd left town, felt like they traveled back in time to their adolescence when they were around their parents, and within the walls of their childhood bedrooms, as if the pictures of Marilyn Monroe and Joey McIntyre taped to the wallpaper were ready to jump straight back into their ongoing conversation. That was easy, coming home and being a kid again, because presumably they got to be an adult the other 360 days a year. When you were in your childhood house on a regular basis, it was harder to separate the past and the present— nostalgia only worked with distance.

Porter was excited to see Cecelia, the second-best thing her little brother had ever done, after teaching Porter how to properly roll joints when she was in high school, despite the fact that he was younger than she was. He'd always been like that—preternaturally confident in his own abilities. He must have practiced in the dark for hours, but Porter hadn't seen it. She'd thought about telling her brother that she was pregnant—he would be the most enthusiastic member of her family, she knew—but even though Porter could vividly remember the day that Cecelia was born, her brother's experience now seemed like a remote continent, too far away from her growing belly to speak the same language. Nicky had been twenty-three, still a kid himself. There was nothing about his experience that was the same as hers. Same with Elliot, who had a wife and a plan and checklists and a hospital bag sitting by the door at twenty-five weeks. It was easier to keep the secret in. That's where the baby was, after all.

Porter could see her mom's behind waggling in the air by the counter, her elbows ahead on the kitchen island, the phone snuggled in between her ear and shoulder, a 1950s teenager. Astrid was whispering.

"Mom," Porter said again, coming close enough to lightly touch Astrid on the back. She didn't want to scare her—Astrid was almost seventy, and even though her mother had always seemed strong and fit, to an almost immortal degree, Porter had heard about Barbara Baker from Wesley Drewes, and sudden death seemed closer, though of course statistically it had just moved further away. In any case, Porter was nervous.

Astrid swiveled around. "Oh, hi! Hi. Okay," she spoke into the phone. "Listen, Porter just walked in the door, I'll talk to you later, okay? Okay. Yes. Me too. Thanks so much, okay. Bye-bye."

"Where's Cecelia?" Porter asked, setting down a box of pastries on the kitchen island. Astrid wound around her, following the cord back to the wall, and hung up the phone.

"She's upstairs, taking a shower, I think. Listen, you're not going to believe this, but I called Bob—you heard about Barbara, didn't you?" Porter nodded. "I called Bob to offer my condolences, because I was right **there,** you know, and you know what he told me?" Astrid's mouth opened like a jack-o'-lantern, a wide, gaping maw. "She'd just **left** him and moved in with her mother at Heron Meadows! She was living with her mother! At the old folks' home! Her mother is so out of it, the poor thing, she probably thought Barbara was her new nurse. It's the craziest thing I ever heard." Astrid blew air out of her nose, an involuntary snort.

Porter opened the box and started to eat one, cupping her hand underneath to catch crumbs. "Is this a funny story?"

Astrid waved her hand in front of her face. "Nothing's funny, everything's funny! It's life! Life is finally deciding that your demented—is that what the word is? Dementia'd?—anyway, that your ancient mother is more fun to be around than your husband of thirty-five years, and then getting hit by a school bus! She was probably mailing her divorce papers, do you think? I have to ask Darrell. He delivers mail to Shear Beauty, I bet he'd know. That mailbox has got to be on his route."

"Mom, you sound like an insane person."

"Yes, well"—Astrid adjusted her hair—"I'm a **curious** person."

"There was actually something I wanted to talk to you about, Mom," Porter said. She opened the fridge and felt her arms begin to pimple with goose bumps. She closed her eyes and pretended she was just talking to the eggs. If her father had been there, he would have rubbed his hands together, excited for whatever she had to say. If her father had been there, she would have been too young to have a baby.

"Porter! Hi!" Cecelia slid into the kitchen in her socked feet.

Porter turned around and spread her arms wide, letting Cecelia crash into her. Elliot's kids were actual monsters, creatures who would no doubt go on to commit duplicitous and mean-spirited white-collar crimes, but Cecelia was probably the number one reason that Porter wanted to have a baby—to have someone this smart, this funny, this thoughtful in your life, and have them be obligated to love you forever. She wasn't sure if she wanted to clone her, adopt her, or be her. Maybe all three.

"How was the train? How's my stupid brother?" Porter kissed Cecelia's cheeks, one at a time, the way Juliette did.

"He's okay. The train was fine. I got up to Harry and Hermione going to his parents' house, where the woman turns into the snake. I had a turkey sandwich with a slimy piece of lettuce and a gross tomato and now probably have food poisoning." Cecelia shrugged and then leaned against the counter, collapsing her torso so that it lay flat against the granite. In the months since Porter had seen her last, Cecelia had become a teenager and was slumping toward indifference to most things, right on schedule. The last time she'd been in town—only eight months ago, at Christmas—she hadn't been like this, and seeing a sulking teenager in the kitchen where she herself had been a sulking teenager set Porter's heart aflame.

"Mom, let me take this child to lunch." Porter grabbed Cecelia by the hand. "I am so happy to see you, Chicken."

"Please don't call me Chicken," Cecelia said, but she was smiling.

"Porter," Astrid said, now back to her stern self. "The house is full of food! But fine. I have something I wanted to talk to you about too." Birdie wouldn't mind—Birdie would be thrilled.

"It's nothing," Porter said. Cecelia cocked her head to the side, like a dog. It was exactly like when her parents tried not to fight in front of her, just opening and closing their mouths like fish on land.

Cecelia plucked one of the apple turnovers out of the box and took a bite. "Do you need some privacy? I can wait in my room." She looked to Astrid and then to Porter.

"You are a magnificent person," Porter said. "Seriously. How did you get this wonderful and mature? Yes, great. Want to go have a snack in town? In a few minutes?" Both pregnant women and teenagers could eat an unlimited number of meals in any given day, their bodies working so hard to transform into something new.

"Sure," Cecelia said. Astrid stuck a plate under the turnover and Cecelia hustled back up the stairs. Porter and Astrid both waited for her to vanish,

and then for the **clunk** of her door—Porter's childhood bedroom door—before speaking again.

"I think we should invite Elliot and the family over this weekend for brunch," Astrid said.
"Would you come? I'm going to invite Birdie. You
know Birdie, don't you? And Cecelia, of course."

"I'm pregnant, Mom, and of course I know
Birdie, she's been cutting your hair for years and
you have lunch with her every Monday," Porter said.

"What?" Astrid said.

"I'm pregnant," Porter said. "Or did you mean
about you and Birdie having lunch?"

"Sorry, Porter," Astrid said. "Last I checked,
there wasn't really a danger of that happening.
We had the talk, I remember it well, and Nurse
Johnson always had the bowl of condoms in her
office. **That** was a whole debacle with the town
council, god, those fools! I know that was a long
time ago, but surely you remember the basics.
What happened? Tell me." Astrid smoothed the
front of her zip-up sweatshirt. She pushed her hair
up, patting it like a show dog. Her hair had always
been dark, and now it was a shiny silver instead, a
polished bell. This wasn't what she imagined—she
thought of Barbara Baker again, who had floated
for so long at the edge of her vision. It could all be
over in an instant. She could be different; there was
still time. Astrid thought about Birdie, about how
she felt when they were alone together. She wanted
to be a different kind of mother than she had

been; was that so hard to say? "Lots of women go through this."

"I'm pregnant by choice, actually. I'm having a baby. By myself." Porter felt her body begin to heat up, starting in her chest and moving outward, a swift-moving forest fire. She kept her feet planted in the kitchen, with her hands flat against the cool granite counter, and said what she had practiced in the bathroom mirror. "I thought about this for a long time, and it's the right decision for me. I know it's not something you would have done, but this is my choice, and I hope you can support it. You're going to have another grandchild."

She sounded like an after-school special, but there wasn't really any other way to say it. There was a baby in her body, and she'd put it there. This was another by-product of staying in one's home-town: Parents weren't frozen in amber, fixed at the moment you left, providing a tidy dividing line be-tween parent and child. Porter couldn't distinguish the person Astrid was now from the person she'd been in Porter's childhood. Maybe Nicky could see differences, like she could see differences in Cecelia—absence made contrast plain. Not that it mattered now—Porter and her mother were both adults. Starting the conversation had been scary, but now the train was on the tracks and it was moving and she couldn't jump off. Porter exhaled through her mouth.

"Who is the father? Are you and Ryan back to-gether? It's not Jeremy Fogelman, is it?" Astrid had never liked any of Porter's boyfriends, no one had. She shook her head, as if she could whisk the news away if she disagreed with it strongly enough. "You're only thirty-eight years old. I'm trying to be sympathetic here, I want to understand. Can you help me understand? Girls in New York City don't even get married until now, you're not far behind. You're going to meet someone, and then what? He becomes stepdad? Oh, god." Astrid was doing the math in her head. "How far along are you? You're definitely keeping it? It's not that I'm not **evolved,** Porter, it's just that I actually raised three children, and I happen to know that it's not a one-person job. Why didn't you ever talk to me about this? How long have you been planning to do this?"

"Mom. Of course I'm **keeping** it, I **paid** to have this person created and placed inside my body. And the father is a person. A man. In the world, somewhere. When the child is eighteen, she can contact him via the sperm bank, and then, I don't know, we'll see. I know you're not going to like it, but that's what's happening." Porter took a deep breath. This was why she'd waited to tell her mother. Astrid's standards for everyone else were the same as her standards for herself, which left no room for error. "And why would you even sug-gest Jeremy Fogelman? That's absurd. This is why

I didn't tell you; I knew this was how you'd react, and I didn't want you to talk me out of it. This is **good news,** okay?"

Astrid stared. "You know, you've always been this way. Everything always had to be on your own terms. Remember when you were Harvest Queen and you made everyone else on the float stand on the lower level of the float so that you were the tallest?" Astrid sat down in her chair at the kitchen table and plucked a hard-boiled egg out of a basket. She cracked it firmly on the lip of the table and began to peel. "You think you can do it with only two arms and two hands, maybe you can."

Porter watched her mother make a tidy pile of eggshell. "I have told you a thousand times, the float was **built** that way, there was only space for one person on the top part of the float that year." The theme had been Studio 54.

"Mm-hmm," Astrid said. She shook some salt onto the smooth skin of the egg white and took a small bite. "I liked that you were on top, you looked like the Statue of Liberty in that green dress."

"Thank you?" If Astrid had talked this way to either of Porter's brothers, they would have walked out of the room. Porter thought that it had to do with her being the only girl, always eager to please, conditioned by the outside world to react softly and with a smile to everything short of bodily harm. It was important to get along, and Astrid had her ways. Nicky had run off to avoid her, and Elliot only wanted to be like what he remembered of their father, which was a twentysomething's view of an adult man, a Ken doll with bills to pay. And so that left Porter and her mother.

"Do you need a doctor? Who are you seeing?" Astrid asked.

"Dr. Beth McConnell, at Northern Dutchess," Porter said.

"I know Beth," Astrid said. "She spoke to the hospital board at our annual luncheon last year."

"And you can't believe she didn't call you." Porter rolled her eyes.

Cecelia bounded back into the room, swinging her backpack in a large circle. Astrid looked up from her egg and waved a finger.

"We'll talk more about this later," Porter said. "Bye, Mom."

"Goodbye, dear. Wear your seatbelt." And with that, Astrid stood up, swept all the pieces of eggshell into her palm, and then blew half a kiss with her free hand, the most spontaneous affection she'd given Porter since her last birthday. It was a start.

Chapter 9

Little Red Riding Hoods

Northern Dutchess Hospital was one town north, in Rhinebeck. It had been built in the 1980s and had the glass bricks to prove it. Porter parked in the covered lot and made her way through the lobby, which was painted in various pastel shades and felt less antiseptic than most hospitals, and more like being at a gender-neutral baby shower. The ob-gyns were on the second floor. She'd gone on a tour of the delivery rooms, all of which overlooked the parking lot, probably because people didn't stay very long and weren't likely to complain about the lack of a view when they had a new baby to stare at. Porter was ten minutes early and picked a chair in the corner.

Waiting rooms full of pregnant women and women who wanted to be pregnant were more full of codes than a spy's briefcase. Porter had been taking notes on her phone, theoretically to remember the experience, mostly because she was always there alone and most of the women were with their partners and she wanted to look busy. The only women who truly seemed not to give a shit were the ones with one or two kids already at home, who took calls from babysitters and answered questions about cookies and iPad time and then spread out their belongings like it was a day at the spa, so happy to have no one touching them, no bottom to wipe, no mysteriously sticky fingers to clean. Some young women came with their partners and stroked their baby bumps like enormous diamond rings, their nerves assuaged by the doting of their loved ones. It was all races and ages, within the scope of human reproduction. Sometimes there were jittery teenagers, holding hands like they might push a button and find themselves in line to see a movie, just on a regular date, instead of sitting on padded chairs and waiting for a doctor to call a name. Sometimes couples fought silently, the woman's face a knotted fist of anger, and Porter would amuse herself by trying to imagine what her husband or boyfriend had said. She liked those couples best.

Then there were women who came alone, like her, and who seemed to be having their first babies. Those women were tighter knots, biting their nails, new lightning bolts of worry crisscrossing their foreheads. She always checked their fingers for a ring, and most of the time, there was one. When their fingers were bare, Porter looked closer. Were they younger than her, or older? Were their bellies big enough that their entire bodies had begun to swell, including their fingers? There were, of course, those pregnant women, who had to temporarily remove their rings because their fingers had gotten too fat. She'd then check for a chain around their neck. She didn't want to care. She actively was trying not to care. There was one Single Mom by Choice group that her doctor had recommended, in addition to a slate of doulas and pediatricians, but Porter hadn't done more than a cursory googling. In her almost five months of pregnancy, she had only clocked three other women who fit her profile.

Porter pulled her tote bag onto her lap and reached in, feeling around for her book. She was trying to be the kind of woman she'd want to have as a mother—well-read, open-minded, that sort of thing. Harriet was in a book club in Oregon and always sent over recommendations. This one was a novel about a bookstore in Paris that hid Jewish children who had escaped the Nazis, and there was a magical talking bird. Porter knew all that from Harriet's email—she herself was only on the fifth page, where she'd been for some time. The book was six hundred pages long—at this rate, she'd finish when her yet-to-be-born child graduated from high school.

A nurse came out and called a name. One of the cuddling couples across the room got up and walked forward, beaming like they'd won the lottery. Porter rolled her eyes and someone laughed. Porter jerked her head to the side, a sort of tucked-away corner of the waiting room, the place where the saddest-looking women tended to seat themselves (the sad women in any ob-gyn waiting room were always the ones with no bump, not even the deflating basketball of a former bump, those who were still swearing to themselves on the toilet when they got their period each month). She saw a woman chuckling.

"I saw that," she said. "Hi, Porter Strick." The woman was about as big as Porter, with just a waxing moon of a belly. She smiled widely, showing a gap between her teeth.

"Oh my god, Rachel, what are you doing here?" Porter stood up fast, knocking her book to the floor. She toed it out of the path and left it there.

Rachel had been Porter's best friend in the seventh through eleventh grades. They had worn matching Halloween costumes (Little Red Riding Hoods, candy corn, vampiresses) three times. Her parents had moved to Chicago during their junior year, and they'd lost touch. It was before the internet; it was no one's fault. Rachel had been back for a few years, Porter knew, but they hadn't gotten together. They each had their friends, and their lives, and there were always excuses. Or rather, there had never been a reason to try to jump back into the double dutch of their friendship.

"What do you think I'm doing here, my taxes?" Rachel stood up to embrace Porter, and their pregnant bellies bounced together with a satisfying **boing**. "Let me see you!" She backed up, still holding Porter's two hands, to take her in. "You look so great. So great. How many weeks are you?"

"Twenty."

"Me too! Well, twenty-one. Twins! Us, I mean. I'm not having twins, thank god. Anyway, I love it! This is so exciting! Where are you living now, near your mom? I'm, um, we're on the north side, Clapham Heights-ish, but farther away from the water. Toward Bard." Rachel's cheeks were pink. She was wearing a Fleetwood Mac T-shirt and looked a little bit sloppy, like she was probably wearing two different socks, not on purpose, and Porter felt immediately flooded with remembered and renewed love: shortcut love, muscle memory love.

"And your husband, what does he do again?" Porter knew a little bit, from Facebook—she could picture someone small and dark-haired, like Rachel, but didn't know any details.

Rachel held up her hand—Porter hadn't checked—and wiggled her unadorned fingers.

"At the moment, he does stuff with other people, I guess. Not really sure." And then she burst into tears and loud hiccupping sobs that echoed through the room. **They should have soundproofed for that,** Porter thought, as she took Rachel into her arms. It had to happen all the time.

After their appointments, Porter and Rachel sat in the hospital cafeteria and caught up over a mediocre feast of macaroni and cheese, iceberg lettuce salads, and potato chips. Some years were easy enough to sum up in a sentence or two— Chicago was cold but fun, Rachel had gone to Vassar, her younger brother was married and lived in Oakland, she taught English at Clapham Junior High, and mostly loved it ("Oh! Maybe you'll have my niece, Cecelia!" Porter interrupted, clapping her hands)—but the recent past took a while.

As it turned out, Rachel and her husband, Josh, had been together on and off for five years before they got married, and then started trying to have a baby pretty quickly. She had a miscarriage, then another, and finally, it turned out that she had what she described as a "funky uterus," which, coupled with Josh's low sperm count, made conceiving hard. They did IUI, to no avail, and then IVF, which took three rounds. Porter knew what that looked like—all the needles, all the blood tests, all the peeing into tiny paper cups. She murmured sympathetic noises. When Rachel finally got pregnant, she was relieved and happy and exhausted, sleeping every hour of the day that she wasn't at school, just the way things were supposed to be. Then one day she looked at her husband's phone and saw page after page of texts with a woman whose name she didn't recognize.

"What kind of texts?" Porter asked.

"Not the good kind. Not, like, oh, you're a woman and also my friend, so what should I buy my wife for her birthday? The bad kind. Like, I want to lick your asshole while you sit on my face."

"Noooooooooooo," Porter said, crinkling her nose.

Rachel shoved a handful of potato chips into her mouth. "Oh," she said, chewing. "Yes. And he couldn't lie about it, because what was he going to do, rip the phone out of my hand and give me the amnesia drug they give you before a colonoscopy? I don't think so."

"So what now?" Rachel swiveled the bag of chips around on the table to make it easier for Porter to take some. She was going to be a good mom. Porter put two of the sweet and salty chips on her tongue and closed her teeth, crunching down like a monster with someone in its trap. There was a tiny part of her that was excited about this story. It was an ugly part of her, a shameful part of her, but it was beginning to glow and dance just the same.

"I kicked him out. He's staying at his idiot

friend's house in Kingston. My mom came and helped me settle in, and she'll be here when the baby's born. Stay for six months, maybe, I don't know. It's just too much to deal with. I want to feel protected and happy and ready. I am not fucking around. Doing this alone is not exactly what I imagined. No offense. So, can I ask?"

Porter slapped the crumbs off her hands. "Ask away." She couldn't imagine Astrid moving in with her in a million years. She could imagine Astrid giving her the telephone number of a reputable nanny agency, or a woman who helped babies learn how to sleep, but not actually moving in herself, no, not that. And if she did move in, in some alternate universe, what would she do? Would she point out all the things Porter was doing wrong, all the empty teacups scattered around the room like clues to a child's scavenger hunt? The way that Porter should be eating while the baby ate or sleeping while the baby slept? Astrid always knew the best way to do everything and it was exhausting.

"Who's the father? Or did you go to a sperm bank? Is that a very rude thing to ask?" Rachel looked at her with wide-open eyes, curious both specifically and in general. Porter could see the future so clearly: Rachel was going to make things out of construction paper and cardboard boxes, she was going to make pancakes shaped like elephants. Whoever her jerk of a husband was, he didn't matter. Rachel was going to be great.

Porter hadn't told anyone except her mother. Her OB knew. Her RE knew. The nurses knew. But no one else. In a funny way, being pregnant meant exposing one's private parts and information to an enormous number of people, all of whom happened to be strangers. It was harder to tell someone who knew about other parts of her life in addition to her uterus. "It's not rude, you asked first. I went to a sperm bank."

"You know, I can honestly say that that has never sounded more appealing to me than right at this exact moment. Like, my husband's genes are fine; he's handsome, I love his parents, whatever. But the idea that I could have those things without ever having to speak to him again is, like, wow, yes." Rachel lifted her can of seltzer water.

Porter blushed, more relieved than she realized to have told someone she cared about and for them to have had a positive reaction, and clinked her can against Rachel's. "Thank you. I mean, we'll see. I'm sure it'll mean some serious conversations with my child down the road, but everyone has those— adopted kids, kids whose parents split up, parents who have to tell their kids that their grandmother was run over by their school bus. It was the right thing for me, and it was the right time. You know what's funny? Because I'm one of three, I always thought that I'd have three, but I can't imagine I'll have another. I guess it could happen, but the odds seem against it."

"Wow," Rachel said. "Yeah. I always assumed that we'd have a few, but now, I don't know. Man, I hadn't really thought about that."

"Don't mention it, though, okay? Obviously you wouldn't. Just please don't. Okay? I haven't told anyone about the baby. Or the donor." Porter worried that she sounded ashamed, or embarrassed. She wasn't either of those things, she was just thinking ahead. For the moment, the baby still felt like a secret hidden inside her body, and she wanted to protect both of them from the outside world, whatever the weather.

"To sisters doing it for themselves," Rachel said, and then took a long swallow of her water, letting out a demure little burp. "Next time, with booze. Oh, you know who I saw the other day, in the grocery store? Jeremy. Your boyfriend."

"When we were in high school." Porter's cheeks burned.

"Yes, but still. I don't know if it's my hormones or what, because I mostly hate all men at the moment, but he looked like an ice-cream cone. He was always a dick, but he's a cute dick."

"Yep," Porter said. "He's cute all right. Always was. He has a cute wife and cute kids too. Cute dog. Probably cute mice in the floorboards." An image of a half-naked Jeremy appeared in her mind's eye. She had heard that pregnancy made women horny, but until this moment, it had seemed unreasonable, as she had heretofore been horny only for antacids and Saltines. But there he was in her brain, Jeremy Fogelman, her first love, as sexually formative as Phoebe Cates coming out of the swimming pool in **Fast Times at Ridgemont High,** or a Judy Blume novel. So much of becoming an adult was distancing yourself from your childhood experiences and pretending they didn't matter, then growing to realize they were all that mattered and composed 90 percent of your entire being. If you didn't remember how you felt during that one game of Truth or Dare when you were a sophomore in high school, who were you? It was nice to know that those twangy feelings, deep inside her body, hadn't vanished for good. And part of the truth of staying close to home was that you were never very far from other people who remembered everything you'd ever done. It was like being surrounded by an army of terra-cotta soldiers, only they all looked like you—the time you threw up at Homecoming, the time you bled through your pants in math class, the time you got caught stealing condoms at the pharmacy.

"'Tis a pity," Rachel said. "Next time with martinis."

"Next time with whiskey **and** martinis," Porter said. "Let's get out of here."

Chapter 10

NFG

Astrid wanted everyone to show up at eleven, but Elliot's twins napped at noon, so brunch was at ten A.M. They were nonstop, Aidan and Zachary, and Astrid knew that Wendy cherished those solid hours in the middle of the day when they were asleep. Of the three of Astrid's children, she'd always thought that Elliot would be the one to have a truly big family, in part because he was the one least likely to actively parent on a daily basis, and so what was the difference between one and five children except a decibel level at mealtimes, but he was thirty-eight when the twins were born, and Astrid was pretty sure that Wendy was closed for baby-making, in part because she wanted to go back to work someday and also because the boys were such hellions that only a fool would willingly ask for more.

Sometimes, when more than one of her children were in the same room, Astrid thought about their father walking in—their father, her husband, Russell, who hadn't made it to the twenty-first century, who had never had a cellphone. Sometimes Astrid thought about that, about Russell traveling to and from his home and office, landline to landline, and it seemed impossibly quaint. She had lived most of her life without one, too, of course— she'd had a flip phone until Cecelia was born, and she understood the pull of always having a camera in her pocket—but Russell never even touched one, she didn't think. One of his college friends, a rich show-off who they had occasionally visited in California, had a car phone the size of a shoebox, and it was something that they laughed about, this hotshot fool who thought what he had to say was so important that he needed to be reachable even in his **car**. She'd had a dream about sitting at a restaurant with Birdie and seeing Russell walk by outside, and running out the door to catch him, but by the time she got outside, he was gone, and it turned out that she was barefoot anyway, and then the restaurant was gone and she had to walk home. Dreams didn't mean anything. Nicky thought they did, but Nicky had always been so good-looking that he believed in all kinds of things that less good-looking people weren't allowed to believe in, because people would laugh at them. No one laughed at gorgeous white men. It was a design flaw in the universe.

Before Barbara died, Astrid had thought about telling her kids about Birdie, but it never seemed to matter. Now it was time. It was time. They were adults, and so was she. Astrid could say the words.

It was 10:20 and no one had arrived yet. Even Cecelia was still in her room, though Astrid heard her clomping overhead.

Maybe it wasn't fair to compare daughters-in-law, just like it wasn't fair to compare sons, but Astrid couldn't help it. Children were the people they were from the beginning and, with the exception of a few social mores (public nose-picking, chanting about poop), rarely changed drastically from toddlerhood on. Nicky had always been a leaf in a river, content to float. His ease in his own skin had made him irresistible to other people, all his life. Elliot was the opposite—he tried so hard to be big enough, smart enough, charming enough, that he was none of the three. He was dedicated to the idea of perfection. As a boy, he'd whined for the largest toy, the biggest scoop of ice cream, the starting spot on the JV basketball team, no matter his skill. And both Nicky and Elliot had found the partners they needed. At least they'd found partners, unlike their poor sister.

It felt something like haunting the house of your widower and his new wife, to see the needs your adult children possessed and the people who filled them. Nicky met Juliette at a party, and they were married at City Hall two weeks later, their fingers always clutching and unclutching like mating spiders. She was decisive and focused, if self-destructive, she was **French,** and once Astrid met Juliette, she could see it all: the love affair, the unplanned child, the swan dive into normalcy, the gradual separation, the end. She felt psychic with visions of doom. Never mind that they were still married—they were trying to live some easygoing fantasy concocted in a forest ceremony, guided by a crystal. It was hooey, and everyone knew it but them. With Elliot, it was the reverse. Both Elliot and Wendy lived to check the boxes of adulthood. They had an engagement party. They had a wedding with two hundred people, three-quarters of them Wendy's enormous Chinese family, and a reception with a costume change halfway through. They had a baby shower, a gender-reveal party, and at each one of them, Elliot and Wendy would smile in the exact same way, even and false, their hands light on each other's backs, and Astrid would think, **What the fuck?** In some ways, Astrid thought that Wendy was just like her, a perfectionist, and was flattered that Elliot had looked for his mother, in some ways, just like the Greeks said. But Wendy's perfection didn't have anything to do with Astrid, not really—she cared about nutrition, not taste. She cared about calories, not exercise. But mothers-in-law don't matter in marriages except as points of contrast.

Russell Strick had never understood a single word that Astrid's mother had said, her English both heavy with Romanian and low in her throat, but he had liked her kasha varnishkes. His mother had been quiet, a dormouse, and Astrid knew that he liked having a wife who was not afraid to speak. Their mothers were not part of their daily lives, as parents. They were not on the rug in their socked feet, playing with the children, the way grandparents were nowadays, the way Astrid's children expected her to be. Russell had been the softie of the two of them. He would have let Cecelia cover his face with stickers, would have let the twins use his body as a trampoline. What would Russell have thought about Birdie as his successor in Astrid's bed? He would have liked her, and then he would have handed her his dirty plate to take back to the sink. He wouldn't have understood. Russell was the kind of man who met women who had lived with another woman for fifty years and thought, **Oh, how nice, roommates**. But Astrid herself had changed in the last twenty years—no doubt Russell would have too. That was a melancholy mystery: how his chest hair would have grayed, how he would feel about gender-neutral bathrooms, what he would make of Donald

Trump. Some days, Astrid felt like she was the same person she'd been when her husband died, but most of the time, that person felt like a distant relative, a cousin in another time zone, seen mostly in old photographs wearing unfashionable clothing.

The menu was simple: pancakes, bacon, scrambled eggs, toast, jam, fresh-squeezed juice, fruit. The twins were gluten-free, as was Wendy, so Astrid made a small batch of gluten-free pancake batter as well. She'd never heard of children with a gluten insensitivity before the twins were born, and it wasn't that she didn't believe it—she knew some celiac people, real ones—it was just that the twins weren't it, and neither was Wendy. She was helicoptering eating disorders into existence, and Elliot wouldn't say a thing about it. He was like the family dog that showed up at mealtimes, tongue out and panting. Both bowls of batter sat ready on the counter, each with its own ladle. The bacon sat cooling on a long oval plate. Astrid picked up a piece and ate it with her fingers.

The doorbell rang, and Astrid hurried to the foyer, even though no one coming would wait for her to open the door. When she got to the door and it was still closed, she looked through the glass panel on the side of the door and saw Birdie, with both arms wrapped around a bowl covered with plastic. The fruit salad.

Astrid pulled open the door. "You're the first guest! Everyone is late."

Birdie leaned in and kissed Astrid on the cheek. "Good morning."

"Good morning," Astrid said, already softening.

Birdie nudged Astrid back inside. "You sure you're ready?"

"Ready or not, here I come. Who knows when the next school bus is coming 'round the bend." They walked back into the kitchen, and Birdie set the fruit salad down on the table.

"There are lots of ways to do it. One at a time, all at once. I came out to my parents when I was twenty-five, even though I'm sure they'd known since I was twelve. I wrote a letter, and then they wrote a letter back all about how sorry they were that I was going to go to hell, and we never spoke of it again. Which was pretty good, I thought." Birdie picked up a strawberry and examined it.

"Well, I think that's horrible," Astrid said. "I'm going to tell them all at once, and they can cry or rend their clothes if they want to, but then it'll be done and we'll have pancakes." She shivered, not wanting to feel nervous but feeling it all the same. Feelings were the problem, really—if you asked her children, Astrid didn't think they would report that she had any, outside of the basics. Certainly not fear. Control: that's what Astrid had always had. Was control a feeling? The summer light filled the kitchen, with stripes of yellow banded across the hardwood floor. It would be a hot day, but it wasn't yet.

Astrid and Birdie's friendship had been fast, and unexpected. Birdie took over for Nancy at the salon five years ago, and Astrid could hardly believe it, that Birdie and Russell had lived in the same town, that they had both touched her body, the same body. Birdie had arrived so long after Russell died that the wounds weren't even fresh, it wasn't a topic of conversation for months. Had Russell ever touched her head? He had given foot massages. He had touched her body, he had touched her cheeks. But Astrid couldn't remember her husband ever touching her hair. Maybe to push it out of the way on a windy day? She couldn't remember. It had been so long that she didn't feel sad anymore, about the things she'd forgotten. Astrid remembered what she remembered, and that was enough.

When Russell died, everyone reached out to Astrid, in the way that polite people do—they sent cards, they called and offered to do "anything," which really meant nothing beyond the extraordinary gesture of putting said card in the mailbox. Nicky was a senior in high school then, the star of the spring play, and Porter was twenty, fat and happy from beer and independence in the dorm. Or at least she had been happy, until Russell died. Elliot was already out of college, applying to law school, trying on suits for size. Whatever else he did, Astrid didn't know about it. The four of them went to see a grief counselor, at the suggestion of Nicky's school counselor, a woman who, like so many people, took one look at Nicky's cheekbones and wanted to nestle him into her bosom, metaphorically speaking. His movie, **Jake George,** was about to come out, and the potential for it was heavy in the air, like the biggest and heaviest ornament on a Christmas tree. Porter and Nicky had both cried, and Astrid and Elliot had remained steady and then it was over. It hadn't done a thing.

But talking was nice, it was true, if the talking wasn't always so focused on the one thing, like every widow was a robot of sadness, and so all those years later, when Nancy moved to Florida and Birdie took over the salon, Astrid asked if she'd like to have lunch. That was how it started. Every Monday, Astrid and Birdie went to Spiro's for omelets, or the serviceable vegetarian place on Columbus Street for salads and iced tea, and talked and laughed, and it made a difference in her mood. Astrid didn't need a therapist; she had Birdie.

Their first kiss didn't happen for another two years. It was February, close to Valentine's Day, though Astrid hadn't thought of it at the time. Weeks later, when Astrid had pointed out the coincidence, Birdie had laughed and said, yes, Astrid,

I know. Astrid had been seduced, and she didn't even know it was coming. **Chocolat** was playing, for the holiday, at Upstate Films in Rhinebeck, and Birdie suggested they go, which sounded just lovely to Astrid, who was used to being home in the evenings, as if her children were going to wander in and need to be fed and tucked in. It was freezing cold and windy, and Astrid remembered holding her hat to her head so that it didn't blow away as they walked from the car to the theater.

The movie was well-photographed nonsense. She'd missed it when it came out the first time. The actors had extraordinary faces and sometimes that was enough. Birdie snickered often, and Astrid didn't shush her. Russell had also loved going to the movies—any movie with gangsters, with the Mafia, with machine guns, he loved it. This was different. Birdie leaned close to make comments about Johnny Depp's gypsy character, about the dialogue, about the way the characters rolled their eyes in ecstasy when they tasted the chocolate. At one point, Birdie ran into the lobby and came back with a package of M&M's, unable to resist. Toward the end of the movie, when Birdie reached out and put her hand on top of Astrid's, she gave her a look, playful and curious, and as soon as Astrid felt their skin touch, she understood what had been brewing, that it had been there all the while, just under the surface, like a child who understands a language fully before they can speak it.

When Birdie kissed her good night after the movie, she kissed her on the lips, and Astrid was ready. That was the story she wanted to tell her children, in some parallel universe, where all things were equally appropriate. Where she'd been a different sort of mother. For the last five years, she and Birdie had been best friends. When Elliot's twins were born, she bought soft-edged dump trucks in two different colors, thoughtful and generous. No one ever thought about their mother's lunch dates. Clapham was LGBTQ-friendly; all the guidebooks said so. There were rainbow flags hanging out of shop windows and restaurants. It turned out that Astrid was even friendlier than that.

The doorbell rang again, and Astrid jumped.

"I'll get it!" Cecelia called, running down the stairs. She pulled open the door and Elliot's boys ran inside without a moment's pause, each of them wielding a large plastic sword. The boys weren't identical, but Wendy had somehow kept them dressed in nearly identical clothing every day of their lives, and it took slowing both children to a complete halt and holding them side by side in order to tell which one was which. Wendy put a **Z** and an **A** on the toes of their sneakers, which they then sometimes swapped, just to mess with their minders.

"Hi," Wendy said, stepping over the doormat. "Sorry. Hi." She had a heavy-looking nylon bag on each shoulder.

"Thanks! And don't worry, I'll catch them!" Cecelia scampered off after the boys, happy to have actual targets for her energy.

Elliot followed Wendy into the kitchen. They were both in their weekend attire, which meant chino shorts with belts and polo shirts. They could golf at a moment's notice, like rich superheroes.

"Hi, Mom," Elliot said, and gave Astrid a dispassionate kiss on the cheek. He looked at Birdie, who was standing behind Astrid, and paused. "Birdie," he said. "Good to see you."

"I get my hair cut in Rhinebeck," Wendy said, apologizing, as she had every time she'd been in the same room as Birdie, as if Birdie's job required a follicle confession. "I've been going to my person forever." Wendy had been at the top of her class in college, and then the top of her law school class. After the twins, she'd gone back to work part time at a law firm in New Paltz, but her specialty— corporate law—had been downgraded to small businesses, and Astrid knew that it did not fill her with fire and passion. Her most successful client was a man who owned most of the Hudson Valley's Dairy Queens.

"That's okay," Birdie said. "They're doing a great job, your hair looks terrific. So full. It's hard, after childbirth, most women lose a lot of volume."

Wendy looked pleased. "It's expensive, but hey, it's worth it, right?"

Elliot picked an apple out of the bowl on the

counter and took a big crunching bite. "Your hair always looks the same." Wendy flicked him on the shoulder, her fingernails clicking against each other.

"It looks great," Astrid said. "That's what he means."

There was a knock at the door, and then Porter opened it, holding more food. Some Clap Happy cheese, of course, and probably a nice crusty loaf of bread. Astrid liked things prepared, things with ingredients and recipes, but everything that Porter cooked or made was—what did they call it now?—rustic. Porter ate all her meals out of a giant bowl, like one of her goats, just everything piled on top of everything else. Astrid watched her daughter wade through the bags that had been dropped by the door, the toys that Aidan and Zachary had somehow already strewn about, and one of Cecelia's shoes. Astrid felt full of love for her daughter, who had brought things and was going to stay. Birdie told Astrid that she should tell her children things like that, when she had little moments of appreciation, that it was nice to know your mother thought nice thoughts about you, even if they were tiny little things that didn't matter. Astrid had always kept tiny little things to herself, in addition to most things that weren't tiny or little at all. It wasn't small, being in love—she was in **love**—for the second time in her life, and at this point, when falling in love seemed less likely than, well, getting hit by a school bus. Astrid reminded herself of that, watching Birdie fill the kettle at the sink, her dark curls lying against her neck. When they met, Birdie's hair had been mostly brown, and now it was mostly gray. Maybe all her life she'd been waiting for someone with curly hair to arrive.

"Everyone, I have something to say," Astrid said. Porter set her things down on the counter, and Cecelia poked her head out of the hallway.

"Whoa whoa whoa," Porter said, shaking her head. She drew a line across her neck with her finger. "Mom, don't."

"No, Porter," Astrid said. She wasn't in the business of telling someone else's secrets. Porter took a breath and nodded. That was something, right there! She would have to remember to tell Birdie, it was an anecdote in the making, something she could tell her grandchild when she was born, her last grandchild, no doubt—**your mother thought I was going to tell everyone about you, but Gammy would never**. Elliot and Wendy were having an almost-entirely silent conversation about him taking the car, and her getting the boys home; no one was paying attention to her. The boys were running up the stairs, shouting, "POW POW POW." Life wouldn't slow down more than this. Astrid cleared her throat and continued. "Birdie and I are in a romantic relationship and have been for quite some time. And after seeing Barbara, well, I don't know, it didn't interest me to keep it from you any longer. If you have any questions, ask away. But brunch is served."

"What did she say?" Elliot asked Wendy.

Porter let out a giant laugh and then clapped her hand over her mouth. She buried her head in Astrid's shoulder. "Wow," she said, and kissed her mother on the cheek. "Birdie, you are in for it." Porter walked over to the sink and gave Birdie a hug. "Or you've **been** in for it, I guess." Porter shook her head. "I love it."

"Mom, are you serious?" Elliot kept his voice low. "This is totally crazy. What are you saying?" He scrunched his face and turned toward Wendy. "What are we supposed to tell Aidan and Zachary, that Gammy has a special friend? I can't believe you're springing this on us like this. Honestly, I'm angry." He clenched his jaw. "How long have you been lying to us?"

"Oh, El. And, yes, you can tell the boys that Gammy's friend Birdie is a special kind of friend, they'll only care if you do. And why would you? You don't need to put a name on anything. We're not running off to join the circus. I'm not getting a tattoo on my forehead." Astrid felt her cheeks burn, but she kept moving and put a stack of plates on the dining room table. She had expected this, even the word **lying,** as if that one slippery word could contain everything she felt for Birdie, everything she felt for her children, everything she'd wanted to share, and everything she wanted to keep to herself. "Please, help yourself. Bacon, Cece?"

Cecelia hadn't moved from the edge of the hallway. Astrid couldn't quite read the expression on her face. She slowly made her way through the foyer and into the kitchen, picking up a plate and a handful of bacon. "I thought," Cecelia said, carefully, with just a hint of a smile on her face, "that I was here because it was a stable home environment."

"Trust me," Birdie said, picking up her own plate. "There is nothing more stable than—forgive me, Astrid—an elderly lesbian." Birdie was nine years younger than Astrid—only fifty-nine years old. Those nine years would have meant something, once upon a time, different schools, different phases of life, but now nine years felt like a blink. In the not-too-distant future, nine years would be a lot again—the difference between eighty and seventy-one, the difference between ninety-five and eighty-six, but for now, they were floating through time together, both healthy and active, both breathing.

Elliot exhaled through his mouth. "I'll get the boys and tell them it's time for pancakes. Can we please cool it with the L-word, please?" He stomped toward the stairs and called their names, to which the only response was a high voice bellowing, "I'M GOING TO KILL YOU IN THE

FACE WITH MY SWORD!," which could have been either twin. Wendy hurried along after.

"I wouldn't call myself a lesbian," Astrid said. "Just to be clear, I'm bisexual. I think that's the word one would use. Not that I'm using a word!" Though it did feel electric to say out loud, and Astrid looked forward to saying it again, in private, just for fun, to see if it zipped up her spine again, like the county fair game with the hammer and the bell. Birdie kissed her on the cheek.

"I have to say, Mom," Porter said, "I really thought you were going to let me be the complicated one in the family for a few more minutes. Honestly, I'm impressed."

"NFG," Cecelia said, and then tightly pursed her lips, as if she could swallow back something she shouldn't have said. Birdie and Porter and Astrid all looked at her expectantly. Cecelia rolled her eyes. "Don't make me say it," she said. They didn't move. "No fucks given."

Astrid let out a whoop. "I love it! That's my new motto, my dear. NFG, Birdie, you hear that?" When had she last whooped? What else was she capable of? Birdie made her feel like she could parachute out of an airplane like George Bush on his ninetieth birthday. She watched Porter's eyes fly open with surprise and, she thought, amusement.

"Mom, if you start saying the F-word in front of Elliot or his children, he will actually die." Porter stuck her finger into one bowl of the pancake batter and then put the finger into her mouth. "What is this garbage?"

"Gluten-free," Astrid said. "Try the other one. And I'll be good, promise." Porter ladled out the regular batter onto the hot griddle and the room filled with the smell of warm butter. Birdie put her hand on Astrid's back and left it there, where it glowed and hummed for several minutes, until Aidan and Zachary were finally dragged downstairs under punishment of death and they all sat at the table and ate, except for Elliot, who excused himself after seething for fifteen minutes, not to be seen again.

Chapter 11

Secondhand News

The weekend before school started, Porter took Cecelia shopping. Starting eighth grade at a new school in a new town was less than ideal but it did offer a certain unanticipated chance at reinvention, and where better to start than with one's clothes? Porter thought about all the women she could have been if given the opportunity to have a drastic change in her life even once a decade—a shaved head, a semester in a country where she didn't speak a word. Porter knew so many people, both men and women, who lived as if their parents were just faraway ghosts, with no gravitational pull, no say over their behavior. That sounded like a lovely way to live, and Porter was sure she'd enjoy it, if she someday moved to Mars.

(Though, in truth, if Porter figured out how to get to Mars, Astrid would be waiting in her space-suit on the other end, picking her up in a sensible Rover, having already found the **only** place one should buy astronaut ice cream.)

The store Porter liked most, Secondhand News, was up the block from the Clapham train station. Unlike Boutique Etc? and the other stores for women who had reached the chenille-tunic stage of life, Secondhand News was cool. It was small but packed, in an old Victorian house, with furniture and housewares on the first floor and clothing—faded T-shirts and gunnysack dresses and polyester disco gowns and vintage Levi's—on the second. The real reason that Porter wanted to take Cecelia, though, was that she was friends with John and Ruth Sullivan, the best-dressed couple in town, and she knew that their son was also going into the eighth grade at Clapham Junior High. Maybe "friends" was a stretch—John had been in Elliot's class in school, though they hadn't been friends, and when John turned into an interesting adult man, with an even more interesting wife, Porter found she didn't always know what to say, but they always smiled and greeted each other warmly and sometimes that was enough. Everyone in town wanted to be friends with John and Ruth.

Porter pushed Cecelia through the creaky door of the shop and heard the little bell tinkle, announcing their arrival. She had emailed to say they were coming—it was her first attempt at a setup, and she wanted to make sure August would be there. It was funny, to think about people roughly her age having teenage children. Nicky had been so young when Cecelia was born, and it had happened so completely by accident, as if he and Juliette had no clue how human reproduction worked. They hadn't thought about how fully it would transform their lives, and then somehow it hadn't—yes, they'd had a baby strapped to their body at all times, but they'd taken her everywhere, to dance performances and museums, to parties and restaurants. By the time she was three, Cecelia had slept in more bars than a lifelong alcoholic. If Porter had had a baby when she was young, it wouldn't have been like that. She would have been measuring ounces of milk and counting diapers and calling the pediatrician every time the baby sneezed, full of anxiety, the way God intended. That was the part that Porter was ready for now, even if it meant saying goodbye to the freedom she'd enjoyed her adult life thus far—she had five months left. Not that it was death row, but still—it was a line that she was going to cross, and once she was on the other side, there was no coming back. Porter looked at Cecelia's pink cheeks and remembered how it felt to feel simultaneously embarrassed and taken care of by someone else.

"Hello?" Porter called out. The store smelled musty and sweet, and even though the shades were all open, the house was perched in such a way that it was still cool and dark inside.

"Hey, be right there," John called from somewhere invisible.

Cecelia wandered toward a lone rack of dresses in the center of the room, and Porter lingered nearby. Everything about how a woman approached clothing came directly from her mother—if she loved it, if she hated it, if she knew how to iron pleats or tie scarves. Astrid was functional and sartorially conservative and so Porter was functional and ridiculous—she wore nubby fleece zip-ups and corduroy pants, socks with cartoon characters on them. She dressed like a preschooler, really, much to Astrid's chagrin. Juliette shopped like a French person—though she'd never had money, she always looked like she did. Because her body was the same as it had been when she was a teenager, her clothing lasted forever, while Porter's closet was littered with mountains of things she no longer could wear, the way a snake's shed skin littered the bottom of its cage. Porter watched Cecelia pull dresses out to look at them, and then push them back in. She wasn't a magpie like so many little girls, just drawn to shiny things. Juliette's maternal influence was still there, inside.

There was a **clump-thump-clump** cascade of steps on the stairs, and then John was in the room.

He was wearing glasses that Porter thought he didn't need. It seemed like a professional hazard. In addition to running the store with him, John's wife, Ruth, volunteered for the Clapham Chamber of Commerce, planning the village's various festivities and fairs. Ruth and Porter worked together every year on the Clapham event where all the summer people came back for a crowded weekend full of apple picking and cider donuts, and where Porter would set up a booth for Clap Happy to give away samples of all her varieties, on Costco Triscuits and tiny bamboo spoons.

"Hi, John, yay," Porter said. "This is my niece, Cecelia, remember? She's starting at CJHS. I thought August might be around?"

"Sweetheart!" John kissed Porter on the cheek and then hollered in the direction of the stairs. "Come say hi!"

Cecelia froze. "Is this a setup?" she whispered to Porter. "You said we were just going shopping."

"We are," Porter said. "We're shopping for clothes **and** friends."

"August is very nice," John said. "I promise."

"What do you need, you think, Cecelia?" Porter asked, moving next to her niece. "Jeans? I kind of love bell-bottoms again; is that weird, John?"

"You know how it works," John said. "If you're old enough to have worn it the last time around, it's probably ready to come back. The nineties were a fertile time for sailor jeans."

"I'm old. You're telling me that I'm old." Porter mimed strangling herself. "But, really, I like them." She had worn bell-bottoms on her first day of high school, with a shrunken baby-blue T-shirt that read SKATEBOARD on it, even though she'd never ridden a skateboard in her life.

There was another set of footsteps on the stairs, and then August appeared with a weightless leap. He was all arms and legs, like a puppy with comically large paws—his body, like Cecelia's, was still in the midst of figuring out what it looked like. His face was just like Ruth's—he had dark eyes and a pointed chin and eyebrows like em dashes across his pale forehead. His hair swung out from behind his ears, and then settled onto his shoulders like a medieval prince in slow motion.

"August, this is Cecelia, Porter's niece. Show her around?"

August mimed irritation with an eye roll, which made Cecelia's shoulders contract into her body like a pangolin rolling into a little armored knot; Porter watched it happen. But then he nodded amiably and tugged her on the elbow. "Let's start with T-shirts." He spun on his heels and headed toward the stairs, Cecelia following behind like a person being sent to death row.

"We're going to run across the street and grab some coffee," John said. "Okay?"

"Okay," August said.

John patted Porter on the back. "It'll be easier without us, trust me."

She had so much to learn from him. Porter would have stayed to shop, but apparently that wasn't what parents did.

"Want to look at clothes?" August said, not unkindly. "Come on." He was so comfortable in the space that Cecelia had no choice but to pretend she was too. She'd never really been friends with boys, not since she was in preschool. Even then, there always seemed to be a threat of kissing, or being punched, like boys had no agency over their own bodies and were being controlled by tiny aliens who lived in their brains. Of course, now the girls were even worse, and the boys at her old school now seemed like stuffed animals in comparison, docile idiots for whom pizza solved any emotional difficulty. Maybe it was time to give boys another try. Upstairs, August flipped quickly through the racks. Cecelia wondered if she should start making a list of all the times in her life that she'd felt left behind. How long would it take to run out of paper and ink? The bell tinkled again downstairs, which meant that she was now alone again, with this new person. She watched him from behind, his thin fingers moving so quickly they were nearly blurry. He didn't turn or acknowledge her presence for a few minutes, which actually made Cecelia feel better about the whole thing, as though he might have forgotten that she was there, and she could slowly back out the way she'd come.

"Try this one," he said, slipping a shirt off its hanger and tossing it over his shoulder.

Cecelia stumbled to catch the flying cotton ball, and then unwound it to look. It felt like it had been washed a thousand times, as soft as a piece of clothing could get before total disintegration. There was a drawing of the Statue of Liberty, and underneath, in script, NEW YORK CITY.

"I love it," Cecelia said, Lady Liberty waving at her from home. They—her parents—hadn't said how long this would go on, their little experiment, removing her from her native environment to see if she would grow roots or wilt in the new soil. A year, she guessed. But they hadn't said. A tear began to form way down at the base of Cecelia's throat and she swallowed and swallowed until it disappeared.

"I'm good at this," August said. "It's my summer job. And my fall job. Et cetera. If a job can be something you don't get paid for."

"That's so cool," Cecelia said, and then wished she hadn't. She didn't understand what made something cool, but she did understand that calling something cool instantly undid whatever magic had been at work. August turned to look at her and raised an eyebrow. "I mean, if you're into, like, wearing stuff."

"Right," August said. "And Clapham's nudist scene is really coming along, I don't know if your aunt told you." He tossed something else.

"What?" Cecelia said as she caught it.

"I'm joking." He moved on to the next rack and pulled a few more things off hangers, placing the empty hangers in a neat pile on the floor. "Here, try them on." August shoved aside a heavy velvet curtain and put the things on an overstuffed chair. Cecelia waited for him to leave before she walked in.

It had been six months since Cecelia's best friend had met someone. Met someone. As if that was a normal thing for a seventh grader to do outside the confines of school or gymnastics class or someone's birthday party. Katherine was the first to get her period, first to get a bra, first to get a phone, first to kiss a boy in Truth or Dare, first to get her own Snapchat account.

The guy said he was in high school at Brooklyn Tech, which was only a few blocks away from their school. He said this in her DMs, and then he said it to her in person at the coffee shop on Fulton Street, and then he said it to her again at his apartment by Prospect Park, an apartment clearly occupied by a single adult man with no parents in sight. Katherine had told Cecelia this in the same tone that she'd used to tell her about stealing a Juul from a Starbucks bathroom, where she'd found it resting on the lip of the sink. She was excited, as proud as a peacock fanning its stupendous feathers.

Cecelia looked at the pile of clothing August had left for her—T-shirts, mostly, plus a few mystery items. He kept thrusting things over the metal curtain rod, and they fell on Cecelia's head like enormous snowflakes, if snowflakes smelled vaguely of mothballs. She peeled off her T-shirt and stood there in her bra, looking at her reflection in the cloudy mirror. She was taller than she had been at the beginning of the summer. She had a mole on the left side of her stomach, which she thought made it look like she had two belly buttons, like someone from a realistic science-fiction movie, where the world was mostly the same except that people had extra body parts and machines could talk. Her boobs were still pathetic and, Cecelia was pretty sure, disfigured. Her mom's nipples were brownish little polka dots on her boyish body, but Cecelia's were soft pink, hardly darker than the rest of her skin, and that just seemed wrong. It also seemed wrong that a boy was standing right outside the dressing room and knew that she was at least partially naked. Sometimes Cecelia had fantasies about moving to rural Pennsylvania and living with the Amish, canning fruit and making pies and swimming in a floor-length dress. Covered up. That sounded so much easier. Maybe a burqa.

She reached down and grabbed the first thing on the pile. It was a vintage jumpsuit, flame red with orange stripes running from shoulder to wrist. Cecelia stepped into it and zipped it up. It fit her perfectly and made her legs look three miles long. She turned around to admire the gathering in the back. She could do a karate kick. She could jump. She could fix a car, or fight crime, not that she knew how to do either of those things. Cecelia looked like a badass, which was not something she'd ever looked like before. Cecelia thought about her body as a thing totally disconnected from her brain, a tadpole with feet, only halfway to where it needed to go. The jumpsuit made her feel like a whole frog. She could even leap. Cecelia pulled aside the curtain and August bowed, pleased.

"See, **that's** cool," he said. "Like, David Bowie. I mean that as a compliment."

"Thanks," Cecelia said. She knew that her mother loved David Bowie but Cecelia didn't know any of his songs or what he looked like, and so she just tried to put on a neutral expression.

"I made my best friend, Emily, try that on, but it didn't fit," August said.

"Oh," Cecelia said, surprised to discover that it

felt like she had been poked in the abdomen with a stick.

"She always comes to visit during the year. She lives in Westchester, Dobbs Ferry. We go to camp together. It's been, like, four summers. Her parents are therapists and love to talk about feelings and sex and stuff, but, whatever, they let her sleep in my room."

"Oh," Cecelia said again, hoping that her face made it look like she'd had even a smattering of the life experiences August had had, and that she absolutely understood his situation. "Cool."

"So, you live with your aunt?" August asked. He was putting things back on their hangers, and Cecelia hurried back into the changing room, to try on the rest of the pile, and to make sure she left everything hung up and folded. She didn't want to leave a mess, she wanted to help.

"My grandmother. I mean, for now." The weirdest part of the whole thing was that for the first time in her life Cecelia saw her entire future as a giant question mark. That was what she pictured—before, it was another year of her middle school, then vying for a spot at one of the good public high schools, and then college. She thought she'd want to stay in the city, maybe, or maybe not. But that was five years away, and five years ago she was eight years old, and so five years sounded like an eternity. Now, instead of any of that, there was just a giant empty space, like her future had been abducted by aliens. A question mark floating in the sky.

"What happened?" August asked, gently.

"I don't know," Cecelia answered. It had gotten away from her, that was the truth. "Stuff."

Downstairs, the bell tinkled again, and Porter called out, "Yoo-hoo! Anybody home?" and Cecelia wondered if her parents would let her sleep at a boy's house. They probably would, because the notion of it being anything other than a **Sound of Music** sing-along would literally never cross their minds, or, even more likely, they wouldn't understand why any parent would say no. Juliette had tried to talk to Cecelia about making love (her words) the day that Cecelia got her first period, which made Cecelia bury her face in a pillow and scream. At that moment, Cecelia was pretty sure she didn't know anything about anything, and that she was the most pathetic teenager who had ever lived, but at least she knew what she was going to wear on the first day of school.

Chapter 12

Condolences

Astrid made two loaves of banana bread and two trays of turkey meatloaf. It wasn't exactly summer food but who cared, they were both dishes she could make with her eyes closed and one hand tied behind her back. Barbara had grown up on the Connecticut shore, Astrid knew, but had moved her mother to Clapham a decade ago, when her health began to decline. Lots of people did that, moved their aging parents closer instead of clearing out a room in their own house, the way previous generations had. Of course in a marriage, such decisions were fraught and almost always told you who held the most power. Barbara and Bob were childless, and Astrid imagined that Barbara had made the case for her mother to be their roommate, but maybe she was wrong. It was impossible to know what went on in anyone else's home, behind closed doors and behind closed mouths.

The Bakers lived on the east side of town, away from the river, in a small yellow house with a Little Free Library in the front yard, a birdhouse-size wooden box where neighbors could exchange books. Astrid peeked inside and saw three romance novels, two self-help books, one spider, and half a cookie. She guessed that Bob had little to nothing to do with it, and that the library would languish and die much more slowly than Barbara herself.

She rang the doorbell and waited, and when still no one came, she rang again. Astrid set the things down on the porch and turned to walk back to her car when Bob pulled open the screen door.

"Hi there," he said. He was dressed in a white T-shirt and jeans, the waistline of which hung low beneath his belly, Santa Claus in the off-season. "I appreciate it." Bob stepped backward into the house, propping the door open behind him. A wiry orange cat darted out and ran down the front steps. "She'll come back," he said, unalarmed. "They always do. Come on in."

Astrid waved. "Oh, no, I couldn't." But then when Bob didn't budge, she did, bending low to pick up the dishes and then plodding slowly into the house.

She'd been to the Bakers' home once, for a holi-day party, maybe thirty years ago. It was funny, to think of a house outliving a person, but of course they usually did. All Barbara's things still sat in their places of honor on the mantel: her basket of yarn and knitting needles, the framed photographs of her and Bob on their wedding day, Barbara's face thinner and beaming. Women were so much better at this than men—she didn't know a single widowed man who had cleaned out his wife's closet by himself. Astrid had kept Russell's watches and tie clips, his date books and high school yearbooks, his wedding ring, an album of childhood photographs, and that was it. No sweaters, no shoes, no pajamas. Why should she—why should anyone—keep drawers full of clothes that would never be worn again? It wasn't just sentimental, it was stupid. Not that Bob should have done it already, but Astrid knew that when the time came, and Bob succumbed to whatever it was that would kill him (for we would all be killed one day, one way or another), Barbara's drawers would still be full of her well-worn cotton underpants and thick marled socks.

"Thank you for this," Bob said. He took the food into the kitchen, leaving Astrid alone in the living room. She stood silent, holding her hands in front of her body like a choir girl. Bob hurried back, patting his hands against his thighs. "Barb's sister is planning the service, she got here yesterday."

"I didn't know that Barbara had a sister; that must be a big help," Astrid said. She herself was an only child, and she found old people with siblings somewhat ridiculous, as if they were eighty-year-olds who still wore water wings in swimming pools. Siblings were for the very young and needy. She had given her children siblings to occupy each other in childhood.

"Carol drove down from Vermont. Her kids are grown, and her husband is retired, so he can mind the dogs. She's a breeder. Havanese. They love animals, the whole family." Bob's eyes went twinkly with moisture.

"How lovely," Astrid said, and nodded solemnly. She looked at the unvacuumed floor, at the basket of knitting needles, at the half-empty drinking glasses on the cluttered coffee table. Bob blew his nose.

"The cats don't know what to do," he said. "When she left for Heron Meadows, Barb would still come back every day to visit, but now they're just climbing the walls. They know she's gone."

"Creatures are such a comfort in times of need," Astrid said, though she believed pets were useful only in teaching small children about death. She knew this was an unpopular opinion. For the first years of their relationship, Birdie had had an ancient, lumbering dog, a big galumph who slept at her feet, and Astrid thought that her sensitivity to Birdie following the dog's eventual, gradual, endless passing showed that she'd made great strides as a person. If she'd bought dogs for her children, she might have been a better mother, though that was what the siblings had been for. "Well, to your health, Bob."

Bob nodded. "Thanks again." The ceiling was low, and the room was crowded with too much furniture by half. There were woven rag rugs everywhere, no doubt to keep Barbara's feet warm as she walked from cat to cat, mewing motherly encouragement. Astrid didn't want to hug him, so she didn't, and she hurried out quickly before Bob started to cry in earnest.

Heron Meadows was set back from the road, with a large wooden fence and a tiny gatehouse for the security guard, whose job it was to make sure that no one's granny escaped in a nightie and bare feet. Astrid parked in the lot and walked in, greeting everyone she passed. Russell's mother had lived at Heron Meadows for the last ten years of her life, and Astrid knew the halls well. No one wanted to outlive their children, and so after Russell died, Astrid made an extra effort to bring the children to visit. It was the least she could do, nearly, just after not bringing them at all.

Like most dedicated residences for old people, Heron Meadows had a vague odor of bleach and urine, and framed reproductions of famous paintings (Monet's **Water Lilies**, Van Gogh's **Starry Night**, no Picasso or Caravaggio) hung on the

walls. Fake plants were here and there in large
terra-cotta pots, evergreen. Astrid asked at the desk
where Birdie was cutting hair and wandered off to
find her.

The Meadows was shaped like a tarantula, with
a fat middle and long legs extending outward, each
hall occupied by residents' rooms. In the middle
section, past the desk, were an exercise room and
a physical therapy room, a television room, and a
bingo room. Birdie's setup at Heron Meadows was
in the bingo room, which was otherwise used for
bridge games and singletons doing word search
puzzles in cheap newsprint books. Astrid peeked
through the open doorway (doorways needed to
be wide, to allow for wheelchairs) and observed
Birdie in action.

There was a woman in the chair, with her back
to the door. Her white hair was damp, and Birdie
was running a comb through it, catching strays.
There was a large plastic mat on the floor, to help
with cleanup. Her various instruments waited on
a round wooden table nearby: two hand mirrors,
a spray bottle of detangler, a spray bottle of water,
a hair-dryer, combs, brushes, clips, and three different pairs of scissors. The residents could sign up
in advance, or they could just show up and wait.
No one was in a rush. By the end of the day, the
room would be full of men and women just waiting patiently, as if for an airplane flight home after
Thanksgiving, full of pie and tryptophan. Birdie

was quick and efficient and, like all hairdressers, adept at the kind of small talk that young people hated but old people loved. Astrid watched Birdie work, her back hunched over in a tight curve, her knees bending slightly. She moved like a boxer.

"Coo coo," Astrid called. "Little Bird."

Birdie looked up, her glasses wedged halfway up her forehead. She waved with a pair of scissors. "Almost done with Doris," she said. "Right, Doris? Almost done?" Doris offered a beatific smile with pink gums and no teeth.

"I'll do a lap," Astrid said. Barbara's mother, Mary Budge, was around Heron Meadows somewhere, and Astrid was going to find her. She went back to the front desk and asked for directions to Mary Budge's room and then walked her tote bag full of food down the wide hallways until she found it.

The doors were never locked at Heron Meadows—that was a safety precaution. And since so many residents were hearing impaired, each room had a doorbell that, in addition to making a small tinkling noise, illuminated a flashing light inside, like a buoy in the ocean. Astrid rang the bell and waited. After a few minutes, the door swung open, and there was Mary Budge. She looked exactly like Barbara, only shrunken 15 percent in a xerox machine. Her shoulders, round as truck wheels, pitched forward, as if she was always halfway through an attempt to touch her toes.

"Hi, Mrs. Budge, I'm Astrid," Astrid said, patting herself on the chest. "Might I visit with you for a few minutes? I knew your daughter, Barbara."

Mary nodded and closed her eyes. She opened the door wide and gestured for Astrid to come in.

The room was identical to all the other rooms at Heron Meadows, some of them mirror images instead of exact replications. Mary's room was the same model as Russell's mother's room had been, L-shaped and tidy, with each dusted knickknack in its place of pride. Barbara's hoarding had not been born from nothing, Astrid saw.

Mary shuffled back toward her recliner and then sat down with a soft squish, covering her knees with a crocheted blanket. Astrid thought to herself, **I will never be that old,** even though that was one of the basic tenets of human existence: stay alive as long as you can. Heron Meadows wasn't the only place for old people in or near Clapham—there was a residence facility near the hospital, for those needing more constant medical attention, and there were a few of what Astrid thought of as boardinghouses for old broads. The men died first, of course, in Clapham and everywhere else. When the apocalypse came, there would be only old women left, with hard candy and clementines in their bags. Some of her older friends (everything was relative, even age, even now) had started to fail, to crumble; some had died. She was still young enough (again, relative) that every death felt like a wrong, cruel blow, and not yet like the eventual and unavoidable mercy that would come for everyone. Mercy! Astrid was not anywhere near mercy. Women her age were still working, even if she wasn't. Astrid had worked at the Clapham Local Bank after Russell died, first as a teller and then as a financial adviser, because she loved telling people what to do with their money. She'd retired at sixty-five, because there were younger bankers, and she wanted to spend more time in the garden. But look at Ruth Bader Ginsburg! Astrid had decades, she hoped.

Mary Budge sat quietly, her hands cupped on the crocheted hills of her knees. Astrid sat across from her on the daybed, which, she realized just after sitting down, must have been where Barbara had been sleeping.

"I brought some things to eat," Astrid said, and took some things out of the bag and waved them around.

"Sandwiches," Mary said, though they weren't, and smiled.

"I'll leave everything by your kitchen," Astrid said, putting the tinfoiled loaf back into the bag. "I'm sorry about Barbara."

"Yes, Barb," Mary said.

Astrid's mother had died thirty years ago, before Russell, before Russell's parents, before anyone else who mattered to her. It had been sickening, the very worst kind of surprise, one that proved

instantly the cruel randomness of the world, as if
famine and genocide and car accidents hadn't already. Her mother had always seemed older than
she was, but she'd never actually been old. Astrid
wondered what her mother would have thought
about Porter's baby, about Birdie, about the way
she'd renovated the kitchen cabinets, about each
summer's crop of flowers, which had survived,
which had grown. Her mother and Russell now
lived in the same neighborhood of her mind,
which felt like a remote Norwegian fjord, or Fiji, a
place that it would take so long to travel to that she
would never go in person, and so hard to imagine
the time difference that it was never convenient
to telephone. They were both **there,** still, inside
her brain, and sometimes she would wake up in
the middle of the night and think, **Now, now, if I
could just pick up the phone right now, maybe
I could catch them**.

"I'm in love," Astrid said.

Mary nodded, smiling.

"With a woman."

Mary nodded again. There were only a dozen
men in the building at any moment, Astrid
guessed, most of them on staff. Maybe all Mary's
friends had gone lez in their widow queendom.
Most women over the age of forty were misandrists
when you got right down to it. They wanted their
husbands around for manual labor, but what else?
And of course, once husbands started dying off, it

was all women anyway, and who cared who slept with whom, who cuddled close or shared a precoffee kiss? Nobody. Astrid felt emboldened and kept talking.

"My daughter's having a baby with a ghost," Astrid said. "Not an actual ghost, but with a negative space, with no person."

Mary nodded. "Mm-hmm," she said.

How long had it been since Mary Budge had held a baby? Human lives were so long, it was hard to stretch a net wide enough to hold all of a person's experiences. What did Mary remember? Did she remember her wedding? Being a teenager? Did she remember Barbara losing a tooth for the first time, and how she'd tucked a crisp $2 bill under her pillow, fresh from the bank?

"Your daughter and I didn't always get along," Astrid said. "But we knew each other for a very long time." Astrid hadn't thought about what she was going to say, but now that she was talking, she knew what she wanted Mary to know, or at least what she wanted Mary to hear. "I didn't always like her, but she was a good person. You did a beautiful job." There was nothing else that mattered, was there? Whatever other accomplishments she'd ever had, Astrid had foisted three human beings on the planet. Had they made it better? Had she? Barbara had tried, in her nosy, nudgey, self-righteous way. Was this what getting old meant, realizing that the people she had always judged for being too much had been in the right, and she had always done too little?

"Barb, yes," Mary said. Her eyelids looked heavy, as if she might fall asleep. There was a light knock at the door, and then a nurse came in with a tray of pills.

"Mary, I see you've got a visitor," the nurse said, kindly. She patted Astrid on the shoulder. "Mary usually naps around now, I wouldn't take it personally."

"I'll go," Astrid said. She stood up and touched Mary on the hand. "I'm so sorry," she said. "For Barbara."

The nurse held Astrid's elbow and walked her to the door. Her grip was firm. "We're not sure how much Mary understands about her daughter," she said.

"I see," Astrid said. How stupid—of course, she should have checked. She should have thought about what Mary knew, if she would be upset or confused. The nurse was still holding Astrid's elbow, which felt both generous and serious; this was a woman who was used to holding people who were shaky on their feet, used to helping people who wouldn't or couldn't ask. Astrid half wanted her legs to give out, to fall in order to be saved, but she stayed upright. "I left her some things," she said.

"Mary says thank you," the nurse said, and opened the door for Astrid to leave.

Freezing cold air blew from the air-conditioning vents in the hallway ceiling. A woman in a wheelchair sat outside a room down the hall, and Astrid waved. The old ladies all looked alike, like babies all look alike through a glass window, lined up in bassinet after bassinet. If Barbara Baker were still alive, and she turned the corner to go visit her mother, and Astrid had been standing right there, what would she have done? The truth was that Astrid thought about Barbara all the time—it wasn't just her death, not at all. Barbara's death was the splash in the water, but for the last twenty years, Astrid had been watching her bounce on the diving board.

People talked about coming out like it was one thing that happened, like it had to do with who you wanted to have sex with, full stop, the end. But there were other things, too, that one needed to say. Fear controlled so many things. Astrid put out her hand and rested it against the cool wall, a ballast.

Elliot had been fourteen, and small for his age. He was in the ninth grade, on the basketball team, getting good grades, and popular enough, as far as Astrid could tell. No trouble. Not like Nicky, who fell asleep at the wheel of her car coming home drunk from a party and nearly killed himself. Even Porter had had her troubles, of the dramatic teenage girl variety, but Elliot was on the honor roll, the class treasurer. So Astrid had been surprised when Barbara Baker called her.

Barbara was a crossing guard then, not at the corner by the elementary school, but two blocks over, in a mostly dead zone beside the river and the train tracks. It wasn't a busy spot, and why they put her down there, Astrid had never understood. But Barbara was calling to say that she had seen Elliot and his friend Jack—a beautiful boy with sandy hair, a soccer player, the son of academics who threw dinner parties and listened to Miles Davis on vinyl—playing on the rocks by the river. It's so dangerous, you know, down there, that's what Barbara had said. It looks still, but the current is strong. She was thinking of their safety. When Barbara was halfway to where the boys were, they hadn't seen her yet. The river was noisy that day, and so were the trains, and they were teenage boys who thought they were alone in the world. Barbara was young then, god—if Elliot was fourteen, she must have been in her forties, like Astrid was, and there was no reason on earth two teenage boys would notice a woman like that. They wouldn't, and they didn't. So she got closer, finally close enough to tell them to quit horsing around, and then she saw. They were kissing.

———

A male nurse wielding a large garbage can on wheels came down the hall and greeted Astrid. She moved out of his way and hurried down the hall to the front door, which was heavy and solid, designed to keep people in. Astrid pushed and stumbled out into the bright sunshine. She'd forgotten how hot it was outside, but it was too late, she was already there, and couldn't actually make her legs take her anywhere else. She sat down on the nearest bench, next to a woman with a portable oxygen tank.

Barbara had waited, politely, for Astrid to respond. Nicky had always piled on top of his friends like they were all puppy dogs, but Elliot never had. She—Astrid, his mother—had never noticed anything like what Barbara was describing. He was her eldest—she had spent the last fourteen years paying more attention to him than his two siblings. She could name every teacher he'd ever had, every friend he'd ever made. But this—she hadn't seen this.

There wasn't a moment of conscious decision making. There was just a wall, erected in an instant, that hadn't been there before. That was the truth about parenting, at least as Astrid had done it—most decisions weren't plans, they were tourniquets, immediate responses to whatever problem was at hand. Astrid said—she had said this—**No, Barbara, you are mistaken. Thank you**. And then Astrid had hung up the phone. It was the second most shameful moment of her life. She didn't tell anyone—not Russell, not Porter or Nicky, nobody. And when Elliot came home from school that day, Astrid told him that she'd had a phone call, without saying who from, but that someone had seen him, and that he needed to be careful. Did she say **careful**? She told him not to. She told him not to do it in public. **It,** she'd said. She told him that she was embarrassed. And that was the most shameful moment of her life. At the end of the year, Jack's mother got a teaching job in Berkeley and they moved to the West Coast, and then he was just gone, and you know how it is, when you're a kid. Especially boys. She didn't think Elliot even tried to keep in touch—and why would he have? And so then Jack was just gone, and Astrid was relieved. She'd thought about that call from Barbara every time she'd seen Barbara since. Sometimes she was angry at herself, sometimes she was angry at Barbara—what a cow! Who did that? Who tattled on a teenage boy who wasn't hurting anyone? But they were both cows, of course, she and Barbara: Astrid could try to blame it on her generation, but that didn't hold much water. There was no excuse, except for the excuse that perfection was impossible, and failure inevitable.

People without children thought that having a newborn was the hardest part of parenthood, that upside-down, day-is-night twilight zone of feedings and toothless wails. But parents knew better. Parents knew that the hardest part of parenthood was figuring out how to do the right thing twenty-four hours a day, forever, and surviving all the times you failed. Astrid felt like she had cursed her own child, like she had set the marble on the track with that one conversation, and that Elliot had just rolled. She could imagine the life that Elliot would have had, if she had said something else. If she had said nothing, even that would have been better. In a parallel universe, she and Elliot had something in common, they would be close, but in this one, she had missed her chance. People always said that life was long, but really they meant their own memories. Barbara's death meant that Astrid had missed her window at a full recovery, at ever really righting that particular wrong. There were probably other wrongs, too, not just for Elliot but for each of her children. Astrid didn't know what they were, but they were there, undoubtedly, places she'd greased the track for other marbles without even realizing what she was doing.

The woman with the oxygen tank pointed across the green lawn to a heron tiptoeing toward the oversized birdbath. Astrid tried to paint a polite expression on her face.

When Barbara was hit, this was what Astrid

had realized, somewhere in the murky depths of her brain—she would have to have only one of the two conversations. She would have to apologize only to Elliot, and not to Barbara too. It was such a sad, pathetic excuse of a feeling, and Astrid felt ashamed again—ashamed thrice!—admitting it to herself.

The heavy front door creaked open, and Birdie stuck her head out.

"Hey," she said. "I'm taking a break, and they pointed me this way. God, it is **hot** out here. Want to get some ice cream?" Birdie's apron had small hairs clinging to it, whole galaxies on the thick blue cotton. Astrid wanted so badly to deserve her.

Chapter 13

Clap Happy

Porter was excited to introduce Rachel to her goats. Clap Happy's twenty-five Nubian and Alpine does lived in a large red barn, with a fenced-in pasture full of grass to eat and bins of alfalfa hay set off the ground. They had piles of rocks to climb—what Porter referred to as "the jungle gyms"—and climb they did. The goats were amusing, rambunctious, and affectionate. Astrid had never allowed furry pets—Nicky had had a lizard for a few years, and Elliot had asked for, received, and then returned a snake—and Porter sometimes thought that if she had grown up with dogs or cats, she would be a happier adult.

Kids were born starting in the late summer. Clap Happy wasn't big enough to keep all the kids, but

Porter loved watching them being born, watching their skinny legs and knobby knees straighten and bear weight. She had two human employees— Grace and Hugh—and they were inside turning the enormous vats of milk into cheese. Rachel wanted to see where the magic happened. It was a field trip. Porter leaned against the fence and stuck a straw of hay in her teeth when she saw Rachel's car pull up.

"You are really going for it, huh," Rachel said, and laughed.

"This is how we do it in the country," Porter said.

"Oh, please. They're so cute!" Rachel stuck her hand through the fence, and two of the Alpines came over to nuzzle her fingers.

"That's Boo Boo and Cassius Clay," Porter said.

"You name them?" Rachel looked surprised. Rachel's parents were city folk, through and through. Porter was surprised that Rachel had decided not to be, that she'd come back to Clapham.

"Of course I name them; I see them all day long, I have to call them something."

"Aren't they all women? I mean, female? Because they're for milk?" Rachel was getting licked.

"I don't believe in gender norms," Porter said. "That's why her name is going to be Elvis." She rubbed her belly.

"You're joking." Rachel stopped and looked at her.

"I am. But maybe she's a he, who knows? I'm

open-minded. Come on, let's go in." Porter opened the gate and led Rachel to the jungle gym, where two more goats were playing.

"Do you ever feel like you just swallowed a lava lamp?" Rachel asked. "You know, like, little balls of goo floating up and down?"

"Ha, yes," Porter said. "Also like hearing a squirrel just inside a wall, like, just tapping and trying to find its way out."

"Also like I'm going to give birth and it's just going to be the most massive poop in the world, with no actual baby." Rachel stopped and put her hands flat against her belly. "I'm sorry. You're not poop."

"I love you," Porter said. "Why are we the only normal people in the world? I'm so sick of all the books and apps that are like, golly gee, it's an avocado!" She scratched Cassius Clay on the ear. "Do you actually have a name yet?" This was one of the reasons Porter was sorry not to have a partner—there was no one to bounce names off, no one to quickly rule out Jezebel or Strawberry or Loretta. Friends and family all had opinions, but their opinions didn't matter, not really. This is what partners were for. She did have names on her list, real ones, but they existed only on a small piece of paper in her bedroom: **Athena Cassiopeia Ursa Agnes Eleanor Louisa.** She added to it and crossed things out but had yet to actually assign a single name to the person in her body.

"My husband's friend just had a baby and named him Felix, which I really like," said Rachel. Rachel didn't know what she was having, a choice that Porter respected in other people but could never have handled herself, like being a marathon runner or going camping in the winter.

"I like Felix," Porter said, crossing it off her future boy list in her head. Almost every woman she knew had been keeping lists like that since they were twenty. She and Rachel had talked about baby names when they were fourteen! It had been baked into both of them, this desire. It wasn't for everyone, but Porter and Rachel had both been the type to plan ahead. Sometimes Porter looked at the most popular girl names for New York State just to rule things out. She didn't want her daughter to have a name that six other girls in her first-grade class would have, one of many. She wanted to choose a name that would work for a Supreme Court justice, or an engineer, or a stern but fair high school English teacher, the kind of person who would have a library named after her someday.

"You know what I've been thinking about?" Rachel asked, extending her hand to get snuffled by Boo Boo again, a true glutton for attention, as most of the goats were. "All the people I could have married. Not that anyone else asked me! But all the strangers I could have chosen to have a baby with. Like, **Sliding Doors,** but with my life, instead of Gwyneth Paltrow. Is that the most depressing thing you've ever heard?"

Porter shook her head. "Yes. I mean, no, it's not the most depressing thing I've ever heard. It's my entire life. It's also a fun game to play for other people. The good news is that I think you have to stop when you have children, because you know that whoever you give birth to wouldn't be there if you'd made different choices. And when Elvis is born, or Felix, or Tallulah, or whoever, you and I are going to look at them and say, fuck, I'm glad you're here, and not someone else, and whatever choices you made led you to that person, your little person, and so the past becomes perfect. The future can always change, but not the past. I don't know." She shrugged. "At least I hope so."

Rachel shuffled over and wrapped her arms around Porter's middle, the gentlest tackle. "Thank you for saying that. Why did we ever stop being friends? It's so nice to be your friend. Right? Am I crazy?"

"You're not crazy," Porter said, and hugged her friend back. The goats gathered around their legs, a happy herd, always looking for more treats, more fun. One stepped on her foot and then wagged its tail. "I don't know why. I mean, it's not hard to keep in touch. I guess it's easier than it used to be. Texting."

"Oh, let's be text friends, yes," Rachel said. "Let's

text each other all day long. I'll text you when my students are driving me crazy because they won't stop texting." She laughed, still hovering around Porter's bump.

"In my head, I'm already texting you," Porter said. "There, I just sent another one." There had been reasons, though not good ones. Were there ever good reasons, for not being a good friend? She remembered a slumber party with six or seven girls, all of them in sleeping bags on the floor of her bedroom like hot dogs on a grill, lying next to each other, eyes wide open in the dark, talking about love. Each girl, in turn, proclaimed the boy she **like** liked, and then all the other girls would shriek and laugh. Rachel went before Porter, and she'd said Jeremy's name first. When Porter said his name a minute later, all the other girls **oooooooh**ed, because, of course, only one could win. It was like voting in a primary election: You could support only one friend's crush on a boy. You couldn't back two candidates in the same race. Was that when their friendship had begun to wane, that night? They had both sworn it was nothing and had banded together, but a few months later, when Jeremy had saved a seat for Porter in the last row of the school bus, Make Out Row, as it was called, she had zipped onto the pleather cushion as fast as her legs could carry her. It was nothing, of course, just a high school romance, kid stuff. Friends understood. Porter could say that to

Rachel now, that she'd been a jerk, and it would be okay. Everyone made mistakes, especially when they were full of hormones and lust, the molten core of every teenage girl. And after that, Jeremy had been her primary relationship, the most important thing, and everything else had suffered, though she hadn't mourned it at the time. She could tell Rachel that too. She would, when the right moment presented itself.

What Porter couldn't (and wouldn't) say was how often she imagined going back in time and marrying Jeremy Fogelman, how many times over the year she had punched things in her bedroom and thought, **What the fuck, twenty-year-old Porter? Who were you waiting for?** Because then she could have a person who she loved instead of just borrowing him illicitly, on and off, over the last eighteen years. She hadn't told anyone. Everyone—her mother, Rachel, John Sullivan— knew that Jeremy had been her boyfriend when she was a kid, but no one knew that it had gone on well after Jeremy got married. They often met at the barn, but sometimes, when they were feeling a little luxurious, they went to Manhattan, and got the smallest room at the best hotel they could afford. Vets had annual conferences, too, in sexy locations such as Minneapolis in February! Memphis in August! Porter could always find a handy excuse. It came back to planting the flag: He was hers first. Whatever came after got layered on top, like whipped cream and sprinkles. Whatever she and Jeremy were to each other, it was the base. They were the bananas in the banana split.

The last time they'd slept together, almost two years ago, they'd gone into the city—all the way to Brooklyn, where people their age were still finding themselves. They did what they usually did, which was that Porter checked into a hotel (this time a new and glossy place that was shaped like an upside-down pyramid), and then she and Jeremy would "run into" each other at either a bar or a restaurant or a movie theater and sit next to each other, shocked and amazed at the coincidence. Then they'd go back to the hotel, have sex a few times, take a shower, and then Jeremy would leave and Porter would watch bad television and sleep alone in the clean hotel sheets. It was a pretty sublime arrangement, if you didn't think about it too much.

But this time was different. Porter had had something on her mind. They'd had dinner at a Mexican restaurant nearby, and she'd had three strong margaritas, each one making her tongue more wiggly in her mouth.

"So," she said. They were stumbling down the hallway in the hotel, bumping into the walls and each other. "I've been thinking."

"Me too," Jeremy said. "I've been thinking about taking off your pants and licking your clit until you scream."

"Stop it," Porter said. "I mean, that sounds good, let's come back to that in a minute. But I'm serious." She slowed to a stop, bracing herself against a doorframe. "You aren't happy."

Jeremy laughed. "How can you say that? I have everything I could possibly want." He came closer, squeezing her sides with his big hands. Porter put her palm flat against his chest.

"You don't have me, not really."

"Of course I do, look at us!" He leaned forward and started kissing her neck.

"But you also have Kristen."

Jeremy straightened back up. "Come on, Port."

"I told you, I've been thinking. You aren't happy in your marriage, and I'm right fucking here! You always said that you would be okay with me finding someone, and I have. I found you. I want to cut the bullshit, Jeremy. I want to have babies before I'm too old, and who would I have babies with, if not with you?"

But Jeremy had already had his kids. He'd also had a vasectomy, years ago, when his youngest was four. And that was it, she'd drawn the line, a line carved with her own wants and frustrations, and he wouldn't (or couldn't) cross it. They'd gone into the hotel room and had sex twice in a row, which Porter had understood as a mutual admittance that they would never have sex this good again, with anyone. After that, there were no more hotel rooms, no more well-lit lobby bars in remote cities, no more midmorning fucks in the barn, her back against the grainy wood. The one positive aspect to breaking up with a person you weren't married to was that it could all vanish in a puff of smoke: there were no lawyers, no shared assets, no bookshelves or record collections to peel apart. And so Porter had moved on. She dated people she didn't care about. She swiped right. What had he said? It was timing. When they met, they were too young, and she wasn't ready. When he was ready to get married, there was Kristen, Kristen who had been born with a wish-list registry, who had a favorite diamond shape. Porter didn't care about jewelry. That was the very worst part of being an adult, understanding that there was no fairness in the world, no unseen hand on the Ouija board. There was only the internet and the paths you chose for whatever stupid reason that seemed right at the time, when you had one extra drink at a party, or were feeling lonely at exactly the moment that someone else was too. And wasn't everyone, always?

Rachel put out her hand and Boo Boo licked it again, and finding nothing there, turned tail and ran away, bleating, as if warning the rest of her friends that these two round humans had nothing to offer. Rachel coughed, and then laughed. "Do you have a human bathroom here? I think I just wet my pants."

"Right this way," Porter said, leading her inside.

Chapter 14

Cecelia's First Day

Clapham Junior High, from the outside, was a brick fortress. It had green grass and a flagpole and a parking lot. Cecelia's school in Brooklyn had been unremarkable in different ways—crowded, diverse, with kids from a thousand different countries; inedible, bland food in vast quantities—but she had yet to discover the center of the Venn diagram in which the schools overlapped. Lockers? Hallways? It wasn't a long list. She'd gone into the school building exactly once, with Astrid, for a new-student orientation, an hour-long chatty tour by a seventh grader named Kimberly. Why did schools not understand that the best person to introduce kids to a new school would be someone who acted like it was no big whoop? No one wanted to be singled out for anything. All anyone in the middle of puberty wanted was a larger rock to hide under, and the spotlight pointed somewhere else.

August had told her that his stop was before hers on the bus, and that he'd probably be on it, depending on his parents. Cecelia was trying hard to play down her attachment to the idea of their being friends. He might not even be on the bus, she kept telling herself, and if he wasn't, she'd be okay, she'd just choose an empty seat, or sit next to a girl who smiled, literally any girl who smiled. The girl didn't even need to offer teeth, just lips in the shape of a shallow crescent. It didn't mean anything. It was just a bus ride.

Her old school didn't start for another week, and Cecelia was keeping abreast of her former friends' lives on Snapchat and Instagram. There were the Finstas and the Rinstas—the fake and the real, the accounts that your parents could see, where every kid posted things about school and new haircuts and cute dogs on the street, and the accounts where you could see more bare skin and authentic teen misery. Katherine had blocked her on both, but some of the peripheral friends in their group hadn't, and so Cecelia could catch glimpses of what was going on in her old life. Sonya had cut her hair and dyed it pink. Maddy had been posting more pouty selfies than usual, which probably meant that she'd broken up with her boyfriend, a friendly toucher who offered to give everyone back rubs in the hallway but then always put his hands just a half-inch too close to your boobs. Cecelia wanted to comment but was afraid that Katherine would respond and then a hole in the earth would open up and Cecelia would have to jump in. She already felt bad enough about the whole thing, sort of, even though she knew what she'd done (tell her parents, tell Katherine's parents, tell their teacher) was the objective Right Thing to Do. Sometimes doing the right thing sucked.

Gammy had agreed to wait inside the house, and not watch her get on the bus, but Cecelia saw her face in the window, though Astrid had quickly disappeared behind the curtain. The bus had clearly been serviced since the accident—it had a gleaming new paint job, bright yellow with black letters so glossy they looked wet. The door folded open, revealing a skinny woman with pale skin and hair dyed as dark and wet as the black painted letters. She looked nervous, which Cecelia could understand. It probably wasn't easy to step into a job recently vacated by a vehicular manslaughter, even if it meant the bar for surpassing the previous standard was rock bottom.

"All aboard," she said.

"It's my first day," Cecelia said.

"Me too," the driver said, her face screwing into a facsimile of a smile. Could she sit there, right next to the driver? Could she operate the shifter knob, the way every kid at a train museum gets a turn to be the conductor?

Cecelia ran up the steps as lightly as possible, trying to project an air of easy self-confidence. This was the plan: pretend to be the person you'd like to be. No one knew any better, and so Cecelia could be confident and cool if she said she was. It wasn't that she wanted to lie, or to be fake—she didn't want to do either of those things. Cecelia just knew how things worked and knew that projecting confidence was her only hope for survival, the way some harmless snakes had almost identical markings to very deadly ones. The bus was about half full, and she immediately felt every eyeball on her. Cecelia quickly scanned the rows— scowls, to a person. The girls looked her up and down, inspecting her outfit's every detail, the boys inspected her face and body with the same x-ray vision, and Cecelia felt the weight of every stare— until she saw August waving in the back.

"Oh, thank god," she said, when she'd finally reached his row. The cool exterior she'd been holding in place melted into a genuinely relieved puddle.

"Yes, well, welcome to hell. It's lovely here, isn't it?" He handed her a muffin. "My dad baked."

Cecelia slung her backpack around her body and collapsed onto the bench seat next to him. "My parents don't bake. For a while, they were into making their own almond milk, and then their own sourdough bread, using this space alien they kept in the fridge, but not normal baking, like with butter and sugar."

"That's too bad," August said. "Butter and sugar are two objectively good things in the world. Maybe your parents just don't like carbohydrates."

"Or thoughtfulness," Cecelia said, taking a bite. The muffin was still warm. "If my grandmother loses it, I'm moving in with you."

"I always wanted a sister," August said.

"Me too," Cecelia said, and took another bite. "Do you ever feel your parents forget that they're your parents and not just, like, your buddies? Mine are major buddies. Not so great on the discipline. Not that I want discipline, just . . ."

"Rules. I get it." August nodded.

The bus bounced over a bump in the road, sending Cecelia and August an inch into the air. They rounded a corner and slowed to a stop. A clump of long-haired girls got on, an optical illusion of homogeny. It took Cecelia a few moments to realize it wasn't three copies of the same girl, but three different girls in identical clothing, down to the holes in the knees of their jeans and the visible belly buttons poking out from beneath their cropped tank tops, with identical expressions of boredom on their dour faces.

"Are they sisters?" Cecelia asked, pointing with her chin.

"No, they wish. Just spiritually. And by that I mean, they have given their souls to their same succubus."

The girls piled into a row near the front of the bus, the only empty seat left, two on the seat and the third on their lap like a baby doll.

"Two to a seat," the driver said, after she'd cranked the door shut. "Find another seat, miss."

The girl on top rolled her eyes, and there was some whispered negotiation, and then the three all switched places, a game of human three-card monte, and one, the tallest of the three, got spit out into the aisle.

"That's Sidney, at the window," August said, "and those are her henchmen, Bailey and Liesel. Liesel's the one who got the boot." Booted Liesel had sulked back two rows, and now was sitting next to a girl with large headphones who had not acknowledged her existence.

Cecelia leaned back against the squeaky vinyl of the bus seat. They didn't look like her friends at home, not really—compared to Brooklyn, Clapham was about as white as a snowstorm in Vermont—but seeing them all together, a posse, reminded her of what she didn't have anymore. She felt simultaneously grateful to be on this weird murderous school bus and mad that she was the one who had been deemed least important and kicked to the proverbial aisle.

"Are you okay?" August asked. "You look kind of green."

"I'm fine," Cecelia said.

"Well, we're here." The bus rounded another corner and pulled up in front of the school. It slowed to a stop, and everyone stood up and lumbered off, the exact opposite of people hurrying to get off an airplane. It seemed to Cecelia that if this new bus driver had taken off and kept driving, everyone would have sat back down and been willing runaways. August and Cecelia were the last ones off the bus, and when Cecelia hit the pavement in front of the school, the clump of identical girls was standing a few feet in front of her, each one checking her makeup in her phone's forward-facing camera.

The second-in-command, Bailey, made eye contact with Cecelia through the screen, and then whipped her head around. "What?"

This made the other two girls turn as well. New students, in a school of any size less than gigantic, meant potential ripples in the social hierarchy. They had to make sure Cecelia wasn't a threat.

"You're new?" Sidney asked. Up close, Cecelia could see the differences between the three girls. Liesel was a good four inches taller, a fact that she tried to correct with terrible posture, with a rip in only the left knee of her skintight jeans. Bailey was the blonde, with a face as round as a full moon, and rips in both knees. And Sidney, clearly in charge, had an upturned nose like a sniffling pug that had been told it was beautiful every day of its butt-sniffing life. Reality had no bearing on her power. Cecelia recognized her type immediately—it was the same look Katherine would have given her, the Queen Bee stare, and somehow identifying it as such did not lessen the impact.

Cecelia nodded. "Yeah, hi!" She waved, her heart beating fast. Friendliness was key to survival.

"Um, okay," Bailey said, and turned back to her phone.

Liesel and Sidney followed suit. When they walked by, August leaned over and whispered into Sidney's ear, "She's a **witch**," and then he hooked his arm through Cecelia's elbow and they walked into school. Once they were safely through the front door, Cecelia laughed nervously.

"Don't worry," August said. "If she really thinks you're a witch, she'll at least give you a little distance. You're not, are you?" He paused for effect and then pretended to be relieved when she shook her head. Cecelia crossed her arms over her chest. The jumpsuit was a little heavy for the day, but she'd worn it anyway, like a suit of armor. It was okay, it was okay. Cecelia often felt like she was late to things—late to her period, late to attempting to put on eye makeup, late to her life—but maybe she was showing up in Clapham at the right time. Maybe those girls weren't so bad. Maybe, just

maybe, Cecelia would always know August, even
when they were fifty years old, even if August
moved to Buenos Aires and became a flamenco
instructor, even if he became a Rockette, or a doctor, or an astronaut. It was a reassuring idea. Just
because her last friends hadn't stuck around didn't
mean it would happen again. She could be cool
this time; she could roll with it, whatever it was.
Friendship was so weird. People spent so much
time talking about falling in love, but making
friends was just as hard—if you thought about it,
it was crazy: Here, meet some total strangers, tell
them all your secrets, expect no hurt or humiliation to come of it.

"Not that I know of." She looked down and realized she was still holding half a muffin in her
hand, and so she stuffed the rest into her mouth
and crumpled the wrapper in her hand, holding it
there like a good luck charm.

The eighth grade had four different homeroom
classes, each with thirty students. Thirty sounded
like a lot but the rooms were enormous and spa-
cious, with a tidy, labeled desk for each of them,
all with their own narrow pencil grooves. Cecelia's
seat was in the second row from the back—
alphabetical. That seemed in some way discrimi-
natory, or at the very least, rude. What if she had
terrible eyesight? What if she had a quiet speaking

voice? In her Brooklyn school, where half the students had teacher's aides to assist with their ADD or ADHD or their autism, the teachers arranged the room over and over again like a game of Jenga, always trying to make sure that so-and-so didn't climb out the window, or that so-and-so's parents didn't call to complain about her treatment in the great educational machine of New York City. Clapham Junior High looked, on the inside, the way her Brooklyn school looked in 1960, probably. The carpets were clean, with earth-toned concentric circles. The water fountains shot springy geysers high into the air. The bathroom's tampon machines worked. August was in another homeroom, which meant that she had to say goodbye after he helped her find the office and jimmy open her locker, and now she was alone. Alone with twenty-nine other kids and one adult, her new homeroom/English teacher, Ms. Skolnick, Cecelia slid into her seat and gently put her empty notebook down on the desk.

Ms. Skolnick was pacing the narrow corridor between her large desk and the blackboard. She was short and smiley, with an unseasonably bulky sweater. She held a piece of chalk in one hand, balanced in between her fingers like a cigarette. Some students grunted greetings when they came into the classroom, but most didn't. Cecelia watched from her seat. An air-conditioning vent was directly above her, blowing freezing cold air, and Cecelia was glad, finally, to have worn the jumpsuit.

"I have an extra sweater, if you need one." It was Ms. Skolnick, who had somehow made her way down the side of the room to Cecelia's desk. "This seat is the Arctic Circle. I've complained to maintenance a thousand times, but there just doesn't seem to be a way to temper the temperature, if you know what I mean."

"Okay," Cecelia said. "I didn't know, but I'm warm enough."

"Didn't know that your assigned seat would be a Popsicle stand? Four demerits! I'm kidding," Ms. Skolnick said, looking at Cecelia's face. "We don't have demerits here. We have detention, but no demerits."

"Am I in trouble for something?" Cecelia asked.

"No! Why? Have you done something?" Ms. Skolnick widened her eyes. "I am just introducing myself, saying hello, offering a port in the storm. It's cool. Welcome! I moved a few times as a kid, too, so I know the whole new-school-yikes feeling."

Behind Ms. Skolnick, a bell rang, and at the same time, Sidney and one of her cohorts—Bailey, the blonde—appeared in the doorway, which startled Cecelia, but the expressions on the girls' faces didn't flicker; they split up without a word, homing pigeons who knew the way. Cecelia had never felt that confident, not even in her old school. Even if her desk had had a photograph of her printed on the seat, she probably still would have asked if she was in the right place.

"That's my cue," Ms. Skolnick said. "Morning, Sidney." Cecelia watched as Sidney slid into the seat right next to her. She made eye contact with Cecelia, but when Cecelia smiled in what she hoped was a very normal and friendly way, Sidney kept her lips in a tight, flat line and turned toward the blackboard.

Cecelia shivered. Her phone vibrated in her pocket, and she took it out as little as possible, just to see who had written. **Dad,** it said, in those big block letters, as if her dad was the same as anyone else's, as if he were a sitcom dad, with a basketball hoop and unflattering jeans and a toolbox full of things that weren't weed or other herbs to be used medicinally. **Hey,** the message read. **I miss you, sweet pie.** Sweet pie. He couldn't even call her a normal nickname. Cecelia felt her eyes fill with tears and daubed the corners of her eyes in a way that she hoped looked nonchalant. Her father had flown back to New Mexico, probably sitting cross-legged somewhere with his eyes closed. It was weird, to be a part of a whole that was no longer whole, and to be the part that was missing. Cecelia didn't want to be missing. She wanted to be in her pretend room in her small apartment with her parents, and to push a button and to rewind a little bit, so that everyone could handle things differently. She wanted her mother to join the PTA and to bake American apple pies and to scream at the top of her lungs when an absurd suggestion was made, like Katherine's parents.

"I'm not a witch," Cecelia said. Sidney raised an eyebrow, as did a few other kids sitting nearby. "I mean, obviously."

Sidney leaned over. "You know who would say that? A witch." She laughed and turned toward the front of the room with her arms crossed over her chest. Cecelia started to sweat.

That was why they'd sent her to Gammy's, Cecelia thought. She wasn't good at handling things on her own, and neither was anyone else in her family. If her father had been sitting next to her, he would have nodded, or even chuckled. He wouldn't have made a cutting remark back. Her mother—a teenage version of her mother—would have scared Sidney to death. But her actual mother would just have rolled her eyes and thought it beneath Cecelia to feel stung. Her parents—her loving, delusional parents—seemed to believe that if Cecelia was at Astrid's, it would feel almost like an extralong Christmas vacation, a cozy nap on the couch, but clearly that wasn't true. She was here because no one had said or done the right thing. When the guidance counselor had suggested that another school might be healthier for her, for the **bullied,** in order to prevent more bully**ing,** her parents had nodded. She was thirteen. There was no world in which the decision was up to her. And so when her parents had sat there the next morning, at their tiny kitchen table, and asked if she was okay with the idea, she had nodded too—what else could she do?

A book landed on her desk with a soft **thud**. **The Catcher in the Rye.** Ms. Skolnick was handing them out one by one.

"This looks boring," said Sidney. "It doesn't even have a picture on the cover. What's it about, baseball?"

Some of the other kids chuckled, not wanting to seem dumb for not knowing, but equally clueless and willing to scoff.

"No," Cecelia said. She'd read it the previous year. "It's about a kid who gets expelled from school and wanders around New York City and he's kind of crazy but he's also funny and it's a really good book."

"Spoiler alert, Cecelia!" Ms. Skolnick laughed. "But yes. Not about baseball, strictly speaking. Everyone read the first two chapters tonight, and we'll get started."

"Teacher's pet," Sidney said under her breath.

"Whatever," Cecelia said. "I've just read it before."

Ms. Skolnick clapped her hands. "Okay! Now let's do a little Getting to Know You Freewrite!

Everyone take out a piece of paper! And a pen! Five minutes! Write anything you want, I will never look! No one will ever know! You are free little birds, free!"

Sidney rolled her eyes. "I bet you love this, witch. Be free! Cast spells!"

Cecelia raised her hand. "May I go to the bathroom?" Ms. Skolnick nodded and pointed toward the door.

"You're doing great," she shout-whispered as Cecelia walked past the big desk. "Great first day so far, right?"

"Right," Cecelia said. "Just peachy." She stepped into the hallway and pulled the door closed behind her. The linoleum floor was spotless and shiny, an Olympic ice-skating rink. Cecelia dragged her sneakers until they squeaked. She was in no hurry. The hall was wide and empty, with lockers on either side. The bathroom was fifty feet ahead, and she ambled, peeking into the small classroom door windows as she went. Children were differently bored in every room. Bored in math class, bored in French class. Heavy eyelids; it was still so early in the morning. After a whole summer of sloth, the students weren't used to filling their brains at such an hour. Television, yes. Irregular verbs, no. They would all adjust, in time.

On the wall beside the bathroom door was a large bulletin board, filled with printed-out computer paper advertisements for extracurriculars, athletic team tryouts, fall musical auditions, and clubs. At her old school, Cecelia had done debate, but that didn't seem to be on offer. She scanned past the comedy and tragedy masks—the play was **The Music Man,** which seemed awfully on the nose for a small town. She had no interest in soccer or volleyball, inane exercises in futility. Dance, at least, offered artistic expression and beauty, but that wasn't for her, either. No, the only thing that caught Cecelia's eye was the sheet of paper in the lower-right corner of the board, clearly the loser's spot: PARADE CREW! HELP DESIGN AND BUILD THE FLOAT FOR THIS YEAR'S HARVEST FESTIVAL! NO SKILLS REQUIRED, and below that, Ms. Skolnick's name and homeroom, which Cecelia already knew how to find. Building a float for a parade was something no New York City school could offer. Take that, cosmopolitan elite! Cecelia pictured herself with a hammer and some bunting and buckets of glitter. Why not.

Chapter 15

Strick Brick

When Astrid felt unsatisfied about the time she was spending with her children, she would just show up and pay for a meal. It had worked when they were in college and subsisting on packaged Ramen noodles and peanut butter, and it worked now, at least on Porter, who could always be swayed by the promise of risotto and a glass of wine in the middle of the day. Because she did it when she had nothing in particular to say, Astrid thought it might also work when she did. Astrid did not like to apologize. She did not like to admit that she'd done anything wrong. It had gotten easier to forget about apologizing after Russell died—without a spouse to bicker with, Astrid was down to apologizing for accidental toe-steps and bumping into people with her shopping cart.

Elliot's construction company, Strick Brick, was housed in a building of their design, which was just outside downtown, and therefore out of the landmarked zone. The building was bright blue and hideous, with the upside-down proportions of a North Carolina beach house, spindly stilts lifting the structure twenty feet in the air, with an open-air carport underneath. A small house had been there for decades, but Elliot had bought it, torn it down, and replaced it with a gleaming new building, built to the very edges of the property line. Some people had complained, and Astrid admitted, in unguarded moments, that if it had been someone else's son, she would have been very put off by the building's incongruousness to its neighbors, but because Elliot was her son, and the project meant so much to him, she was proud, or at least said so in public.

After college, Elliot had badly wanted to go to law school, but his LSAT scores had been low, and he hadn't gotten in anywhere he wanted to go, and it had taken him a while to figure out what he wanted to do. Russell had been a lawyer, and that was part of it, of course—Astrid could see it, the direct line that Elliot had always imagined, and that line breaking into pieces. He'd worked construction during summers in college; all his Clapham friends did. It was outdoors and sweaty and they got paid in cash and their muscles got bigger, everyone won. And when he took a job in construction after graduation, it was supposed to be temporary, until it wasn't. Seven years later, Elliot had his own company. Most people would see that as success, but not Elliot.

Astrid parked her car outside his building. "I'm here," she said. "Come out, it's lunchtime." Five minutes later, Elliot jerked open the front door of the office and barreled out onto the flagstone sidewalk.

"I don't have much time," he said.

"Good," said Astrid. "Neither do I. Just give me directions, anywhere is fine."

He pointed to the right, and they walked quickly up the sidewalk, occasionally ducking under low branches. Elliot was half a foot taller than she was, but Astrid moved double time and kept up.

"Lunch with the boss!" Astrid said as she hurried alongside him. It was warm and sticky out, the air nearly humid enough to see. Her voice always got a little bit higher around Elliot, compensating for his often sour baseline mood. Perkiness was not her natural habitat, and she could hear how odd she sounded, but she could never quite figure out how to fix it.

"I have eight employees, Mom, not eight hundred. You don't have to act like that."

"Plus the construction crews! You don't have to be modest for me, El, that's a lot of people." Astrid grabbed Elliot's arm, rubbing it briskly. Nicky had been an affectionate boy and was an affectionate man, kissing her on the cheek to say hello and goodbye when he was around, sometimes even for no reason. Elliot didn't touch his mother more than he would touch a kind old woman he met at an acquaintance's wedding. It was different, being a mother to different children. Not just the gender lines, trucks versus dolls, though the pink aisle conundrum had driven Astrid to madness as a young mother. There were also the varied ways that adolescent creatures either cried or hid, and those differences followed along when the children became adults too. When Nicky got married, he'd sent out postcards with the announcement, which meant that Astrid found out just after their mail lady. When Elliot got married, Astrid, who had always been best at performing tasks, had been forced to sit back and watch—a spectator! She'd always thought that Porter would be different, that there would be a way into her adulthood that she hadn't found with the boys, but now even that ship seemed to have sailed clear across an ocean. Where was the door that she'd missed? Astrid believed in giving people space, in giving her children space. Wasn't that what everyone wanted? Two of Astrid's friends had been in the delivery room with their daughters, watching as they pushed through the ring of fire and became mothers themselves, that ultimate magic act. Astrid wasn't sure what she wanted, but she knew that wasn't it, watching blood collect in a plastic bag under her daughter's bottom as she pushed. When she got home, Astrid was going to ask Cecelia more questions about her day. She was going to sit closer, to follow her up the stairs to her bedroom, sit on the floor, even.

Elliot nudged her up the sidewalk in the direction of The Spot, a restaurant Astrid hadn't been to for a decade, following an unsatisfying tuna melt. It had a dingy awning and plastic tablecloths in addition to the mediocre food, but Astrid wouldn't complain.

"Let's go here, they have sandwiches," Elliot said, opening the door and holding it ajar for his mother.

They sat at a table by the window. The menus were enormous and laminated, and Elliot took a quick look and then put it down on the table, turning expectantly to look for the server.

"Hmm, tomato soup, that sounds good. I wonder if it's warm or cold. A cold tomato soup sounds delicious, doesn't it? I wonder if it's pureed. Or cream based. I'm not really in the mood for a creamy soup, though." Astrid folded the menu closed to look at the back. "Or they have specials! Did you see? Maybe I'll have a soup and a half sandwich. I think I'll do that. Did you see the lunch specials?"

"We're ready to order," Elliot said, waving to a woman in an apron walking toward them. "I'll have the turkey club and an iced tea. Thanks."

"Sure, hang on, just give me a minute," the woman said, drawing a pad out of her apron pocket.

"What's your tomato soup like?" Astrid asked. "Too heavy for a warm day?"

"Jesus, Mom, it's just soup!" Elliot put his head in his hands.

The server raised her eyebrows. "It's a little chunky, cold. Really good."

"I'll have that, please, and half a grilled cheese. Thank you." Astrid handed over the menu and then knit her fingers together on the table.

"Sorry, I'm just a little stressed," Elliot said.

"I can see that," Astrid said. "What's going on?"

"Nothing. Work stuff. The boys are fucking terrors." The server came over with Elliot's iced tea, and he nodded a thank-you.

"They're just little boys," Astrid said. "You were a little boy once."

"I wasn't like this. They tell me they hate me. Aidan told me he was going to kill me in my sleep. And then he laughed, like an actual psychopath. I want to send them to military school, where they can channel their anger into discipline. I don't know." Elliot shook his head. He removed the straw from the iced tea and put the wide glass to his lips, sending ice sloshing against his skin. "They are ruining my life."

"It's just a phase," Astrid said.

"Yeah, well, it's a bad one," Elliot said. "Anyway, why did you want to have lunch? Do you have cancer? Anything else I should prepare for?"

"El," Astrid said, shaking her head. She spread her hands flat on the table, no cards hidden. "Do you want to talk about Birdie?"

"No, I don't want to talk about Birdie, Mom. It's just weird, don't you understand that? I'm allowed to think it's weird."

"It's not **that** weird. It's just a relationship, like any other. Between two adults." Astrid leaned back against the hard back of her chair. Elliot looked red and sweaty, and his neck, thicker now than in his youth, strained against his shirt collar. It wasn't middle-aged spread; it was the gym, his muscles getting bigger, not everything else getting bigger when muscles were ignored. But Astrid thought that too much of anything was probably a sign that something was amiss. If Porter had some of Elliot's workout regime, if Elliot had some of his siblings' ease in their own bodies, if Nicky had some of Elliot's inertia, and if Porter had some of Nicky's charisma, then she might have one perfect child. They were all perfect, of course, in their own ways, insomuch that they were each perfectly their own tangle of positives and negatives, but together, if plucked just so, they could have made one flawless human. Astrid knew it wasn't a fair way to think about her children, but there it was.

"Yeah, but the other adult is your female hairdresser, which is what makes it weird. I mean, god, don't you see how that could be awkward? For all of us?" Elliot waved his now empty glass at the server.

"I'm sorry that it makes you feel that way," Astrid said.

The server swanned to their table holding a wide tray against her shoulder. She put down their plates with an elegant knee bend and took Elliot's glass. "Be right back," she said. Elliot and Astrid both waited silently for her to go before they spoke. Elliot pulled his phone out of his pocket and tapped out an email with his thumbs.

"Whatever," Elliot said. "It's your life. It's just that it affects my life too. I guess I'm surprised that you're not more aware of how it could matter to me, and to your family, how people view your actions."

Astrid sat still and stared into her soup. It wasn't actually the kind of gazpacho she liked at all. Astrid hated dishonesty in restaurant workers, in the "specials" that were really just to use up ingredients that were about to spoil, and people who said that every dish you mentioned was one of their favorites. The soup would be edible. It would be fine. But it wouldn't be any good. It didn't matter. She wouldn't come back to this place. It was just a meal. "Okay," Astrid said. "I understand."

"Things are just kind of fucked right now, Mom," Elliot said. "The office is busy, the house is a mess, Wendy is mad at me, it all just kind of sucks."

"I'm sorry to hear that, honey." Astrid picked up her spoon and tasted the soup. It was better than it looked. She watched Elliot tear his sandwich apart with his teeth. He ate as if he'd missed his last several meals, the way he had after swim lessons as a kid, his body needing the calories instantly. She had wanted to talk to him, to really talk to him, but it was so hard to know where to start. All of a sudden—forty years of parenting in!—she felt like she was on shaky ground. If her son felt this way about his children, if they were making mistakes, how many other mistakes must she have made without admitting them to herself? Her children were the way they were because of all the things she had done and all the things she had not done.

"I love you," Astrid said. She reached out and touched the tip of Elliot's finger. He moved his hand back on top of his phone and flipped it over.

"I have to get back to work, Mom," he said.

Astrid patted the sides of her mouth with her napkin and then laid cash down on the table.

There was no precedent in their relationship for what she needed to say, just like telling him about Birdie, which had not gone well. Astrid decided that she would try again another time; today was not the day.

Chapter 16

FOGELMAN

It was not accidental, the way Porter found herself standing on the sidewalk in front of Jeremy Fogelman's place of work. Porter didn't want to admit that her mother's falling in love had tweaked her, but it had. If Astrid Strick could find love again, against all odds and personality deficits, then maybe Porter could too.

After their first official breakup at age sixteen, Jeremy had continued on a clear, well-lit path for lo these many years. He had been the Homecoming King, paired with Jordan Rothman, their classmate whom Porter had detested since preschool for her toxic combination of beauty, athleticism, and healthy self-confidence. Jeremy had then stayed close to home and gone to SUNY New

Paltz, where he had studied veterinary medicine, and then he had become a vet, like his father, in order to save ancient cats and tumorous dogs and pet turtles and the occasional wild thing found in someone's backyard. Jeremy had married Kristen when they were twenty-three years old, and his children were now coltish humans who could be found wearing jerseys that read FOGELMAN on the back, forever running back and forth across soccer fields. Porter went to the other vet in town, in part because she was closer but mostly because it would have seemed too obvious to have a reason to see Jeremy so often. It didn't make sense, but Porter had always liked the subterfuge.

The East Clapham Veterinary Clinic had once been white and was now somewhat less than that, a dirty snow-colored building with a wide ramp to the side door and a squeaky screen door banging in front. Porter stood outside and wished that she still smoked cigarettes, the way she had when she and Jeremy had first been paramours. It was so funny, looking at a grown man and knowing what his body had looked like as a teenager, how smooth his hairless chest had been, when just a few brave curls had started to announce themselves. No matter how well his wife thought she knew him, no matter what friends he had now, and how many times they went out to dinner and talked about the boring details of their daily lives, Porter would always know him better. It was almost maternal, knowing a body for so long, and watching it change. **Or no—not maternal,** Porter thought, shaking her head. **Almost marital**. His body belonged to her; Jeremy belonged to her. But maybe she only thought that because she'd never been married.

"Porter Strick, as I live and breathe." Jeremy was walking up the sidewalk, coming around from the parking lot behind the building. He grinned. Living in the small town you grew up in meant sometimes politely ignoring people you'd known for decades, because otherwise you'd never be able to finish your grocery shopping. Over the last two years, Porter and Jeremy had looked past each other in public successfully hundreds of times, always keeping their bodies from touching, a planetary ballet.

"I have goats," Porter said. "Do you do goats?"

Jeremy laughed, which was generous. Once you decided someone was funny, you were likely to laugh at any old thing they said. "Sure. You see Dr. Gordon, over at Clapham Animal, right?" He knew where she went, of course. He was agreeing to be an actor in her play, curious about where she was going with it. Jeremy crossed his arms over his chest. He was wearing a button-down shirt tucked into his jeans. Rachel was right—he looked like an ice-cream cone, a hundred percent lickable, just as he always had been. She felt everything at once: the way his breath had always smelled like scrambled eggs on the school bus; the way he held her hand while walking down the hall; the way he'd tried to finger her for the first time, nearly slipping his hand in the wrong hole entirely; the way he'd looked at her during his wedding reception and on their last night at the hotel.

Jeremy's college and Porter's college hadn't been so far apart, and in those early days, when they were both still clinging to their youths, when anyone who had known you before seemed preferable to a stranger, they had stayed in touch. There had been brief visits facilitated by Greyhound buses, visits that ended with UTIs from too much sex and hickeys to be covered with makeup. Their encounters were irregular, which is to say at irregular intervals, but they were always mutually satisfying. It was almost better, not being exclusive, not being "together," because it meant that every time they saw each other, in whatever months had passed between, both Jeremy and Porter had picked up a few new tricks from other people.

"Yeah, I see Dr. Gordon, but I thought, hey, might be time for a change." Porter wondered if she looked different to him than she had before. "And I was just in the neighborhood, thought I'd say hi." She could have been saying anything, she could have been speaking gibberish. Right now, Jeremy was trying to figure out why she had come, and what she wanted. Once he did, he would know what to do.

"I was going to get a coffee before I went in; want some coffee?" Jeremy pointed down the block. In the morning sunlight, Jeremy's brown eyes looked golden. His wife was a blond stay-at-home mom who designed her own art projects with Popsicle sticks and felt. Porter had seen them together too many times to count, but she and Kristen had met only a handful of times: at their five-year high school reunion, before Kristen and Jeremy were married; at their wedding, at which Porter had gotten supremely drunk and danced with all the small children; and only once by accident, when she wasn't expecting it, at the mall in New Paltz, when they were trying on clothes in neighboring changing rooms at the Gap. Kristen was the kind of woman who murmured sweetly to strangers' screaming children in elevators, when everyone else turned their eyes toward the ceiling and prayed to be sucked up by a tractor beam from outer space.

"One cup," Porter said, not meaning it, never meaning it, not with Jeremy, with whom there were no limits. She followed him back around the building, to his car, and when he opened the door to the passenger's seat, she got in.

"I need to pick something up at home first, is that okay?" Jeremy waited, his hand on the shifter knob.

"Yes," Porter said, and they were off. She'd never minded a little white lie.

———

There were several distinct neighborhoods in Clapham: Clapham Village, which contained the commercial stretches and all the homes within a two-mile radius of the roundabout; Clapham Heights, where her mother and Elliot lived, up the hill; Clapham Valley, where she lived, at the bottom of the hill; and then there was Clapham Road, which led out of the valley and into towns south. Jeremy lived halfway between Porter's house and the farm, and though she had driven by a number of times, and occasionally been invited to large parties there, Porter had never so much as parked in front.

She was pregnant. He was married. It was not a date. Jeremy pulled the car into the garage and shut the door behind them.

"Where is everybody?" Porter asked. She didn't budge.

"Nobody's here," Jeremy said. "Come inside." He waited for her to get out of the car, and then he walked around to her side of the car and gave her a small, friendly shove toward the door into the house.

She'd seen the inside of his house thousands of times, in photos on Facebook and Instagram, in videos from when his children started walking or when the cat did something funny. She knew what his kitchen island looked like, what color the paint was in the living room, his outdoor furniture. Walking into it felt like walking into a children's book she'd loved, shocking to have things suddenly three-dimensional.

The house was small and tightly packed: cleats and flip-flops by the door in an overflowing basket, jackets haphazardly flung onto hooks. The living room was lined with bookshelves, with two well-used sofas, one of which held a sleeping dog, the other, a sleeping cat, each curled into donuts. Before Porter made it all the way across the living room and into the kitchen, she knew what she would find there: overflowing bowls of snacks and fruit, a Sharpie'd height chart on the wall. The whole house was a diamond ring.

"So where's the family?" Porter slid onto a stool at the kitchen counter.

Jeremy shrugged. "A mediocre hotel restaurant with a dozen smelly children, I'm guessing? Soccer tournament, the travel team."

"Aha," Porter said. "And you don't have to be at work right now?"

"This seemed interesting enough to take a break for." Jeremy opened the fridge and pulled out a bottle of white wine with one hand and a bottle of seltzer with the other. "Thirsty?"

"It's ten in the morning, what's wrong with you?!" Porter said. "Fizzy water is fine. And are you really going to? What if you have to operate on someone's cat?"

Jeremy shrugged and put the water in front of Porter. "Keeps things loose," he said. "I'm kidding." Being in someone's house was like having immediate access to their private world. Not just their things, their objects, but also what they fed themselves, what they made with their own hands to fill their body.

In all their time together, Jeremy had never made Porter a meal—the opportunity had never presented itself. She had no idea whether he could cook or not, which seemed like an enormous thing not to know about someone you'd had sex with so many times. Porter popped a cashew into her mouth before she'd fully taken in the bowl in front of her. There were things to eat everywhere, it was heaven. She wondered what kind of sheets Jeremy had, if he had a ceiling fan, if there was a place to sit in the backyard, if he thought about her when he masturbated, if his wife ever watched him, the way Porter sometimes did in hotel rooms. There was a wedding photo on the bookshelf, and Porter looked away quickly. It was harder to ignore his other life when she was sitting in his house, where she was surrounded by proof of it, but she wasn't interested in changing direction now.

"Egg sandwiches?" Jeremy pulled open the heavy stainless steel door of the fridge. Had that fridge come with the house? It looked new. Shopping for appliances—that was something they'd never done together.

"Okay," Porter said. "I'll be your assistant." It felt more like when they were teenagers than it had in years. Jeremy's parents' house had been carpeted everywhere—the kitchen, the stairs, even the ceiling of the basement rec room. The house had always smelled like the inside of a kennel, which it was, more or less, with one or two wounded animals always limping around. Porter looked around Jeremy's messy kitchen. What did his wife complain about? Porter couldn't think of one thing, not counting the sex he'd been having on the side. And that wasn't a problem anymore, which made it vanish into the air, a rain cloud pushed farther across the sky.

Jeremy left the fridge open and walked away, across the room to the screen door, which he then propped open, revealing the backyard, with a wooden playhouse, a stainless steel grill, and a small table with benches. A bird feeder hung in the nearest tree. It was almost too much.

"Not bad," Porter said, peeking through the doorway, as if she hadn't seen a thousand photos of him and his kids frolicking in the patchy grass.

Jeremy walked back to the fridge and started piling things up on the counter—a loaf of bread, two eggs, a hunk of what Porter recognized as her own cheese. He'd thought of her, before the second she showed up outside the clinic. She wondered if he ever dreamed that she was sleeping next to him and woke up surprised to have his arms

around his wife. Jeremy leaned over Porter to reach
a pan and then turned on the stove. She stood next
to him, their bodies almost touching, and side by
side, watching the eggs cook.

"So, Porter," Jeremy said. "What's the story?"

Porter thought about it. She hadn't had sex
with anyone for so long—more than a year—the
longest dry spell in her adult life. Her body was
only getting bigger, and once the baby came, what
would dating be like? This was what her mother
worried about, Porter knew, among other things,
and it killed her that she agreed. No one really
knew what changes motherhood could bring—to
the body, to the sex drive, to anything. It was like
going to another country and knowing that you
could never go home again. In the not-too-distant
future, everything would be different, and Porter
could no sooner imagine it than she could imagine
life after death. But standing in the warm morning air, Porter knew what the story was, the story
happening right at that moment. Jeremy slid the
eggs onto the bread.

It was not a date, it had not been a date. She
stood next to Jeremy and stared straight ahead at
the food in front of them, her stomach grumbling
with hunger she hadn't known was there—and
then extended one hand and put it at the lowest part
of his back. Jeremy closed his eyes, a butter knife
in his hand. He let the knife fall to the counter

and pulled Porter's hand around to his stomach, putting it flat against the cotton of his T-shirt. It wasn't sudden if you counted the last twenty years as a very, very slow courtship, or if you blinked and the last two years disappeared like a bad dream.

"Hmm," Porter said.

"Hmm," Jeremy said, and slid her hand farther south until it rested against his newly sprung erection.

They were kissing, and then they were peeling clothes off each other like they were being timed by a trainer with a stopwatch. His tongue was clumsy, so eager, slipping in and out of her mouth. Porter was grateful for the light coming in through the open door to the backyard, and through the windows. She licked his belly button; she couldn't help it. Being in Jeremy's house was sexier than a thousand pristine hotel rooms, which by design felt temporary. Being in his house felt like the moment in the A-ha video where they step out of the cartoon. This was real life.

"Are you . . . ," he said, his eyes on her belly.

"I'm pregnant," she said. "On my own." Porter didn't want to wait for him to ask, for him to imagine that there was someone else, which was of course ridiculous, but there it was.

"Okay, I can see that," Jeremy said. "You look so beautiful, Porter. Goddamn. I mean it. Does that mean I can skip the condom?"

Porter thought about it. "Yes, just stick it in, do it, before I change my mind and ask you too many questions."

Jeremy didn't have to be asked twice. The rag rug in the kitchen felt good against her back, but then she remembered the baby and rolled Jeremy over so that she was on top. She came in minutes, and Jeremy quivered under her. Porter lifted a knee and he rolled away and then carried her over to the sofa, where he laid her back and went down on her with such mastery that she laughed.

"You are fucking efficient," Porter said. "I'm sorry that I'm pregnant, if that's weird. I mean, I'm not sorry that I'm pregnant, I'm happy that I'm pregnant. I just mean that I'm sorry I didn't officially tell you before I took my clothes off."

"Being pregnant is nine months without a baby. It's cool." He'd done this before, of course. It was both comforting and disconcerting to remember that Jeremy had had sex with a pregnant woman before. Marriage was something that Porter didn't quite understand, a fact for which she blamed her mother. Or rather, she blamed her father's death, and then her mother's ease with being alone. Her father had died before she'd moved out of the solipsistic period of youth, when parents existed only in relation to their children, not to each other. They'd been so close to the empty nest, her parents, and to whatever phase would come next. Porter felt sorry for her mother, for the very first time—Astrid would be horrified, maybe even more horrified than she would be about what Porter had just done on the Fogelmans' kitchen floor.

For her whole life, Porter had imagined she'd have a marriage just like her parents—**fine**. They fought but only sometimes. They were affectionate but only sometimes. They rolled their eyes at the dinner table and saved their big arguments for when the kids were out of earshot. That seemed like the goal—another person to help manage the logistics of a full, busy life, someone whose face you liked, someone you could live with for fifty years without throwing each other out the window. Nicky made marriage look like an art project, and Elliot made it look like prison. Porter could count on one hand the number of married couples whose relationships she actually coveted, and most of them were famous people (Mel Brooks and Anne Bancroft, Barack and Michelle Obama), so who knew what was really happening behind closed doors.

She looked at Jeremy and tried to remember why she hadn't wanted to marry him when she was twenty. She was too young, that was all. What a fucking ridiculous choice, what hubris! To think that there would be an unlimited number of willing suitors, like on **The Bachelor,** an endless line of men stepping out of a clown car limousine. Porter hadn't seen Jeremy's bedroom and so she just pictured his teenage bedroom at the top of the stairs of his adult house, the posters of Patrick Ewing and Pamela Anderson at her **Baywatch** best. His children—full-size humans with enormous backpacks and orthodontist appointments—didn't matter to her. They were something else entirely, as remote a concept as having been born a boy, or with three eyeballs. His wife wasn't there, and Porter banished her to the outer limits of her psychic galaxy. There was only so much room inside her body. Pregnancy was so bizarre, so full of unanticipated effects and side effects and side-side effects that Porter felt both connected to every woman who had ever lived and also like she were the first person on earth who this had happened to.

"So why did you come to see me?" Jeremy asked, his head half buried under the blanket over her lap. "I fucking missed you, Porter."

Porter petted Jeremy's neck, following its smooth curve down his spine. "I missed you too." The dog—it was called Ginger, she remembered— woke up and ambled over, pressing her wet nose into Porter's palm. She closed her eyes and pretended it all belonged to her: the dog, the house, the boy. Maybe it still could. It was delusional, she knew, but Porter also knew that this was her last chance at delusion. Soon she would have to shape up, to get her head on straight, to set limits on candy and screen time and curfews and whatever evil thing came down the pike that no one had even heard of yet. Right now, she was still just herself, just one person, with no one to answer to. And so if she wanted to fuck her ex on his kitchen floor, she was going to. Porter didn't believe that everything happened for a reason—that was absurd—but she did believe that one thing led to the next. Her mom had fallen in love with no consideration of the consequences, Porter had run into her old best friend, and all that had led her to Jeremy's office, and then his car had led her to his house, and then their bodies had come back together in the way they had always, always done so well, that had led them here, to this moment, which felt like a beginning or at least the opening of a door.

When Jeremy drove them back to his office, and Porter got back into her car to go home, she put her forehead against the steering wheel and cried. She was happy. Doing stupid things didn't have to be wasted on the young.

Chapter 17

Wendy Wakes Up

It was 12:30 P.M., which meant that Wendy had just begun to enjoy two full hours of silence. The boys were freshly three, and she knew they wouldn't nap forever, and maybe shouldn't even still be napping now, seeing as they woke up at five A.M., but Wendy would rather be up before dawn and get a break in the middle of the day. Next year, they would be in school, and they would be someone else's problem, then they could stop napping. Oh, how Wendy hated her friends who had daughters, dutiful little creatures who could sit quietly at a table with nothing more than a piece of paper and a cupful of colored pencils. If her children were awake, they were running at top speed, screaming like Mel Gibson in **Braveheart**. She wore earplugs when the pitch got too high, which was often. She now hid pillboxes of earplugs in nearly every room of the house, like an addict hiding their stash.

Wendy sat in her home office, a room with no purpose other than organizing their lives. She worked twenty hours a week, a minuscule amount, in New Paltz, and she loved those twenty hours like she loved oxygen. She loved the boring parts, the tedious parts, the scrolling through emails until she forgot what she was looking for. She loved the watercooler, mostly because it was never her job to change it when the supply was getting low. She did not buy the toilet paper; thrillingly, she didn't even replace a roll when there were only a few squares left. She was responsible for neither making her co-workers' lunch nor ensuring that they ate it. Her home office was supposed to be a place where she could do work if she needed to, and she did answer an email inside its walls from time to time, but really it was just a nicely designed closet. It was where all the family's papers were filed, the things no one wanted to look at but were afraid to throw away: previous years' taxes, health insurance forms, bank statements. The room had a window overlooking the backyard, which was strewn with large plastic toys in primary colors, oversize baseball bats, and shrunken basketball hoops. Elliot wanted them to be athletes, though thus far both boys had shown an aptitude only for total destruction. It was a beautiful day outside, and a breeze blew the tree branches. Wendy wondered how much wind it would take to blow the whole house down.

She had pushed for Chappaqua, Bedford, Scarsdale, something that would have made the commute into the city seem like a doable crunch, and not the soul-crushing plot of a deranged workaholic, as it was from Clapham. This was before she was pregnant. Elliot had almost agreed. Mintybreathed Realtors had driven slowly past town landmarks, past top-rated public schools, past quaint houses and brand-new ones. She nearly had him, but then she'd gotten pregnant sooner than she thought—Wendy was pragmatic and had planned for trying for at least a year, at her age, with her history (every woman had a history). But once the egg had implanted and she'd told Elliot, Wendy knew they weren't leaving Clapham. He called his mother first. Wendy asked her mother to come when the baby was born, and then before too long they knew that the baby would be two babies, and she was needed all the more.

Living in Clapham was like living in a Strick museum. **This** was the house where her husband had lost his virginity. **This** was the field he and his friends used on the Fourth of July to send illegal fireworks zooming into space. **This** was the restaurant with the best hamburger, **this** was the bar with the best booths. He was the expert in their lives, and she was his tourist. When they had the twins, she became an expert in them, which was enough, for a little while. Aidan would sleep for only forty-five minutes at a time, Zachary preferred applesauce and yogurt mixed together in an equal ratio. Aidan would pee on the potty but not more, Zachary would always, always go in a diaper, until she took the diapers away and threw them into the garbage with a grand flourish, as she had previously done with the pacifiers. Elliot would come home and announce his amazement at her work. Her "work." It was work, of course, but when he said it, she knew that he whispered those quotation marks, that he thought anything that took place inside their house's walls was playtime. As if children's playtime was playtime for their parents. As if it wasn't work, to keep the house and the children from bursting into flames, to keep herself from lighting the match. Men understood so little.

When Wendy was seven months pregnant, her mother arrived from San Francisco—twins came early, and both Chan women liked to be prepared. Wendy's father stayed at home—truthfully, was there ever a more useless figure than a grandfather? Vivian Chan chose the bedroom next to the twins', though there was an au pair suite on the first floor, by the garage, with its own door and a small kitchenette. She would move down there when the boys were sleeping through the night, she

said, and she did, when they were six months old.
Wendy had always loved her mother, in her own
way, the way one loves an airplane for not crashing
into a mountainside, but once the boys were born,
she appreciated her too. The two women spent
days together without speaking, passing things
back and forth without more than a nod: a diaper,
a pack of wipes, a bottle, a swaddle. They were
synchronized swimmers. Elliot was their absentee
coach, who occasionally wandered into the room
and found them each holding a sleeping child and
offered an enthusiastic thumbs-up, wandering out
again before he could ask if their arms had fallen
asleep, if they were hungry or thirsty, if they could
reach their phones. When her mother had returned to San Francisco after the boys' first birthday, Wendy wept more than she had ever wept in
her life.

Just as Wendy had turned into something else
when the children were born, so had Elliot, only
she had taken a step toward the rest of human experience, and he had taken a step back, shaken as
he was by the visceral fluids, the menial tasks, and
the tedium. He had no training—he'd said that
to Wendy, incredulous at her request that he help
her change Aidan one morning, when her mother
and Zachary were already downstairs, and Aidan
had produced an incredible, bright yellow dal of
a bowel movement, which covered his lower half,
his back, the changing table pad, and Wendy's

two hands. He'd said this to her as if **her** classes at Princeton had included Home Ec and Childcare 101. As if there were a manual, and she'd read it. (There were manuals, of course, hundreds of contradictory books, and she'd read dozens of them, but that wasn't the point. The point was that she always left the books, underlined and dog-eared, on his side of the bed, and he'd never opened them.)

Wendy was deciding what to do: She could nap on top of the made bed, she could fold laundry, she could make meatballs for the boys' supper, she could do one of her exercise videos. She decided to nap, or at least rest her eyes, and walked back over to the master bedroom, which was a suite of its own—his and hers closets, even his and hers toilets inside the master bathroom. Astrid had been appalled when they'd showed her the plans—it was the biggest house Elliot had ever built, and like his office, significantly bigger than the house it was replacing. There were so many big **old** houses in Clapham, houses just like the Big House, that was Astrid's argument, as if she were telling them to remember to recycle their paper and plastic garbage. But they hadn't wanted someone else's house. Wendy liked things clean as much as Elliot did, fresh, and it was his job, to build new things. Astrid had never understood Elliot—it felt cruel to Wendy to even think that about another mother, but it was true. It also felt good to remember that she and Elliot were united on some things, the way they used to be with everything. She fell back onto her side of the bed and scooched upward until her head was on the pillow. She could nap this way, without mussing herself or the sheets, for at least thirty minutes. Wendy had just closed her eyes when she heard the garage door peel open.

She scurried over to the window—no one should be coming in, unless something was wrong. She got to the glass just in time to see the back bumper of Elliot's car pull in. Wendy looked in the mirror and patted her under-eye bags, squeezing the skin on her cheeks. She walked down to the kitchen and found Elliot sitting at the table.

"Hi," she said.

"Where's everybody?" Elliot said.

"The boys are asleep." He could know the details if he listened.

"Okay," Elliot said. He looked sweaty. September was still summer, after all, and still hot enough outside to make anyone glisten if they stood in the sun for more than a few minutes.

Wendy crossed her arms and waited for him to tell her why he was sitting at their table, and not at his desk, in his office. Instead, he leaned forward and rested his forehead on the wood.

"Are you sick?" Wendy looked at the clock—they had an hour left, maybe less. Did he not understand that her entire life was more carefully timed than a parking meter?

"Not exactly," Elliot said. He sat up and made a face like he might have to put his head in a plastic garbage can. "I have good news."

"You could have fooled me," Wendy said. She cocked her head to the side. "What kind of good news?"

He gestured to some glossy folders spread out on the counter. "I got an offer. A real one."

Wendy's eyebrows shot up.

Elliot had bought the parcel of land on the roundabout a year ago. It was hard to keep a secret in Clapham, and hard to keep a secret in real estate, but it could be done. Still, Wendy was amazed that Elliot had managed to keep it from his mother. Astrid thought that she knew what was best for everyone—for Elliot, for the twins, for the whole town.

The idea was this: Bring Clapham into this century. Build the town a new anchor. Make it a destination. Elliot had a long list of things the town needed: an upscale boutique hotel, a bar that didn't have a neon Budweiser sign, a Shake Shack, one of those movie theaters where you could eat dinner in your seat. Elliot had a million ideas and he wanted to build them all. He loved his town but not as much as he loved the idea of what it could become. It was what his father would have wanted for him: to make his mark.

"Who?" Wendy asked. For months, Elliot had been courting as many potential bidders as he could. It had been harder than he'd imagined, to transform Clapham into his vision of the future. He changed his pitch depending on who he was talking to—Clapham was the new Westport, the Hudson Valley was the new Hamptons. In the last year, six different businesses had made proposals: a Tractor Supply store, a vegan bakery, a store that sold model trains for adults, a pet groomer, and a Mexican restaurant. Some of them had slipped proposals under the door, others had mailed packets of paper to the address listed, Wendy's parents' house. Elliot knew both the Tractor Supply guy and the pet groomer—they'd both talked to him at the counter at Spiro's, not realizing.

"Beauty Bar."

"Shit."

"What? They're huge, it would be the destination for every woman in fifty miles!" Elliot still looked nauseated.

"Right, and it's big and glossy and will be right across the street from your mother's girlfriend's salon. Is that not what you're thinking about?" Wendy reached over and picked up the black folder—she could see the back-to-back lowercase **b**'s of the Beauty Bar logo embossed on the cover and ran her fingers over it. "Expensive."

"It's a good deal, I think. I need a lawyer to read it, but the person I spoke with, Debra, she told me it's a really good deal. They want me to build it, they want to rent for ten years, they'll pay more than anyone is paying on Main Street. Twice as much, maybe more. Enough for us to buy more buildings, to do the shopping center by the gas station." Elliot wanted to make the valley into the Strick Brick Corridor, with his buildings and businesses running from New York City to Albany.

Upstairs, a wail, and then a **thump**. The twins should have slept another forty-five minutes, at least.

"I'm a lawyer, you know," Wendy said.

"I'm going to figure it out," Elliot said. He swallowed a pocket of air.

"Let me read it. And why don't you talk to your mom about it? It's your decision, but you don't want to do something you'll regret."

"Why the fuck would I ask my mother? Jesus, Wendy!" Elliot's cheeks were blotchy, and his nostrils flared. "It's my decision!"

"Yikes, okay," Wendy said, putting up her hands in surrender.

"It's my decision!" Elliot said again, as if she could have misheard him the first time.

Over their heads, Wendy heard one set of feet turn into two sets, a small herd. She could see the rest of the day: Elliot locked in his office, making phone calls, or maybe just tapping golf balls in the backyard, his Bluetooth headset on, while she wrangled Aidan and Zachary from nap until bedtime, with Daddy swooping in for a good-night kiss. If he wanted to live somewhere else, they could have lived somewhere else.

One of the boys—it sounded like Aidan—let out a full-throated scream.

"Are you going to go see what the hell is going on up there?" Elliot asked her.

"No," Wendy said, now loving the sound of the word in her mouth. "Give me the proposal, show me what they actually said. I'll go read it."

"What the fuck? It's a workday, Wen!" He was still sitting, an impatient customer at a restaurant.

Wendy picked up his keys from the table. "I'm doing you a favor, you can just say thank you."

Elliot's mouth fell open with such stupid shock—the insult!—that Wendy laughed. "If I had to guess, it would be that Aidan had to poop. Check the potty when you get upstairs, unless you want to spend the next hour cleaning waste off the walls and the floor while two children climb all over you. I will be home soon, to help. Definitely by bedtime."

Elliot sputtered. He was scared, Wendy realized, of his own children.

"You'll be fine," she said, and was out the door.

Chapter 18

Family Meal

Astrid believed in a proper dinner, she always had. First, when it was just her and Russell, it had felt like playing house, with cloth napkins and candlesticks; and then with baby Elliot, who had been a solemn, reedy creature, like a tonsured monk, content to gnaw on a single hunk of bread for fifteen minutes; then Porter, who squawked and sometimes threw handfuls of peas but would eat anything within reach, even slippery oysters; then baby Nicky, who loved the feeling of soft food mashed against his skin and so had to be bathed after every meal, Astrid rinsing off the pureed carrots, the peanut butter, the creamed corn, whatever it was that they'd put on his plate. Those were the best years, the years when the children were all growing, when the differences

between them were so vast (one learning to do mul-
tiplication tables, one sorting out the rabbit ears of
shoelaces, one walking, on two feet, all the way
across a rug) that Astrid and Russell were filled
with genuine marvel for at least five minutes each
day, no matter how hectic and frustrating the other
one thousand four hundred and thirty-five minutes were. When Elliot left for college and Porter
and Nicky were teenagers, that was when the roller
coaster ducked into a dark tunnel, and before they
could come out the other end, Russell was gone
and the tunnel was permanent. Astrid had been
looking forward to coming out the other side—
flying to foreign countries and huddling around a
tour guide holding aloft a colorful flag, renting a
houseboat, who knows. It was easy to say it would
have been a wonderful and exciting chapter in their
lives now that it was purely hypothetical.

Adding Birdie and Cecelia felt good, a return
to form. Astrid had tired of cooking only for herself—so many things seemed no longer worth the
trouble. Goodbye, short ribs, goodbye, coq au
vin. Each configuration had fit around the same
two tables, the massive dining room rectangle or,
more often, the small kitchen table tucked into the
corner. Cloth napkins at every place setting. She
wasn't sorry when the children got big enough to
help clean up, and when they stopped throwing
food on the floor. Every parent had spent enough

time on their knees trying to scrape day-old pieces of elbow pasta off their floor.

Why hadn't Barbara Baker had children? Astrid had always thought it was strange—not that a woman could or would choose not to, though it was less common when they were young, harder to defy expectations. But Barbara in particular had always stooped over to talk to her small charges as they crossed the street, she'd put M&M's in her homemade Rice Krispies treats for town hall events, she'd dressed up for Halloween. Not to mention all the pets. In many ways, Astrid thought that Barbara seemed better suited to parenthood than she was—more patient, probably, more willing to have endless conversations about dinosaurs, more dexterous with child-friendly scissors. Astrid knew her limits—of course she did. Limits were important. That was why her children were polite to strangers.

Cecelia was reading at the table. Astrid was surprised they still taught J. D. Salinger in school—he had slept with a teenager, hadn't he? They should just be reading Toni Morrison. It seemed so easy, to cut out the creeps and sexual predators, just by cutting out all the men. Sure, you'd lose some decent people, but the net result would be so positive, who would complain? Still, it was nice to see a small face tucked behind a paperback, elbows splayed on the wood. Astrid paused at the counter and just watched. This was what she'd wanted—this was what everyone wanted. To have your children's children around, to be young enough to watch them grow, and for them to be self-sufficient, within reason. Grandparenting wasn't the same as parenting, thank god, even in cases like this. She couldn't quite imagine Elliot's sons getting to this point—she'd be old, or dead, by the time they could sit still and read books. But Cecelia was right here, an easy guest. It meant that she'd done something right with Nicky after all, whether he'd admit it or not. She looked so young to Astrid, clearly still a child—when Porter was thirteen, Astrid had seen her as a young woman, closer, as she was then and now, to Astrid's own age. When Porter was a teenager, Astrid's own teenage memories still felt like a relevant part of her DNA, whereas now, those same memories seemed like a sad, dull movie whose plot she couldn't quite remember. Cecelia was a kid. Astrid hoped that she had known that when her children were teenagers, though she didn't think she had. Everything was so much easier with distance.

A timer dinged, and Birdie perked up. She'd been mixing a salad dressing—tahini and yogurt, Astrid's new favorite. "Roasty toasty!" Birdie said, as she swung open the oven door and slid out a baking sheet of caramelized butternut squash and red onions. Astrid watched as Birdie shook off her oven mitt and began making plates for the three of them.

There had been other moments when Astrid had considered telling her children about Birdie. Porter, at least. Last Christmas, and on her last two birthdays. But then Birdie went to her sister's for the holiday, and her children never showed up at the same time for her birthday, if they showed up at all, and so really Astrid would have been telling Birdie about Birdie and of course she already knew. It had never felt necessary, and Birdie had told Astrid over and over again that it was entirely up to her what she told her family and friends. They were happy together, that was what mattered. Astrid sometimes thought that if she had liked Birdie half as much, she would have told people twice as fast.

"It's so nice to cook for more than one person," Birdie said.

"It's so nice to be fed," Astrid said.

"It's so nice that you guys forget that pizza was invented." Cecelia put down the book. "I'm just kidding." Her parents were usually vegetarians, and Cecelia was used to mushroom and tempeh feasts.

Birdie handed the full plates to Astrid, who walked them the few feet to the table. Astrid sat in the chair opposite Cecelia's bench seat, leaving the chair next to her open.

"So, what's school like, Cecelia? Find anyone else you like yet?" This was an ongoing conversation. Birdie hadn't been around a teenager since she was one and was genuinely curious. Astrid wanted to explain that teenagers didn't talk, not really, but it was sweet to watch her try.

"It's okay. My English teacher is okay." Birdie and Astrid shared a look.

"Anyone under the age of twenty-five?" Birdie asked.

"She might be under twenty-five, she might be fifty, how am I supposed to know? She's a teacher. And August."

"Other than August?" Astrid asked. Girls needed girlfriends for a million reasons: because they carried tampons, because they liked to talk on the phone, because they always wanted to talk about how you were feeling. Nicky had always liked to talk about his feelings, too, but he'd been a unicorn.

"Nope."

"I was thinking," Astrid said, changing the subject, "about going to see the bus driver."

"The new one? She's super weird. Like, very nervous." Cecelia picked up a fork and dragged some roasted squash through Birdie's thick, delicious dressing, which Astrid had glopped on top.

"No, the old one. He's in jail, awaiting trial. My friend who works at the county clerk's office told me." Astrid looked for the pepper grinder, her fingers waggling over the table like a star-nosed mole sniffing out a meal.

Birdie and Cecelia made eye contact with each other and then both turned to Astrid.

"Why on earth," Birdie said.

"That is crazy," Cecelia said.

"I'm just curious! I think he may have had a motive. Not that he was looking for Barbara specifically, necessarily, but that he was looking for someone. I think he wanted to feel that power. It's always white men, you know, nine times out of ten. It's white men who turn to violence against their families, against strangers, against the world." Astrid forked some dinner into her mouth.

"Sure, yes," Birdie said. "But what does that have to do with anything? You're not Miss Marple! Are you out for vigilante justice? He's already in jail, Astrid. He did it. Everyone saw it. It's not a mystery."

"What would you even say?" Birdie offered Cecelia some salad, and then Cecelia poured them all full glasses of water.

"I would ask him why! I would ask him how he was feeling. Clearly there are mental health issues there." Astrid popped back up. "Napkins!"

"Gammy, I really think that's a weird and bad idea. If it's that important to you, I will make more friends," Cecelia said, taking a cloth napkin from her grandmother.

"I agree with Cecelia," Birdie said. "He went

crazy. Or he was just on drugs! He's not going to do it again. Whatever the reason, it wasn't a hit job on Barbara. I know it's not fair, but that doesn't mean there's some secret reason behind it." She put her hand on Astrid's shoulder. "Really."

"It was just an idea! I think I just want something to fix. I had the worst lunch with Elliot," Astrid said. She winced at Cecelia. "I shouldn't say that in front of you."

"It's okay," Cecelia said. "He's not my dad. You can say bad things about uncles. I'm going to babysit for the twins, Wendy asked me."

"What does your father say about me, Cecelia?" Astrid asked.

Cecelia looked at her expectantly, her fork hovering in the air two inches in front of her face. Birdie raised an eyebrow. "Astrid!"

"What do you mean?" Cecelia asked. The roasted onions were sweet, and she lowered them into her mouth like a sword swallower. "What does he say about you when?"

"I mean, if your mother were to ask your father if he'd spoken to me, what would he say? What expression would be on his face? I'm curious."

Birdie clucked her tongue. "Astrid."

"What! This is a unique opportunity." She looked at Cecelia. "You don't have to tell me."

"Um," Cecelia said. "You mean you want to know what bad things he says about you? Like, his complaints?"

"Or not! The good things, too, of course!"

Birdie frowned at Astrid. "This is not the kind of thing that ends well."

Astrid leaned over and kissed her on the mouth. "I'm trying a radical new approach to life. It's called asking questions."

"Honesty can backfire, just so you know," Cecelia said. "I don't know if you're ready, Gams."

Astrid nodded solemnly. "I can take it."

Cecelia set her fork down on the lip of her plate and daubed her mouth with a corner of her napkin.

"Stop stalling," Astrid said.

"Jeez! Fine! Fine." Cecelia rolled her eyes. "I think that my dad thinks that you're a little, um, rigid."

"As in strong?" Astrid felt her eyelids flicker.

"As in, um, fixed? Like, you know. Immovable?"

"A bit stiff, maybe?" Birdie added.

"Gasp!" Astrid said, pinching Birdie's thigh. "Traitor!"

"I'm just trying to help her out!" Birdie picked up her chair by the seat and slid closer to Cecelia.

"He would definitely say that you were really organized. Neat. I know he likes that, even if he can't do it himself," Cecelia said. "My parents are always fighting over whose turn it is to do the dishes even though neither of them wants to do it."

"See, that sounds like me," Astrid said. "Okay, that's not so bad." She would show Nicky that she was a flexible person. That she was fun. That she was not only capable of housing and feeding his daughter, but that she was capable of providing substantive care. Astrid hadn't had time to be warm when her children were small—there were three of them, after all, and she didn't want to go insane. When they were teenagers, they didn't pay attention to her, anyway—Astrid remembered picking out flowers for Porter when she was one of the Harvest Queens in the annual school parade, an honor that Porter took about as seriously as a fart, and Porter hadn't even thanked her. When Russell died, Astrid had had to be tough. A sniveling, destroyed widow wouldn't do, would it? Astrid didn't think so. But now, maybe now. She could try.

"Okay, I think that's enough food for the bear, Cecelia, don't you?" Birdie asked. "Want some ice cream?"

"Yes, please," Cecelia said, a child again, holding up her empty plate.

Chapter 19

Twenty Weeks

Pregnant women saw their doctors more than they saw their friends, or at least Porter did. Almost more than she saw her goats. But Porter loved Dr. McConnell. Beth McConnell was an African American woman from Albany, with enormous tortoiseshell glasses and a gap between her front teeth, the smartest, nerdiest girl in any third-grade class made good. What Porter loved most about Dr. McConnell was that she swore ("Oh, shit, I forgot the goo, I'll be right back") and was unpretentious, but best of all, she was Porter's age and unmarried.

The day's appointment was for the anatomy scan, which zoomed in on each part of the baby's body, a detailed, slow-moving movie in real time about the completely natural and simultaneously utterly alien reality of growing one human inside another. Porter was nervous.

"So you'll be able to see everything. Truly everything." Porter had known for weeks that she was having a girl—mothers over thirty-five had to take extra blood tests, as the risks for all kinds of terrible birth defects skyrocketed, as if in punishment for the delayed procreation, as if the eggs themselves were in revolt, salty at not being invited to the party sooner.

"Yep," Dr. McConnell said. "The chambers of the heart, the blood, the kidneys, the toes, the spine . . ."

"Hopefully not in that order." Porter lay back on the chair and lifted her shirt up to the top of her rib cage. For a long time, she had just felt like she was getting fatter and softer, her whole body squishier everywhere except for her breasts, hard little rocks that dreamed of becoming boulders. Now her belly curved out in a proper parenthesis, even when she was lying flat on her back.

"Oh no," Dr. McConnell said. She rubbed her hands together briskly. "I know it's not cold outside, but the AC is pumping in here, and my hands are freezing, sorry." She poked around Porter's belly, the pads of her fingertips pressing firmly at her pubic bone—"Here's the bottom of your uterus"—and a few inches below her sternum— "and here's the top, that's great. You're measuring

perfectly." She readied the machine for the sonogram, back so soon in her routine tasks.

The word **perfect** made Porter's eyes water.
Dr. McConnell probably said it all the time, but
Porter was grateful anyway. The idea that anything about what she was doing in life was perfect was a new one. It would have been a nice
thing, Porter imagined, to hear that every so often.
Rachel's parents were always cooing about her accomplishments—on Facebook, Rachel's feed was
littered with posts from her mother—baby photos, newspaper clippings, pictures of hippos cuddling in muddy rivers. The subtext was always **You
are perfect**. Maybe she'd always done it, or maybe
she was making up for Rachel's husband, but it
didn't matter. She was still doing it, and there was
no way Rachel had asked. Astrid sometimes said
things like that to Nicky. Not the word **perfect,**
because that wasn't how she rolled, but she'd say
things like, "Oh, I was at Susan's Bookshop and
these two young ladies at the register were talking
about some new book, and then one of them said,
'It's just like **Jake George!**' And then they both
put their hands over their heart and swooned." She
never said things like that about Porter, though
Porter knew her mother was proud of her hard
work, and what she made. But if Dr. McConnell
said that Porter was measuring perfectly, that
meant both she and the baby were right on track.

"Well, let's take a closer look, then. I'm sure you want to see her." She scooted her wheeled stool over to the wall and flicked off the lights. By the time Dr. McConnell had zoomed in on the first body part—the spine—Porter was already crying.

"I'm sorry," Porter said. The baby's heartbeat flickered on the screen like an airplane moving across the night sky, strong and steady.

"I'm not," Dr. McConnell said. "She's gorgeous."

Porter sniffled through the rest of the exam, dabbing her eyes with a tissue every thirty seconds. The baby was curled up like a shrimp, her legs kicking gently, her bent arms pointed toward her face.

"You could always bring someone, you know," Dr. McConnell said. "Your mother? A sibling?"

Porter pictured Astrid sitting next to her, holding her hand. Would she be crying? Would Porter be crying, if her mother was there? She pictured Elliot, checking his phone in the corner, nodding every so often in a fake show of support. Nicky might have cried. Cecelia too. She could have invited Rachel—why didn't she? They could be each other's plus ones! Rachel's mother was her plus one already. Maybe Jeremy would come? She'd seen him three times now, at the barn, at her house, and once in the back of the vet clinic in the middle of the night. They didn't talk about the baby, not really, though he did put his hand against her belly, much like the doctor had just done. Of course—he knew what he was feeling for. Dr. McConnell moved the wand, and the baby's face came into full view. She pushed a button on the machine, and the image changed into a 3-D landscape. The picture was muddy brown, pixelated like the information had to travel a great distance, which, Porter supposed, it had—all the way through her skin, from the inside out. Porter thought about all the men in the world who got to pretend that they had done the work just because they were now losing some hours of sleep. They hadn't done this. Women were always alone, alone with their babies. There were some burdens—some **experiences**— that couldn't be shared. Porter stopped crying and watched the baby hiccup, her little body floating inside her but already having a life of her own.

Porter went back to work and then called her brother from the middle of the pen. It usually took six tries to get Nicky on the phone—Porter always assumed she'd have to leave a few messages before actually reaching him—and so she was surprised when he picked up after three rings.

"Puerto," he said. "Mom told me about the baby. It's great."

Porter shooed a goat away from her shin. "She told you? I was going to tell you! So why didn't you fucking call me, you freak?"

"It's great, I said! It's been busy! I love you!"

Nicky coughed. He was always, always smoking weed. Porter assumed it was something he would grow out of, but he was thirty-six now, her baby brother, and marijuana was as much a part of his life as when he was a teenager. If he were a different kind of guy, he'd be planning a CBD oil empire or a field of marijuana plants as high as an elephant's eye. But not Nicky—he was just enjoying it. Not many people could walk away from being a Famous Actor, but that was her brother. Weed, yes. Fame, no. There were so many things that other people enjoyed that Nicky had turned away from—Hollywood parties, being famous enough to have his picture in magazines, casual sex—but never marijuana.

"It's a girl."

"Girls are the best. How's mine?" He inhaled.

"She's great, no thanks to you." It wasn't a nice thing to say, but Nicky was her brother, and that's what siblings were for, target practice. And she knew he wouldn't take the bait.

"She is, it's true. Always has been. Took me a while to understand that—they are who they are, from the second they're born. She and Astrid getting along?"

"They seem to be. I don't think Mom is driving her crazy yet." It was a glorious day—inching toward fall, but warm and light. If there was a place like Clapham in mid-September year-round,

Porter would have moved there. And Northern California didn't count, it was too far away.

"That's good. I keep calling, but it's hard to get her on the phone. Don't laugh," he said, but Porter was already laughing.

"Pot, kettle," she said. "I miss you."

"I miss you too. I really wish I could see you pregnant. It's crazy, Puerto. You're gonna be great. And don't listen to Astrid, you don't need anybody. I mean, you don't need a husband. You need a community, you need friends who can come over with food and wash dishes and do the laundry. But you don't need a husband. Trust me. We're not that great."

"You're not so bad." Porter reached into her pocket and found a chocolate bar she didn't remember buying.

"And you're feeling okay? No morning sickness? Juliette threw up, like, four times a day for months. God, I haven't thought about that in years. She used to carry mints in her pocket, in every bag. For years, whenever we used a bag, there was a little package of barf mints in the bottom. That's what she called them, barf mints."

Porter was quiet. She could tell her brother wasn't done, not quite.

"It's so weird, having Cecelia not be with one of us. It's like being in a constellation. You can't see the whole picture when you're one of the stars, you know? That's what I feel like right now. The point of an arrow. The bottom corner of a spoon. Nothing. Juliette and I are doing our thing, you know, here and there, together, alone, whatever. But without Cecelia here, it feels like pretend, like we could both just spin off into our orbit and no one would notice or care. There's no weight holding us together."

It was also how Porter felt about herself and her brothers, that they were three parts of a whole that had somehow gotten untangled. She remembered being little and loving her brothers more than she loved anything else in the world, thinking (before their father died) that the three of them could run away and have adventures and that nothing bad could ever happen, because they had each other. Nicky and Elliot were so different from each other now, and they had always been, but the proximity of childhood had made the differences seem unimportant, just a part of their comedic timing, like rivals on a sitcom. Nicky was their wild little mascot, and Elliot their de facto leader, and Porter was the peanut butter, the glue. They both loved her more than they loved each other. When Nicky had been in the movie and people paid attention to him, out of nowhere, a bolt of blue, Porter and Elliot had swooped in like two bodyguards. He was the first to break away, and then when their dad died, it unhooked the rest, and Porter had spent her whole adult life trying to figure out how

to put it back together. Jeremy had told her a thousand times that brothers didn't matter—he didn't
speak to his brother more than once a year, and
who cared—but Porter had never wanted to give
up. She never called Elliot, and he never called her,
and when they were together, Porter felt more irritated than anything else, but still. But still.

"Love you, Nicky." He would have cried at the
ultrasound, he would have held her hand. He
would have said something about their dad that
she'd forgotten. It wasn't fair when people moved
away—they took so much of you with them, without even meaning to.

"Love you, too, sis," Nicky said. "Hug that girl
for me, will you?"

"Of course," Porter said, and she wrapped her
arms around her own body too. Sometimes she
wondered if she'd been too successful at convinc-
ing everyone in town that she was as tough as her
mother, as tough as her brothers. She was so tough
that no one ever checked on her, just to make sure
she was doing okay, because she was always doing
okay. That wasn't true, of course, but no one ever
bothered to find out. That was another thing
Porter was going to do as a mom—she was going
to ask her daughter how she was, and what she was
feeling, at least once a week, if not once a day. She
would wait for the answer.

Chapter 20

August Tells the Truth, Part One

The first way August made sense of it was thinking about the moment when cells began to come together and multiply, every human their own private science experiment. August's parents explained it one day after school in the third grade. Making a baby was like baking a cake, August's mother, Ruth, had said, with ingredients, and a specific order in which to do things, and then you had to wait and see if the recipe worked. **So,** August thought, **maybe they got part of the recipe wrong, and put in too much of my mom and not enough of my dad**. Maybe that's where the feeling came from. Later, August would be embarrassed by this thought, which was wrong in a thousand ways, but kids were kids. August had been only eight.

———

Not wrong. Just different. The way two different people can follow the same recipe and make two different cakes, depending on how much vanilla you put in, what kind of butter you use, how long you mix things together. How patient you are. How many times you open the oven, just to check.

The clothing helped—the shop was always full of different possibilities. August's parents thought of them as costumes but August knew better.

When August was ten, the family drove to summer camp for the first time. August had begged to go—already a good researcher, August had found the camp online. It was progressive, even for Clapham, even for the Northeast, even for people like Ruth and John who sold old clothes and composted with worms. The camp T-shirt read SUNSHINE VILLAGE CAMP IS NONCOMPETITIVE, NONRACIST, NONHOMOPHOBIC, NONTRANSPHOBIC, NONSEXIST, NOT FOR PROFIT. The word zinged in the middle and electrified August's eyeballs every time it appeared. The camp was hidden in the woods of Massachusetts, only a few hours away, but when John turned the car down the private road that led to the camp, a collection of old barns and converted farm buildings, August felt nauseous—this summer was a test to see if anyone else noticed, to find out what happened if anyone knew the truth.

At camp, everyone was experimenting with something: macramé, bisexuality, slime, ultimate frisbee, French kissing, makeup, shaving their legs. August decided to start with a new name. August was one of twelve kids in a bunk called Evergreen, everyone equipped with two sets of sheets and a sleeping bag and a canteen and four pairs of shorts and eight T-shirts and two sweatshirts and as many pairs of underwear as they had. August's bed was a bottom bunk, which was coveted, though August thought sleeping on top seemed like more fun, and so when August offered to swap with a kid named Danny, a curly-headed blond from Brooklyn, August was thrilled and hugged Danny, saying, "Dude! You rule!" When the bunk gathered for their first circle time, where everyone introduced themselves and said where they were from, August announced, as confidently as possible, as if it wasn't the first time, that at home, no one actually used the name August, but Robin instead, and that they should too. And so they did. Easy as that. It felt like a tiny shaft of light piercing a pitch-black room.

Sometimes a lie wasn't a lie when it got you closer to the truth. Sometimes a lie was more like a wish, or a prayer.

Robin Sullivan. The kind of name where you couldn't tell. It was an in-between name, a practice name, maybe. The girls in the bunk next door were August's closest friends, and when August ran over to their table in the dining room every morning, they sang out "Rockin' Robin, tweet, tweedly twee" in unison, and August's eyes rolled back from pleasure, like a dog getting its tummy rubbed. They weren't like the girls in Clapham, who all wore capri leggings and let their long hair grow to the middle of their backs and rode pink bicycles with pink and purple streamers and bought the same color lipstick at CVS as soon as their parents said they were allowed. The girls at camp were different. One girl had a buzz cut, one girl had three holes in one of her ears. The women counselors were different too: Some wore baggy jean cutoffs and had nose rings, and some wore tiny flowery dresses and had Rapunzel hair. One, who everyone called Goose, bragged that she'd never cut her toenails. The black girls slept with their hair wrapped in silk scarves. All the girls farted noisily and then laughed. August hadn't been sure before, because being a girl had always been so specific, so narrow, but the girls at camp weren't all like the ones August knew at home, and they weren't all the same. They all thought August was gay, and it seemed silly to correct them. There were lots of gay kids at camp, and some of the older ones paired up and held hands and kissed at the end of the weekly dances, or behind bunks, when they thought no one was looking, just like the straight couples. It was like once you passed through the gate, all the rules about how things were supposed to work got erased, and instead they could just work however they wanted, in whatever way felt best, and no one ever got teased. It felt like another planet.

August had picked the camp, in part, because no one from Clapham went there, and once John and Ruth drove away, there would be no one paying attention to the things August said, no one judging those things against what they knew to be true. Or things that they thought they knew, because August had never said otherwise.

The weeks passed quickly: The kids canoed, they sang around a campfire, and they each got browner and more freckled in the sun. August's lower bunkmate, Danny, snored evenly, like a human white noise machine. John and Ruth called once a week and sent letters every day, so August didn't miss anything at home.

Parents' day was a week before camp was over. August told John and Ruth they didn't have to come, but they wanted to, of course, and August couldn't argue too much.

During the days, August tried things: a friend's top with flouncy sleeves. A beaded necklace. Everyone painted each other's fingernails, even the most handsome boys who played basketball shirts versus skins, so comfortable in their own bodies that they didn't mind if other people looked.

Every night, lying in bed, August asked questions to the air:

What's the difference between your body and your brain? Nothing? Everything?

What's the difference between what you are and what you say you are?

What's the difference between a lie and a secret?

What's the difference between fear and shame?

What's the difference between the inside and the outside?

What's the difference between a meteor and a meteorite? The meteorite hits Earth. It makes contact. Was there a word for a meteor that had to choose when and if it hit?

August wasn't the only one.

The most popular activity at camp was Cloud Watching, and all you had to do was lie on your back on the big sloping hill and stare up. Sometimes there were lots of clouds to watch and sometimes there weren't, but it didn't matter. There would be a counselor there, reading a book, or just lying on their back with closed eyes, and all the kids would surround them like petals on a flower. The counselor who most often offered Cloud Watching was tall and skinny, with a freckled nose and curly brown hair that pointed in all directions at once. Her name was Sarah, and according to some of the kids in August's bunk, Sarah had been called another name before. A boy's name. Her dead name, was what the campers who had been there for several summers called it, which made it sound like a ghost story. But that's what Sarah called it, and they all loved Sarah, and so no one used the dead name, not ever. August always did Cloud Watching when it was with Sarah, and hurried along, to make sure to get the spot closest to her, the tops of their heads almost touching. Some of the boys teased August gently (okay, so there was teasing, sweet teasing), saying that he had a crush on her, and it was true, in a way, but not the way they meant.

The morning that the parents came, everyone was nervous and excited. They knew the summer had changed them—all summers did. That was why the kids at school looked different in September. Being a kid meant being in a constant state of transition, no matter what. It was true when you didn't want it to be, in addition to when you did.

August thought a lot about what to wear, and finally decided: a swap with Emily, a Clapham High School Tennis sweatshirt of John's for a long striped dress with short sleeves. It was nautical and made August look tall and slinky, like a dancer in a 1940s movie that took place on a ship. That's what all of August's friends said, and when August walked the length of their bunkhouse like it was a runway, they all cheered. Robin was wearing a dress on parents' day. All the campers waited on the main lawn for their people to arrive. One by one, a kid would jump up and run across the grass and leap into their parents' arms. Even the kids who claimed not to have suffered a second of homesickness leapt. Everyone had a well of feelings that were hidden from view; August liked that.

——

August saw John and Ruth when they rounded the corner, holding hands. A thousand kids were running a thousand directions, and August saw Ruth jerk her head to one side and then the other, searching. John cupped his hand around his forehead to block the sun. They were thirty feet away, then twenty, then ten. August walked toward them, and Ruth gasped, and ran straight, her arms wide. August was as tall as she was but it didn't matter, she would always be big enough to hold her baby. The dress was long and could stretch only so far. August was in her arms and then John piled on top of them, a happy clump. August held on tight. While they were hugging, there could be no questions, only love.

There was some free time, then lunch, when your parents could take you out if you wanted, then there was the camp play. The idea was that by the time the parents left, everyone would be so tired from the day that no one would be sad.

August led Ruth by the hand around the bunk, showing her where everyone slept, showing her the crevice in the wall where all her handwritten letters were stuffed. She crawled up on top with

August while John went to the bathroom ("Smells like twelve boys have been peeing on the floor all right!" he said when he got back) and they whispered.

"I like your dress," she said, and touched the fabric by August's knee.

"It's my friend's," August said. "I'm just wearing it."

"Okay," she said. "It looks nice on you."

"Thanks," August said, and touched the wooden walls, where generations of kids had written their names, and the years they'd slept there. Sometimes it was a girls' bunk and sometimes it was a boys' bunk. August touched the spot where someone had written **Zoe** in bubbly letters, two tiny purple dots above the **o**.

"Who's Robin?" she asked, her voice quiet. "Is that what everyone is calling you?"

August wasn't sure they'd notice. "Yeah. It's a nickname thing."

"Do you want us to try it too?" She was whispering. "At home?"

"Maybe," August said. "Maybe not. I'm not sure."

"What are you guys talking about up there?" John said, his face level with the mattress. He pressed his nose against the tiny bit of August's knee that was against the wooden slats of the bed like a dog nuzzling for a treat. Everyone else was sitting out on the lawn, waiting for the talent show.

Evergreen was singing a Beatles medley, with Sarah playing the guitar. She'd started to teach August, just a few chords here and there. August watched her every move.

"We'll talk about it later," Ruth said, looking August in the eyes. "Unless you want to talk about it now?"

"Let's talk about it at home," August said.

"I don't want to miss the show!" John said. He had loved summer camp, in the way that some adults do, where they could break into some made-up song at the drop of a hat.

"Yeah, me neither," August said. Ruth turned around and went down the ladder, and then both stood there at the bottom, the two of them waiting for August like firefighters with a trampoline.

"Careful," Ruth said. "It's harder in a dress."

"You can do it," John said. "And we're right here, in case you fall." August turned and followed, lowering one foot down, down, down, until it felt something firm.

Chapter 21

Dead Birds

The plan was this: Cecelia would get off the school bus, hop on Astrid's plush cruiser bike, and then ride over to Elliot's house, where either he or Wendy would be waiting by the open front door, the sound of screams echoing off the walls of the foyer. She would enter, and they would exit, to return at six o'clock. In between those hours, Cecelia was responsible for keeping Aidan and Zachary alive. For this, she would earn one hundred dollars, more money than she had ever gotten from her parents for doing any kind of chore, and so it seemed like a great deal all around.

Before she moved in with Gammy, Cecelia had probably spent a grand total of three minutes alone with Elliot—if that much. She saw him in the doorway as she rode up the semicircular driveway. He paced back and forth, a six-foot Ping-Pong ball.

"Hi!" Cecelia said. She swung her leg off the back of the bike and glided to a stop.

"Hey, thanks for coming," Elliot said, and Cecelia wondered if he'd forgotten her name. Elliot and Porter seemed so much older than her dad. Maybe it was just that she knew him better, but Cecelia didn't think so. It was as if for every year between them and their baby brother, Porter and Elliot were one step closer to the previous generation. Her uncle seemed old-fashioned, like he didn't entirely understand how the internet worked, or know that calling a woman he didn't know "sweetheart" was bad. Maybe it was because she'd never had a grandfather, and he was the oldest man in her family. "Let me give you a quick tour." He turned and walked back inside before the kickstand hit the ground. Cecelia could hear war cries emanating from an inner sanctum of the house.

Elliot and Wendy and the boys lived only a few blocks away from the Big House, but unlike Gammy's house, which showed its age in the creaks of its staircase and the elaborate moldings, the heavy doorknobs that often didn't work right, the nightly groans, as noisy and irregular as an old man with a head cold, Elliot's house—she could feel it the second she walked in—didn't even whisper. It was the Anti–Big House, the inverted version, but with roughly the same square footage. The walls were taupe, the sofa was beige. Astrid's house wasn't cluttered, but it was lived in—art hung on every wall, there were books in every room. Elliot's house was empty, if you didn't count all the enormous Legos dotting the carpet, which was also shades of tan.

"Nice house," Cecelia said, just as Zachary crashed into her from behind. It felt like a hotel or the set of a soap opera. The only things on the supersize mantel were fake candles that went on with a switch. Her parents would have laughed. Her parents referred to the houses that Elliot built as McMansions, which was not a compliment.

"Ha ha ha ha ha, your butt!" Zachary said, and ran off again in the opposite direction.

"The kitchen's in here," Elliot said, walking and pointing. "Bathroom's over there. Their room is upstairs, they can show you. It's an enormous mess—you cannot possibly believe what a mess it is. The door to the backyard is here, I recommend pushing them out of it and then closing the door behind you." He crossed his arms. "What else. Let them eat anything from the fridge, it's Wendy's problem if they don't want to eat dinner." He winked. "Don't tell her I said that. I'll be back, or Wendy will. There's cash on the counter, and my number, if you need it."

Just then, both boys ran at full speed toward the door to the backyard and smacked into the glass.

"We're birds!" Zachary said.

"Dead birds!" Aidan replied, gleefully.

"We've had some problems," Elliot said. "The windows are too big, the birds don't understand that it's just glass." He frowned. "As far as I know, none of my clients have had this problem, but who knows, maybe they just didn't say anything. You sure you'll be okay? Oh, also, I lost my phone somewhere in the house, so if you could keep an eye out for it, that would be great. It's here somewhere, because I've been in prison with them for two hours, and now somehow I can't find it." He patted his front and back pockets again, as if the thing might materialize.

"Absolutely. Let's go outside, guys!" Cecelia said, in her best imitation of a camp counselor voice. She waved to Elliot. "See you later!"

The backyard was wide and flat, with a tall wooden fence on the three sides not facing the house. The twins raced past the swing and to the very back of the yard, where they began to build something out of sticks. Cecelia wandered in their direction but stopped and sat on the tire swing. She lay back and stared at the clouds passing back and forth over her head.

Elliot looked a lot like her dad. Or, he looked the way her dad would look if someone got him on a TV makeover show—tighter clothes, neat, short hair, no beard, real shoes. Their voices even sounded alike: higher than average, with a touch of caramel on the back of the tongue. Her father was a great singer—Smokey Robinson, that sort of thing. Cecelia wondered if Elliot ever sang. She couldn't imagine it—according to her dad, Elliot had always been uptight, and everyone knew that uptight people couldn't sing. (She herself was too shy to sing in front of anyone, and understood.) Families were the weirdest thing in the world. Her dad and Elliot and Porter, all living in one house? Eating breakfast and dinner together every day? Sharing a hotel room on family vacations? It was like a video game—stick all these people together and see which one survives. One of the boys cried out, and Cecelia sat up. They seemed perfectly content from a distance, but when she wobbled to her feet and took a few steps closer, she could see that one of the twins—Zachary, if the shoes were on the right person's feet—was bleeding from his face.

"Shit," she said, moving faster now, with both boys running in her direction. "Shit shit shit shit shit."

There were no Band-Aids in the bathroom Elliot had pointed to, nor in the kitchen drawers, which

Cecelia opened one at a time, slamming them open and closed while holding the bleeding twin on her hip; he weighed at least thirty pounds, maybe more, and the other twin kept trying to climb onto her other side.

"Let's look upstairs, it's okay, it's okay," Cecelia said, not remotely sure that it was the truth. She watched as tiny drops of blood fell onto her shirt, onto the carpet in the living room, onto the gleaming hardwood floor. Zachary wailed—the cut was just underneath his eye, a straight line, about an inch long. An inch looked like a mile on a small face. Cecelia humped him higher up onto her hip and held Aidan by the hand, dragging him along.

Elliot's bedroom was spotless. Cecelia didn't think that she'd ever seen a real bedroom with no clothing piled up in one place or another. Zachary buried his face in her chest, leaving smears of blood on her shirt. Cecelia set his butt down on the ledge of the sink and opened the medicine cabinet. There were Band-Aids and tubes of Neosporin and tweezers and more bottles of skin cream than she'd ever seen outside of a Sephora. She pulled down a box and quickly unwrapped a Band-Aid. Zachary stopped crying long enough to watch her with suspicion.

"Are you going to take out his eyeball?" Aidan asked, his chin level with her hip bone. He sounded hopeful.

"What?! No, he just needs a Band-Aid," Cecelia said. Aidan pinched her thigh to express his disappointment. Zachary whimpered while Cecelia held the corner of a towel to his face to stop the bleeding. The towel looked clean, like everything else in the house, and surely they wouldn't object to a stain from their child's blood. She let the towel drop to the floor and put the Band-Aid on the cut. He looked like the Shrinky Dinks version of Rocky. "You'll be okay," she said. "I promise. Let's go watch some TV."

Zachary didn't need to be told twice. He leapt to the ground and ran down the stairs, not slowed for a second, with his brother two strides ahead of him. Cecelia stooped down to pick up the towel, and after opening and closing a few doors, found the laundry room. She pulled open the door of the washing machine and, just before she let go of the bloody towel, noticed an iPhone sitting in the steel basin. This seemed like the universe evening itself out a little bit: one downside, a child was bleeding, but on the upside, she'd found Elliot's missing phone. Maybe she wasn't the world's worst babysitter after all. She'd been half surprised that he had asked, given her new status as a ne'er-do-well. Maybe losing the phone was a test, and he was checking to see if she was a thief in addition to whatever else.

Downstairs, the sound of **Paw Patrol** filled

the house. Kids knew how to do everything now. Cecelia poked her head into the room next door—an office. Instead of the beiges of the rest of the house, the room was filled with thick dark wood and a heavy desk that was meant to look old but clearly wasn't.

Cecelia looked for a piece of paper to write a small note on—there was a pad on his desk, clearly made by Wendy, with photos of the smiling twins at the top of every page. Cecelia tore off a sheet and opened Elliot's desk to look for a pen. In the drawer, just behind some loose pens and pencils and the odd penny, there was a glossy black folder. Cecelia reached for it without thinking—it was shiny, with the Beauty Bar logo. Elliot didn't seem like the Beauty Bar type, though Wendy did. When it had opened its first branch in Brooklyn, Katherine and Cecelia and their friends had gone and tried every sample, regardless of their need for it: lipstick, wrinkle cream, blush, volumizing spray, cuticle ointment. The stores were as glossy and black as the folder, with floors that looked like pools of wet ink. Cecelia opened the folder and looked at the drawing on the first page. It was a drawing of the roundabout, with Susan's Bookshop and Spiro's and Shear Beauty and the hardware store all in their spots, steady as Beefeaters outside Buckingham Palace, but in the upper-left corner, next to the pizza place, was Beauty Bar. It dwarfed everything else—the building was taller, wider, darker, like a hurricane that had decided to stay put.

"Ugh," Cecelia said. She pulled out the top sheet of paper and kept reading. When she was done, Cecelia scribbled a small note, left it and the phone on Elliot's desk, and then she walked down the stairs and found Aidan and Zachary horizontal on their designated monogrammed beanbags. She squeezed in the narrow place between them, and each boy moved his head a few inches closer to hers.

"So what's this show about, anyway?" It was after her time, which was sort of nice to realize, that her childhood was far enough away that new cartoons had been invented. Eventually, she'd be old, too, just like Elliot, and Aidan and Zachary would have to explain all the things they automatically understood, just like she took it for granted that gay people could get married, or that Google could answer any question in a split second. She looked forward to there being things that young people would have to laboriously explain, their eyeballs rolling skyward. The boys didn't answer, too deep in their simultaneous pleasure comas, and so Cecelia just watched with them until they'd seen five and a half episodes and she knew all the pups by name and the theme song and the ancillary characters that cycled through Adventure Bay to ensure that the pups weren't always just rescuing themselves. When they heard Wendy's key in the door, Cecelia swam back to the surface, kissed the boys goodbye, and then got back on Gammy's bike to ride back to the Big House, her pocket fat with cash.

Chapter 22

Lady Date

Porter picked up Rachel before dinner—there was no reason for them both to drive.

"You be the designated driver on the way there, and I'll be the designated driver on the way back," Rachel said, as she slid into Porter's passenger seat. "Or maybe we can find someone drunk and drive them home, too, instead of just wasting our sobriety on each other. Like the Guardian Angels of Dutchess County."

Porter wanted to take Rachel to The Yellow Owl, a farm-to-table restaurant in Tivoli that was a few years old. It was one of a dozen or so places that catered to the Brooklyn escapees and the food photographers, meaning it had kale and crudo and expensive bowls of ragout. The inside of the restaurant was so dark and the space in between the tables so narrow that Rachel and Porter bumped into nearly every table on their way to their own, like Tweedledee and Tweedledum.

"That was harrowing," Rachel said, once they were seated. A trio of tea lights sat in the middle of the small table. She picked up the menu and scanned it quickly. "I'm having the pasta. All I want is pasta, three meals a day."

"It's good. They use my cheese for their ravioli." Porter gnawed on a breadstick. She watched Rachel rub her belly in time to the song playing on the stereo. "Raviolo. It's just one giant ravioli. It's kind of weird, I don't know."

"Have you heard from your husband?"

Rachel rolled her eyes. "Yes. I was going to text you, but then it just seemed too pathetic and sad. He keeps calling me. Writing me these huge, long emails. It's like he was addicted to sex and now he's addicted to apologizing. He showed up the other day too."

"Showed up where?"

"At my house. It was like something out of a Julia Roberts movie from the nineties. You know the one I mean, where she has to learn how to swim in order to get away from her abusive husband? Like he's following me. Which he is. I mean, he knew where to find me, obviously, but also obviously, I wasn't responding to him and had no interest in seeing him." Rachel took one of the breadsticks and crunched it between her back teeth. "This is good."

"Did you talk to him?" At the next table, a couple was on a date. They looked maybe twenty-five and were holding hands over the middle of the table, tea lights be damned. Porter wondered what they had done right that she and Rachel had so clearly done wrong.

"No, I wasn't home, thank god. He got my mother, which is, like, his worst nightmare. Even when he and I were on good terms, she was his kryptonite. Now, forget it. You have never seen a more satisfied angry person than a woman who's been waiting her whole life to be a grandmother." Rachel laughed. "She told him to take a long walk off a short pier. I don't know, he cried. If I was there, I would have felt bad. But my mom did not feel bad. It's kind of awesome."

Porter nodded. "Do you think you'll change your mind? And want him to be around?"

"When the baby's born, you mean?"

"Yeah, or after. I mean, I'm on your side, obviously, but I just wondered if you ever considered his behavior being, like, a temporary insanity. Some men are really afraid of it. **It** being us, looking like this, and whatever comes after. Stretched-out vaginas, breast milk. You know, the perks." Porter put her hands on her belly.

Rachel thought about it. "Maybe. I don't know.

The idea of it being my mom and me in the delivery room does kind of kill me—like, he got me into this, and he's not there for the screaming and the pain? For my hemorrhoids? To tell me that my stretch marks are beautiful? That's fucked up. He should have to suffer. This way, it's like he gets a prize. Like, you don't have to wake up in the middle of the night, congratulations, motherfucker! I don't know, man. I think I will talk to him eventually. He's my husband, you know? Like, he might be a total assface, but legally, he's **my** assface. But then I feel like I want him around just to punish him, as if having the baby is a punishment, which it isn't. I just know that it's going to be hard and I want help, but I'm still so, so fucking mad. Fuck!" The couple at the next table turned to look at her. "Sorry," Rachel said. "Hormones."

"I had sex with Jeremy," Porter said. She blurted it out and then made a face. The waiter came over and asked them if they'd like anything to drink, and Rachel stared him down until he left. "I've been having sex with Jeremy. For a long time, and then not for a while, but again, now. Not right now, obviously. But we did. Sorry! I'm kind of nervous to tell you, I feel like this is coming out weird."

"Are you joking right now?"

Porter hadn't thought this through, she realized, as she watched Rachel's facial expressions cycle through surprise, anger, and hurt. She'd been looking forward to telling Rachel about the sex itself, which was sort of hilarious and new, but also about her current fantasy. It was a fantasy, mostly—Porter knew that—but she also couldn't help herself from daydreaming: Jeremy would finally split up with Kristen, move into a new house with Porter, and be a doting, sleep-deprived parent with her. The timing wasn't great, but life wasn't perfect. He would get on board, she could see it all now. Jeremy's whole job was to care for small creatures! He wasn't grossed out by anything. He had two kids already. The man was practically a doula. Porter hadn't said this out loud, but she wanted to try, to see if it sounded completely delusional or if it sounded like a **New York Times** Vows column. She wasn't sure.

"No," Porter said. "It just happened."

"What does that mean, it just happened? Were you hypnotized? Roofied? What, I'd really love to know." Rachel crossed her arms on the table, her mouth clenched. She put down her breadstick cigar.

"I ran into him, and we had lunch, and then we had sex. It was like riding a bike? Sort of? I know that sounds very rushed, but really, it just happened, and because it had happened before, it didn't seem like such a big deal." It did not sound great, it turned out. In fact, the whole situation all sounded much worse when Porter said it aloud, more premeditated, which she supposed it had been. She had pictured him naked when they were standing in front of the vet clinic, she had run her tongue over her upper lip. She had wanted to get into his car, to have him drive her somewhere. She had wanted every minute of it. "What we had was serious. For a long time. I think it still is. I think he's the love of my life. I know that sounds weird and cheesy, but I think it's true."

"I don't care if it sounds cheesy, Porter. Cheesy is fine! We're pregnant! You don't think it's cheesy that strangers call me 'Mommy' on the street? That my relatives have started to send me onesies with baby ducklings on them? What I care about is that he's married, Porter. With kids, right? Which makes you, pretty much, the same as the woman whose asshole my husband was so interested in." The couple at the next table may as well have been Mormon missionaries, they looked so aghast over their small-batch cocktails and chicken with preserved lemon and spiced lentils.

"It's not the same thing," Porter said, arguing because she didn't want it to be true. "They're not happy. And he was mine first." This was a bad argument, she knew, but it was how she felt.

"How do you know if they're happy? All you know is that they're married, and have a family, and that he had sex with you anyway, which, no offense, is not a great sign. You're about to be somebody's mother. And if I remember correctly, didn't you already do this with him?" Rachel stood up with an **oof**. She scraped her chair aside and worked her way out from behind the table. "This is fucked up. I'm sorry, but I just can't. This was always your problem, you know that? Like, you're not still the Harvest Queen, riding on a float. You're a grown-up."

The restaurant hummed. Only the couple next to them noticed, and the waiter, when he returned. "Oh, just one?" he asked, meaning nothing but the number of menus needed. Porter nodded. "Just one." She looked at the menu. Everything and nothing looked good. She wanted chicken soup, or pasta with meatballs. She wanted pancakes at Spiro's. Rachel didn't know what she was talking about—just because her husband had slept with someone else didn't mean that Porter and Jeremy couldn't have something real—the fallacy of moral superiority was embarrassing. Porter was a grown-up! She was. If anyone wasn't a grown-up, it was Rachel, for thinking everything and everyone could fit into neat little parking spaces. It was entirely possible that Jeremy was finally going to leave his wife. **Leave** her. Even that language was regressive, and 1950s, as if Jeremy was going to pick up a suitcase and never see her again. This was Clapham, in the twenty-first century. No one left their children anymore, or their spouses. People hosted their exes for Christmas and posted pictures on Instagram. #Blended, #consciousuncoupling. It was like Prince Charles and Camilla—Diana had the beauty and the charm, but deep down, everyone knew that Camilla was the right choice. Porter didn't want to be Camilla, and she didn't want Kristen to die in a horrible car accident, but she would be lying if she said that the scenario had never occurred to her, midshower. She would be a doting stepmother. It could happen. Everyone else could fuck off.

"I'll have the pasta," Porter said, when the waiter came back. "And the steak." The baby needed food. She was going to be a good mother, she hoped. And if the couple next to her was alarmed that she was crying while eating, well, that was too bad for them.

Chapter 23

Elizabeth Taylor

August wasn't sure about the Parade Crew. "It's just, not, I don't know . . . ," he started, saying plenty.

"You can be honest," Cecelia said. "You think it's lame."

It was study hall, and they were sitting at the very last table in the library, with August's phone propped up behind their American History textbook. August had taken it upon himself to educate Cecelia about Elizabeth Taylor, his favorite actress. They had already watched several clips from **Cat on a Hot Tin Roof** and **Cleopatra** and had moved on to clips from **Giant,** which was August's favorite. They were sharing one pair of headphones, with one tiny bud in August's right ear and the other in Cecelia's left.

"Don't get me wrong—I love to build things and to decorate things," August said. He was so wonderfully careful with his words. "It's more that the Harvest Festival Parade is always full of girls like Sidney and her posse, who always wear the same strappy dresses and strappy shoes with dumb beauty-queen curls, like they've never even seen a magazine. I think it would be way more fun to build, like, an alternative parade that happened on the same day on the other side of town."

"As my one friend, don't you think you should be encouraging?" Cecelia snuck a gummy bear out of her pocket and passed one to August. "And you could probably make the float like a hundred times better! Why don't you do it with me? It's easier to change things from the inside out, right? And what if **I** was a Harvest Queen? You know what they say—if you can dream it, you can do it." Elizabeth Taylor made Texas look about as sultry as Wisconsin, but Cecelia was into it anyway.

"What about me? I could be the Harvest Queen too! At least I'd wear something interesting. Fine, fine. Join. Don't let me keep you from your dreams."

Nicky and Juliette weren't big on holidays—there were usually flowers and chocolates on Valentine's Day, and celebratory pancakes on birthday mornings, but Christmas and Thanksgiving they usually spent at other, more organized people's houses. No tree of their own, no turkey of their own. The one holiday thing they had always done, though, since the year that Cecelia was born, was take the subway to the Museum of Natural History the night before Thanksgiving and watch all the balloons get puffed up. That it happened at night made it always feel half secret, even though there were hundreds or thousands of other people there too. Cecelia never cared about the crowds. It was like a giant version of being in your school after dark, a little bit sneaky, even if nothing sneaky was going on. She would hold hands with both of her parents—why would anyone want to be anything other than an only child? She was in the middle, clutching them both, at the very center of the world. That was why she wanted to build a float. Maybe if the float was big enough, or glittery enough, she could make her parents wake up, get on a train, come to the Big House, pick her up, and take her home. It was a humiliating, childish desire, and she would rather die than admit it out loud, but there it was. It was as if she had proven just **too** challenging, after twelve years of perfect, normal, easy behavior and then several months of a handful of confused calls from the guidance counselor's office and tears and conversations with other parents that weren't just about playdates. Her parents needed a time-out from being parents. That was how she saw it— betrayal masked as concern. Katherine's parents, in their leather shoes and buttoned-up clothes, had forced the school to apologize, had threatened to sue, had kept their daughter home for a week's suspension and then had started tidying their private school applications. It was nothing.

"I just want to learn how to do things," Cecelia said.

"Fair enough," August said. "Now, look at her **blouse**."

"You're the only person under fifty who uses the word **blouse,** August," Cecelia said.

"Yes, well, you can learn from me too." He bowed.

The library was quiet—only a third of the eighth grade had study hall, and it was still nice enough that they were allowed to sit outside, on the lawn, which was what almost everyone else had decided to do. A few studious girls were doing math homework at the next table toward the door, and then there were a few kids sitting alone, reading. Cecelia felt flushed with appreciation for August, for her aunt Porter, for the universe. Having friends was not something to take for granted.

Liesel appeared in the open doorway of the library, and even though Cecelia couldn't see who she was talking to in the hallway, she could guess. She nudged August's elbow and then they both watched Liesel make her way down the low bookshelves until she'd reached their table. She held out a folded square of paper, and Cecelia took it slowly, as though it might bite. When she'd taken it, Liesel turned quickly and hurried back into the hall.

"Let me see that," August said. He took the note out of her hand and carefully unfolded it until it was a creased but mostly flat piece of paper.

A WITCH IS BETTER THAN A SNITCH, BITCH.

Cecelia gasped. "How the hell does she know?"

"I don't know, the internet? How does anyone know anything? Wait, there's more," August said, dragging his finger down the page until the whole sheet was unfolded. It was also possible, August supposed, that he had told his mother and that his mother had told Sidney's mother, because they took yoga classes together, but he didn't want to admit that he might very well be the source of the leak. Better to blame it on Sidney's Insta-stalking, which she was no doubt doing. At the very bottom, in smaller letters, it read:

AND YOUR DAD USED TO BE SUPER HOT, WTF

"Oh, god!" August said. "This is, like, bad, even for them! This is the kind of note someone gives you on your prison lunch tray right before they stab you with a pointy toothbrush!"

Cecelia let her head fall into her hands.

"What exactly happened, anyway?" They hadn't talked about the details, just the really broad strokes, because the details didn't make sense, and it was easier to keep things neat with new friends.

On the tiny rectangular screen in front of them, Elizabeth Taylor was getting older in three-minute increments. Someone had taken the trouble to put the whole three-hour movie on YouTube, and they were watching, skipping every few minutes so they could get through as much as they could in forty-five minutes. Cecelia just wanted to see everything at once, to know how things would turn out. Everything took too long—school, her parents' fights, puberty, summer camp, the line at the bagel store on weekday mornings. Cecelia wanted the Hollywood version of her own life—fast-forward, with wrinkles made out of papier-mâché. It was too hard to wait and see.

When Cecelia was small, and her mother was dancing more than she was teaching, Juliette was often away in the evenings at bedtime. Nicky was always around, his job being more or less make-believe, and her dad would fill the tub with bubbles and tell her stories about mermaids until her eyelids began to flutter closed. She didn't object, because it was nice to have time with her father, too, but Cecelia remembered the day she finally understood: Her mother was gone because her mother was **somewhere else**. She hadn't just evaporated for the night, she had gone **somewhere else,** to do things with **other people**. It was heartbreaking. Her father didn't understand why Cecelia would cry so much, because she couldn't quite explain—it had to do with the unfairness of being a child in a family of adults, of being left out, of being left behind. Juliette was always there in the morning, but in the morning, Cecelia would be tired, and still clutching on to her anger like a security blanket. No kid wanted their parent to belong to the outside world, not really. No one wanted an independent mother. Those nights when she was small, Cecelia had often put herself to sleep by saying, **fast-forward, fast-forward, fast-forward,** because the sooner she went to sleep, the sooner she would wake up, the sooner time would pass. She didn't want to get older, she just wanted to be on the other side of whatever it was. Whatever her mother was doing, she wanted it to be over.

"I told you. My friend Katherine," she said, "she got me in trouble for getting her in trouble, basically. She met a guy who turned out to be something else. Like, a grown-up. And I told because I didn't want her to get murdered, and then she accused me of bullying her, even though I wasn't. And now she's still getting me in trouble, which was the whole reason my parents wanted me to come here, so that it would just be over, erased, as if life works that way. Why do I know that and they don't? It's like, guys, the internet exists. The internet doesn't care what zip code you're in. There is literally no escape. Maybe Antarctica."

August shook his head. "I don't know."

"I'm going to do the Parade Crew." Cecelia folded the note back up and put it into her backpack. She didn't want to throw it away and have the librarian find it and start the whole thing all over again.

"Okay," August said. "I'll do it with you."

"Really? Thank you. You are a good friend. Thank you," Cecelia said. She crossed her ankles and watched Elizabeth Taylor lean against a doorframe. She looked like she wanted to push the opposite button. Rewind. Wash it all off and start again. Maybe someday Cecelia would want that, too, but not today.

Chapter 24

Hot Time in the City

After they put Cecelia on the train, Nicky had taken a cab to JFK, where he was scheduled to fly to Albuquerque, with a layover in Dallas, but as soon as he walked through security, Nicky knew he couldn't go. He turned around, pulling his small wheeled suitcase behind him, and went to the back of the taxi line. Being apart from Cecelia was strange enough; he didn't want to be apart from Juliette too. The two of them walked around the apartment in circles for days, dueling somnambulists, avoiding conversation but happy for the companionship. Finally Nicky did what he always did when he felt terrible—he went to the Russian baths on Tenth Street and tried to sweat it all out. When he was in Taos, Nicky liked to drive out to the banks of the Rio Grande, where there were natural hot springs, small, stone-lined pools of hot water; but there was no calming river in New York City, no empty, quiet space, and so instead Nicky took the train into Manhattan and walked to the East Village and traded his street clothes for a pair of one-size-fits-all shorts and a shvitz.

He'd first come to the baths during college, in between when he shot **The Life and Times of Jake George** and when the movie was released eight months later. It was Jerry Pustilnik's idea, the actor who played his father in the movie, who had played the father to half a dozen other teenage heartthrobs, as well as scores of police detectives, and criminals of several denominations, due to his mirthful belly and round cheeks, which could look either stern or menacing. Jerry went to the baths every week he was in the city, and he told young Nicky that it was a life-changing experience, and so they made a date to go. Nicky brought his bathing suit in his backpack, not knowing what to expect, but before long they were surrounded by Russian Jews with bellies that made Jerry's look petite. In one of the saunas, Jerry paid a guy ten dollars to smack his back with giant oak leaves and then they ate pickles and borscht, Jerry's skin now electric red, and Nicky was sure that Jerry had been right. The purposeful discomfort—in a community set-ting, no less!—had a numbing effect on the mind, because all you could think about was how every drop of water in your body was trying to come out.

The space had been upgraded slightly, but there was no removing the smell of mildew, which clearly lived behind every tile and beneath every floorboard. Faucets ran twenty-four hours a day, cold water to splash on yourself when the heat became unbearable. It was still mostly bare bones, despite the much-changed demographic of the East Village and despite the burly Russian man who had taken his money at the door. The shorts were the same, and though it didn't seem possible— Nicky hadn't been in at least six months, maybe a year—he recognized the faces and bodies of some of the men in the sauna room. He lay his towel flat and then stretched his body out on top of it. It was a co-ed day, no one's favorite except the rich guys who came with their model girlfriends, couples for whom physical discomfort and awkwardness seemed part of the plan. It was too hot for human bodies, and so the sweat just came. The true-blue bathers covered their chests and legs with a layer of Vaseline, making it even harder for the sweat to push through. Nicky closed his eyes and breathed, every cell in his body telling him that this was a very bad idea. That was part of the pleasure of it, fighting against the urge to leave, but he'd spent the last twenty years meditating, and this was the same thing. Sit with the discomfort. Sit with yourself. Just sit.

When he was eighteen, Nicky's body could do anything—he could run for miles without tiring, he could play a new sport adequately well having only just learned the rules. He wasn't competitive but loved team sports—when he first saw Juliette dance, the night they met, at an engagement party for mutual friends who were now divorced, she and her friends danced with such total abandon, their arms and legs poking and sweeping and jutting and shaking all to make one another and themselves laugh, he understood. He had understood her, the way she moved through the world, body first.

They had come here together, from time to time, though Nicky came less often when the demographics of the place began to change faster. He liked the assortment of ages and bodies, the Hasids, the union guys who came after working all night, each of them trying to burn something out from under their skin. When he first came with Jerry, Nicky was sweating out grief—his father's death had been sudden and his mother's response was like closing a door to keep out the chill. It was done; it was over. There was no meaningful discussion. When their teachers had pushed for some sort of family counseling, Astrid had rolled her eyes but acquiesced, clearly just to check it off the list, and to satisfy the due diligence. Nicky remembered what the room had been like—a dark purple corduroy couch, a glass coffee table with a box of tissues sitting in the middle, some cracked-leather chairs on the opposite side. Porter and Nicky had sat together in one corner of the couch, with Astrid perched forward on the far end and Elliot across from them in a chair, bouncing his knees. Nicky and Porter had curled into each other's bodies and sobbed. Only the therapist had thought to slide the box of tissues within their reach.

Acting had never been particularly interesting to Nicky, but it was something he could do. He could remember lines, and he could speak in public, in dark rooms, with a light pointed at his face. The eighth-grade performance of **South Pacific** had been spotty—Jamie Van Dusen, who played Nellie, had a thin, timid voice and gave a little half chuckle whenever she was about to break into song, as if in acknowledgment that she knew she wasn't going to be terrific, but she was going to do her best. After the performance, Russell had rushed up to Nicky, leaving Astrid and Porter with the flowers, and embraced him. Nicky could feel his father's warm breath in his ear, could still hear him say, "Son, that was **wonderful,**" as if the wondrousness wasn't due to Rodgers or Hammerstein but as if he, Nicholas Strick, were solely responsible. Encouragement could do anything. Encouragement and a natural inclination. Russell could have encouraged Porter to be an actress every day of her life and she still would have turned beet red and tried to swallow her own tongue at the prospect.

Nicky admitted that much, that there was something in him, some true match that his father had seen. After that, Nicky was in everything: **My Fair Lady, RENT, Our Town, The Crucible**. And when his high school drama teacher recommended Nicky audition for a film, Russell slapped his hands together. He knew Nicky would get the part—they were looking for a charmer, a flirt, someone who half the audience would pretend to kiss in their bedrooms at night and the other half would imitate in the halls at school. Russell would have loved the movie, though it was passable at best, and now seemed horribly dated. But Russell would have loved seeing his son's face in **People** magazine. Imagine, Nicky Strick, in every dentist's waiting room in the country! Russell would have tapped strangers on the shoulder. He would have beamed. Instead, he'd died in between filming and the release, suspended in the time when anything could happen, or nothing could happen. Russell would have been proud either way.

Someone touched Nicky on the foot, and he opened his eyes. It was a young man with a blond buzz cut.

"Massage?" he asked. Everyone who worked at the baths was related to everyone else—Jerry Pustilnik had told Nicky the whole saga once, how it had been owned by brothers who had had a falling-out, and how they now ran the space on different days, how if you bought a ticket from

Dmitri, you could only use it on Dmitri days, that his brother, Ivan, would frown and turn you away. The rest of the staff were members of their family that remained agnostic, like so many children of divorce. This young man was someone's nephew or cousin. Nicky had always wanted that kind of family, so big that you could never quite work out if you were someone's second cousin or third cousin once removed, because it didn't matter, you were family, and that was the only label that counted. But you needed so many people on board to make that happen, generations of joiners, and the Stricks were not that.

"No thanks," Nicky said, and the young man moved on to the next potential victim. Across the room, Nicky watched two young women murmur to each other—they were closer to Cecelia's age than his, much closer. Cecelia, who'd been an adult all her life. Astrid had been horrified when he'd told her that they let Cecelia take the subway by herself when she was ten years old, but Cecelia was ready! She was cautious, she paid attention, she never fell asleep on the D train and woke up in Coney Island like he'd done in college. That's why the whole thing with her school and her friends had been so confusing—as if, after so many years, he and Juliette had the blindfold pulled off and were shown that Cecelia was, in fact, only a child. They'd never thought of her that way before.

Nicky couldn't say precisely what Cecelia had

done. Her best friend, Katherine, had said that they'd met someone on the internet. She and Cecelia, together. That they had chatted with a man, who they thought was a boy. That they had gone to his apartment. Cecelia said she hadn't but Katherine said that she had, and then Cecelia said she'd gone but waited outside, or picked Katherine up, and she had **known,** she had known all along, and just the fact that this could happen, that there were local men impersonating teenagers in a place (the internet) where they could interact with his daughter was too much. Nicky did what any parent would have done: He pulled the rip cord and got her out of there. Was that better or worse than leaving her in a toxic puddle, no matter who made it? You couldn't ask kids to change. You could sooner change the weather.

Nicky knew better than to blame. You could expect only so much from anyone, even parents. Maybe even especially one's parents, the people who cared the very most, and who saw themselves so much in every reflection. When the movie came out, Nicky had just moved into the dorms at NYU, as if his life had anything in common with the way it had been a year earlier, when he'd applied to schools. He was a boy about town, trying to fill the hole left by his father with whatever he could put into his mouth: with body parts attached to beautiful girls, with endless joints, with bullshit party small talk, shouting over the DJ at

Don Hill's while young actresses danced around him, all of them starring in a live production of **This Is Fun, We're Having Fun,** staged around the city twenty-four hours a day.

The director of **Jake George,** a midwesterner with large, square glasses, had told Nicky that he wanted to introduce him to a friend of his, a director who made artsier films. The friend—Robert Turk, a legend already, though he'd made only three movies—had seen some early footage from **Jake George** and loved Nicky. Phone numbers were exchanged and Robert called Nicky on a Friday night and said he was having a small party, nothing fancy, just a few friends. Nicky changed his clothes three times before getting on the subway uptown.

Robert Turk lived in a doorman building on West End Avenue and Eightieth Street. The lobby was white marble, with one attendant at the door and another behind a desk, both wearing uniforms and hats.

"Hi," Nicky said. "I'm here for the party? Turk?"

The men didn't smile but nodded toward the elevator. "Sixth floor, end of the hall on the right."

It was ten o'clock. Nicky could remember, only a year ago, when ten o'clock would be closer to the end of a party than the beginning. He had a couple of joints in his wallet, because he knew it was rude to show up to a party without anything, but his fake ID was for shit, and he didn't know any of the delis uptown and didn't want to risk it. It might not be a pot kind of party, but it might, and it never hurt to be prepared. When Turk had called, he told Nicky not to bring a posse, because it was an exclusive party, and so Nicky had come alone. He didn't mind. Everyone was always alone, anyway, whether they realized it or not.

Nicky knocked on the door, 6E. Someone shouted to come in, and so he turned the doorknob and pushed. The apartment was more modern than he'd expected—low lights, spotless surfaces, framed movie posters on all the walls.

"Hello?" Nicky called. He took a few tentative steps down the hall.

"Hey," Robert Turk poked his head out of a doorway. "In here."

Nicky took off his backpack and set it down in the hall. He wrung his hands together. "Am I too early?" He got to the doorway and saw it was a narrow galley kitchen. The windows overlooked a courtyard and all the other apartments. They were all lit up like Christmas trees, and almost none had curtains, as if everyone in the building had tacitly agreed that light was more important than privacy. Robert handed Nicky a glass of wine.

"I know; it's better than television," he said. He clinked his glass against Nicky's and took a long sip. "I'm so glad you came."

There was no one else there, it was clear. Nicky

drank his glass of wine and looked at the books on Robert's bookshelves and tried to understand if what was happening was weird or not. His cheeks were feeling flushed already. Robert was walking around behind him, watching him, from two feet away, the way you sometimes walked the same path as an animal at a zoo, to get a better look, to see what they looked like from other angles. "Can I make a quick phone call?" Nicky asked. "I'm sorry, I forgot, I was supposed to call my girlfriend, she's going to be so pissed, do you mind?"

Robert pointed toward a bedroom. "There's a phone in there. Go for it." He settled onto a couch and crossed one ankle over a knee.

Nicky ducked into the room and shut the door behind him. He didn't have a girlfriend. He picked up the phone and called his mother.

"It's practically midnight," Astrid said, after Nicky had identified himself, his hand cupped around the phone. "What's going on?"

"I'm at this director's apartment," Nicky said. "I don't know, he said it was a party, but it's just me, and it's kind of weird."

"Okay." Astrid must have been in bed already, reading a book. Nicky could picture her, eyes closed, the book tented open on her middle.

"Do you think I should leave?"

"You're an adult, Nicky! How should I know? Do you want to leave?"

"I don't know." He wanted her to tell him to leave. He wanted her to tell him that she would call a car service and have it waiting downstairs, that he should run if he wanted to, that his comfort was her fire alarm, that there was nothing to be afraid of, that she was there, always awake and waiting, like when he was little and woke up in the middle of the night with a bad dream. "I don't know what I want you to say."

Astrid laughed. "Nicky, sweetheart, I'm going to sleep. I trust you. Have a drink! It'll be fine."

Nicky opened the bedroom door and Robert smiled. He shifted on the couch, and Nicky could see a tentpole in his jeans, poking skyward.

"She's super pissed," Nicky said. He set his wineglass down on the coffee table. "I should go."

"Are you sure?" Robert stroked his inseam with a finger. "I'd really like to get to know you better, Nick. I think we could do some really great stuff together. And we could get started right now." He gave half a wink, and Nicky understood that he did this all the time, and that it usually worked.

"Yeah, thank you, thanks, I'm sure." Nicky scooped up his bag and held it against his chest as he hurried back toward the elevator. It took forever to come, and his heart was beating so loud that he thought Robert might be able to hear it from inside the apartment.

It was windy on West End when he pushed past the doorman, and Nicky pulled his coat shut as he ran to Broadway. He didn't know why he was running. He could call Jerry, or a friend, but why? All his life, people had treated Nicky like a paper doll, something they could dress up or down, a cute, flat toy. It didn't matter what he wanted, not really—he had become an actor because his father had had tears in his eyes. He had become a movie star because he'd gotten the part. He had danced and kissed beautiful girls because they were beautiful but mostly because they were doing the same thing that he was doing, pretending that the roles they were given had been doled out fairly, that they had any choice in the matter. Photographers snapped pictures of his hand on a model's thigh, and then they were dating, and then she was his girlfriend, and then they'd broken up, all before they'd shared a meal or knew the names of each other's siblings.

The Russian baths were slick and salty, every surface wet. Nicky's pores were wide open. He could feel it all coming out, every angry feeling, every time he'd let himself down by saying yes instead of saying no. He watched himself storm out of that apartment a hundred times before he opened his eyes, and through all the steam and heat watched himself sit down next to Robert and let him play paper dolls. Nicky didn't know then if he'd ever be a parent, if he'd ever get married, anything like that—but he did know that if he did, if he **did,** he would always listen for the tiny voice inside the

big voice, and try to answer all the questions, the
ones being asked and the questions hiding behind.
Nicky pushed himself up to standing, filled up his
bucket, and poured ice cold water over his head. It
was time to go.

Chapter 25

Working Together

The contract wasn't as solid as it seemed. Wendy went through all the points quickly. They were alone in Elliot's office. This was why they needed extra help with the kids—because in addition to her part-time job, Wendy had taken on a pro bono client: her husband. Beauty Bar was offering more money than the other businesses on Main Street, it was true, but they were offering only a five-year lease, with an option to renew, with rent increases of only half a percent for the entire length of their lease. They wanted the landlord to pay for everything else—snow removal, air-conditioning, the rent during the time it would take to build the store, which could be up to nine months, much longer than the standard three.

"So, no way! Right?" Elliot had shut the office door so that they were talking in private. He'd built his career by building houses, which was just managing crews and couples, basically, and usually the architects and interior designers got the brunt of those problems. The most trouble he had was when people wanted to move outlets and bathrooms, without understanding that both power and water came from somewhere else and didn't just appear in a wall by magic.

"This is a first offer," Wendy said. "They're testing you."

Elliot nodded. "Okay. Okay. So now what?"

"You make a counteroffer, and take all this garbage out, and tell them what you actually want, and if they don't come back to it, I will give you a million dollars. Do you know how much money they have, El? This company makes billions of dollars. They can pay for everything. They just don't want to if they don't have to."

"And what if they take it?" Elliot looked out the window, where a pair of squirrels were chasing each other up a tree. "Then we have to do it?"

"You don't have to do it until you've signed a contract," Wendy said.

Elliot put his hands on his jaw and rubbed. "I think I've been grinding my teeth." He paced. "On the one hand, I want it," he said. "It would change the whole town, and I would be the one who did it. But on the other hand, it would change the whole town, and I would be the one who did it."

"There will be other offers," Wendy said. "We could do more research, take some polls, you know, find out what people want. Do they want beauty products? Sure. But maybe there's something they want more. I'm telling you, El, this not-great offer is the sign that they will eventually make you a really, really good offer. I can feel it." Wendy opened her laptop and started typing. "I'm just taking everything out and starting over. I love this. I feel like an assassin."

Elliot raised his eyebrows. "Oh yeah?"

Wendy didn't look up.

"That's kind of hot, Wen."

Now she looked up. Elliot walked slowly back over to his desk. His office manager sat outside, down the hall. Out of eyeshot and earshot, especially when the door was closed.

"I'll tell you when something's hot," Wendy said. A twitch in her lower lip gave her away. "Sit down."

Elliot wheeled his chair so that it was next to hers, both of them facing away from the door. Wendy unbuttoned her own pants, and then his.

"Ask me if you can touch me," she said.

"Can I touch you?" Elliot asked.

"Yes."

Wendy took Elliot's hand and snaked it past her waistband.

"I'm not going to ask you," she said. "I'm just going to do whatever I want to you, and you're going to like it."

"Yes," Elliot said, his eyes fluttering closed in concentration. It was just like when they were in the library in college, so hungry for each other's bodies that they'd have sex in the unisex bathrooms. It wasn't that the children had taken away Elliot's desire for his wife, or his appreciation of her body and all the things it could do—it was just that they were always so fucking tired all the time. In the land before children, Elliot had loved Wendy like crazy—how smart she was, how beautiful she was, how confident she was. She had always been out of his league, but somehow, she'd loved him back. They had both wanted children, but it felt so good to remember, before that, how much they had both wanted each other. How did anyone with kids under six do anything at all? This was how, maybe. They did things during the day—legal things, pleasurable things, any thing. He wanted to do what she said forever.

Chapter 26

Join the Parade

The Parade Crew met in seventh period, when the school day was officially over but when all the sports teams had their practices, and the halls filled with the sounds of student musicians wheeling their cello cases across the floor. Cecelia waited in the hall until just before the bell rang, then walked into her homeroom. She was in no hurry.

Ms. Skolnick was sitting on her desk with her knees wide apart, a folding table in front of her. There were half a dozen kids scattered around the room, no one that Cecelia recognized. One boy in the back of the class seemed to have a five o'clock shadow, which would have made him look like an adult if he hadn't also been wearing a tie-dyed Pokémon T-shirt and CJHS gym shorts. A girl with long black hair sat in the front row, hands clasped in front of her like she was on her knees in church. A boy and a girl sat in the second row, holding hands across the space between their desks. The boy had a crown made out of duct tape. August, already rolling his eyes, clapped.

"Cecelia!" Ms. Skolnick said, with genuine enthusiasm. "Yes! Come on in!"

Cecelia made her way to the seat next to August and tucked her bag by her feet.

"Now, hello! As most of you know, this club will move to the woodshop next week in order to get down to business, but we'll spend the first session planning in here. It's a remarkably quick process, and superfun! Let's start by brainstorming! For those of you who weren't here"— Ms. Skolnick winked at Cecelia—"last year's theme for the float was **Lord of the Rings**. Anyone care to start? Anyone want to take the chalk?"

The boy with the duct-tape crown sprang to his feet, held his palm open for the chalk, and then spun back around.

"My lady," he said, and dropped to a knee. He held the thin white piece of chalk over his head like the world's tiniest sword.

His girlfriend, a redhead with a **Fortnite** T-shirt, bowed and then slid out of her desk, took the chalk, and walked to the blackboard, swinging her hips like she were a Victoria's Secret angel.

"WTF," Cecelia whispered to August.

August leaned closer. "Oh, yeah, it's like that. Megan and James have been going out since fifth grade. They're probably going to get married. She apparently goes down on him in the bathroom every Friday during lunch. Not that I want to spread rumors! But that is what people say. They do theater tech, and that includes floats, I guess."

The redhead, Megan, got to the blackboard and cleared her throat.

"**Bob's Burgers**!" said the kid in tie-dye. Megan wrote it down slowly, in bubbly letters.

"**Into the Woods**!" said James. "Or, just more generally, fairy tales."

"Elizabeth Taylor," August said. When Cecelia turned to look, surprised that he'd spoken, he said, "What? As long as I'm here, might as well contribute."

Fifteen minutes later, the following list was on the board: **Bob's Burgers, Into the Woods**/fairy tales, Elizabeth Taylor, **1001 Arabian Nights**, Rock and Roll, the 1980s, Shakespeare, the Empire State, and Clapham FTW. August got up to go to the bathroom, and as soon as he was gone, the girl sitting in front of Cecelia turned around.

"Hey," the girl said. She was the one wearing all black, down to her fingernails and eyeliner. "You're Cecelia, right?"

It didn't sound promising. "Yeah?" Cecelia said, as though she were unsure of the answer.

"I'm Melody," the girl said. "Seventh grade."

"Hi," Cecelia said.

"Can I ask you something? Well, two some-things, really." Melody waited.

"Okay," Cecelia said.

Melody leaned halfway across the expanse be-tween their desks, and after a moment's hesitation, Cecelia leaned in the other direction to meet her there, their heads nearly touching.

"You're friends with August, right? Is he gay? He's gay, right?" Cecelia's eyes were level with Melody's temple, and she watched the thin skin move in and out as Melody breathed.

"I don't know," Cecelia said. It actually hadn't occurred to her, which instantly made her feel very, very stupid, even though of course she didn't know if it was true. Her generation—at least at home—had been open-minded, at least that's what her father said, with awe, **you kids are all so open,** even though the alternative seemed like choosing to live in a previous incarnation of the world, like the people who were into steampunk and wore stovepipe hats. But who knew if that was true here. This was how rumors worked—no mat-ter if something was true or not, if it **sounded** like it might be true, and was something you hadn't actually imagined yourself, then truthfulness seemed triply more likely. Who cared if Megan and James really had sex, or did whatever, in a bathroom? If everyone said they did, what was the difference? That was how she'd ended up in

Clapham. Obviously Cecelia hadn't understood as much as she thought she had about the way her generation worked.

"Okay, fine, whatever," Melody said. "Second question. Is it true you got kicked out of your old school for sleeping with someone you met on the internet? How did they find out? Your school, I mean. Because . . ."—here Melody paused and took a breath—". . . because I've been talking to a guy who's a freshman in the high school and he's friends with my older brother and nothing's happened yet but he said that in two years, when I'm a freshman and he's a junior, he wants to take me to junior prom, which actually seems sweet, but he's not, like, my boyfriend, and I definitely don't want to get kicked out of school. What do you think?"

Cecelia sat back up and shook her head. "No, I didn't."

Melody stayed where she was, clearly still waiting for an answer.

"I don't know," Cecelia said. "That doesn't sound like something that could get you kicked out of school. Tell your parents, maybe?"

"Oh, they know," Melody said. She nodded vigorously. "But good, good. Okay. Thank you!"

Ms. Skolnick had pushed herself off the desk. She grabbed a mug, checked to see that it was empty, and said, "Okay, everyone! Time to vote! Grab a piece of paper, write down your vote, then pop it in!" Cecelia was happy for the interruption.

She tore a small corner of paper out of her notebook and hunched over. August slid back into his seat.

"Voting time? You better vote for mine." He hunched over, too, as if they were taking a test and he didn't want her to cheat off his page. Maybe they were.

Ms. Skolnick walked up and down the aisles, holding her cup out like a beggar, until everyone had dropped their folded choices in. When everyone had put in their vote, she walked back to her desk.

"Anyone care to tally?" Megan sauntered back to the board like a bored Vanna White.

In the end, it was a gentle victory for Clapham FTW, which had squeaked ahead by a single vote.

"Well, okay," Ms. Skolnick said, surprised. "Not really sure what that means, but we can make it work."

"Maybe it can be round, with a gazebo in the middle," Cecelia heard herself say. "You know, like the town? I don't know. Maybe that's dumb." More than anything else, Cecelia was mad at her parents and Katherine for making her second-guess her every decision.

August gasped. "That is actually a really good idea."

Ms. Skolnick nodded, and the rest of the Parade Crew turned around to look at Cecelia, their dark horse.

Chapter 27

Wendy Asks for a Hand

Wendy had called and asked Porter to meet her at Spiro's, which wasn't like her at all. Porter didn't actually think she'd ever seen Wendy eat a meal in a Clapham restaurant, and she'd been married to Porter's brother for a decade. Drink iced coffee, maybe, while cutting grapes in half for her sons or asking questions about the provenance of the meat in the hamburger, but never actually just dig in and eat. Porter was curious but also hungry. She left the house twenty minutes earlier than she needed to and started driving.

Now that she'd been inside Jeremy's house, parking in front didn't seem like such a big deal. She put the car in park but didn't turn off the engine, just in case. It was a weekday morning, and she assumed that Jeremy was at work, but his wife could be home. She could be at the grocery store, or at the YMCA, or at the bank, or getting a manicure, or volunteering at their kids' school, or cooking at a soup kitchen. Porter spent a considerable amount of time picturing her doing each of those activities and more, each one getting more and more virtuous until she couldn't help but believe that Kristen was donating a kidney to a stranger while simultaneously reading to the blind. Kristen was good and she was bad. Kristen was beautiful and she was ugly. Kristen was thin and she was fat. Kristen had made all the right choices, right from the very beginning of her personhood, including but not limited to what kind of underwear to wear under which clothes, what kind of haircut to get, what kind of sex to have on which date, what to say after someone told you they loved you, what to say when someone said they wanted to marry you. She had done everything right, and Porter had limped along, making her silly, stupid mistakes, all the while thinking that there would be time to correct the course. Now she was pregnant and sitting in a running car like a getaway driver, her eyes fixed on the front door.

The light shifted; something inside the house had moved—the cat, maybe—and Porter drove away before waiting to see what it was. She drove past the clinic, slowing down enough to make sure that Jeremy's car was in the lot. She thought about the cloth seats of his Honda, stained from years of abuse, and wondered how Kristen's labors had been. Her pregnancies. Had she been sick, had she slept? Had she delivered vaginally, with no drugs, a Madonna of the birthing center? Or had she circled a date on the calendar and gotten a bikini wax in preparation for surgery, just to look nice? Porter felt a wave of nausea roil through her esophagus and pushed the button to roll down the window. It was sick, what she was doing, and she knew it. It was sick but it was also giving her the same kind of tingly feeling she'd had in high school and college when she saw someone she had a crush on, and no one else had to know, not yet. Humans deserved things they kept private. She wanted what she wanted. Everyone had their kink, right?

By the time Porter circled back to Spiro's and went inside, she found Wendy already taking up prime real estate at one of the large booths. Wesley Drewes was on the radio, his sonorous voice talking to callers about the Clapham Harvest Festival, and the annual hordes of leaf-peeping tourists that would soon descend upon the Hudson Valley, taking up parking spots and restaurant tables, filling hotel rooms and campgrounds. The festival was in mid-October every year, and it was a big weekend for the town, and for Clap Happy. If every person who came to Clapham that weekend bought one of her cheeses, Porter could retire at forty. The highlight for Porter was the parade, which featured floats built and helmed by students. The year she rode on one as the Harvest Queen was a disaster, but as a spectator, she always enjoyed it.

Porter squeezed into the booth opposite Wendy, who had half a grapefruit in front of her, and a plate of toast and cottage cheese.

"Hi," Porter said. "How are you? How's everybody? Gorgeous day outside, isn't it?"

Wendy shook her head. "You don't have to do that."

Olympia swanned by with a stack of dirty dishes in each hand. She paused. "Pancakes?" Porter nodded.

"Okay," Porter said, relieved. "Are you okay? Why did you want to see me?" She ran a hand over her belly. It was something she'd observed in other pregnant women, too, the insatiable urge to touch yourself, as if to simultaneously remind yourself of your double existence and as an attempt to connect to the person on the other side, like someone touching one side of the glass in a prison visiting room. "Birth tips? Parenting advice?"

Wendy shook her head. "Not really, but we can certainly talk about that, if you like. I know you're more, well, **earthy** than I am, but so much of it is unnecessary: the essential oils, the eye mask, the mix CD of birth songs, doulas. There is stuff you should actually take to the hospital: socks, pajamas, a good breastfeeding pillow, a change of clothes for . . . Oh, I guess you don't have to worry about that."

"For my imaginary husband? Yeah, I don't think he needs extra clothes." Porter felt irrationally annoyed. "So what was it? That you wanted to talk about?" She could be having breakfast with her goats, or sitting in her car in front of a veterinary clinic, she didn't need this. If she wanted judgment, she could call her mother, or Rachel. And there were plenty of women who had had babies who could tell her what was bullshit and what wasn't.

"Okay. Two things. So, one of the things that Elliot and I had been putting off forever, for whatever reason, is making a will. But I decided that I would go ahead and do it. Which was fine. It's just a piece of paper, right? I'm a lawyer, we know how it works. But the one thing you have to do is choose someone who will be your children's guardian if you die." Wendy paused and then hiccupped. When had she started to cry? Porter had never seen either Wendy or Elliot cry, not at their wedding, not at the birth of their children. Elliot hadn't even cried, at least not in front of her, when their father died. "And we choose you. If you agree to be chosen. I know that you're about to have a baby, and that you are one person, so feel free to say no. Astrid is too old, my parents are too old, and on the other side of the country. I don't have any siblings. Your brother Nicky is a pothead. Which leaves you. You're local, so they wouldn't have to move and leave their whole lives. You love them, they love you. They might not always show it, but they do. We would make sure that you had enough money for everything you needed. The house, if you wanted. Or the money from the house. If we're dead, we don't need it, you know?"

"Wow," Porter said. It was not a thought that had ever crossed her mind. When her father died, Porter remembered Astrid sitting them down and telling them that they all belonged to one another, that if she were to die, Elliot and Porter would both be Nicky's legal guardians, and their finances would be handled by Mr. Chang, at the bank, Astrid's favorite co-worker. Porter had sometimes had dreams that her mother was dead and that the three siblings would have to move in with Mr. Chang, even though they were adults and could theoretically take care of themselves, and that Mr. Chang and his wife would teach them things that their parents never did, like how to play the piano and make pasta from scratch, and when Porter woke up, she would feel guilty about enjoying her new parallel life.

"So, if you both died, the boys would live with me."

Wendy nodded. "And the baby. So you'd have three. Which is a lot of kids. Especially for a single parent. If it's too much, please, say so." She was still crying, silently except for a few errant hiccups here and there. Porter had never understood her sister-in-law, but she could imagine a world in the not-too-distant future where they could actually be friends, like how in postapocalyptic worlds ruined by plagues and zombies, you could be best friends with someone you'd otherwise never encounter. Maybe this was motherhood, a feeling of benevolence for all human beings.

Porter took her hand off her belly and reached across the table. "Of course," she said. "Just in case you get hit by a school bus. Out of curiosity, is there a reason that my brother isn't the one asking me this?"

Wendy wiped her cheeks with a finger. "Let's hope it never happens, but yes. And your brother is a man, that's why. Do you think any man has ever been the one to take care of things like this? No man I've ever met. We talked about it years ago and he said he'd ask and here I am."

"Fair. But you'd trust me? With your kids?" Porter asked. "I'm sorry, that's not what you want to hear. I'm saying yes, I'm not saying no. It just means a lot to me. That you think I can do it."

"Of course you can do it," Wendy said, snapping back into her more familiar mode, as crisp as a carrot stick. "Women can do anything. All the things that men are useful for—think about it, what are those things? Lifting something heavy? Taking out the garbage? Grilling steaks? Please.

Elliot has never properly cooked a steak in his life. And I have to tell him when it's garbage day. And I can pay someone to move a couch."

"I guess you're right," Porter said. "I think I like you, Wendy."

"Well, thanks," Wendy said. "I'll draw up the paperwork." She took a long, slow drink of water. "If you ever need someone, you know, like an extra pair of hands, you can call me. I don't want to sound like your mother, but it is a lot. A friend of mine from law school who had a kid on her own hired a night nurse for the first three months. This lovely woman came over every night, and my friend got to sleep, unless she was feeding the baby. There are ways to make it easier."

It didn't seem fair, after spending so much time thinking about wanting to get pregnant, figuring out how to get pregnant, and being pregnant, that you would so soon also have to think about the reality of having a child on the outside of your body too. Yes, one thing led to the other, of course—Porter understood human reproduction—but to reduce the physical and mental state of pregnancy to a way station, like waiting for a bus, seemed suddenly so deeply misogynistic that Porter felt offended on her own behalf, at no one. At people. At men.

"Okay, so what was the other thing?" Porter asked. Inside, the baby did a somersault. Outside, Clapham was enjoying the afternoon. The gazebo in the small grassy center of the roundabout was a makeshift jungle gym for a couple of kids with long, tan arms and legs.

"It's about that, actually," Wendy said, pointing.

"The gazebo?" Porter watched the kids climb all over it like she and her brothers had done when they were kids, taking turns jumping off the hand-rail into the center, zooming toy cars around the wooden plank seats. Her brain had just started to picture Aidan and Zachary and her nameless daughter, some years in the future, all siblings of a sort, when she realized that she recognized the children.

"Elliot bought it. Not the gazebo, the building across the way. The empty one."

"Fogelmans!" she said, not quite hearing what Wendy had said.

"Excuse me?" Wendy said, following Porter's gaze.

"Those kids," Porter said. "I know their father." The girl, Jeremy's daughter, was the elder of the two, and had long blond hair like her mother. It swayed back and forth as she clung to the top of the gazebo. She had never seen the children this close up—they were older than she thought, probably close to Cecelia's age. Why weren't they in school? And then Jeremy strode up, camera in hand—a real one, the kind people bought to take on safari, not just his telephone held sideways. He crouched down to take her picture.

"Are you okay?" Wendy raised an eyebrow.

"I'm fine. So, wait, what? Elliot bought that building? What's he doing with it? Astrid is going to flip. I'm sure he knows that. You should have heard her when there was a rumor that Urban Outfitters was going to take over the Boutique Etc? shop. It was like when crazy moms in the eighties thought that Judas Priest records were trying to make their kids worship Satan."

Olympia came back with an extra-tall stack of pancakes. This was something a mother was supposed to know how to do—Porter's were never that good, not half as good as Astrid's. Not enough baking soda, maybe? She'd never tried to figure it out.

"I know. He's really worried about it." Wendy spooned a tiny amount of cottage cheese into her mouth.

"Why doesn't he just build something himself? Or move his office there, I don't know." Porter sometimes thought about her brother like an alien creature who had crash-landed into the Big House during puberty. He looked the same, but he didn't act the same. Everyone Porter knew would have benefited from whole-family therapy for their entire lives, but who did that? Sibling relationships were as complicated as any marriage, without the possibility of divorce. What would estrangement do, when your parents died, and you were sitting across from each other, sorting through decades of photographs and mismatched cutlery?

"I mentioned the idea of him asking your mom what she thought," Wendy said, and then turned to look out the window. "And he kind of freaked out. I don't know if it's Birdie, you know, and your mom's whole new thing, but it was really weird. I think she would have good input—no one cares about Clapham more than she does. Do you know that she knows every UPS guy's name?"

"You don't know your UPS guy's name?" Porter asked. "Elliot's a grown man. He should build what he wants. What's the big deal?"

"I know **our** UPS guy's name. Astrid knows them **all.**" Wendy shook her head. "I'm not sure Elliot knows what he wants."

Porter looked at her sister-in-law. "Huh," she said.

"What?" Wendy said.

"It's just funny. You know him. I mean, of course you know him, you're married to him, but it's funny that you know the same person I know. That sounds strange. Do you know what I mean?" Porter felt the baby do a flip. It felt like the split second without gravity on a roller coaster, the moment before the drop.

"Yes," Wendy said. "I do. Would you talk to him about it? He wouldn't ever ask me to ask you, but I think Elliot likes being told things, don't you? He likes having permission."

"Listen, my brother does not give an **F** what I think," Porter said. "I'm the mess, haven't you heard? At least El and Nicky gave mom weddings and babies. I'm just giving her a solo geriatric pregnancy. I don't think he'd want my advice." She folded an enormous piece of pancake into her mouth, leaving a trail of maple syrup drops across the table, her napkin, and then, yes, her T-shirt.

Wendy leaned her elbows on the table. "I hope you know that's not true. I don't want to be disloyal, Porter, but I'll just tell you right now, that's not true."

It was hard to respond to sincerity, and so Porter just chewed. When she had swallowed, she took a long sip of water. "Well. I suppose I could try."

"Thank you," Wendy said. She scooted out of the booth and dropped a twenty-dollar bill on the table. "It's on me."

When Porter left Spiro's, she could see Jeremy and his kids still taking pictures in the gazebo. She wouldn't have said hello otherwise, but now that they were all outside, and it was more or less on her path to her car, it seemed silly to avoid them. Jeremy was crouched down in the grass, his camera lens pointed skyward.

Jeremy's daughter was in her Clapham Junior High School sweatshirt, and the expression on her face said something between **drop dead** and **go away,** both possibilities that made Porter immediately appreciate Cecelia even more than she had before.

"Hi," Porter said, tapping Jeremy on the shoulder.

"Hey," Jeremy said. He turned awkwardly, then dropped to his knees and pushed himself back up-right. He gave her a hug and a kiss on the cheek, nothing more or less than anyone would give an old friend. "Sweetie, want to say hi?" His daughter offered an eye roll to end all eye rolls, but then slumped toward them as if being pulled by an invisible chain. Porter stood still, a polite smile plastered on her face.

"Sidney, this is my friend Porter, the one who makes the cheese you like."

"Nice to meet you," Porter said. She stuck out her hand, but Sidney crossed her arms. "Do you go to CJH? My niece, Cecelia, just started there, in the eighth grade. Cecelia Raskin-Strick, do you know her?"

"Um, yeah," Sidney said. "We have homeroom and English and math together."

"Oh wow! Are you friends? That is so awesome!"

"Um, no," Sidney said, and then ran back to the gazebo, where her younger brother was waiting. Porter wondered what kind of siblings they were, if they held hands when they were frightened, if Jeremy yelled, if they punched each other when their parents weren't looking.

"Sorry," Jeremy said, his voice low. "She's pretty much a total asshole right now."

"That's okay," Porter said. It had somehow never

occurred to her that her child might also be an asshole. That seemed like a stage of parenthood she hadn't imagined yet—being far enough in to think they were being a dick. There were always more levels, like the Super Mario Bros. ascending to higher and higher clouds.

"It'll pass," Jeremy said. "That's my one parenting truth that I can give you. Everything passes. The good stuff, the bad stuff, everything. Nothing lasts." He shrugged.

Sidney was jumping up and down in the middle of the gazebo. "Dad!" she said. "Come onnn!"

"What are you doing, anyway?" Porter asked. She put her hand on his arm lightly, the way you might before you asked a stranger for directions. She and Jeremy had made their thing work for such a long time, and no one had gotten hurt. They'd made each other happy, and everyone wanted to see their parents happy. That's what children of divorce always said—no matter how bad or ugly the actual divorce, it was better than living inside a sad marriage, or worse. Of course, Jeremy hadn't gotten a divorce.

"She's running for Junior Harvest Queen," he said. "Weren't you Harvest Queen once?" The vote seemed entirely due to her brothers' popularity, but Porter had won, a prize that involved a short ride on a pickup truck filled with hay, and a sash, and a scepter made out of corn on the cob. She'd been sixteen, a junior in high school, and both her parents had been tearfully proud, as if she'd actually **done** something, which made her feel both dopily happy and totally furious. If she'd known that in three years, her father would be dead, she would have enjoyed it more. Porter's biggest pet peeve was when people complained about having to do things with their families—Thanksgiving at their in-laws', a birthday party, a formal baby shower for their mother's friends. Did those people not understand that death was marching toward everyone, every single day? Porter thought about making a line of greeting cards that just said, "Surprise! You're dying and so is everyone else! Get over yourself!" They'd be good for any occasion.

"I should go," Jeremy said. "But it's good to see you. Can I see you? Again?" He raised an eyebrow, as if such a cue were necessary.

"Always," Porter said. "Call me. Or just come by, whatever." She tried to be casual. "If you want."

Jeremy winked and then jogged over to the gazebo, where Sidney was tapping her flip-flop on the wooden floor and staring into the small screen of her telephone. When her father approached with the camera, she widened her mouth into a plastic smile and flipped her hair over one shoulder. She was beautiful, after a fashion, like a catalog model, with all the parts in the right place but nothing extraordinary that would distract you from the shorts she was selling. Jeremy crouched down to take her photo, and Sidney changed positions every few seconds. The littlest Fogelman, a towheaded boy with earphones in and an iPhone, slouched against the opposite wall of the gazebo, his head nestled in a peony bush. Porter waved like a pageant queen, elbow to wrist.

Chapter 28

August Tells the Truth, Part Two

Painting a million three-inch-long pieces of wood white gave Cecelia a lot of time to think. Parade Crew turned out to be lots of tiny art projects put together, like preschool parallel play, where you were mostly doing your own thing but near other people, and Ms. Skolnick played good music, and it was fun. Cecelia's hands had white flecks, her jeans had white flecks, her hair too. But she didn't mind. She liked sitting in the drafty woodshop and making things.

"I think this is why adults are into coloring books," August said. "I feel like my brain is in a jar on the table."

"I know what you mean," Cecelia said. And she did, sort of. But more than that, she understood that that's how August felt. How **she** felt, with her busy hands and quiet mouth and all the extra oxygen that the Hudson Valley had to offer, was that her main problem was trying to be agreeable. A good girl, whatever the situation. Flexible with her parents, flexible with her friends. She didn't ask questions if she thought the answers would lead to conversations she wasn't ready to have. The goal of life, Cecelia thought, was to be conflict-free, to get along well with everyone. That was what her father spent years learning to do by meditating. Her mother couldn't have cared less about getting along well with people, or about being agreeable, but Nicky was so agreeable that Juliette didn't have to be. And since Cecelia knew she couldn't change anyone else, she tried her best to be open to whatever someone else had in mind.

That was why, when Katherine first told Cecelia about the guy she'd been talking to online, Cecelia hadn't said anything. Yes, the internet was full of dark, scary corners, but it was also full of kids just like her, and Cecelia chose to believe Katherine, or at least she chose to believe what Katherine had chosen to believe. The guy's name was Jesse, @jdogg99 on Insta, and he only posted pictures of graffiti and sunsets and dogs. Cecelia pointed out that if Jesse was born in 1999, that made him eighteen years old, which wasn't **super** gross, but still, not the best. An eighteen-year-old who wanted to talk to a girl going into the eighth grade was weird. Even the ninth graders she knew, like Katherine's older brother, Lucas, and his friends, called them babies and wanted at least ten feet between them when they walked down the street together. But Katherine had insisted that Jesse was cool. And so Cecelia hadn't said anything else.

It got to the point where Jesse and Katherine were texting all the time. She put him in her phone under the name Jessica, just in case her mom looked. Before school, after school, all night long. Cecelia got used to sitting across a tiny Starbucks table, just watching Katherine smile and chuckle, her fingers moving at the speed of light. Every now and then, Katherine would lower her phone to the table and say, you have to hear this, and would then read off a string of messages. She never actually took her hands off the device, though, as if by doing so, she might lose contact forever. Cecelia had known it wasn't going to end well—she had seen it. He kept asking her how old she was and saying how she couldn't tell anyone about them. Would an eighteen-year-old say that? Maybe. But deep down, Cecelia knew it was worse than that. But she didn't want to upset Katherine. And so she just watched it all unfold, even though she could see it in slo-mo.

"Are you okay?" August asked.

Cecelia looked up at him. "Yeah, why?"

"Because you've been painting the same Popsicle stick over and over again. I think that one's good."

He pointed with his paintbrush. Sure enough, the piece of wood that Cecelia had been painting was permanently shellacked to the newspaper underneath it.

The first time that Jesse and Katherine were supposed to meet up, Cecelia went too. Katherine—admitting some form of weakness, or maybe just because she'd watched **Dateline**—asked her to go along, and to just stand in the background, so that if Jesse was watching, he would think that she was alone, as they'd agreed. They were supposed to meet at Grand Army Plaza, on the stone benches right in front of the entrance to Prospect Park, where the farmers' market was on Saturday mornings. On Saturday nights, it was empty, with a few smushed tomatoes on the ground. People everywhere. That was the idea.

Katherine had stood there for almost an hour before she gave up and skulked back to the bench that Cecelia was sitting on. She should have told her parents then. **He must have come,** Cecelia thought, **and seen more than one girl**. There were cops around, too, just hanging out next to their squad car. If Jesse was really a teenager, he would have sloped up to them like Katherine's older brother would have, with a dumb look on his face and eyes full of fear. That was when Cecelia should have told. The next time anyone told her anything, she was going to shout it from the rooftops. She was going to be clear and direct. It was the only way.

August and Cecelia walked together to the bus stop after school. They'd stayed late to help Ms. Skolnick put away things after they dried, and to help prep the next round of things that needed to be painted, which meant cutting out tiny doors and windows for the float, and August was going to come over for dinner. The sun was hanging above the trees, turning the sky purple and pink, and they both cupped their hands around their eyes to stop the glare.

"Can I ask you something?" she said to August, who was rearranging things in his backpack.

"Mm-hmm," August said, without looking up.

"Are you gay?" Cecelia felt her heart beating fast. She was nervous. What a crazy thing to ask someone, just flat out, outside, in the middle of all this light and air.

August looked up. It didn't seem to be the question he was expecting. "Did someone tell you that?"

"A girl asked me, in Parade Crew. The seventh grader with all the freckles. I said I didn't know." Cecelia closed her eyes, her resolve gone at the first clip. "I'm sorry, that was a crazy way to ask that. You don't have to tell me anything you don't want to."

August zipped his bag back up and slung it over his shoulder. A lock of hair got caught under the strap, and he tugged it out gently. "People have been asking me that for a long time. For a while, I thought I was. But I'm not."

At the other end of the driveway, a kid drove their car too fast and screeched to a stop at the light. It was a miracle anyone survived childhood, really.

"I have a friend at camp who's trans, do you know what that is?" August was speaking quietly. He stood up straight and took a step closer, so that she could hear him.

Cecelia nodded. She'd known a few kids, back in Brooklyn, people who had asked the teachers to say **She** instead of **He**, but none of them had ever really been her friends, just figures of interest at school. She stared ahead, to the wall of trees, to the purple sky, to the neat lines of birds sitting on the telephone wires. This was important—**Don't fuck this up,** she told herself. **Whatever you did before, don't do that now. Don't lose your only friend. React perfectly. Whatever that is, just do that, and nothing else.**

"Trans is when you're born into a body that doesn't match what's in your brain. My friend was born looking like a boy, so everyone treated her like a boy, but inside, she always knew she was a girl. Like, always. From preschool. She always knew she was a girl." August shifted from side to side.

He was nervous, too, Cecelia could tell. Some kids pushed through the main school doors, some fifty feet away, and were laughing loudly. Their voices echoed into the trees.

"Okay," Cecelia said. "She."

"She," August said. "Yeah. But it's hard to tell everyone, so she hasn't yet. Just at camp, and when she's alone with her parents, for now."

Cecelia shifted her body so that they were standing next to each other instead of opposite each other and pressed the side of her body into the side of his body, and together they stared out, as if to designate that they were united in this space, that they were a human oasis from the Sidney Fogelmans of the world. The tip of Cecelia's elbow touched August's, two points in the dark. "This sounds like a close friend."

"Really close," August's voice was small, just above a whisper.

"Like how close?" Cecelia asked, whispering. "Like your best friend? Emily?"

"Like, closer than Emily. Like, inside my body close," August said, now almost inaudible.

"Does she have a name? Like, a different name?"

People said that the past and the future didn't exist, but they did. Just not at the same time. The past was right there, if you wanted to look at it. The only trick was knowing that your past was never the same twice, and the past was never the same for two people. Everyone looked at things through their own eyes, and also through every single thing that had happened before that moment. Even the present was iffy.

"Robin," August said. "It's my middle name. It goes both ways. It's used for both boys and girls, I mean."

"Nice to meet you, Robin," Cecelia said. "I won't tell anyone, I swear. Not anyone in the world, as long as I live, not until you tell me it's okay." It was important that August knew that—that Robin knew it. She was done telling secrets. Not for her friends, not for her grandmother, not for anybody. Cecelia leaned sideways, until their heads were touching. She wasn't the only one who wanted to fast-forward, she understood. Maybe everyone wanted to zoom through space in one direction or the other, and the trick was finding people who wanted to go the same way you did, to help pass the time. The bus came around the corner, circling back to pick up the kids coming from after-school activities, and the driver offered a friendly honk, acknowledging that she'd seen them waiting. Cecelia felt like a much larger alarm should sound every time someone in school said or thought or did something enormous and life-changing, something that their adult selves would remember for the rest of their lives, every time a bowling ball began its heavy roll. But of course then that alarm would sound constantly, all day long, and no one would be able to learn anything at all.

Chapter 29

Barbara Baker, Rest in Peace

Barbara had been a Quaker, and so the memorial service was at the Clapham Valley Congregation of Friends, with the reception to follow in the basement. Astrid dragged Porter and Cecelia, promising to take them to a movie afterward, all three of them stuffed with homemade caramels and snickerdoodles and salads with mysteriously pink dressing, the only foods that Astrid had ever been served in a church basement of any denomination. Birdie was going to meet them at the church. It made Astrid nervous in a way she didn't like to think about. She and Birdie had been to a thousand places together—at the shop, at the movies, at every restaurant in town, at the dry cleaner, at the bookstore, at the garden center, at Heron Meadows. There were lots of gay and lesbian couples in Clapham and the surrounding towns, many of them gray-haired just like Birdie and her, eating breakfast at Spiro's, arguing over which new hose to buy at Frank's hardware store, browsing at Susan's Bookshop, all the things that made up the days and lives of anyone. But somehow this felt different—it was An Occasion, the kind of event where people held hands with their spouses and thought about their own funeral arrangements. Astrid was nervous.

"What are Quakers?" Cecelia asked under her breath, as they pulled open the light wooden door. "I mean, like, where do they fall on the heaven/ hell scale?"

Porter shrugged. "I think they're kind of like the do-unto-others religion," she said. "No heaven or hell."

"Heaven!" Astrid said. "Why not believe in heaven? It's absurd, but so is everything else in life. It's dessert, right, heaven? What you get at the end, for being a good person?"

"Do you believe in heaven, Mom?" Porter stopped in her tracks. "Seriously? Like, angels?" On the other side of the door, a large crowd filled nearly all the pews. The room was simple, with diamond-shaped windows of red, yellow, and green. It felt how Porter imagined preschool would look in Sweden. Pale, and light with the sun.

"Of course not, not in a literal sense," Astrid said. "But I'm not a humanist. My grandparents left their country in order to have more freedom." She rolled her eyes. "Of course, Barbara believed in people doing good for goodness' sake. Good god, it's the lyrics to 'Santa Claus Is Coming to Town'!"

Bob Baker was standing a few feet inside the entrance, greeting mourners as they entered. Standing beside him was a woman who looked just like Barbara, only with a feathered blond bob, her bangs winging out to the sides like a host on the Home Shopping Network, a woman who had found Her Look in 1984 and was sticking with it, come hell or high water. Astrid shook her head. "It's the sister."

"Barbara's sister?" Porter asked. "Does she live here?"

"Vermont," Astrid muttered through clenched teeth. "Dog breeder."

"Isn't that kind of like being a pimp?" Cecelia asked. "Like, haven't we all agreed, as a culture, that the concept of 'purebred' sounds like eugenics, and that we should just adopt? What kind of creep chooses genetic material?"

"Um, hello? First of all, could you be a little less smart, please?" Porter asked, and then pointed to her belly: "And second of all, some of us need a little help, you know."

"Why didn't you adopt, Porter? That's actually an excellent question, Cecelia." Astrid paused. "Did you ever consider it? No judgment. I'm just curious."

Porter rolled her eyes. "We are at a funeral. Can we talk about my decision to carry my biological child later?" She shoved Cecelia in the back.

"I was talking about dogs," Cecelia said.

"Are you a dog lover too?" a voice asked. The three Stricks turned around to find Barbara's sister mooning at them. There were embroidered dogs all over her sweater. Barbara never would have worn anything so garish.

"I have goats," Porter said. "But, yes, big dog lovers, all of us. So sorry for your loss."

Astrid stuck out her hand. "Very sorry for your loss. These events aren't easy, I know. I lost my husband. People expect you to be the host, when all you want to do is stay in bed. Bob told me you've been a great help."

Barbara's sister nodded. "He's a wonderful man. They were a great couple. One for the ages." She looked skyward. "I think we're going to start soon, if you'd like to find seats."

"Thank you, we will," Astrid said, and guided Cecelia by the shoulders to the last row, nearest the exit. "I bet you a million dollars that Barbara hated her sister. Two million. One for the ages, my ass. Do you think her sister knew that Barbara was living at Heron Meadows? I doubt it. You think all those cats of Barbara's are purebred? No way." Astrid looked toward the door and saw Birdie.

She was as dressed up as she got. Birdie was wearing a navy blue button-down shirt and some

pin-striped pants, with a skinny silver bolo tie.
The tie made the silver streak in her hair—a blaze,
Astrid had learned it was called, like Susan Sontag,
or Cruella de Vil—sparkle. At least that's what it
looked like to Astrid. She stood up and waved,
smiling perhaps a little too broadly for the occasion.

It came and went, her courage. She had felt it
this morning, a little cloud floating above Birdie's
side of the bed. Birdie, who had always been herself. Astrid had never lied, but she had also never
been loud. She tried to imagine what Russell would
have said, if she'd told him that she had sometimes
imagined being with a woman. Not more often
than she imagined being with a man, just sometimes. Every so often, once every five years or so,
there would be someone who caught her eye, and
Astrid would imagine a first kiss with that person,
and having sex, and being married, and after a few
months, the feeling would pass. Porter's fifth-grade
teacher had lingered; he had been tall and brawny,
and once Astrid had had an extended fantasy
about him taking her camping in the Catskills,
and what he would do to her body in the tent at
night. Another was a woman with beautiful dark
eyebrows who had worked at Susan's Bookshop
and then left to go to library school. Russell had
been sensitive, self-conscious, and he would have
been hurt if he'd known. But if he had lived, she
would have stayed married, and she wouldn't have

ever told him anything. That was the truth of a successful marriage that Astrid understood: All you had to do was not get divorced or die! Everything else was fair game. Taken was taken. All love settled. Not settling for something less than you deserved, just settled down, the way breath settles in a sleeping body, not doing more than necessary. Was that what Nicky and Juliette were trying to avoid, the boredom of an average marriage? Was that why Elliot and Wendy seemed so miserable? Astrid understood. It sounded old-fashioned, and depressing, but that's how things used to be, she wanted to tell her children. All three of them needed to hear it! This is how it was! Do you think your grandparents and your great-grandparents and your great-great-grandparents were always in love? You heard about those couples, the ones who danced beside their dining room tables every night, who held hands every day until they were ninety years old and then died two days apart because they couldn't bear the loss, but those were the exceptions, weren't they? Astrid thought so, but she couldn't be sure. She and Russell had been a good couple but not an extraordinary one. He listened to terrible music. They argued and pointed fingers; they had both spent nights sleeping on the couch, too angry to stay in bed beside the other one. If he were still alive, they would no doubt be fighting still. And would she and Birdie have started going out to lunch? Would they have gone to the movies and shared popcorn, their hands digging into the buttery bag at the same time, knuckles knocking against each other? And would Astrid have felt a tiny zip up her spine? She didn't know, she didn't know.

"Gammy, I think you're a Barbara stan," Cecelia whispered.

"What is that, a country? Afghanistan?" Astrid craned her neck, watching Birdie make her way through the crowd to their row. Memorial services were exactly like weddings—you never talked to the people whose names were on the invitation, and you spent the whole time catching up with acquaintances while holding disposable plates and paper napkins.

"No, it means stalker/fan. You're her stan."

"I see," Astrid said. "Now, be quiet, both of you." She stood up and scooched Cecelia and Porter over so that Birdie could sit on her other side.

"Hi," Birdie said, when she'd finally reached them. "Got the cheap seats, I see."

Astrid laughed and then kissed Birdie lightly on the lips. Birdie looked pleasantly surprised, which made Astrid feel simultaneously horrible that it had taken her so long and joyous that she'd finally done it. They squeezed into the pew and faced forward, attentive. Astrid wondered if anyone had seen, if she'd hear about it later, gentle questions on the sidewalk in front of the grocery store.

A woman with a black robe and a rainbow-colored

woven scarf walked up to the podium and nodded at everyone, making eye contact until the crowd hushed.

"We are here to celebrate the life of our friend, neighbor, sister, and wife, Barbara Baker," the woman began, and much to her own surprise, that was all Astrid needed to burst into tears. Birdie reached for her hand and intertwined their fingers. They'd never done that before, not in public, not like this, in the middle of the day, surrounded by the entire town. That made Astrid cry harder. Now that she'd told her children, she could tell anyone. And it was Barbara Baker, unlucky Barbara Baker, who had made it all possible, somehow. A woman in the row ahead of them—Susan Kenney-Jones, who owned the bookstore and whose children were roughly the same age as Astrid's, but living elsewhere—passed back a travel-size package of Kleenex. Susan's bookstore was two doors down from Shear Beauty—they saw Susan every day. Astrid had known Susan even longer than she'd known Barbara. Susan's husband had died, too, maybe four years ago. Brain cancer. More tears. Astrid had never cried so much, not in public or in private. Porter looked over, alarmed.

"Are you all right?" Birdie whispered into Astrid's ear. "We can go, if you want; the girls will be fine."

Astrid shook her head and commanded herself to get it together.

The pastor went on. "For those of you who have not attended a Quaker service before, we will all sit in silence for the next hour, creating a community through our bodies and our breath. If you feel moved to speak, please stand up and do so. That is all. Thank you." She bowed her head, and everyone else did too.

Astrid came from a family—two families, really—for whom being lost in your own thoughts during a religious service was something you weren't supposed to admit. She liked the pretense of paying attention to someone with a strong voice, an expert in the field of faith, telling a roomful of people what they should believe and why. This felt sort of like not getting one's money's worth, as a religious experience. Was it a religion? She should know this. Astrid wiped her eyes and then turned to look at Porter. She'd shut her eyes tightly and had a faint smile on her face. Her hands roamed her belly. She was midconversation, clearly, the constant nonverbal dialogue that first-time mothers had with their unborn children. Astrid remembered being pregnant with Elliot, how terrified and excited she'd been, how she had whispered to him in the middle of the night, before he had a face, before he had a name. Was Elliot listening then?

A woman sitting on the other side of the room stood up. She brushed her hair out of her eyes and said something about Barbara's potato salad, and then sat back down. Porter's eyes flickered open and then closed again. Every few minutes, someone else would stand up, say a few words, and sit back down. Astrid felt herself getting agitated, and shifting in her seat. After a long pause, she straightened her legs.

"Hello," she said. She held on to Birdie's hand. Both Porter and Cecelia looked up at her, surprised. "My name is Astrid Strick, and I've known Barbara for forty years. I've never done this before, so apologies if I'm not doing it right, but what I want to say is this: Barbara told the truth." All around the room, people nodded in agreement. "And that's not an easy thing to do. That's all I want to say." Astrid gave an awkward wave with her free hand and sat back down.

"Good job, Gammy," Cecelia whispered, nuzzling her face into Astrid's bony arm. Astrid lifted her arm and hung it around Cecelia's back. What would have happened in her life if she had been honest from the start? With her children, with herself, with her husband, with Birdie. What if all the fuzzy-type mothers had been right, and she'd been wrong? Astrid felt full of things she wanted to announce to a silent, respectful group. It was yet another example of Barbara's earnestness winning out over whatever it was that had ruled Astrid's life heretofore—triage, was how she thought of it. It had been triage with three small children, and then it had been triage as a young widow. She hadn't had time to plan things perfectly, or to parent intentionally, the way some women she knew had, with well-considered questions on the tours of local preschools. Astrid had always been trying to survive one day so that she could live the next. It was something she had always thought she'd grow out of, but somehow, there always seemed to be so many things to do in a single day. Barbara had seemed to have time for everyone, if not herself.

Bob Baker sat in the front pew, surrounded on both sides by gaggles of women, each of their backs curled into a seashell, the stance of any woman putting a Band-Aid on a child's boo-boo. They were easy enough to identify from behind—Astrid counted at least two widows in the bunch, plus a woman whose husband lived at Heron Meadows. There were some people who just needed to be married, who felt like they were only wearing one shoe when they were alone. Astrid had some friends like that—or she had had some friends like that. Women who needed a partner that badly tended to be unreliable friends, Astrid found, which was why they needed a new partner so badly when their first one died, smothered by all the marital attention.

The point, surely, was not to look around the room at everyone else, but Astrid couldn't help it. She felt like she was on a ship, sailing across an ocean. In addition to Susan from the bookstore, there was Olympia, from Spiro's, and the ditzy yoga teacher who'd been there when Barbara was hit. What would happen when she, Astrid, died? Would Birdie and Porter organize a service together? **It would be just like this,** Astrid thought, **a roomful of old ladies and kind community members**. Which of them would actually care that she had died? Cecelia would care, the sweet girl, but who knew where she'd be by then—back in Brooklyn, off at college, or somewhere else, too busy for her grandmother. There weren't very many men in the room, and so Astrid started to count them. She started at the left-hand side of the room, all the way at the end of the aisle, and when she'd made it three-quarters of the way around the room, she counted Elliot as number four.

He was sitting alone—that is, he wasn't with anyone she knew, but flanked on either side by white-haired ladies. Astrid gestured in the air, trying to get his attention, but Elliot didn't notice, and instead Astrid got some weird looks from other people. Eventually the pastor stood up again and pronounced the service over.

"Come, come," Astrid said, hoisting both Cecelia and Porter up by their armpits, and then guiding them into the aisle. Birdie followed behind, the caboose. "Excuse me," Astrid said, and squeezed her way into a thicket of mourners. Astrid tried to get across the room to where Elliot had been sitting but was instead herded into the stairwell and down into the basement reception area. They were pushed toward long folding tables with carefully arranged cheese plates and brownie bites. She dodged Barbara's sister by the pitchers of lemonade and iced tea, still swiveling, trying to find her son. When he finally made it through the crowd to them, Astrid found that she was sweating, and when she hugged him hello, she said, "It's so warm in here, isn't it?"

Porter shrugged. "I'm always hot, I'm growing a person."

"Kind of," Cecelia said.

"Not really," Elliot said. "But women are always hot or cold."

Porter smacked him in the chest. "That is so sexist, shut your face."

"I didn't know you were coming, honey, you should have come with us!" Astrid pushed aside Porter's fist. "Why did you come?" Her face felt hot. He couldn't know, about Barbara, about the phone call, could he? Astrid searched his face for clues but found nothing. Aside from Barbara, Elliot was the only one who knew that she was a hypocrite.

"Bob works for Dutchess County Electrical, we've done a lot of work with them." He was looking over her shoulder at the snacks. "Porter, grab me one of those cookies? Yes, those. Holding hands in public, it's a big step." He nodded at the clasped knot of Birdie's and Astrid's hands. She wondered who else was clocking them, who else was taking note, which book club would be gossiping about them over caprese salads and pesto pasta. **Let them talk,** she thought, and pulled Birdie even closer.

Astrid watched as Elliot folded a whole cookie into his mouth. Elliot coughed and then shoved in a second. Wendy would not have approved. Once she'd served a half watermelon in place of a birthday cake at the twins' party, claiming that they didn't like sugar. "I have to get back to work."

"So soon?" Astrid said. "You have to go?"

"Mom, I have to go. Bye, all." Elliot scooped up one last cookie for the road, and they all watched him weave his way through the silver- and white-haired attendees, until he vanished back up the stairs. Astrid wanted to stop time, to run outside, to be his mother, properly. How many chances did she have? That was the point, wasn't it? That was what Barbara had meant—the bus, not the phone call—Astrid watched the back of Elliot's head disappear and knew that, once again, she had lost her shot to say the right thing.

Chapter 30

Alarm Bells

When Porter was feeling low, the goats always cheered her up, and when she was feeling giddy, their nuzzly noses made her feel positively euphoric. She bent over to dust some goat slobber off her calf and felt a sudden pain in her belly. The closest bathroom was inside, a Sheetrocked corner of the office that she'd been meaning to turn into a nice bathroom for years, but it worked well enough, and so she hadn't. Porter sat down on the toilet and leaned forward, her elbows digging into her thighs. It felt like cramps, but it couldn't be cramps. She reached between her legs with a wad of toilet paper and drew her arm back slowly, revealing a small archipelago of blood. Porter had her telephone in her other hand

and dialed Dr. McConnell. In five minutes, she was on her way to the hospital. She texted Rachel on the way, even though they hadn't spoken since their dinner. **Fuck,** she dictated into the air of her car. **Scary stuff happening, heading to doc, if you're free, I would love you there. I miss you.** When she didn't hear back right away, she texted her mother too, and told her where she was going. Then Porter started to cry.

Only one woman was in the waiting room when Porter arrived, knitting a powder-blue baby blanket, the expanse already knit lying over her mountainous belly. She was making warmth in real time, inside and out. Porter hovered at the desk, waiting for someone to appear, clutching her hands to keep her from ringing the small bell that was there to be rung. The receptionist came back, a woman old enough to be a mother, a woman who might be a mother, and Porter reached for the lip of the counter to keep herself standing. It wasn't pain that was pulling her down, it was fear. With Jeremy and Astrid and Birdie and Cecelia, so many distractions, Porter had let herself forget how much she wanted this. She'd spent years thinking about it, imagining her body pushing out to a smooth curve, imagining a tiny, soft person of her very own. She wanted it. She wanted the baby. She wanted to be someone's mom. The lack of sleep, the frazzled nervous system, the sore nipples, who cared! She wanted those too. Porter was sick of seeing old friends and having them humble-brag about their early wake-up calls, their spit-up—stained T-shirts.

"Strick?" the woman asked. "Room three. Dr. McConnell will be right in."

Porter hurried into the room and lay back on the chair, her hands pressed against her belly. It didn't hurt anymore, not the way it had at the farm, which made Porter feel both relieved and scared—what if it didn't hurt anymore because no one was there? You heard about things like that, heartbeats fading to black.

There was a quick knock at the door, and Dr. McConnell poked her head in, followed by Astrid. "I found your mother in the hallway; can we come in?" Porter nodded. Astrid hurried to her side and gripped her hand, a worried look on her face.

"What's going on? Let's take a look. You said there was some blood?" Dr. McConnell sat on the wheeled stool and put on gloves.

How emotionally tricky, to be a doctor. Any other profession had the leeway of white lies, of truths softened by hopes and niceties. Doctors couldn't lie. They gave you the results, which were never graded on a curve.

"Yes," Porter said. When her animals were hurt, she did not waver. She called Dr. Gordon and took stacks of blankets into the pen and they would be there, together, until the trouble had passed. She could do that for herself too. Stay calm. Keep breathing.

Dr. McConnell had her strip from the waist down and put a thin hospital blanket over her knees. Porter lay back and thought of herself as an animal. Dr. McConnell was quiet, just listening to Porter's belly with her stethoscope, pressing different spots and asking if it hurt. Astrid looked away from any bare flesh, as if she hadn't seen every inch of Porter's naked body, as if Porter's naked body hadn't passed through Astrid's own naked body.

"I'm going to do a quick pelvic exam, just to make sure everything's okay, Porter, all right? Everything seems fine so far. A little blood is scary, but it's just blood. It doesn't mean anything is wrong. If it continued, yes, like a heavy period, or if the pain increased, yes, but right now, you feel okay?" Porter nodded. "And the bleeding seems like just a tiny bit of spotting, is that right?"

Porter nodded. She closed her eyes. She could hear Dr. McConnell and her mother breathing, and the squeak of her stool moving around the floor. "Okay, that all feels fine, let's take a quick look." She squirted a little pile of warm goop onto Porter's belly and spread it out with the sonogram wand. Immediately, the sound of a heartbeat filled the room, a horse galloping. Porter opened her eyes and watched the baby perform an elaborate water ballet. Astrid gasped and squeezed Porter's hand even tighter. When Porter looked up at her mother, her eyes were damp and twinkly. "Wow," Astrid said. "There she is! Oh, honey."

"There she is, looking and sounding totally healthy and great," Dr. McConnell said. "You're fine, she's fine. Nothing to worry about. Are you feeling stressed otherwise? Anything going on?" She left the wand in place, so that any and all conversation would occur over the comforting percussion. Some doctors were better than others. Porter felt a brief twinge of pity for any pregnant woman with a male obstetrician.

There was a question. She'd been thinking about it all morning. Porter looked at her mother, who was now holding on to her shoulder lightly, the way a queen holds the edge of the king's throne.

"Mom, don't have any kind of reaction, please," Porter said, "but because of my abortion . . ." Porter paused here. She didn't look at her mother, but she didn't have to look to hear Astrid's sharp inhale. "You know. I had an abortion, a long time ago, and afterward, there was bleeding, and this morning, that's what the bleeding reminded me of. But that's not happening, right? I'm not losing this baby, right?"

"No, you're not," Dr. McConnell said. "Your uterus is beautiful, your pregnancy is healthy, everything is fine. There's a lot going on in there, you know? And there's a lot of blood in your body, moving around, and doing its job. A little bit of spotting can be alarming, but it does not mean that anything is wrong. You did the right thing, by coming in, and now we know for sure, all is well."

"What about sex?" Porter asked.

"Sex is totally fine during pregnancy," Dr. McConnell said. How did people have such incredible straight faces? There must have been whole semesters in medical school where doctors had to say things that would make any normal human being laugh, and then not laugh. Porter could picture it, rows of future doctors staring into each other's eyes while saying the words **penis, vagina, testes, feces,** et cetera.

Astrid let go of Porter's shoulder and crossed her arms over her chest. "Porter. This is why I asked about Jeremy Fogelman. Don't think that I don't have eyeballs."

"Never mind, Mom! But she's okay? I'm okay?"

"You're both fine." Dr. McConnell handed Porter a washcloth, to wipe off the goo. It was the color of toothpaste, an unnatural blue, and no matter how thoroughly she scrubbed, she knew she would find bits of it later, caked into the band of her underwear or just under the lip of her belly button.

"How do you know if you're going to be good at it?" Porter asked.

"Good at what?" Dr. McConnell was cleaning up. There was no doubt another patient was waiting, another woman to be reassured.

"Being a mother." Porter sat up, her belly now cold and damp. She tugged her shirt back down, where it stuck to her skin in spots. "You know, just that."

Astrid cleared her throat. She had hardened back into her normal shape.

"Are you worried about something specific? There are some great childbirth classes in town, and newborn care support groups, lactation specialists . . ." Dr. McConnell trailed off.

Porter laughed. "Yes, sure, all of that. But mostly I'm afraid that I'm not going to be enough. Good enough, smart enough, patient enough. That sort of thing."

Dr. McConnell nodded. She had heard this before. "Here's what I can tell you—most of the time, if you are concerned that you're not being a good enough parent, it means that you are a good enough parent. If you are self-aware enough to worry about your child's mental and emotional health, you are also going to be supportive of it. I'm not worried." She put her hand on Porter's forearm. "Just try to relax. Take good care of yourself. Prenatal yoga. Acupuncture. Meditation. You're in a dialogue with your baby all the time. Talk to her. Tell her how you're feeling. You're going to be in it together, you know?"

"Okay," Porter said. She stared down at her bump.

"I'll see you in a few weeks, okay? Astrid, good to see you. Take care of your baby, too, okay?" Dr.

McConnell hugged both Porter and Astrid and then vanished into the hallway. Porter could hear her welcome her next patient into an exam room. That was parenting, too, helping so many women (and their partners, she supposed) move from one side of their life to another, to cross this profound barrier. No one Dr. McConnell saw was the same when they were done with her. Rachel had told her that she'd heard that giving birth was the number one reason women became doulas or midwives, that they felt so altered by the experience of pregnancy and childbirth that they were like junkies, loath to leave the cozy, warm zone of uteruses.

When she got into the hallway, Porter expected to see Rachel—Porter would have come, if she'd gotten a text like that, but Rachel wasn't there. Friendship was as mystifying as love, with none of the rules. Or maybe there were rules, but Porter didn't know them. She had never been a bridesmaid. That seemed, suddenly, like a shameful admission of failure. Out of all the brides in the world, how had not one of them wanted her by their side? She called, she wrote emails, she sent baby gifts, she made dinner dates. Some people seemed to move through life in herds, surrounded by friends like baby elephants surrounded by their mothers and aunties, protected from life's dangers. Porter felt—had always felt—like she was alone. Maybe her mother was right, and having this baby was foolhardy, but even Astrid didn't understand why. Porter wanted to love someone fully, and to have them love her back. She wanted to be so indispensable to someone, to be so important that a casual erasure was impossible. Other people had that with their partners, didn't they? The legal webbing that made a knot that much harder to untangle? Porter was happy to be tangled up with her baby, their bodies working so hard together, already a team. Was she a good mother or a bad mother? Porter wasn't sure she believed Dr. McConnell, but she wanted to. **I love you,** she said, on the inside. **I love you I love you I love you.**

Porter and Astrid walked slowly back to the elevator.

"You never told me that you had an abortion," Astrid said. "Why didn't you tell me?"

"Oh, sure," Porter said. "I'm sure that would have gone over **great**. Like, the day after I was Harvest Queen, want to take me to Planned Parenthood? I'm sure you would have been super excited." She didn't want to sound like a petulant teenager, but she couldn't help it.

"It's not about being excited, Porter." Astrid stopped walking. "It's just a big thing to have carried around on your own for so long."

"Well, you had a secret. I'm not judging your secret. So don't judge mine. Would you rather that I had had a baby when I was in high school? I'm sure your gardening friends and town council friends and tennis friends would have loved it. Oh, and Dad too. That would have been great, for Dad to have known. It might have killed him even faster!"

"Porter Strick!" Astrid covered her eyes with her hands. "Stop! Stop it."

A massively pregnant woman waddled down the hallway toward them. She took slow, small steps, and every few steps, she paused to breathe with her eyes closed.

Porter was just about to ask if she needed help when a man with an overnight bag and a breast-feeding pillow tucked under his arm leapt out of the elevator and took her elbow.

"We're almost there, honey," he said, and led her down the hall toward labor and delivery.

"Can we just not, please?" Porter said when they were gone, and she pushed the button for the elevator. "And how long have you known about Jeremy?"

Astrid rolled her eyes. "A long time. And to be clear, yes, it is okay to have secrets. Everyone has secrets. We're human! We don't like to tell everyone everything. That's fine, I understand. And we're not the most effusive family in the world, I know that too. But, Porter—I love you. And you could have told me about it. I would have gotten you hot water bottles. And Vicodin. Whatever you needed." Astrid reached up for her daughter's face. At first, Porter resisted and pulled away, but Astrid's hands refused to let go. Porter let her mother turn her face.

"I love you. I love this baby." Porter chewed on her lips, a habit that Astrid had always hated. "I'm sorry that I made you feel like you couldn't tell me."

Porter nodded. She had thought about telling her parents, but it made as much sense as hiring a skywriting airplane to fly over Clapham and puff the words out in smoke. Who would it have helped?

"I'm sorry," Astrid said again. She pulled Porter's face even closer, knocking them both slightly off-balance. Porter wasn't used to her mother hugging her, and so it took them a few minutes to figure out which arms should go where, but they did it, eventually.

The elevator dinged and its doors shuddered open. Porter and Astrid took a step closer, and all of a sudden, both Porter's and Astrid's telephones began to trill and beep.

"What the fuck?" Porter said. "Cell service in this town sucks. Can you not call someone to fix that?" Porter held the phone to her ear and started listening to a string of messages. "Oh shit," she said. "It's Cecelia's school."

Astrid nodded, pointing to her own phone, also at her ear. "Me too," she said. "Let's go. Port, drive to my house, and we'll go to the school together, okay?"

"Okay," Porter said. She looked down and realized that she was digging her fingernails into her own palm.

Chapter 31

Cecelia Winds Up

It was the last period of the day, which, on Fridays, meant math. The junior high had tracked math classes, just like her school in Brooklyn had, which meant that the kids who were good at numbers were in one class and the kids who couldn't add their way out of a paper bag were in another. Cecelia and August sat next to each other in the very last row, where they absorbed little to no lasting knowledge, which they both felt fine about. There were people who truly needed higher math, in order to become adults who did great things of a particular type: scientists, astronauts, professors who would someday be played by a sallow-skinned British actor in a movie adaptation of their lives. Cecelia and August were not those people.

Sidney Fogelman sat one row closer to the

blackboard, separated from her cronies by aptitude, and spent the entire forty-five-minute class
period putting her hair into a high ponytail and
taking it out again.

August slid his notebook toward the edge of his
desk, and wrote: **I think Sidney counts by imagining My Little Ponies jumping over a rainbow.**

Cecelia laughed and wrote in her notebook:
**I don't think there are even numbers on her
phone, just emojis.**

Their math teacher, Mr. Davidson, was twenty-
two. That seemed like math worth paying attention to—they had asked on the first day. A male
teacher was always cause for a low-level celebration, or at least an interested **oh** from a parent, but
neither of Cecelia's parents had asked about her
teachers, not specifically, not by subject, not actually thinking about the fact that she was interact-
ing with all these adults every day and they had no
idea who they were. Katherine would have loved
Mr. Davidson. He was tall and thin, with a mustache that clearly existed just to demonstrate that
it could. He wore pants the color of New England
clam chowder, and New Balance sneakers.

There was an elaborate algebraic equation on
the board, lines and squiggles that Cecelia could
hardly make sense of. In most ways, she was a good
student, and it seemed fine that in this one way,
she was merely passable. As long as she passed. She
raised her hand.

"Yes, Cecelia?" Mr. Davidson said.

"I'm sorry, could you explain that again? I got lost at the **x/y**."

"Does anyone want to come up to the board and take a crack? Explain as you go?" He waved the chalk around the room.

"I'll do it," Sidney said, pulling her hair back into a ponytail, the way a fighter might take off her earrings before a sidewalk brawl. She turned around and gave Cecelia and August a nasty look. "You guys are fucking morons."

She sauntered up in between the desks and accepted the chalk from Mr. Davidson with more than a smidge of lasciviousness, as if he had selected her, and not the other way around. She squeaked out some figures, handed back the chalk, and then dusted off her hands while Mr. Davidson checked her work.

"Great, yes. Now, can you explain how you got there?"

Sidney rolled her eyes. "It's easy. You just have to factor for **x**, and then multiply everything that's left."

"Yes, sort of," Mr. Davidson said. Sidney seemed satisfied and walked back to her seat. She nestled herself back in and worked on her ponytail until the bell rang. When they all stood up, shoving their things back into their bags, Sidney spun around on her heels and stared at August.

"You think you're pretty slick, don't you?" She

was smiling, which would have been worrisome on its own.

"Well, I'm no math genius like you . . . oh, but wait, you're in the dumb class with us! Never mind!" August slapped his forehead. "My mistake."

"I have a friend who goes to Sunshine Village, did you know that?" Sidney crossed her arms over her chest. "She told me some crazy shit. **Robin.**"

"That's his middle name," Cecelia said, the words coming out fast. "My middle name is Vivienne, and sometimes people call me that. Especially the French side of my family."

August was breathing hard. Cecelia reached down and held his hand.

"Wait, so if you dress up like a girl and call yourself a girl's name and"—here Sidney pivoted her body to face Cecelia directly—"and you hold hands with girls, does that mean, oh my god, are you gay too? Like your grandmother? Your family is **so** crazy, I swear." Sidney leaned back and let out a great big whinny of a laugh. She pulled her phone out of her bag. "I can**not** wait to tell everyone."

"Wait," Cecelia said. She let go of August's hand.

"Cecelia, it's okay," August said.

"Don't!" Cecelia said. "That's not fair! It's none of your business, none of it!" She wanted to scream but gritted her teeth instead. She was not going to let it happen again. She wasn't going to tell secrets, but she also wasn't going to lie down and let another steamroller flatten her into the ground. It wasn't about truth, it was about protection. That's what she was trying to do for Katherine, and that's what she was going to do for Robin too.

Sidney rolled her eyes. "I'm in the business of entertaining myself, and this is better than an episode of **Vanderpump Rules**."

Cecelia looked at August, who had turned the color of unbuttered Wonder bread. "I'm sorry," she said to him. "I have to."

"You have to what, try to kiss me? Do it now, I'll do a Boomerang." Sidney puckered up and held her phone at arm's length. "You get in here, too, **Robin,** all the girls in one picture!"

"Okay, that's it," Cecelia said, and pulled back her right arm until her fist was touching her shoulder, and then she let it fly, straight into Sidney's nose. There was a sharp noise, like an aluminum can being crushed. A thin stream of blood spurted out of Sidney's nose, like a single ketchup packet, and she gasped, in pain, surprise, or both, bringing her hands to her face. Cecelia and August stood patiently while Mr. Davidson quickly made his way to the back of the class, the smile fading from his face as he realized they were fighting about more than equations.

The middle school principal's office had a carpeted waiting room, and that's where Cecelia had been sitting for an hour. August's parents had come to pick him up, leaving with damp faces and a little affectionate squeeze of Cecelia's hand after a brief private conversation in the office, and then Sidney's father had come and taken her home after a second private conversation, and still, there Cecelia sat, alone with the principal's receptionist, a plump woman named Rita who was much beloved around the school for having a wide selection of Entenmann's cookies sitting on her desk, free for the taking. So far, Cecelia had had three. The principal herself had vanished with her leather briefcase some time ago.

Rita held the phone to her ear, shook her head, and set it back in its cradle.

"Still no answer, honey."

"Did you try my aunt Porter too?"

Rita consulted her notepad, ticking off names with the sharp tip of her pencil. "I tried your grandmother, your aunt, your mother, your father, then your aunt again." She frowned. "I'm so sorry, sweetie. I'm sure one of them will call us back super soon."

"I could still make the late bus," Cecelia said, looking at the clock.

"It's just school policy, sweetie, after an incident, to have an adult take you home." Rita wore one pair of glasses on her face and another on a chain around her neck.

"Maybe you could try Shear Beauty? Ask for Birdie?" Cecelia looked at her palms. There was also Elliot and Wendy, but she didn't want to sit in between the twins' car seats and get hit by flying objects or, worse, sit in a totally silent car with her uncle.

The door opened, and Ms. Skolnick blew in, her arms full of books and a stack of paper between her teeth. She stuck the papers in her mailbox, which was next to the door, and then saw Cecelia and did a double take.

"Hi!" Ms. Skolnick looked at Rita. "What's going on?"

"There was an altercation in Mr. Davidson's eighth-grade algebra class," Rita said. "We're just waiting for a parent to pick her up. A family member."

It was funny, to have adults talk about her over her head, but Cecelia had gotten used to the idea of having no say in her own destiny. If she could have chosen anyone to walk through the door, she didn't know whom it would be. Gammy, she supposed, because that was the current arrangement. That was what was supposed to happen. If it had been her mother or her father, who she wanted to see so badly, so badly that she might do something crazy like punch a mean girl in the face, then it would mean something dramatic had happened. The irony was not lost on her, that her rage about being unfairly blamed had led to her doing something that was, without question, her fault.

Ms. Skolnick tiptoed across the carpet until

she was behind Rita's desk, where she crouched down beside Rita. She cupped a hand in front of her mouth like she was testing for bad breath, and spoke too quietly for Cecelia to hear, which she assumed was the point. Rita nodded.

"Do you have house keys, Cecelia?" Rita asked.

"To my grandmother's house? Yes." Cecelia dug them out of her bag and waved them in the air.

Rita looked at Ms. Skolnick again, who nodded. "Well, since the principal has already gone home, and I can't seem to get ahold of anyone, we'll have a meeting next week, okay, dear? Ms. Skolnick has offered to drive you home. Would that be okay with you?"

"Sure," Cecelia said, and before she knew it, Ms. Skolnick had hooked her by the elbow and was pulling her out of the office, down the hall, and out the front door.

The faculty parking lot was at the back of the building, next to the soccer field. It was full of well-loved Hondas and Nissans, with an occasional Ford. The sky was pink and orange, with the sun already hanging low on the horizon.

"Sorry about this," Cecelia said.

"It's fine! No trouble at all." Ms. Skolnick started to jiggle some keys.

"Yeah, but it's just really weird that she couldn't get in touch with literally anyone. It's not your job,

I know. I have an enormous family. Sort of. I mean, there are a lot of people in it." Cecelia chewed on a fingernail. How enormous could a family be if not one member could come pick her up? She had some cousins in France—maybe she could get on a plane. She spoke enough to get by.

"I am happy to do it, really." Ms. Skolnick put her hands on her belly as they walked—she was clearly pregnant. Cecelia had noticed before, but she'd been well trained to ignore such things unless she was on a crowded subway train. "Whew, sometimes she kicks me so hard that it feels like she's trying to audition for **American Ninja Warrior,** and the obstacle course is just getting out of my body."

"Congratulations," Cecelia said. Talking to a teacher outside of school—even just in the faculty parking lot—felt like acknowledging something that everyone spent their lives pretending wasn't true, which is that teachers were people with whole lives, not just puppets who slept in their supply closets, eating only apples and dreaming of lesson plans.

"You just socked Sidney Fogelman in the nose, is that right?" Ms. Skolnick stopped. They were standing next to a small blue car. Ms. Skolnick unlocked the driver's side, climbed in, and then pulled up the lock on the passenger side. Cecelia looked at her blankly. "This is how cars used to work, in the olden days. Get on in."

A few other teachers were in the lot now, and Cecelia could see cigarettes and vapes in their hands, ready for the second they were off school property, or maybe in the safety of their vehicles. Mr. Davidson had put on a denim jacket, which made Cecelia feel sad, for reasons she couldn't quite identify. She walked around the back bumper and pulled the door open. Ms. Skolnick was already blasting the air-conditioning, pitched forward as far as her belly would allow.

"She really deserved it," Cecelia said. "I can't say why, but just believe me. She's pretty much the devil. Like, if there are nice people, and then there are medium-nice people, and then there are people who would trip you at the top of the stairs, I think that last one is Sidney."

"Unofficially, I don't doubt that. Officially, I am equally supportive of all my students." Ms. Skolnick moved her face from side to side. Her cheeks were magenta. "I'm friends with your aunt Porter, did I tell you that already? How is she doing?"

Cecelia fingered the zipper on her backpack. Gammy hadn't yet followed through on her offer to teach her how to drive, and Cecelia wasn't sure she wanted to learn, anyway. It seemed like too much responsibility for one person, being in command of so many thousands of pounds of steel. Horsepower, they called it, as if a horse could do to a human body the same thing that a car could.

"I think she's okay," Cecelia said, knowing the

minute that she said it that she had no idea how her aunt was, not really, not in this topsy-turvy world where grown-ups were allowed to act like teenagers. "You know, pregnant."

Ms. Skolnick shifted the car into reverse and they sped backward onto the street.

Cecelia had never punched anyone before. Not in boxing gloves, not in jest, not ever. Her knuckles hurt. Sidney had been so surprised that she'd dropped her phone, and it had clattered to the linoleum floor, the glittery pink rubber case winking up at them. August had slid behind Cecelia's back, and someone toward the front of the room had cheered. Whether they were cheering the fact that Cecelia had punched Sidney or just the fact that there had been a punch at all—talk about spicing up math class!—she wasn't sure. She definitely would have been kicked out of school in Brooklyn for this—it happened from time to time, fights, and that was it. Zero tolerance. When that wasn't mentioned immediately, Cecelia felt like she'd crossed into the twilight zone. It was a genuine math problem—whatever she hadn't been guilty of before, was she guilty of it now? If her biggest sin had been the threat of exposure, and she had just thwarted exposure with violence, was that in the plus column? She didn't know.

What made her feel the most weird was that Cecelia felt, not for the first time in her life, that she had been not only neglected in the way that bohemian parents sometimes did, letting their children fall asleep in their clothes at a restaurant dinner party, small body lain across a pile of coats, but also in the less glamorous way, where her parents just couldn't focus on her, couldn't focus on her, couldn't focus on her, and so instead forgot about her instead. Where the fuck were her parents? They texted and sometimes called, but what the fuck? August's parents waved at him—at **her**—when he—when **she**—got on the bus every morning, and made her dinner at night. Even jerky Sidney's dad had hurried over to school, as if he'd been sitting in his car, key in the ignition, just waiting to be called into action. But her parents— separately!—hadn't even picked up the phone. Cecelia imagined herself as a ten-foot-tall dragon, red-scaled and fire-breathing. She imagined herself as Godzilla, stepping on the Big House and crushing it with one giant webbed foot. She imagined walking through the Hudson River until she got back to Brooklyn and then crushing it too. The whole thing. Parents were supposed to be there. That was their whole job. Good, bad, whatever— the very lowest job requirement was to be there.

When they rounded the final turn into the Big House's driveway, Ms. Skolnick screeched to a stop. Astrid's car was barreling out backward and stopped just a few feet in front of Ms. Skolnick's windshield. Cecelia took a deep breath. "Go on," Ms. Skolnick said. "They aren't going to hurt you," as if she knew such a thing, as if that was a promise anyone could make, but Cecelia opened the door anyway and stepped out, her sneakers crunching the gravel. Astrid swung open the driver's-side door to her car, and Porter swung open the passenger side, and they both sprang out, hands reaching for Cecelia. She watched them move toward her cautiously, hunters tracking a new species: Girl in Trouble—place of origin: Methodist Hospital, Brooklyn, New York. She didn't smile. She wanted to make this second last as long as possible, when all the adults in her life were waiting on her next word.

Chapter 32

Friendship Loveship

Porter hugged Cecelia first, quickly enveloping her niece in her arms, and then asked what had happened.

"This is my homeroom teacher, Ms. Skolnick," Cecelia said, now casually stepping out of Porter's arms. "I guess you two know each other?" A few strands of hair were plastered to her forehead; she looked a bit wild-eyed. Porter stroked Cecelia's cheek with her thumb and waited for Rachel to get out of the car. The driver's door swung open, and Rachel planted her feet on the gravel and then pulled herself up to standing.

"Hi, Rach," Porter said.

"Rachel Skolnick, look at you! Must be a boy, you're all belly!" Astrid said. She pointed, as if

Rachel might be confused as to which belly she was talking about.

"You never say that to me," Porter said.

"You're having a girl!" Astrid said.

"I meant about being 'all belly,' what am I? All hips? All arm fat?" Porter rolled her eyes.

"Hi, Porter; hi, Astrid," Rachel said. It was true; she looked wonderful, which was not how Porter felt except in fleeting moments when she caught sight of her current silhouette in the mirror or a shop window. Porter wanted to hug her but Rachel stayed on her side of the car. "Nice to see you both," Rachel lied politely. "Cecelia is a wonderful student."

"I am?" Cecelia asked.

"Of course you are!" Rachel said. "And it's been great to have her in Parade Crew too."

"You're doing Parade Crew?" Porter asked. "Like, building a float? Why didn't you tell me?"

"Such a joiner!" Astrid said. "Porter was Harvest Queen." She squeezed her daughter's arm. It was a fact that sounded almost like a compliment.

"We don't have to talk about it," Cecelia said.

"Would you like to come in, Rachel?" Astrid asked. "Let me pull the car in, you can park in the driveway." She didn't give Rachel a chance to respond before jumping back into the car and zipping back up the drive.

"I'm so sorry, we didn't have any cell service," Porter said. "What happened? Are you okay?"

Rachel gestured for Cecelia to answer.

"The short version is that my hand collided with someone's face." Cecelia immediately covered her own face with her hands.

"What?!" Porter grabbed Cecelia's forearms and moved them aside, like curtains.

"Now tell her the longer version," Rachel said.

Astrid honked the horn and then slammed her car door shut. "Come on, let's go inside, I don't want to miss anything, and there's no reason that everyone else should hear," she said from the front door, as if there were more foot traffic than her dog-owning neighbors jogging by twice a day. Rachel dutifully maneuvered herself back behind the wheel of her car to pull up the driveway, and Porter and Cecelia walked behind it up to the house.

Cecelia sat down at the kitchen table, and the other women filled in around her. Astrid quickly grabbed a bowl of blueberries from the fridge and shoved it in front of her, then thought better of it, took back the bowl of blueberries, and replaced it with a pint of ice cream and a spoon.

"I should punch people more often," Cecelia said.

"You **punched** someone?! They didn't say that on the message! They just said that you'd been in a fight and needed to be picked up!" Astrid put her hands to her cheeks. She turned toward Porter. "Do I take away the ice cream?"

Porter waved her hand. "No, don't be ridiculous. What happened, Cece?"

Cecelia picked up the spoon and dug into the hard surface of ice cream, scraping off a quenelle of chocolate. "There is a very mean girl in my math class, and we had a disagreement. She thought that it was okay to try to shame and humiliate someone, and I disagreed." She put the spoon into her mouth and pulled it out clean.

"Who is this girl?" Astrid asked. "What did she say? This is shocking, Cecelia! It sounds like you held the moral position, at least until you hit her. You can't hit people, you understand. I'm sure your father will be horrified. Hitting! He never killed a bug." She turned to Rachel. "Nicky's a Buddhist."

"I didn't kill anyone, Gammy. It was one punch." Cecelia dug out some more ice cream and then offered her spoon to Porter, who slid into the chair next to her.

"So who is this cow, anyway?" Porter asked. "I am fully prepared to hate her with you, I don't care if she's a child."

"Get ready," Rachel said. "This is actually the best part." She looked at Cecelia—"I'm here as a family friend, not as your teacher."

Cecelia rolled her eyes. "Her name is Sidney Fogelman. And I think she might have a broken nose. But probably not. It probably takes a lot to actually **break** a nose, right?"

Porter coughed up some ice cream. Astrid

looked at her, eyes wide. "Fogelman? Is that Jeremy Fogelman's daughter?" She put her hands flat on the table. "Oh dear."

"Is he sort of good-looking, for a dad, and smells like a wet dog? That's who picked her up. Strangely, he didn't introduce himself." Cecelia held out her hand for the spoon. Porter was still coughing into her napkin. Rachel sat back, put her hands on her belly, and laughed.

"No, yeah, I'm fine," Porter said, her mind reeling. "I'll be right back, are you guys okay? I have to pee. I'll be right back. Don't hit Gammy, Cecelia, okay? Rachel, you're in charge." Porter patted Cecelia on the head and then rolled her eyes at her mother.

Rather than go into her old bedroom, which was of course now occupied by Cecelia, Porter went into what had been Elliot's room. It looked much the same as it had when Elliot was in high school: neat as a pin, with a much-used dartboard hanging on the back of the door and several New York Yankees pennants hanging on the walls. Porter thought that his love for the Yankees might explain most of her problems with her brother: more than anything else, more than money, even, he wanted to win. Now he was trying to win a contest with himself, a contest that he (clearly, so clearly) was destined to lose.

The full-size bed was made, as always, with a plaid bedspread and fourteen pillows too many for a normal person. Porter flopped backward onto the bed gently, the way a scuba diver had to fall into the sea. She pulled her phone out of her pocket and then rolled onto her side, shoving two of the pillows in between her knees.

Jeremy answered after two rings.

"Hey," Porter said. "I just heard."

"About Sidney's nose? You're lucky I'm a doctor! Otherwise I'd charge your crazy brother's ass."

"I mean," Porter said, her voice lowering, "you're not a **doctor** doctor."

"Oh, you want to be like that, do you?" Jeremy asked. He was purring. "Is this how you apologize?"

"I thought I could apologize later," Porter said. "If you're free?"

"I'll meet you in the barn at ten," Jeremy said. "I anticipate a sick animal. An emergency call."

"SOS, and sorry," Porter said, "about the nose." She waited for Jeremy to hang up, and when the phone clicked to dead air, she stared at Elliot's bookshelf, which was full of paperbacks he'd read in high school, several volumes of **The Guinness Book of World Records,** sports trophies, and no sign of a personality whatsoever.

There was a knock at the door. "Yeah?" Porter called, still horizontal.

Rachel opened the door. "Hey."

Porter struggled to sit up elegantly and failed. "Hi," she said. "Sorry, I was about to come back down."

Rachel shut the door behind her and leaned against it. "Pretty funny that Cecelia punched Sidney Fogelman. That girl is a **dick**."

"You know, I got that impression," Porter said. "Is Cecelia going to get in trouble, you think?"

Rachel shook her head. "I'm not sure exactly what Sidney said, but I think it's covered under the umbrella of 'hate speech,' so if anyone is in deep shit, it's her."

They were quiet for a minute.

"How are you?" Rachel asked. "You said you were at the hospital?"

"I had some spotting," Porter said. "But I'm okay. How are you?"

"I'm okay too," Rachel said. "Josh and I have been talking a little. He came over for dinner. I don't know."

"That seems good," Porter said. "Right?"

Rachel shrugged. "I still want to kill him. I'm just testing it out, just in case I might not always want to kill him. How about you?"

Porter wanted to tell her friend the truth, she did. And even more than that, she wanted to be the kind of woman who wouldn't stand for bad behavior in herself or anyone else. She wanted to be a woman with standards. And she would be. The dividing line was so clear—the finish line,

the checkered flag, the whole thing. That was how
Porter saw it—an expiration date. She had until
the baby was born—until she grunted and pushed
her way from one kind of person to another. She'd
push it all out—along with the baby, she'd push
out this part of herself, the part that was juvenile
and selfish and on the wrong side of her own history. Just not quite yet. "I haven't seen him much.
What was going to happen, really?" Porter was
going to say more but found that she couldn't.
Rachel walked over and gave her a tight hug. Lies
by omission weren't as bad, Porter told herself, and
she willed herself to believe it.

Chapter 33

Shear Beauty

Cecelia's punishment, such as it was, was to help Birdie in the salon: an internship, for which she would not be paid. August, who very much supported the punch, volunteered to join her, and so Birdie now had two eighth-grade assistants. Two other hairdressers had chairs in the shop—Ricky, who would only say that he was "older than he looked," with tight jeans that were always cuffed high enough to show off his colorful socks, and Krystal, who had cropped blue hair and wide hips and a good loud laugh. As everywhere in Clapham, Shear Beauty was a place to chat with neighbors about the weather, the president, one's offspring, Barbra Streisand, and though Birdie and her employees didn't know about sports, they knew enough to get through a haircut.

August and Cecelia took turns sweeping up the cut locks of hair, and carrying towels and capes to the laundromat around the corner. On the weekends, they ran across the roundabout to Spiro's to fetch coffee and pastries. They practiced shampooing each other's hair, and then helped each other clean up the water they'd accidentally sprayed on the floor. Mostly they chatted up the customers as they waited, which was easy enough, and August quickly taught Birdie how to install a credit card reader on her telephone, so that she could save some of the fees she was currently being charged.

After the fight, Cecelia had asked August what she should call him. In public, in private, in front of her parents, in front of the idiots at school. The answers were clear: Alone, she was Robin. In public, he was August. Not forever, just for now. Cecelia's brain toggled inexpertly, but she understood that it was one thing for her to try to get it right and another, much harder thing for Robin to have to figure out. Mostly they talked about other things, like how cute Mr. Davidson was, and whether Shawn Mendes was beautiful and talented or just plain beautiful, and whether Cecelia's parents were the very worst parents who had ever lived, if cheese fries were better than regular fries all the time or only sometimes.

The salon closed at eight P.M. on Fridays, which meant that Birdie would make sure they had dinner before they went home. Her last client was usually out the door by 7:30, and then they just had to sweep one last time and clean all the brushes and make sure all three stations were well stocked and that the electric teakettle was unplugged and that all the lights were turned off before they locked the door. Spiro's and Sal's Pizzeria stayed open late, but otherwise, downtown Clapham was dark and empty by nightfall.

August was sitting on the chair nearest the window—Birdie's chair—while Cecelia rotated shampoo bottles so that all the labels faced in the same direction.

"What do you guys want for dinner?" Birdie called from the back.

"Mustache pizza!" Cecelia yelled.

August shrugged, swiveling the chair back and forth with his foot.

"Do you think I should cut my hair?" Cecelia asked, coming and standing behind August. She picked up a clump of her hair on each side of her head and held them out to the sides, Pippi Long-stocking. "My hair is so dumb. It's dumb hair. You have great hair."

"It's not dumb," August said. "It's classic. I do have good hair, though." August blew a kiss into the mirror.

"What do you think, Birdie? Give me your pro-fessional opinion." Cecelia tapped August, and they swapped places. Birdie made her way out from the back. She was wearing her reading glasses on a chain around her neck.

"Hmm," Birdie said. "Let's see." She fluffed Cecelia's hair, scratching here and there. Birdie tilted her head to the side. "You know, I think you could have an angle. Or some color. Have you ever thought about some color?"

Cecelia had never considered doing anything to her hair that would make other people notice it. Her hair was a color that no one would ever describe, like a dun-colored female peacock, as drab as mouse droppings and the straw bristles of a broom.

Birdie wasn't finished. "Okay," she said, raising Cecelia's chair with the foot pedal and spinning it around so that Cecelia was facing her. "Okay, I see it. A bit of a chop—chin length. Then, we go for flames. Bright red. **Run Lola Run.** Have you seen that? I think it came out before you were born."

"Oh, yes!" August said. "I have! Cecelia, do it. Why not?"

Birdie picked up a pair of scissors and put her hands on her hips. "August, want to run across the street and order us a pizza? I'll get started." She slid her wallet out of her back pocket and handed it to him.

Cecelia reached for August's arm, pretending to be scared. It felt like she should ask someone for permission, but there was no one to ask. "Don't leave me! Or, no, I want pizza! Do leave me but come back soon!" August nodded.

"Lock the door behind you, will you?" Birdie asked. "My keys are on the desk."

August scooped them up and went out the door, pulling it shut behind himself. Main Street was dark—it was fully fall now and already cool enough to need a sweater. August was only in a T-shirt and thought about going back inside, but the pizzeria was warm. He sat and waited for a few minutes and then, carrying the pizza box out of Sal's, he saw two men walk out of the corner building.

August's parents had a theory: Someone was sitting on it, waiting for big money to come to town. A few years ago, Rite Aid had bought an old grocery store just outside the village line, and everyone lost their minds, as if Clapham would transform into a soulless shopping mall in the blink of an eye. August's parents started a petition, Keep Local, Shop Small. They still refused to shop at the Rite Aid. Ruth and John talked about the place on the roundabout all the time—if someone local had bought it, and was just waiting to have enough money to renovate, Ruth would have known from the town committee. If it were some corporate giant, she would have known that too. Ruth and John were hoping for a really good ice-cream parlor or a great sandwich shop.

The street was mostly dark, but there were

streetlamps every so often, tall shapely ones that made August think of Paris, though he'd never been, wrought iron with a delicate bend that made you forget it was made of something so impossibly hard. There was one puddle of lamplight right on the corner, and August watched as Cecelia's uncle Elliot stepped into the center of the yellow circle, shook hands with another man, and then stood there on the sidewalk as the other man walked away. He then turned toward Shear Beauty, and both August and Elliot looked through the window at Cecelia and Birdie. Cecelia was laughing, and Birdie was, too, and August—Robin, in her head she was always Robin—started to think about what she'd like to do to her hair, someday. She was thinking mermaid hair, like her mother's, the kind of hair she'd accidentally sit on.

"Why don't you come in?" August said. Elliot looked startled. "I'm friends with Cecelia. Want some?" He pointed to the window with the corner of the pizza box.

"Sure, okay," Elliot said. August watched as he ran his hands through his hair a few times and then jogged across the street, taking the pizza from August while he unlocked the door.

Birdie was working fast. There were at least four inches of Cecelia's hair on the floor. "Things are happening," Cecelia said, her face pointing toward the floor.

"Chin down," Birdie said.

"I found your uncle Elliot," August said.

"Huh?" Cecelia said, peering up from behind a wall of hair.

"Hi, Elliot," Birdie said. "What a nice surprise."

August slid a slice out of the box and onto a paper plate and set the plate gently in Cecelia's lap before curling into the chair next to her with his own slice.

"You know, I've been meaning to talk to you, Birdie." Elliot took a slice of pizza and folded it in half.

Birdie looked up, her scissors still. She made eye contact with Cecelia in the mirror. All Cecelia wanted was to stop being a person who other people confided in. Not really, not forever—but temporarily, absolutely. Not that her uncle had confided in her—he hadn't. And she hadn't told anyone about what she'd seen in his desk drawer, which meant that she could plausibly pretend she hadn't seen it at all. It might not exist.

"What's going on?" Birdie asked. Her glasses were halfway down her nose; she was making Cecelia look better, and she was doing it for free. Cecelia had never met her grandfather, so she didn't know what he'd been like, but she liked watching Gammy and Birdie cuddle together in the kitchen when they thought she wasn't looking. Sometimes Cecelia thought that her superpower was her ability to fade into the background like a neutral wallpaper. Katherine had expected her to keep her mouth shut. August too. Elliot had invited her into his house, assuming she wouldn't open drawers. Cecelia was never the subject, she was an object. Even now, Birdie was doing the transforming; Cecelia was just a head in a chair.

"Yes?" Birdie kept working, snipping away. August held the pizza in front of her mouth and let her take a bite before moving it away, so that it wouldn't get covered with hair.

"I've been meaning to talk to you about the space on the corner," Elliot said. "I'm not sure if my mother knows yet, but I bought it."

"Did you?" Birdie stopped what she was doing. "Do you know that Astrid is obsessed? You must know that. Do you? All she wants is for something to open there, and I keep telling her, something will. But it's you!"

"Yes," Elliot said. "It's true."

"That's exciting," Birdie said. "So what's your plan? You know, Susan's Bookshop and I have had the same landlord for eighteen years. Predating my time in Clapham. Spiro's has been there since the dawn of time. Frank too. It's a big responsibility, thinking about the community. Especially because you live here. Most landlords want to stay as far away as they can." She turned her attention back to Cecelia's head and gently pointed it toward the ground.

"Yes," Elliot said.

"What do you actually want to put there?"

August asked. "I mean, when you bought it, what was your plan?"

"It's not that simple," Elliot said. "It's about real estate, not services."

"But you live here," Cecelia said.

"And you must want stuff," August said.

"These are some smart kids," Birdie said.

"I want one of those Instagram museums," Cecelia said. "You know, those places that just exist so people will take pictures and post them on the internet."

"That's not real," Birdie said. "Is it?"

"It is," Cecelia said.

"Do you think that's what people would want?" Elliot asked, his voice searching.

Cecelia and August made eye contact in the mirror and burst into laughter.

"No, I knew you were kidding," Elliot said. He looked miserable. He knew this feeling—the feeling that he was getting it wrong. His brother, Nicky, had never done anything wrong, not really. Even when Nicky did something royally stupid, it slid off his back. Porter too. Both of his siblings could have tried to water-ski with cement blocks, and they somehow would have skidded along the surface. Confidence. That was what they had. Enough confidence to not care about making money, or having a big house, or living a normal life, the kind of life everyone wanted. When Elliot looked at his brother's weird marriage and tiny apartment, or his sister's refusal to just marry someone already, he felt embarrassed for them, but also, he felt embarrassed for himself, that they clearly didn't need what he needed, that they were powered by some internal engine that he did not possess, to move to their own beat, when he'd always been happy with the usual rhythm. Only in his family could Elliot feel like the weirdo for getting married before having children, for having a baby on purpose, for registering for kitchen appliances.

It couldn't all be blamed on one conversation, of course. Or could it? Elliot didn't know how brains worked. One conversation could change the course of a life, though—what about people whose spouses had to tell them they were getting a divorce, or every parent or wife or son who got a call saying that someone had been killed in an accident? Bob Baker's life had changed with a conversation, hadn't it? And so why not Elliot's too?

It was right after his college graduation. Elliot had wanted to take the LSATs right away, as quickly as possible before all the information from all his classes slipped out his ears at night while he slept. After being away at school, it felt good to be back in his room in the Big House. Some of Elliot's friends had real jobs already, either with their family businesses or with consulting firms in Manhattan and Boston. Elliot had asked his father for a job at his law firm, but Russell didn't think it was a good idea, for slightly foggy reasons. He wanted Elliot to get a job somewhere else first. He could work for him down the road, he said. After law school. After working for someone else. As if those things were easier to do than to work for your father.

His scores were just south of mediocre. They weren't so bad that Elliot seemed illiterate, or to have filled something out incorrectly, but bad enough that he wouldn't be able to get into a reputable program. And if you could only get into a fourth-tier law school, who would hire you, anyway? Elliot had a summer job lined up at Valley Construction. He could take the test again in the fall.

The days were hot and long, and Elliot slept like the dead, his tired body crashing into bed, sometimes still in his clothes, and not moving for ten hours. Twelve on the weekends. By the time he stumbled down the stairs in his boxer shorts and T-shirt, his parents were already on lunch.

When there was a breeze, Astrid and Russell ate outside at the small wrought iron table. Russell didn't wear suits on the weekend, but he still never looked quite relaxed, the way that other dads did. He wore collared shirts and ironed his pants. Russell thought denim was made for children and cowboys. Even though he was warmer than his wife, far more likely to crack a joke, or to give a quick bicep squeeze, in some ways he was just like Astrid—precise and clear. Elliot opened the fridge, and the cold air felt good, so good that he leaned forward, pressing his nose against a carton of orange juice. He felt like he had a hangover, but from physical labor instead of alcohol. The house was completely silent—no Wesley Drewes, none of the Steely Dan that Russell played when Astrid wasn't home. Elliot took the orange juice out of the fridge, shut the door and leaned against it. He tipped the triangular spout into his mouth and drank straight from the carton, long, slow glugs. Outside, his father laughed.

Later, that laugh would hurt more and more, once he knew what would follow, but in the moment, on that one, sunny afternoon, Elliot laughed to himself in response. His father's laugh was goofy; higher pitched than his speaking voice, a genuine giggle. Elliot held the carton against his chest and moved closer to the open door to the garden. He stayed out of sight. Porter was somewhere else—if she'd been home, she would have been making a racket, talking on the phone, or eating handfuls of potato chips, sitting in between her parents, egging them both on. He was the only child home, and he wanted to know what his parents were saying.

"Oh, come on," Russell said. "You don't mean that."

"I'm sorry to say that I do!" Astrid said. "I don't want to believe it. But I do. I think he's skated by.

He skated through school, barely graduated from college. And now he thinks he's going to be a lawyer, just because you are? I'm **sorry**. We aren't doing him any favors by flattering him into believing that's going to happen." Her fork clinked against her plate. Elliot turned his face away, but he couldn't bring himself to leave the kitchen. His mother went on. "I just think he's not cut out for the business world. He should open a yogurt shop, I don't know."

"Yogurt!" Russell boomed back. Elliot's breath started to move around his body again—his father was going to defend him, of course he was. "Yogurt's passé. Maybe he'll stay in construction! Build some glittering mansions on the hill!"

"Hmm. We'll see. Maybe if someone else tells him where to put the beams. Not everyone can be the boss, Rusty."

Elliot heard the sound of one of their chairs scraping against the stone patio, and he set the orange juice on the counter and padded quickly out of the kitchen and back up the stairs, where he stayed for the rest of the day.

"Who were you meeting over there now?" Birdie asked.

The corners of Elliot's mouth turned south. "He makes ice cream. He lives in New Paltz. I don't know. He could only pay half as much as some of the other people who've approached me. I don't know. His wife does spin class with Wendy. I don't know how he found out that I owned the building."

"So he's a local and has community ties and also makes ice cream," August said.

"Listen, it's a business decision," Elliot said. "It has to be about business."

"You just said **business** like sixteen times," Cecelia said. "No offense." She thought about the glossy folder and felt more like a local than she ever had before. Astrid was not going to like this, and Elliot knew it. Cecelia willed herself to be brave, but no one liked tattletales. "I'm sure it'll be beautiful."

Elliot looked at her, his eyes wide. Cecelia turned her face back toward her lap.

Elliot took two giant bites of pizza and then leaned against the wall. He exhaled. "Well, Birdie, I should tell you. I did get approached by Beauty Bar. I don't think they cut hair, but they do blow-drying. And sell makeup."

"Keep Local, Shop Small!" August said, repeating his parents' mantra.

"Gross," Cecelia said, pretending that she didn't know, that her words had been a coincidence.

"You two behave," Birdie said, and kissed Cecelia on the top of her head. "It's up to you, Elliot. If I may?" He nodded. "It's got to feel good. My parents wanted me to be a teacher. But I never liked teaching. My two sisters live in Texas, in the same town as my parents, and they're both teachers. I'm not saying they're unhappy. I'm just saying, you need to make decisions you're proud of, and not worry about what other people will say. That includes your mother."

"I think you see a very different side of my mother than I do," Elliot said. "I mean, obviously. But not just that. I'm used to my mother telling me that I didn't do something right. I'm the first-born, you know?"

Birdie pointed her scissors in the air. "Me too. In solidarity."

"Me too," said Cecelia.

"And me," said August.

"No, no, you two are **onlies,**" Birdie said. "That's different. Only children are, all problems aside, treated like porcelain. Eldest children are treated like glass and then promptly ignored for the cuter, newer model. Only children are the prize. Eldest children are the tests. I understand."

Elliot slid another piece of pizza out of the box and sat in the third salon chair. Beauty Bar would make him rich, an actual success, if the people in town didn't boycott. And not saying yes to Beauty Bar, walking away from the most money, would make him a bad businessman. He let his legs dangle beneath him, just like the kids. It wasn't fair, to still need your parents' approval. Nicky definitely didn't need it. Porter didn't seem to need it. Elliot closed his eyes and tried to imagine what that felt like. Wendy said that it was time for him to think about his children more than he thought about his mother, and he did, in terms of the percentage of his thoughts on any given day, but that wasn't what she meant. Wendy thought that one's actions should be driven by the future, which Elliot knew was a brand of optimism he did not possess. He knew that the only thing that really drove anyone—drove **him**—was the past.

Chapter 34

Verbal Confirmation

Farms were good for staying busy: there were always things to do, tasks to complete. Even at nighttime. Something always needed to be cleaned or tended. When Jeremy knocked at ten past the hour, Porter was organizing the mountain of paperwork on her desk, a task she delayed until the stack threatened to topple and cover the floor of the office like a blanket of fresh snow. It had taken a couple more days for him to make his way for the fake sick pet emergency, but what was a few days? Porter called out that the door was open, and Jeremy wandered in.

"Do you not have lights in here?" he asked, which was the only reason Porter realized it had gotten dark, and the only light in the room was the small lamp on her desk.

"Goats don't need lights," Porter said. "They have excellent vision, even in the dark. Did you know that their pupils are horizontal, and that they can see in almost all directions at once? It's like a fish-eye lens."

"So you're saying goats have fish eyes," Jeremy said. He walked behind Porter's desk and scooped her into his arms.

"Ooh, you went to a **good** veterinary school." Porter let him kiss her, his tongue on hers, her tongue on his, both of them slipping in and out like invitations. There was a ratty old couch, for necessary naps, and the occasional night spent, and Porter pushed them toward it. Everything about Jeremy made her feel like she was still a teenager, with only the present moment at stake, only whatever they would do to each other's bodies next. Is this what people meant when they talked about being in love? She thought it was, the rush to connect with another human, above all others. Jeremy peeled the underwear off from under her dress and flicked them across the room and then buried his face where the underwear had been.

"You make me feel like a teenager," Porter said. Jeremy's mouth was busy, and he didn't respond. He made her feel, in fact, exactly like **herself** as a teenager. Porter didn't want to go back in time, not at all, but she did think of that period of her relationship with Jeremy as the last time she was really, truly, just a kid. She wanted her baby, she

wanted to have all the sex she wanted with whom-
ever she wanted to have sex with: Was that too
much to ask, for every part of her life to exist in a
vacuum? She pushed him backward and climbed
on top, slipping him into her body. He didn't care
how big her belly was, he loved her, and she loved
him, and what they were doing was okay.

Half an hour later, Jeremy was getting dressed.
Porter watched him kick out the legs of his pants
before pulling them on.

"Hey," she said. "Should we talk about it?"

Jeremy ran a hand through his hair. "Yeah,
I guess so. I mean, we'll have to sooner or later,
right? I know my wife will want me to."

"Yeah," Porter said. "Of course. What do you
want to tell her?"

Jeremy buttoned his jeans and then searched
through the couch cushions for his long-sleeved
T-shirt. "I guess I'll tell her that we talked about it,
and Cecelia's going to stay away from her? Because
the school isn't going to do anything. They told
me that. Apparently Sidney said some things that
aren't PC enough, even though it didn't sound
that bad to me."

"No," Porter said. "I mean, about us. Do you
want to tell her about us? What do you think she
knows? She must know something, right? We never
talked about it. But she's not a moron, obviously

she must have known something was going on. And I feel shitty lying about it, too, it's not just you." The baby kicked, as if in solidarity.

"Huh," Jeremy said. He sat down on the couch, forcing Porter's legs in the crack at the back of the foldout. "That is not what I was talking about." He put his hands on her knees. "I meant about Sidney and your niece. I told her that I would talk to you and get some reassurance that she wouldn't do it again, and we wouldn't press charges or whatever, you know, not like anything big really happened, just that there could be a formal apology and then we'd all move on. I think that's what Kristen was thinking." He leaned back, using her legs as a human lumbar support pillow. "What do you think?"

"Well," Porter said. "I think that Cecelia and Sidney and the school can probably work out whatever apologies need to be made. No one should get hit, obviously, and no one should say something that would make someone else hit them. I don't know what Sidney said, for the record. Cecelia is actually very discreet." She grunted a little, trying to maneuver her legs from out behind Jeremy's back, and swung them heavily back down to the floor. "What about the rest?"

Jeremy pulled on his chin. "The rest?"

"Yeah. Like us. I don't want to feel like Molly Ringwald here, asking you about prom, but what's the deal?" Whenever she'd had the conversation in her head, Jeremy was smiling. He was crawling across the floor to her, he was holding a ring, he was filling a bathtub with rose petals. That was dumb, of course, and Porter didn't want a grand gesture anyway. She just wanted an audible confirmation, like a flight attendant talking to the people sitting in the exit row.

"Come on, Port," Jeremy said, his head zigzagging like a snake. "You know it's more complicated than that. You know I love you—I have **always** loved you. Do I love you more than I love my wife? Maybe. Yeah, shit, you know what? I do. I fucking do. Being with you makes me feel like I'm sixteen years old, and totally invincible, like I'm fucking Superman. The way you look at me, Porter? When you look at me, I don't feel like a middle-aged loser who sticks his finger up dog butts all day, who has to put cats to sleep just like his father did, you know? I feel like a kid who is going to screw his brains out all night long and maybe all day the next day too. Do you know how often I sleep with my wife? Never. I never, ever sleep with my wife. Maybe on my birthday, or our anniversary, if she doesn't have her period. She wouldn't care if my dick fell off when I was taking a shit and I flushed it away by accident." He leaned over and embraced her. "You mean everything to me. You are amazing, and I love you. Is that confirmation? I want to figure this out. Do you know how happy it would make me to come home every day and have you there?"

Porter wrapped her arms around him. Jeremy was warm and smelled like sweat. She thought she'd wanted to hear it, but she hadn't expected it to sound so sad. When Astrid had cleared her throat and told the noisy kitchen about Birdie, her face had been as full of joy as her face could be without breaking. She was nervous but happy, Porter had seen it. But now that Jeremy had said what she'd asked him to, more or less, Porter felt like she needed to go home and take a shower, like she'd eaten an entire cake, and it would all have to come out, one way or another. "I have to go," Porter said. "We both have to go."

It was almost eleven when Porter got home. Her porch was dark, because she'd been gone all day and hadn't left the light on. She pulled the car in and kept her keys in her hand. The front door was sticky, as usual, and she kicked the bottom with the toe of her shoe, sending the wooden door skidding open. Every old building in Clapham was like that, rickety and full of eccentricities. Porter reached for the light switch with muscle memory, flipped the whole row up, flooding the house with yellow light. There were a dozen pink balloons floating in her living room. She screamed and then clapped her own hand over her mouth.

"Hello?" Porter said, to the balloons, to the otherwise seemingly empty room. It didn't seem like the sort of thing a murderer would do, but she kept her keys in her fist, just in case.

A groan came from the direction of the sofa. There, underneath a blanket, was her little brother, Nicky. "Surprise," he murmured, head still buried deep in her pillow. "Where have you been? I brought dinner. And balloons. It's not easy to get balloons on a train, I want you to know."

Porter screamed again, more happily this time, and then climbed on top of her brother, sitting on his rib cage. Personal space did not exist for siblings. When Porter was angry with her mother, there was always this: Astrid had given her two brothers, including one Porter actually liked. She wasn't alone. "My baby," she said, bouncing a bit, until Nicky cried uncle.

"I'm a total idiot," Porter said. "I can't even tell you. I mean, I can tell you, but you wouldn't believe it. I mean, you'd believe it." She shook her head.

"Me too," Nicky said. "I'm an idiot because I shipped Cece up here because I was scared of some teenage girls and the internet. Why are you an idiot?"

Porter slid off his body so that they were sitting

next to each other. "I've been sleeping with Jeremy Fogelman. Again."

"Again? Yeesh."

Porter grabbed a pillow and covered her face. "I know. It's beyond stupid. But I think I had to just get it out of my system for good. Put childish things behind me."

"It's okay," Nicky said. He put a hand on her shoulder. "We all make mistakes. I won't tell her." He nodded toward Porter's belly.

Chapter 35

And Then There Were Three

Elliot came downstairs in workout pants and a wrinkled, untucked dress shirt, clearly the first two pieces of clothing he put his hands on in the blackout-curtained void of his bedroom. Nicky had kept Porter from honking the horn when it took Elliot more than the three minutes he'd promised to emerge from his front door. It was late—everyone else was asleep. But Porter didn't care. She didn't even care that when they did drive to Buddy's, the only local bar that was open late, she wouldn't be able to have more than a few surreptitious sips of her brothers' drinks. The only thing that Porter cared about was that for tonight, and maybe only tonight, she had her baby brother all to herself, if you didn't count her big brother too.

Elliot shivered on the front step for a minute, blinking at the car, as if he couldn't remember who had texted him sixteen times to tell him that his attendance was mandatory. Nicky rolled down the passenger window and waved. "All aboard, old boy," he said. Elliot jogged over and slid his body across the back seat until he was sitting in the center, with one hand cupping each front seat.

"When did you get in?" Elliot asked, rubbing his eyes.

"Were you asleep?" Porter asked. "What are you, nine?" She was usually asleep by then, too, of course.

"A few hours ago. I was trying to surprise our pregnant sister, but she wasn't home, so I surprised myself with a little catnap on her couch." Nicky reached over and put his hand on top of Elliot's. "It's good to see you."

"Yeah, man."

"Oh my god, El, you're overflowing with love, I can hardly take it," Porter said, rolling her eyes. "Let's get some drinks in you two and see if I can get drunk just by dipping my pinkies in your beers."

"Fermentation is good for you," Nicky said. "A beer wouldn't hurt. Certain beers are actually great for lactation. You need those enzymes."

"That's what I'm talking about," Porter said. "Finally, some familial support."

———

Buddy's always looked closed, despite the large neon sign outside. It was on the bottom floor of a large building, down three shallow steps from street level, sunless and dank at all hours of the day. That was the appeal. The three Strick siblings jostled one another through the narrow door and to a booth at the back of the room.

"This place hasn't changed at all," Nicky said. He made a small stack of damp coasters, a tiny Andy Goldsworthy tower that would crumble with time and moisture. Porter rested her head on his shoulder and closed her eyes. Her belly bumped up against the edge of the table.

"Cecelia's been babysitting for us," Elliot said. His voice boomed, as if he needed to shout over loud music that only he could hear. He sat on the opposite side of the booth. Porter couldn't imagine putting her head on her older brother's shoulder. He was more like Astrid, with an invisible electric fence surrounding his body. Neither of them invited touch. Not like Nicky, who Porter had held in her arms when he was one day old, still soft all over, with no neck to speak of. He was a born cuddler.

"That's great, that's great," Nicky said. He petted Porter's hair. "God, I miss her. It seemed like the easiest thing to do, to send her up to Astrid, but now I don't know. It's so fucking hard to know if you're making the right decision."

Elliot put his hands on the table and pushed himself back up. "Well, if you want to talk about questionable parenting decisions, we'll be here all night. I'll get the first round."

"Seltzer water for me, please," Porter said, to his back, which Elliot acknowledged with a thumbs-up. "He's so annoying," she said to Nicky, though Elliot hadn't done anything. She was always ready to be annoyed by him.

"So you think Cece is doing okay?" Nicky asked.

It felt so nice to have him back, even just for a little while. Nicky had been her perfect doll, her laughing and cooing toy. She'd always wanted to bring him in for show-and-tell, as if he could just sit quietly in her preschool cubby for the rest of the day.

"She's great, Nicky. She really is. I don't know exactly what happened in school this week, but I think she kind of turned into a superhero. I think it's good, I do." She squeezed his arm. "I don't think you have to worry about her. She's such a good kid. Like, a **good** kid. Way better than any of us."

"Hey!" Nicky said, pretending to be offended. Elliot came back, holding three glasses in a well-practiced drink triangle. He set the drinks down and then slid back into the booth, leaning up against the worn leather back. He took a long sip from a short glass, the brown liquid sliding into his mouth like honey.

"So, tell me about Birdie," Nicky asked. "I mean, I get the broad strokes. But how is it? It sounds like it's been going on for a while."

There was a jukebox, and it was playing Hall & Oates. Porter didn't think there was a song on it that was released after 1997. "I think it's kind of amazing," Porter said. "It feels a little bit like watching an episode of **Black Mirror,** but one of the uplifting episodes, not one that makes you feel like the robot overlords have already won. I think Astrid is happy, believe it or not."

Elliot leaned forward, spreading his elbows wide on the table. The coaster tower collapsed to one side. "It's not amazing, okay, it's fucking weird."

"Here we go," Porter said.

"No, Porter, come on! Come on. You really don't think it's weird? After all this time of Astrid being like the Hudson Valley Margaret Thatcher, now she's Ellen DeGeneres? I like Birdie. I like her a lot, even. But it's still weird." Elliot shook his head.

"Oh, is that the face you make when you have to imagine a woman doing something just because she wants to? Do you know what year it is? It's the year of the woman! Again! Women can do anything. We can do stupid things and amazing things and smart things and dumb things. And we don't even need to get a permission slip!" She slapped the table, sending a wave of Nicky's beer onto the already sticky wood.

"That's not what I meant," Elliot said. He shrank backward, as Porter had known he would. Elliot growled, but he never bit. "It's that it's not like Mom. I don't mind seeing her happy, it's just that she never seemed happy before, and it's like, man. I don't know. It's like she's a whole different person."

"I think she was happy," Nicky said. "I think her happiness just lives in a little box, you know? Her happiness has boundaries. And I think it's good. Birdie is younger than she is. Companionship is important. Care is important."

"She's not her **nurse,** Nicky, she's her girlfriend!" Porter didn't think she'd have to scold them both.

"I know that, Puerto," Nicky said, gently. "But getting older isn't easy, and I think that people who do it together are happier and live longer. I worried about her being alone. I know that you two are both here, but from a distance, I'm relieved."

"You are such a kumbaya fucker," Elliot said. He took a drink. "I guess my problem is that she was always so hard, and that was our model, you know? Like, after Dad died, all we had was her, and she was this certain way. It's like the mama duck turning around and telling all her ducklings that they've been waddling the wrong fucking way, even though she taught them how to do it."

Nicky reached across the table and put his hand on his brother's cheek. "You still walk like a duck."

"Oh, come on. It doesn't matter to you because she liked you the most! Everyone did! She didn't even pretend to like us the same. Or be as proud of us or whatever. As if what you were doing was so great or important. **Jake George** was a fucking stupid movie, you know?" Elliot held up his palm, waiting for Nicky to nod, which he did. "See? You know. Everyone else knew. But Astrid's still waiting for your Oscar to show up in the mail."

"And the Nobel," Porter said. "It's true. She still likes you best! I mean, look at us, we're both still here, and she treats us like we're crushing disappointments, and you never even call her and her eyes get all twinkly when she says your name. I'm surprised there isn't a photo of you stuck to her refrigerator."

"Come on," Nicky said. He took a drink of his beer. "It's not like that."

"Like hell it's fucking not," Elliot said. Porter clinked her water glass against his beer. Maybe he wasn't **always** annoying. For a split second, Porter imagined a future in which she and Elliot could see each other on purpose, for pleasure. "Parents are not supposed to do that. I may think my kids are monsters, but at least I think they're **both** monsters."

"All I can say," Nicky said, "is that they were different with me because they were different. If

Juliette and I had had another baby a few years after Cecelia was born, we would have been different parents. You had one set of parents, El, it's true, and then Porter had another, and then I had a third. They just look the same on the outside."

"And what, that just makes it fine? So we all just have to accept the fact that our parents like you more than they like us?" Elliot's cheeks were red, but he didn't look angry. Porter recognized this look of her brother's—it was the face he'd had as a kid when his team had lost after he'd missed a few free throws, or when he hadn't won his class election. Whatever bad feelings Elliot was having, they were all pointed inward. "They were supposed to lie. They were supposed to make us believe it."

"It's not your fault," Porter said. "Just like it's not my fault."

"Fine," Elliot said. "It's not my fault."

"Hey," Nicky said. "It's really not."

"Can I ask you about something else, El?" Porter asked. They were already skating onto new parts of the ice, and so she decided to keep going. Porter sat up straight and cracked her knuckles. "Wendy told me about the building."

"What building?" Nicky asked.

Elliot poured the rest of his drink down his throat. "What did she tell you? When? Did she call you?"

"Wendy and I had lunch." Porter turned to Nicky. "Our big brother bought the building on the corner of the roundabout. But it's top secret." She lifted a finger to her lips. Being in a bar at night with her brothers was enough to make her feel a little bit drunk, even though she'd only siphoned a single sip of Nicky's beer.

"The corner? The wine store?" Nicky asked, turning his face back and forth between his siblings.

"That was one of its recent occupants, yes. Seventy-two Main Street. Next to Sal's. I can't believe Wendy told you." Elliot fumed. "I just didn't want it to be a big clusterfuck, you know, with everyone telling me what to do and what not to do. I'm an adult, and this is literally my job, building things." His glass was empty now, but he brought it to his lips anyway.

"I think that's exciting, El," Nicky said. "What are you going to put there? Are you going to move your office? Or rent it out? Build something new? That's major. Putting yourself right at the center of it. Does Astrid know? She's going to throw a parade. She's going to send an email and not bcc anybody, and we'll all get five hundred replies."

"Oh, god," Porter said. "You know, it might be better if Birdie were actually really young and could teach her how not to do things like that."

"No, Mom does not know. And I would very much appreciate it if you two wouldn't tell her. I'm working on a couple of potential deals, and I just want everything to be set before I tell her." Elliot rolled his glass along the edge of the table. "What-ever choice I make, it's going to be the wrong one, and I'm not looking forward to it."

Bells chimed. Nicky dug his hand into his pocket and pulled out his phone. "That's me, it's Juliette, let me take this. I was supposed to call her when I got in, but then I fell asleep." Porter scooted over and moved out of the way. Nicky nimbly jogged to the front of the bar and pushed open the heavy door back outside.

Porter held out her hand and Elliot waved it away, making his way to standing by himself. They walked to the bar together and leaned against the smooth glossy wood. Another drink appeared in front of Elliot, and another seltzer in front of Porter. She couldn't remember the last time she'd been this close to her brother after dark. She could see him more clearly in the dark, the familiar shape of his nose, the way he held his elbows when he was nervous. Being an adult was like always grow-ing new layers of skin, trying to fool yourself that the bones underneath were different too.

"Why don't you want to tell her?" Porter asked. It felt kind of like being in **Groundhog Day**, being in a family. No matter what happened, the next morning, Elliot would still be her big brother, no matter if they'd had fun tonight or pissed each other off as usual. Her mother would still be her mother. Her brain was trying to do the math to figure it out—if she and Elliot and Nicky had all had different sets of parents, did those different sets continue, on alternative timelines, all the way to the present? Was there a reset button? Their father's dying had been a reset, that much she knew. Maybe that was when Astrid had started to change, and they were all too busy being heartbroken to notice.

"Do you not see how much harder she is on me? Than the two of you? Do you remember when I stayed out too late with Scotty and she made me sleep on the porch?"

"That didn't happen," Porter said.

"It did. I mean, she came out an hour later and let me sleep in my room, but she did it. Do you remember when Dad died and you came home from school and you and Nicky slept in the same bed for a week? I stayed in my apartment." Elliot sipped his drink.

"You never said you wanted to come sleep over!" Porter said. "Were we supposed to read your mind?"

"You don't get it yet. But you will. And who knows, I probably do it to my kids too. At least right now they're too young to remember."

"Well, **that** doesn't sound ominous at all," Porter said.

Nicky breezed back in and kissed them both on the cheek. "Juliette's coming tomorrow," he said. His beard and breath stank of weed. "We'll surprise Cecelia. Oh, before I forget—I have a question for you guys. Who the hell is Barbara Baker? Mom has mentioned her, like, six times, and I have absolutely no memory of her."

"She was married to Bob Baker, you know? He always used to drive the float at the Harvest Parade? What's most fucked about it is that Mom was right there, like **right there** when it happened. It could have been her so easily. That's what I keep thinking about." Elliot took another sip of his drink.

Porter had just opened her mouth to begin to explain that, in fact, Barbara had been more than a wife to her husband and an unlucky stand-in for their mother when, across the bar, a woman in her midthirties narrowed her eyes at them, a look they all recognized.

"Uh-oh," Nicky said.

The woman slid off her barstool and staggered toward them. "Are you Jake George?" Devotees of Nicky's movie were between the ages of thirty and forty, waist-deep in their life decisions, with a pulsing soft spot for their teenage crushes, those dreamboats who had offered glimpses of what love could be. Cecelia had told Porter that some of the kids in her class had seen the movie, too, and quoted lines that were now screamingly racist and sexist at each other—how had it been less than twenty years ago, when jokes like that seemed permissible, let alone funny? Nicky had been horrified then and he was horrified now, but he was polite, and so he stuck out his hand and said yes. The woman squealed and spun her body around quickly to take a selfie. Nicky had a no-selfie policy, but the woman worked astonishingly fast, given her obvious intoxication, and so after the flash he grabbed his siblings and retreated to their corner. Safety in numbers.

Chapter 36

Astrid Is Ready

Astrid drove Birdie to the shop, dropped her off, and kept driving, her big car slow and heavy on the shadow-dappled roads. October was the most glorious month of the year—the summers could be hot and the winters snowy, but fall was perfection. She could drive these streets blindfolded, if there were no people or dogs to avoid, that was how deeply her muscles knew every turn. She drove past Spiro's, past the grocery store, past Clap Happy's red barn, past the YMCA, past Heron Meadows's fat spider body, past the train station, past Porter's house, past the church where Elliot and Wendy had gotten married, past the junior high school, past the high school, and around the roundabout six times, crisscrossing back and forth across town. Nicky had texted to say he was in town, and had stayed at Porter's for the night, and would come over and visit in the late morning. Nicky back at home made her nervous—she knew he didn't like Clapham, or maybe that he didn't like her. With two parents, there was always someone else to blame for being difficult, but with one, there was no cushion. Astrid wanted to make their relationship better, even though whatever she'd tried to do to make it better usually made it worse. Giving him space, not getting angry when he was out late, the way she'd been with Elliot. She had tried to correct mistakes! That was the problem with being part of a family: Everyone could mean well and it could still be a disaster. Love didn't cure all, not in terms of missed communication and hurt feelings during an otherwise uneventful dinner conversation. Love couldn't change the misread tone of a text message or a quick temper.

She had called Nicky and Juliette individually and explained what had happened at Cecelia's school. At **this** school. Astrid knew that she'd been distracted for the poor girl. If Barbara had died earlier, she might not have said yes to their idea of Cecelia's coming to stay at all. Astrid was happy to have her—she loved Cecelia. The problem was Barbara. The problem was that she, Astrid, a woman, a person, turned out not to be made of steel the way her children thought she was.

It was the first time Nicky had been in Clapham since the twins were born. Three years! Astrid could remember when three years seemed like an eternity, when her children had to count their ages using quarters and halves because an entire year was an endless expanse they could not yet see across. Now three years seemed like days or weeks, except that Nicky was her baby, and long or short, fast or slow, any time without him within her walls felt like a tragedy. But who could she complain to? Porter and Elliot were used to living in Nicky's charismatic shadow, and that wasn't fair, she couldn't complain to them. Russell was gone. And two out of three of her children lived within five minutes—Astrid also couldn't complain to any of her friends, whose children had all moved to Los Angeles or Portland or Chicago, places that required airplanes and scheduled Face-Time dates so that their grandchildren remembered what they looked like. Juliette and Cecelia had come to visit two or three times a year, spending weekends here and there just for fun, to hit up the petting zoo and swim in the local pool, when Brooklyn got too sticky. It wasn't that long, really—they weren't **estranged** or anything horrible like that, he just didn't like to come, and he liked to be by himself, and he liked to travel. Once

children appeared, there were not limitless oppor-
tunities to visit. Astrid understood. It felt greedy,
unseemly even, for a mother to hunger after her
adult son's love.

Astrid turned and found herself on Elliot's
street. She supposed that she had been headed
there from the beginning. It was that way with
children—they each wanted different things.
Where one would always want to be cuddled and
hugged, another would want space and silence.
Astrid had tried, she had tried, to give each of her
children what they needed, but it was an impossible job to do perfectly. She assumed he hadn't
seen his brother yet, and Astrid wanted to invite
Elliot over for dinner—she wanted to have all her
children and grandchildren in the house at the
same time. It was such a simple idea—not for a
holiday or a celebration, where one person was the
center maypole, around whom everyone else spun,
but just because they could, because they were all
alive at the same time, and wasn't it a miracle? The
older Astrid got, the more she understood that she
and her parents and she and her children were as
close as people could be, that generations slipped
away quickly, and that the twenty-five years in between her and her mother and the thirtyish years
in between her and her children were absolutely
nothing, that there were still people who had lived
through the Holocaust, which had happened less
than a decade before she was born, but which her

children had read about in their history textbooks. It happened before you could blink. Her children had been children, and now they were adults; they were all adults here, now.

Astrid parked her car in Elliot's driveway and then rang his bell, which was loud and electronic, an ostentatious imitation of bells. No one answered, and so she tried the knob and found that the door was open. The picture window in the living room showed Wendy and the boys outside. Wendy was on her knees tending to someone's boo-boo. She was a good mother—tough but loving. Astrid respected Wendy, who seemed to have endless patience for two children who could be extremely trying. Astrid thought the twins were more difficult than her own children had been, but the 1980s were a different time, and less had been expected of her. They'd barely had seatbelts. She wanted to offer more to Wendy—more babysitting, more advice, more charming tales about Elliot and his siblings as small children, but she knew it would be unwelcome and so she kept her mouth shut. Whenever she had let herself start to babble about something tiny baby Elliot had done, the way he'd plop down on his fat diaper when he was learning to walk, Elliot would narrow his eyes and stare at her like she was asking about the current state of his bowel movements.

———

Elliot's office door was closed. It was such a big house—Aidan and Zachary shared a room, and the other bedrooms, for additional children Wendy and Elliot might have had, were used for absurd purposes that they had brainstormed out of necessity: a home gym, a playroom, a library, for which they had purchased leather-bound, hard-back books by the foot, books that they never even remotely intended to read. Astrid knocked on the door and waited for Elliot's response. She heard him sigh, already exasperated, and then slowly turned the knob.

Elliot was golfing. That is, he was pretending to golf, with a video game on the TV screen. Astrid hated that he had a television in his office. That wasn't an office, it was a clubhouse, a teenager's fantasy of what grown-up life was like.

"Hi, Mom," Elliot said, without turning around.

"How did you know it was me?" Astrid asked.

Elliot bent his elbows back in a faux swing, only a tiny controller in his hands, and whacked a pre-tend ball high into the simulacrum of a blue sky.

A score appeared on the screen, and then Elliot clicked a button, turning the screen gray; he tossed the controller onto his desk. "What's up?"

"I wanted to talk to you about a couple of things, can I sit?" Astrid pointed toward the leather chair opposite Elliot's desk. He nodded, and she sat primly, ankles crossed, with her purse on her lap.

Elliot picked up his phone off his desk and

pressed some buttons. "Sure. I have a call soon, about a thing, but yeah." He sat on the edge of his desk like an impatient high school principal.

Her heart was beating fast in her chest, thumping closer to the surface than usual. She looked at Elliot's body, still as slim as when he was a boy. There was no fixed point in a person's life, no definitive period. Yes, one's friends from childhood always seemed like grown-up versions of children, and work colleagues were hard to imagine as adolescents with elaborate orthodontia, but when Astrid looked at her eldest son, she saw all of him at once: the sporty teen, the charming toddler, the inconsolable baby, the law student, the husband, the new father. All of them here, all of them exactly Elliot.

"I'm sorry," Astrid said. Elliot had moved from the desk to stand before the window. She stood now behind him, both of them staring out at the lawn. Zachary and Aidan were outside, taking turns whacking Wiffle balls off a plastic T-ball stand. They swung their whole little bodies every time, nearly falling to the ground, no matter if they hit the ball or not. Wendy was sitting a safe distance away in an Adirondack chair. The boys were rough on people and things but not each other, and Astrid liked watching them wait patiently and rotate through their batting lineup of two.

Elliot stiffened. "Did Porter call you? Wendy?"

"About what? No, honey, **I** need to apologize to

you." She'd been doing it wrong; he didn't understand. "It's about Barbara Baker, actually. She was the one who told me that she'd seen you, do you remember?"

Elliot turned around to look at her. The sun was shining behind him, which put his face in shadow. "Jesus, Nicky was right, you are obsessed with Barbara Baker. It's weird. Do I remember what?"

For a moment, Astrid wondered if she'd concocted the whole thing, if it had been a dream. But no: She could tell the difference between her imagination and her memory, at least most of the time. "You were in the seventh grade. I told you that someone had told me that they'd seen you. That someone had seen you. On the rocks, by the water. With that sweet boy, the one who moved away. And I told you to stop whatever it was that you were doing. That's what I'm apologizing for." It was too little, of course, too little and too late by decades. But still, Astrid felt something lift off her shoulders the moment the words were out of her mouth. "I'm sorry, my love. It must have had more to do with me than I realized. You weren't doing anything wrong."

Elliot cocked his head to one side. His face—what she could see—was impassive. "I don't remember that," he said. There was a **thunk** outside, but neither of them turned to look. The boys were cheering. One of them had connected and sent the ball sailing through the air. Wendy was clapping, and they could hear the sharp smacks of her flat palms.

"Your friend, Jack? His parents moved to California, to Berkeley, I'm pretty sure. Not too far from where Wendy's from, actually. You don't remember him?" Childhood was infuriating this way—she'd felt it over and over, when one of her children (all three of them!) would inevitably forget the words to a song she'd sung to them five hundred times, or a book they'd read, curled up together, six, seven, eight times a day, and then time passed and they had no recollection, and the information was stuck there in Astrid's head, marked as important. Maybe this was just another **Runaway Bunny,** something that she'd weighed down with meaning over the years until it was an anvil around her neck, when really, it was her own anvil, not his. "Oh," Astrid said. "Well. He was a boy, and you were close friends." She stopped there.

"It's okay, Mom," Elliot said, finally. "It's fine. I'm sure it wasn't that bad, whatever it was." Elliot's phone began to vibrate on his desk, and he jerked himself away. "I have to take this." He picked up the phone and said hello, and then he opened his office door and waited for his mother to leave. Astrid stepped into the hall and then Elliot closed the door behind her. She had done it. She had done it. Astrid lifted her chin and saw herself out.

Chapter 37

Couples Massage

The first time, Porter and Jeremy had broken up in person, and so this time, it seemed fine to do it over the phone. Porter thought that her resolve would be stronger if she didn't have to look at his face. She didn't know why his face was so irresistible to her, but it was. Diabetics didn't have to stare at a fridge full of Coca-Colas when they went cold turkey. Sometimes the easy way out was fine.

It was a weekday, and so Porter called the clinic. His assistant, whose name was either Stephanie or Tracy, Porter could never remember, put him on. Porter's heart was beating fast, but she knew what she had to do.

"Hey," Jeremy said.

"Hey," Porter said. "Again. I know I've said it

before, but this was all my fault, us doing this again. It's not good for either of us. Right? Don't you think?" She hated herself for asking the question, as if it was an open matter, still to be decided.

"That's what you always say." She could hear the smirk in his voice. Jeremy didn't need to be sitting in front of her, Porter could see his face just as clearly over the phone.

"Yeah, well. This time I mean it. Bye, Jeremy." She clicked the phone off before he had a chance to respond. Her tear ducts were dry, but her hands were shaking. Porter closed her eyes and took a deep breath. In the momentary dark, she could see it all: the two of them as idiot kids, herself in the parade, the cold waiting room, the first time they'd slept together afterward, the first time they'd slept together after he got married. Porter wanted to be better than she was. If her brothers were right, parenthood was all about making mistakes. Now that she was so close, Porter wanted to start making them by accident instead of on purpose. Maybe someday she'd tell Elliot that she'd listened to him. She exhaled again and then picked her phone back up. Porter scrolled through her contacts until she found what she was looking for. She hit Call and waited for a few rings. When Rachel answered, Porter got right to it.

"I have a plan."

At four P.M., Porter was standing in a parking lot when Rachel pulled up. It wasn't a Parade Crew day, and so she was free right after school. They were both bigger now, Porter saw, well past the point of plausible deniability. Rachel's coat was open, her belly laughing at the idea of a zipper.

"Hi there, pregnant lady," Rachel said.

"Hello there, pregnant lady," Porter said back. They hugged, and Porter slung her arm around Rachel's shoulders.

"So what exactly is happening here?" She pointed to the building they were standing behind. It was the Seascape Spa, never mind that the sea was hours away. "Pedicures?"

"Oh no," Porter said, guiding her down the stone path toward the door. "You'll see."

The young woman inside took their coats. The sound of a babbling brook came from speakers in every corner of the room, which made it feel less like a brook and more like being caught in the bottom of a drain during a torrential downpour.

"I have to pee," Rachel said.

"What else is new?" Porter asked, and knocked into her shoulder.

The receptionist offered them both mocktail mimosas—orange juice mixed with seltzer. "I think half a glass of champagne won't hurt us," Rachel said. "What do you think, Port?"

"For sure," Porter said. The girl squirmed, clearly uncomfortable, visions of brain damage dancing in her head. "Just the orange juice is fine." The girl melted, relieved, and left them alone in a room filled with overstuffed chairs and a large fake fireplace.

"Mmm," Rachel said. She took a sip and then sank into one of the chairs. "I can almost taste the three drops of mediocre champagne she was thinking about pouring in."

Porter took a sip too. "Oh yes. Hints of citrus."

Two women poked their heads into the waiting room. "Couples massage?" said the taller, sturdier woman.

"Yep," Porter said. She reached for Rachel's hand. "Let's do it, baby."

Rachel laughed. "When you think about it, it's more than a couples massage—it's a quadruples massage."

The tall, sturdy woman and her short, stout counterpart led Porter and Rachel down a dimly lit hallway into an even dimmer room. In it, there were two massage tables side by side, the covers pulled back in crisp identical triangles. In the center of each table was a divot—a hole.

"What in the world?" Rachel asked. She touched the hole with her fingers.

"It's for your belly, miss. If you'd rather not, you can always stay on your side. But some of our clients prefer it."

Rachel looked up at Porter. "You got me a hole."

She began to laugh. Her body shook, a cartoon Santa.

"I'm sorry for being an a-hole. I didn't plan that joke, but I think it works, don't you?" Porter asked.

Rachel offered a generous chuckle. "Wait, I still have to pee." She toddled down the dark hallway while Porter took off her clothes and tried her best to maneuver herself gracefully under the cover. Her belly slid into the hole. It felt like swimming. She closed her eyes and listened to the flush from the bathroom, and then to the sound of Rachel making her way back in, and taking off her clothes layer by layer, with no small amount of grunting. Porter listened to Rachel climb up on the table and assume the same position.

"Aaaahhh," Rachel said, from the face cradle. "This is great."

"It hasn't even started yet," Porter said. She slid her left arm out from under the sheet and reached into the gully between the two tables. "Rach," she said. Rachel picked up her face and saw Porter's hand, then slid her right arm out to meet it. They clasped fingers. Porter wanted to tell Rachel that she'd finally done it, gotten rid of Jeremy, but as far as Rachel knew, she already had long before.

"Ready?" one of the therapists said from the dark hallway, where they were waiting in total silence, like assassins.

"Ready," Porter and Rachel said, in unison.

They let go of each other's hands, and Porter felt happy to be alone, together, each of them in their own bodies, with their unknown passengers floating inside, like ocean liners sailing across a dark ocean. Alone, together, and full.

Chapter 38

Parents Come Home

Astrid and Cecelia were planning to spend the afternoon making sign-up sheets for the newly reinvigorated Keep Local, Shop Small petition—Astrid bought half a dozen clipboards, and a brand-new box of pens. It was Astrid's idea to reinvigorate. The plan was to assemble their materials at home, drive downtown, park the car, and spend the day walking up and down Main Street, collecting signatures. Cecelia had agreed to participate as part of her punishment, though it had become clear that all her punishments existed in quotation marks and could also just be described as pleasant time spent with friends and family. Cecelia had asked August to help, and he had agreed, as long as his parents didn't need him at the shop. They were sitting at the kitchen table when the doorbell rang.

"Get that, would you?" Astrid asked. She pulled down her glasses and looked at Cecelia over the bridge of her nose.

Cecelia shrugged and slumped off her chair. She pulled open the heavy door without looking through the peephole, because no one in Clapham ever used a peephole, because if it was a homicidal maniac, the door was probably unlocked anyway, so why bother.

Her parents were standing on the oversize doormat, a small suitcase behind each of them. Her father had trimmed his beard, Cecelia could tell, and her mother's skin looked brown and freckled, as it always did in late summer and early fall. Their mouths were open in frozen smiles, as if posing for a photograph.

"Mom? Dad?" Cecelia felt a lump in her throat and swallowed over and over again, willing it away.

Juliette stepped forward first, pulling her daughter close to her chest, and when Cecelia's face was buried in her mother's hair, and she smelled her perfume, and her natural deodorant that never worked very well, and the smell of her laundry detergent, a smell she'd never actually thought of before, until she smelled it right at this moment, that was when the lump got too big to swallow away, and she buried her face in farther, so that no one would notice that she had started to cry. Her father

reached around her, closing her into the middle of
a parent sandwich.

Cecelia had so rarely been in the Big House without her parents before moving in, but now it was
strange to have them there, like suddenly having
visitors to a zoo be able to climb over the barri-
ers and into the cages. Cecelia wasn't sure which
animal she'd be—maybe one of the wild ones that
looked just like a regular dog, so kids would get up
to the edge of the enclosure, peer in, and quickly
move on. After coming in and kissing Astrid hello,
both of Cecelia's parents followed her up to her
bedroom.

Nicky walked the perimeter of the room, touching the curtains and the knobs on the dresser and
the scalloped edges of the full-length mirror. He
eventually settled in the cushioned window seat
and sat with crossed legs, his hairy toes wiggling
inside his sandals.

"I always liked this room. It has the best light,"
Nicky said.

Juliette crawled on top of Cecelia's bed with
her. "This is a nice room. It's big!" Cecelia let her
mother pull her close, two spoons of the same size.
Cecelia had her father's face, her father's hair, her
father's skin. Unless your father was Brad Pitt,
that wasn't what you wanted. Cecelia had always
wanted more proof that her mother's beauty had

contributed to her makeup. Having her mother's body so close reminded her of all the ways it hadn't: the way Juliette's ankles looked in sneakers, with a deep hollow on either side, a body part asking to be photographed for a magazine; the way Juliette's shirts hung off her collarbones like a shirt on a hanger. Her body was never awkward unless she wanted it to be. Cecelia felt the exact way about herself, only perfectly inverted. She was always awkward. Even being hugged by her mother, Cecelia wasn't sure where to put her arms.

"So who is this girl at school?" Nicky asked. "What happened?"

"Do we have to talk about it already? She's just a girl who is not very nice," Cecelia said. "I know I shouldn't have hit her. I wasn't planning on it. And I do have self-control, most of the time."

"And she's Jeremy Fogelman's daughter?" Nicky asked, a curious eyebrow lifted.

"Who's Jeremy Fogelman?" Juliette asked, into her daughter's neck.

"Porter's high school boyfriend. A human lacrosse stick." Nicky shook his head and rubbed his cheeks, as if it would will his beard to grow faster.

"What's lacrosse?" Juliette asked. "It's like hockey?"

Cecelia loved the sound of her mother saying English words she wasn't used to—**hoe-key**.

"Yes," Nicky said. "Less violent, more likely to wear boat shoes."

"Hmm," Juliette said. "Okay. But what did she say to you, **amour**? What did she do?"

"She said some really mean things to my friend, August." Cecelia had resolved not to tell August's secret, which made it hard to talk about, but she also thought that August would understand. Not at school, of course, just with her own parents, so that they would understand why she had done such a thing. She closed her eyes and pulled her mother's arms tighter around her body. After a few minutes of pretending to sleep, Cecelia actually did feel herself begin to drift in and out, and she pictured herself floating on a raft in between islands. Every time she got close to one, she would bounce off some undersea rocks and head back out to sea.

At home, when things got so bad that she actually wanted to talk to her parents about it, Cecelia and her father would sit on opposite sides of the bathroom door and talk, their voices only slightly muffled by the wood. It was the only actual door in the apartment. Right now her eyelids were the wood. Cecelia heard her father pad across the rug and then felt the bottom corner of the mattress sag when he sat down by her feet.

Cecelia hadn't wanted to say anything about Katherine—it sounded like envy, she knew, to have a complaint about a friend's older boyfriend. That's what Katherine said, that Cecelia was jealous, that she **wished** guys were trying to meet her online.

It had happened before, people sending Katherine messages. But this was the first time she'd actually met up with someone. Katherine said that Cecelia didn't understand because she wasn't a woman yet—she still wanted to play make-believe. Two weeks later, Katherine told Cecelia that the guy had locked her in his apartment and masturbated in front of her, while she sat on the couch next to him. She'd tried to make it sound funny, like she was in on the joke, and this was what adults did, but Cecelia knew that it wasn't, and she wasn't, and it was most certainly not okay. It was so hard to tell someone what they didn't want to hear, and Cecelia had agonized about telling her parents, knowing that it would turn into her telling more and more people, until she might as well have stood outside Katherine's window with a bullhorn. It was hard enough when it was your own story, but telling someone else's? Cecelia knew it was both indefensible and the only truly right thing to do. She had to betray her friend to make sure nothing worse happened to her. What would happen to August if she whispered to her father? Would her mother make her repeat it, not understanding? Would they call the school? Cecelia wanted to be good. She wanted to have good thoughts and be surrounded by good people. August (Robin!) was her friend, and she wanted to do right by him. By **her**. She wanted to do right by her.

Cecelia felt her father lie down, too, his head at

her feet. The rest of his body folded along the bottom edge of the bed. Her mother shifted to make room for him, and Cecelia exhaled, knowing that parts of their bodies were touching, in silence, and that they had to be feeling things too. It was too enormous to imagine what, like trying to imagine what babies remembered from the womb.

"I'm so sorry, honey," her father said. He propped himself up, which Cecelia could see through her eyelashes.

"She's asleep, love," Juliette said. "Let her sleep."

Cecelia felt the bed shift as her father reached for her mother's foot.

"I just hate feeling like we let her down," Nicky said. He exhaled loudly. "This never would have happened if we'd kept her in school. We could have fought with those fucks. God, I hate Katherine's parents. And we let them win."

Cecelia's heart was beating fast. Her father never said anything bad about anybody. And he never apologized, either. The downside of Buddhism, as Cecelia understood it, and also of years of therapy, was that no one ever seemed to think anything was their fault. Everything was always open to everyone else's feelings, or the ultimate balance of the universe. If the point of life was to let things go, then you never had to be sorry about anything.

"It's okay, **amour,**" Juliette said. "Come."

Nicky rolled onto all fours and crawled up the

side of the bed. Juliette inched closer to Cecelia, and Nicky lay down behind her, three anchovies in a full-size tin.

Cecelia let herself drift in and out of her parents' breath. It didn't matter that they were late or that they had done the wrong thing. What mattered was that they were sorry, and that they had come for her.

Chapter 39

Team Kids, Part One

There were teams in every family, alliances that buoyed the affiliated over the tides of any given trauma or daily boredom. Everyone needed a second-in-command, a buddy, a consigliore. When Elliot was born, it was Astrid and Elliot together against the world. When Porter was born, Russell and Elliot became a duo so that Astrid could feed Porter a thousand times a day, and change her diapers on the wobbly wooden console table in her bedroom. The family shifted like that for years, until all three children were school age and no one had an immediate claim on their mother that overrode the others' needs. Porter and Nicky were thick as thieves, always banding together when a family vote was necessary: if it was time to stop for the bathroom, whether to watch **Alice in Wonderland** or **Robin Hood** for the trillionth time, who got to sit in the **back** back of the car. Of course Nicky went to see Porter first. Astrid could only have been miffed if she'd been surprised. It didn't matter—he was here now, under her roof. It wasn't that Astrid felt **intimidated** by her youngest child, not exactly, but she did feel like by moving away, Nicky had cast doubt on all her parenting choices. It seemed not only likely but probable that he understood something (things!) that she didn't.

Astrid and Birdie went shopping for dinner. It was unclear what Nicky ate—Soup? Vegetables?— but Astrid knew that she wanted to feed everyone. Birdie had spent her whole adult life as a single person, a single addition to Thanksgiving meals and wedding receptions, and she seemed to be enjoying the chaotic nature of parenthood, and the challenge of cooking for a brood. She recommended tacos, which sounded interactive and fun and easy to alter for Nicky's vegetarian diet. Astrid watched as Birdie filled their cart with things she didn't have in her kitchen: three different kinds of chilies, a pineapple, cilantro, cabbage.

"This is nice," Astrid said, walking alongside Birdie, who pushed their cart. "I feel like I'm on a date and you're trying to impress me."

"You are on a date," Birdie said, kissing Astrid on the cheek. "But I don't need to impress you."

They checked out and carried the heavy bags

to the car. The grocery store was on Main Street, two blocks before the roundabout, with a large parking lot set behind a wooden fence. From the front door, Astrid looked straight down Main Street. Clapham was lovely in the fall. The leaves had begun to drop, and the ones on the trees were starting to turn yellow and orange and red. It was a beautiful town. And now it had all three of her children in it. Astrid took a few steps away from the parking lot. Cars slowed as they approached the stop sign before the roundabout and stopped when a person stepped out into the road to cross the street. People were polite here, on the whole. They were rule followers, and do-gooders. They voted in midterm elections. They mowed their lawns.

"Did you ever think about moving back to Texas?" Astrid turned her face but kept looking forward.

Birdie set her chin on Astrid's shoulder. "No. I like winter. When I was a kid, we'd sometimes get these catalogs in the mail that had winter coats in them, and I would fold down the pages. Boots too. I love winter boots."

"Do you think Clapham is an okay place? I don't know, I've just been thinking. Is the town too small? Should I have moved somewhere else, after Russell died?" A woman stepped into the white crosswalk and held up her hand to stop an oncoming pickup truck, as if her small hand could stop all that steel. Astrid held her breath, but the truck squeaked to a stop with room to spare. It was easiest to worry backward, when you couldn't change course even if you wanted to, or sideways, into equally impossible parallel universes. Astrid could no sooner leave Clapham than grow wings.

"It's very okay," Birdie said. "Even nice. And if you'd gone somewhere better, you wouldn't have me." She set down the bags she was carrying and rubbed Astrid's forearms. "Let's go roast some pork, it'll make you feel better."

It turned out Nicky wasn't a vegetarian anymore. Children didn't have to tell you anything. He came into the kitchen when Birdie was expertly slicing peppers with a sharp knife, and he immediately began to help. Astrid sat down and watched Nicky and Birdie work together.

He'd always been like this—easy to incorporate, easy to get along with. Even as a teenager, Nicky had been able to hold long conversations with middle-aged women about gardening and dog training and other things he didn't ostensibly know anything about. He was a good listener.

"I want to have everyone over this weekend," Astrid said. "I don't know how long you and Juliette are planning to stay, but I really want to have all three kiddos and all three grandchildren here at the same time." Birdie had assigned Astrid the guacamole, and she was dutifully slicing the soft avocados in half and scooping the green flesh into a large bowl.

"Sure," Nicky said. He was slicing garlic now, doing whatever Birdie put in front of him. "But I saw Elliot last night. Porter and I made him come to Buddy's with us."

"Buddy's!" Astrid whooped. "The three of you? I had no idea." She felt a pang of jealousy at not having been invited, though of course she was also overjoyed that her children cared enough about one another to get together without her pushing. Astrid grabbed the onion on her cutting board and sliced it in half. Tears sprang to her eyes immediately, as they always did. Why had no one figured out how to fix that problem?

"Yeah, he came with us," Nicky said.

"How does he seem to you? I think he and Wendy are having some problems. I don't know. He just seems so unhappy, and work seems fine, and the boys seem fine. I just assume. I know it's none of my business, but I really think so. I've tried to talk to him about it, but he's so hard to get through to." Astrid wiped her eyes with her sleeve. "Yeesh."

"I think Wendy's fine. I mean, it's an adjustment, them working together, but I don't think that's the problem." Nicky looked up, biting his lip, and waited to see if his mother would pounce.

"She's working with him? At Strick Brick? No

one tells me anything. You know, I do worry that he doesn't have enough business. I know it was so important for him to hang his own shingle, but are people hiring him? Does he have enough projects?" Astrid looked up, her eyes swimmy.

"Oh, I'm sure his business is okay," Birdie said. She lifted a lid off a pot on the stove and the whole kitchen filled with a warm, smoky smell. She looked at Nicky. "Did he talk to you about any new projects?"

Nicky cocked his head to one side. "He did. Did he talk to you?"

"He did," Birdie said, her voice low. "The kids and I were at the shop the other night, and we saw Elliot by the roundabout. Seemed to be checking out some properties."

Nicky locked eyes with Birdie. "Oh yeah?"

"What on earth are you talking about?" Astrid was still crying. She slid out from behind the table and carried her cutting board over to the counter. "Checking out what properties?"

The front door opened. Cecelia and Juliette were laughing—Juliette had driven Astrid's car to pick up some wine in town, after not having driven in a decade. Astrid still wanted to teach Cecelia how to drive—before there was too much snow on the ground, she was going to do it.

"Hi, sweetheart," Nicky said. Cecelia wound her way around everyone and to the stove. Birdie lifted the lid again and let Cecelia breathe in the steam.

"Oh, yum," Cecelia said. "I'm so hungry."

"Doesn't Gammy feed you?" Nicky said. He winked at his mother, knowing the exasperated sounds that would begin to bubble in her throat. "I'm joking, Mom."

"No, wait, I don't want us to get off topic," Astrid said. She put her hands on Cecelia's shoulders, as if to claim physical responsibility, though of course the girl belonged to her parents more. "What did Elliot do? What's the business? What are you talking about?"

Cecelia froze. "You told her?" She looked at Birdie.

Birdie shook her head. "I didn't."

Juliette snuggled her body against Nicky's, no matter that he was holding a large knife. "It's fine, Mom." Nicky made a face at Birdie. "I think?"

"Who knows," Birdie said. "People have tried before."

"People have tried WHAT? Okay, right now, one of you tell me what's going on!" Astrid shouted. "Where do you want these onions, Birdie?"

Birdie gestured. "Just put them there. Honey, it's fine." She looked to Cecelia, and then Nicky. Cecelia covered her ears, but Birdie was calm. "Honey, he's trying. The building on the roundabout. He bought it. Which is great. We actually had a good conversation about it." Cecelia slowly lowered herself to the floor and crawled under the table.

"And I don't want to tell tales out of school, but he's been talking to some big places," Nicky said.

"Big places? Bird, you knew about this?" Astrid looked back and forth between them. "What's a big place? A chain? Which one?" Visions of Clapham as a shopping mall danced in her head. "Why does no one tell me anything? How is it possible that everyone else knows this but me? I am the only person who actually asks him anything, and he tells me nothing! What am I doing wrong? Someone, tell me, please! What am I doing wrong?" Astrid was shaking—it was just like with Porter. How many things had she missed, how many choices, how many mistakes, how many heartbreaks? She had no idea what mattered to any of them, what was boiling inside. She was asking! She had asked. Watching Barbara get hit had made her want to be honest, but it wouldn't work if the honesty went in only one direction. Astrid felt like she were walking through spiderwebs, trying to claw to the surface. Everything she knew about Porter had been about her daughter being carefree and aimless, Peter Pan. Now that she knew about the abortion, did she need to go back and recalibrate, to reinterpret everything that came after? And if Elliot was happy in his marriage and buying up historic buildings in the middle of town, was he happy? She thought she'd done something so awful, this one thing, and maybe it was awful. It was. But what else had she missed with Elliot, because that moment was all she could see?

"Well," Nicky said, gently. "I think you're finally starting to ask the right questions." Astrid looked at her beautiful baby, eyes oniony just like hers. There had to be things she'd done wrong to him too. God. Astrid wished that there was a button everyone could push that immediately showed only their good intentions—how much pain that would save. Nicky could see it, she thought. He kissed her on the cheek.

Chapter 40

The Harvest Parade

The Harvest Festival Parade was scheduled for ten A.M. on a Friday. The rest of the Harvest weekend was for tourists and returning weekenders, putting in one last good-weather hurrah before retreating until Christmas, but the parade was for the town, homegrown and proud. All around the roundabout, and up and down Main Street, people set up folding chairs starting at dawn, staking out their spots. Parents brought bags of snacks for their toddlers and let them run wild in the temporarily closed-off streets. Wesley Drewes was set up at a booth, broadcasting live, and people stopped to take selfies with his gloved hand waving in the background. The air smelled like apple cider and cinnamon donuts, both of which were available at a stand in front of Spiro's,

Olympia ladling out the steaming cider into paper cups. Cecelia, August, and the rest of the Parade Crew stood behind their creation about fifty feet up Main Street, just out of sight. And, oh, what a sight it was.

Cecelia had not had much faith. The float was really just a decorated platform on the back of a small flatbed truck, and Cecelia's only skills were following directions and not gluing her fingers together. August and Ms. Skolnick and the rest of the crew, however, had made something magnificent. Not only had they built a small-scale gazebo that looked exactly like the actual gazebo at one-eighth of the size, they'd made waist-high miniatures of the entire roundabout. There was a tiny bookstore, a tiny Spiro's, a tiny Shear Beauty, a tiny vacant storefront, tiny trees, tiny benches, the whole shebang. Cecelia had helped glue down the AstroTurf grass. She had painted planks of particleboard. August had sewn tiny curtains and cut out hundreds of multicolored leaves. The whole thing sat on a circular platform that could be rotated, very slowly, by a member of the Parade Crew walking alongside the float.

"This could be your job," Cecelia said to August. "Making things."

August rolled his eyes. "That sounds lucrative. But thank you."

Ms. Skolnick shooed them all together. Megan and James, so moved by their work, had their tongues halfway down each other's throats, and their hands shoved into each other's back pockets, cupping and squeezing to their heart's content. "Please, guys," Ms. Skolnick said, lowering her camera. "This is PG." They all smiled and squished together. For the first time, Cecelia could see Clapham—big Clapham—in her future. She and August going to the prom together in complementary gowns, Porter's baby learning how to walk toward Cecelia's encouraging hands. It wouldn't be so bad. It could even be nice. It was like the Thanksgiving balloons, only smaller. The high school had a float, and so did the fire department, and the Elks Lodge, whatever that was. They were all lined up in a row, a tiny armada. Ms. Skolnick handed out branches—real branches with large, watercolored leaves—for the crew members to wave along the route, which sounded both like wholesome fun and complete and total humiliation, depending on your perspective.

"Reporting for duty," someone said, and Cecelia spun around to look.

Sidney stood with her arms crossed, a small beige Band-Aid stretched across the bridge of her nose. Cecelia didn't think that there was an accompanying bruise, but even if there had been, Sidney was wearing enough makeup to cover it and then some: Her eyelids sparkled gold, her lips were magenta, and the rest of her skin had been shellacked into a solid peach mask. No matter that it was high fall, and everyone in front of Spiro's was wearing a fleece zip-up—Sidney was wearing a strapless party dress that flared out at her knees. Her bare arms and legs were already pimpled with goose bumps.

"Oh, great," Ms. Skolnick said. "Right this way, all aboard." She kicked a small stepladder over to the side of the float and held up her arm for balance. Sidney teetered up, her ankles wobbling in heels. When she got to the platform, she lightly rested a finger on the top of the gazebo, which came up to her waist. "Cute." She made a face that neither confirmed nor denied that she was speaking earnestly. Sidney rubbed her arms and bounced on her toes. "Everyone else should be here soon."

She meant the rest of the Clapham Junior High Harvest Festival Court, of which she was the queen. There had been no surprises in the listing of the names: Sidney, Liesel, Bailey. No one had any imagination. But that wasn't what Cecelia was thinking about. She and August walked around to the opposite side of the float and stood behind the model of Shear Beauty. Cecelia peered inside, as if expecting to find tiny models of Birdie and her gammy.

"Hey!" Cecelia said. "Are you sure about this?"

August held up a tote bag. "As ready as I'm going to be. Come back and change with me?"

Cecelia nodded. "Hey, Ms. Skolnick, we'll

be right back, okay? We're just running to the bathroom."

Ms. Skolnick looked at her phone. "We've got ten minutes. Go fast, okay?"

Cecelia and August hurried down the block and into the municipal hall, which had the nicest public bathrooms. They went into the single stall together.

"I'm really nervous," Cecelia said. "Not for me, but for you. Are you sure you want to do this? I know I already asked you that, but I just don't want anyone to be mean to you. Are you doing this because I hit Sidney?"

August set a tote bag down on a chair and pulled a long dress out of it. Cecelia recognized the dress from Secondhand News—it had been on a mannequin in the window. It was pale yellow, from the 1970s, made of polyester, with floaty sleeves, a dress made for dancing. "Cecelia," she said. "This isn't about you."

"I know," Cecelia said. "I know it's not. I just don't want to be responsible for pushing you to do this before you're ready."

August smoothed out the dress and held it against her body. "I promise," she said. "I wouldn't do this if I wasn't ready." Then she pulled her T-shirt over her head. She was wearing a padded bra—Cecelia had the same one, and her heart fluttered a little bit, realizing how much more she and August had in common than she thought, how many things there would be for them to talk about, always. She took the dress out of August's hands and unzipped it, holding out the wide opening for her friend. August rested one hand lightly on Cecelia's shoulder and stepped into the dress before sliding her jeans off her hips. Cecelia tied the string around her neck and then, together, they looked in the mirror. And then there she was. She'd taken her costume off.

"Okay, Robin," Cecelia said.

Robin looked at her in the mirror. They were two girls standing side by side. Robin pulled her hair out of its bun, and it tumbled down past her shoulders. Cecelia could see it all: Robin as an adult being so proud of everything she'd done, of herself, and wishing that she had taken more than one minute to do her hair. Cecelia could see further too: some future Clapham High School reunion, the first one that Cecelia could convince Robin to come to—Cecelia could see Sidney Fogelman sheepishly approach her at the punch bowl, and Robin be as gracious as possible, while patiently waiting to talk to someone she had actually liked in school. She would apologize, Sidney, and that would make the conversation tolerable, until she'd awkwardly try to follow Robin into the bathroom to keep catching up.

Porter stood next to Nicky in front of Shear Beauty. Elliot and Wendy were on her other side, trying to keep the twins from disappearing into the crowd. Astrid and Birdie were inside, and Juliette was sneaking a cigarette around the corner. Being French was like being a teenager forever, gorgeous and immortal.

"Her float is first," Porter said, tugging on Nicky's sleeve. She regretted saying it right away—it must have been hard for Nicky and Juliette to come to town and see that she and her mother knew so much more about Cece's life, that they knew her teachers and her friends. Her friend. They knew something, at least.

"I'm nervous," Nicky said. "I don't know why, but I'm nervous."

Juliette came back and reached her hand across Porter's lap like a seatbelt, and Nicky took it. Porter tried to make herself invisible, but it was hard, especially because the belly that Nicky's and Juliette's hands were clasped around was full and hard, a person-filled balloon. The baby kicked, as if on cue, and both Nicky and Juliette turned toward their hands, as if their touch had caused a tiny earthquake.

"Was that her?" Nicky asked.

Juliette nodded, because mothers know. Juliette held on to Nicky's hand with her left hand, but shifted her body so that she could put her right hand flat against Porter's belly. The baby pressed out, as if in response. **"Bonjour,"** Juliette said, her voice soft. Porter watched as Juliette looked up at Nicky. She watched them remember Juliette's belly, with Cecelia inside, a miraculous, invisible fish. People touched her belly all the time—acquaintances at the grocery store, Dr. McConnell, people she barely knew, her mother, Jeremy—but everyone reacted like meeting a cute puppy on the sidewalk: charmed, sure, but not moved to tears. Everyone who touched her had been closer to other pregnancies before, ones that mattered more to them, and were just using Porter's body as a time machine into their own memories. But Nicky and Juliette cared—this baby mattered to them, which meant that she mattered to them. She was already someone's mother, Porter. It had happened. The baby was there, and growing. She was listening. She was paying attention.

There was applause down the block—the parade had started. Aidan and Zachary cheered, and Elliot and Wendy each hoisted one child into the air. Nicky spun around to knock on the window at Shear Beauty to let his mother know. Porter and Juliette were craning their necks to see the floats begin their slow journey. It was like watching manatees race.

Cecelia and Robin left the bathroom holding hands. Their dresses were long, and they were wearing matching beaded sweaters, but still, the air was chilly and they were nervous. Cecelia thought she heard kids laughing, but the whole town was at the parade, and everyone was in a good mood—who was to say what anyone was laughing at. They forged through the crowd back to their float, where Ms. Skolnick was looking back and forth from her phone to the crowd, clearly searching for them.

"Oh thank god, you guys, come on! We're up first. The queens are restless!" She pointed toward the shivering threesome atop the tiny round-about. Megan was doing an interpretive dance that looked remarkably like Regina George's Santa Claus dance in **Mean Girls,** and Cecelia couldn't tell if it was supposed to be mocking Sidney and her posse or titillating James, but it seemed to be doing both. Sidney and Liesel scowled down at her while Bailey posed for photographs, pictures that the other two would no doubt veto before she posted them, rendering them all but useless. Then Ms. Skolnick noticed that they'd changed clothes. "Oh. Hi. You look fantastic, August. You, too, Cecelia. But August. Truly, gorgeous."

"You can call me Robin. Call me Robin. Could you call me Robin?" She curtsied.

"Robin, yes, I sure can," Ms. Skolnick said. "You know what?" The driver of the truck honked. It was their turn. The Parade Crew had gathered around, rubbing their hands together, waiting for instructions. The only person who didn't look cold was the kid with the beard and the shorts, who never looked cold, not even in February. "How would you feel about riding up top, Robin?"

It would mean waving. It would mean smiling. It would mean standing close to Sidney and Liesel and Bailey, and taking photos. It would mean a picture in the yearbook, with all their names printed underneath. **Robin Sullivan, eighth grade**. It would mean an introduction, a debut, a thousand corrections, confusion, applause. Robin turned to Cecelia.

"You can do it," said Cecelia. "I'm right here, we're all right here. I'll be your bodyguard. Not that you need one."

"Okay, yes," Robin said.

"Wonderful," Ms. Skolnick said. "Sidney, make room!" The three girls already aboard the float scuttled backward. It wasn't a lot of room, especially because the gazebo took up the whole center of the float, and so they had to circle the small white structure with their bodies, which made it harder to see, but nobody cared. Robin stepped up onto the float and smiled.

"Wow," Bailey said. "You look, like, amazing."

"Yeah," Liesel said. She looked Robin up and down. "I love that dress."

"Thanks," Robin said. "I like yours too." Her eyes flickered down to Cecelia's, to let her know that she was just being kind, because it was a kind moment, that Cecelia's vigilance was appreciated but unnecessary. That Cecelia could stand down, at least for now. Cecelia understood: They were Sidney's henchmen, but really they were just stupid magpies, going toward whatever was most glittery. They didn't have any real allegiance to Sidney; they were probably terrified of her. It was just that Sidney was the most beautiful girl in their class, and glamour had power. Bailey and Liesel just wanted a model to copy, to make themselves feel better about the miasma of junior high. And Robin was suddenly the most glamorous person in sight. It didn't mean there wouldn't be mean things said, or bumps along the way, but Cecelia saw that Robin herself was what would make it easy for girls like Liesel and Bailey, who could look at her and see themselves—pretty. Even the shallow could be accepting. It was oddly comforting.

The float started to move, and Cecelia stayed close to the side that Robin was on both for emotional support and physical support, just in case. She was the spotter. Sidney was facing forward and stumbled on her heels when the float started up—she didn't have a spotter, not really, and for a split second, Cecelia felt bad for her. Sidney stared straight ahead like someone trying to drive through a thunderstorm. Cecelia wondered what Sidney was thinking—if she was angry that she had less room, or that her popularity contest wasn't the only thing that mattered, or something else. You never really knew what someone else was thinking. Robin was waving, and the breeze blew her hair off her shoulders. Cecelia wondered where Robin's parents were, but then she saw them, off to the left of the float, standing in the middle of the dead-end street that led from the roundabout to the river. Robin's father had his hands over his mouth and he was crying, crying and smiling, crying and laughing and cheering all at once. Robin's mother was pumping her fists in the air, and Cecelia felt so proud of her friend, and proud of herself at knowing the difference between privacy and secrecy, between being a support and an accessory. Cecelia waved at Robin's parents, having forgotten, for the moment, that her own parents were also in the crowd somewhere.

Porter saw the CJHS float coming, the young girls standing on top in their seasonally inappropriate dresses, as if their youth made them impervious to weather. When she'd been the Harvest Queen, on the high school float, she'd felt like an adult. But she wasn't, was she, no matter what she thought at the time. Her dress had been green, and flowy, made for disco. Astrid had hated it, had tried so hard—with bribery, with insults—to get her to wear something else. Bob Baker had driven the float. Porter couldn't even remember who the other girls were. She'd known her parents were there somewhere, and Nicky, and Jeremy, and everyone, but she hadn't wanted to see them. That just felt embarrassing. But then she'd heard her name and realized it was her parents, standing on the sidewalk in front of the hardware store, both of them waving. She had seen her mother more clearly than her father—years later, Porter would hate that this was true. She should have jumped down from the float like an action movie heroine and run up to him, putting her face just inches away from his and clicked her internal camera right then. She wanted to remember him better than she did. But that day she hadn't minded the fuzziness—it had made things easier. And so she'd bared her teeth and laughed with her mouth open, genuinely happy.

When her period still hadn't come that weekend, Porter told Jeremy to get a pregnancy test and bring it to school. The two pink lines didn't even wait the full minute that the test said they might. Jeremy had thought she was being dramatic—he said he was good at pulling out. When they'd driven to the clinic in New Paltz, Porter had been too stunned to cry. No part of her had wanted a baby. That was never on the table. The way she'd seen it, the rest of her life was on the table—her entire future. This or that, this or that. She couldn't have both. Every year there was at least one girl in school who got pregnant and got bigger and bigger as the year progressed, until one day she vanished, like a puff of smoke. Sometimes the girls came back and finished, but mostly they didn't. You'd

see them around town, pushing strollers, or playing with their babies on playgrounds, sometimes
the same playgrounds where the high schoolers
would meet at night to smoke joints and drink
wine coolers.

"I think we should take a break," she had said,
looking out the window. "When this is done, I
mean." This was what she'd thought: that her parents were more likely to find out if she and Jeremy
stayed together. She was giving him a present. Had
he realized that? She'd given him the present of
not thinking about it, of putting it out of his mind
forever. It had just been an afternoon. That was
how good her body was—she could hold it all,
even the memory of the tiny cells she would get rid
of. When Jeremy drove her home after, her parents
had been out. Nicky had been in her room, smoking a joint out her window, and he was the only
person she told. Next year, the Harvest would have
a new queen. That was the way it went for girls.

"There they are, there they are," Nicky said. He
pointed to the float that was coming slowly down
the street. Cecelia was wearing a long dress, and she
walked awkwardly in it, her legs not able to go as
far as they usually did in a stride. Instead of looking at the crowd and waving as the rest of the kids
walking alongside the float were, she was staring
up. Porter followed Cecelia's gaze and saw Jeremy's

daughter, sullen and blue with cold, standing next to a radiant girl in yellow. Was that August? It was. Porter tried to think about the bravest thing she'd ever done, and after a few seconds of searching her brain, she put her hands on her belly.

"I'm going to the bathroom," Porter said to Nicky and Juliette, who were so transfixed by the sight of their daughter willingly participating in the town's ritual that they both responded with barely audible grunts. The twins were the happiest Porter had ever seen, waving at everyone, and Wendy and Elliot both beamed, at each other and the world. It took so little, truly, to turn a parent's frown upside down.

The municipal hall's bathroom was in the same place as it always had been, and Porter squeaked her way down the hall. There were parents with children everywhere—dads unapologetically on their telephones, as if whatever they had to talk about couldn't wait an hour, and moms chased smaller siblings up and down the hallway, backs hunched over and fingers reaching. There was a short line for the bathroom, and everyone amiably smiled and then ignored one another.

The stall door swung open. The belly came out first—a massive pregnant bump that put Porter's to shame, nearly a full circle. The dress surrounding the bump was skintight, with vertical red and white stripes, a gigantic human peppermint, like something out of Willy Wonka. Porter's eyes traveled up the woman's body until they got to her head. Kristen Fogelman caught Porter's eyes and smiled.

"Oh, hey," Kristen said. She pointed to Porter's belly. "Congratulations. Jeremy told me that you were expecting."

"Yes," Porter said, her mind shouting a host of expletives that she was trying hard to keep on the inside of her body. Her mouth felt as if someone had patted her tongue dry with a paper towel. She sifted through all the words in her brain until she finally spat out a complete sentence. She pointed to Kristen's beach ball. "I didn't know."

"You didn't?" Kristen shook the excess water off her hands. "That's weird. But I guess that's how it is with your third baby. The bloom is off the rose." She wrinkled her nose. "Though I don't feel like a rose so much as a watermelon at the moment."

"That's quite an age difference you've got," Porter said, trying to think if it was possible that Jeremy actually **was** the father of her baby, even though she knew it wasn't true. They hadn't used condoms, she and Jeremy, on four different occasions now, and Porter imagined all his thousands of tiny little sperm hiding away inside her body, finding new eggs that weren't yet spoken for, and taking up residence, waiting for this baby to be born before really taking root. Had she learned nothing? "Is he here? Jeremy?"

"Oh, sure, of course. Sidney and her friends are

the little queens today, so cute. But yeah, I know," Kristen said. "Built-in babysitters!" She straightened up and stepped toward Porter. Kristen came within an inch of Porter and then stopped, her mouth so close to Porter's ear that they were almost touching. "Just so we're clear," she said. "He was never going to choose you. Everyone knows, Porter. You're the only one who thinks you've got a secret. Kind of makes it even sadder, doesn't it?" Kristen put her hands under her enormous belly. "It's fine. You're going to grow up someday. Or you're not." She walked away, hips swinging like a majestic elephant who knew its rightful place in the animal kingdom.

"Right," Porter said. There was a line of women behind her now, all waiting patiently for their turn. When Porter didn't immediately head into the stall, the woman behind her—Porter recognized her, she worked at Croissant City—piped up. "Aren't you going in?" Porter shook her head, and the woman ducked inside the bathroom. He'd come back for more because she'd let him, not because he was unhappy with his marriage. Porter shuffled into the bathroom the next time it opened and sat down. She could hear the sounds of the parade outside, the merriment, the people. Vasectomies were reversible, another win for the male ego. He hadn't told her, of course. Porter made herself a wad of toilet paper and tried to breathe into it, a makeshift paper bag, but tiny fibers flew off and into her throat. She coughed and coughed, forgetting that she was in public, forgetting that she would ever have to get up and move, and see her family. See anyone's family. See August's parents, who were clearly doing the right thing, and her brothers, who were trying. See Astrid, who was in love. Porter didn't know how, after everything, she'd managed to be the biggest failure of all.

"Porter?" a voice called from the other side of the stall door. Astrid's firm knock was unmistakable. "Porter, what's going on? Are you all right?"

"Hi, Mom," Porter said. She leaned forward and unlocked the door. Her mother stared down at her and then took a tentative step into the stall, squeezing to the side until she could close the door behind herself.

"Okay," Astrid said, crouching low, their foreheads now level, their knees knocking against each other. "It's going to be okay. You are strong, and you are brave, and you are going to be a great mother."

That made Porter sob harder. "Those are the three nicest things you've ever said to me. You can space them out, you know."

"I'll try," Astrid said, and put her arms around Porter's shoulders, letting Porter's weight fall against her like she had as a baby.

Chapter 41

Team Kids, Part Two

After the parade was done and everyone disembarked the floats, it was as if Robin had won Harvest Queen. Sidney Fogelman kept her distance, but her henchmen were among those crowding around to congratulate Robin on her bravery. Liesel took a selfie. Almost all the seventh-grade girls huddled around Robin and told her that she looked beautiful in her dress, because she did. Nicky saw Robin's parents—noses running, eyes gleaming—a few yards away and went to say hello. Porter and Astrid came back from the bathroom and huddled together in front of Shear Beauty. So many people were talking that it took Porter's family a minute to realize that something else was going on when she staggered back into the clump of her family.

Elliot leaned over to whisper in his sister's ear. It was noisy, and Porter was having a hard time talking, and so Elliot crouched next to her and waited. Nicky came back up from talking to Robin's parents and then quickly sank down next to his brother. Astrid watched their three heads—from above it was easier to see how they all looked alike, their hair the same shade of brown, their backs all curving the same way—and she felt that surely she hadn't done every single thing wrong. Small victories carried the day, didn't they?

Nicky and Elliot rocketed back up to standing and looked around—past Astrid—and then Nicky pointed toward the other side of the street, which was still mostly closed off to cars and therefore full of people. They jogged across, toward Jeremy Fogelman. He was leaning against the window of Elliot's building, smiling at nothing. Sidney and her mother were receiving guests on the corner like a deposed dictator and her second-in-command, but Jeremy didn't seem to be in a hurry to do anything. Nicky and Elliot appeared in front of him. The street was noisy, and they all had to shout in order to be heard.

Porter watched them and said, "No no no no! No! Guys! No," but her brothers were too far away to hear her. She watched as Jeremy stuck out his hand, and Elliot knocked it away. Jeremy raised his hands in fake surrender. Kristen and Sidney were watching now, and pretending not to. All

Porter could think about was all the therapy that Sidney Fogelman was going to need someday, and how much of it she herself was responsible for. Wendy and the twins had wandered closer to a float to examine its mechanics, thank god. Porter didn't want to feel responsible for ruining everything.

It wasn't as if she'd never thought about it—of course she had. That's why Porter had broken up with Jeremy in the first place. Or in the second place, the second time. As adults. She'd broken up with Jeremy because she wanted to be someone who made good decisions, and who felt valued for more than her willingness to play pretend. She'd made the choice to have a baby, she'd been doing great, and now this? What was it that made her fall back? Porter felt that if she fell any further back, she'd be dinosaur food. It was Cecelia's being in the house, and seeing Rachel, all these things that made her feel like she had time traveled back to her youth, when in reality those years were gone, gone, gone. And she knew she didn't miss them.

"Everyone makes mistakes, Porter," Astrid had said in the bathroom. "You don't have to be perfect. You don't even have to pretend to be perfect." But she wasn't watching the boys.

Elliot's finger was pointed at Jeremy's face, only an inch of air between them.

"Oh, god," Porter said. She pushed herself up and hustled across the street just as Elliot was drawing his arm back. She dodged a large, friendly golden retriever in the middle of the sidewalk and made it to her brother just in time to see Elliot let his fist fly directly into Jeremy Fogelman's nose. Or rather, it would have flown directly into Jeremy Fogelman's nose if Jeremy hadn't ducked out of the way. Elliot's fist, instead, connected with the part of the Plateglass window where Jeremy's face had been.

"You idiot!" Porter shouted. "That is not what is happening here! What the hell are you doing?"

"I'm protecting you," Elliot said, clearly stunned, as a tiny crack formed in the window, and quickly spidered out. Jeremy stepped out of the way, in case the wall of glass was about to come crashing down. Elliot was breathing hard, his fists balled at his sides, unsure what to do next. "Fuck, man, that's my window!" he decided to say. "Damn!"

"I don't need to be protected," Porter said, gently. "And I definitely don't need to be protected from that loser." Jeremy shrugged and hurried away before the Stricks could change their minds.

"I tried to tell him," Nicky said.

"You said he dumped her! And that he didn't tell Porter that his wife was pregnant, which is such a dick move!"

"That is not what I said," Nicky said. "I don't think that's what I said."

"You guys," Porter said to her brothers. "Thank you for trying to stick up for me, but I do not need it. I mean, I do need it, and I will need it, a lot, but not like that. This is not about Jeremy, okay? This is about me."

"All Stricks across the street, right now," Astrid said. She had hurried behind Porter and was hovering, but enough was enough. If they were still her children, then she was still their mother. She clapped sharply and then hurried into the middle of the street, holding a hand in front of her like a stop sign. She waited as her three children and Juliette and Cecelia all crossed, safe from the handful of cautious drivers who had returned to the road, which was still thick with bodies. Wendy and the twins looked up and followed, confused about the family procession, but getting it quickly: The Stricks were on the move, and they were doing it together. It was right here, Astrid realized, that Barbara had been standing. If she could go back in time and escort Barbara back onto the sidewalk, if they could have had a real conversation, standing next to the mailbox, would Elliot's hand be flecked with shards of glass? Would Porter be carrying on like a teenager, would she and Birdie be carrying on like teenagers? Astrid hurried into Shear Beauty and riffled around under the counter until she found the plastic bin full of Band-Aids and antiseptic ointment. Everyone else sat on the bench. The boys went loose in the salon, and Wendy held Elliot's wounded fist and then kissed his knuckles.

"Let me see if I get this right," Cecelia said. "I

try to make sure my friend doesn't get, like, raped and murdered, and I get shipped out of town. I punch someone, and somehow I'm the family role model?"

Astrid jostled back into the narrow hall and handed Wendy the box. "What in the world, truly."

"Can we just focus on me for a second?" Porter asked. "I didn't ask you to hit him. It was my mistake, not his. I wasn't crying because I was mad at him, I was mad at myself." She had stopped crying and was holding her belly.

"I didn't even want to hit him!" Elliot said. "I don't want to hit anybody! I feel like I was just trying to overcorrect in the protectiveness department."

Nicky reached out to Cecelia. "Honey, I am so sorry. I am so sorry. We totally fucked it up. I know you didn't do anything. Before you hit the girl in the face, I mean. You should never hit anyone in the face." Here he glared at his brother, with only a slight twinkle of amusement. "I know you didn't do what Katherine said. I just wanted to get you out of harm's way. But I know how it seemed, like we weren't behind you. We are always behind you, my love. Okay? Always."

Cecelia's eyes stung. She looked up from her father and stared at the wall behind him. She examined a corner of the wallpaper she hadn't noticed before, a line where two sheets met and didn't quite line up, a hiccup in the repeating image. A stuttering bouquet of flowers. When her father had been her age, what had he imagined his life would be? Did boys dream about marriage and children? Did girls? Cecelia didn't. She dreamed about city buses passing beneath her window, and garbage trucks. She dreamed about her friends. She didn't want to be happy or sad, she wanted to be normal, and to have normal parents, whatever that meant. Robin had given her a copy of a book about Elizabeth Taylor and one of her husbands, about their tempestuous love affair, and throughout the book, which was full of airplanes and hotel rooms and fancy cars, there were always her children and pets in the background, wildly ignored while she was busy throwing flowerpots at her lover's head. Cecelia had to stop reading. She preferred Richard Scarry books, where parents of all species were always helping their children brush their teeth or escape a runaway truck full of ketchup.

"Robin invited me over for dinner tonight," she said. "Can I go?"

"Of course," Nicky said. He held up his hand until Cecelia took it in hers, and then he gave a squeeze. "Who's Robin?"

The bell tinkled, and everyone turned to look. Birdie pushed open the door with her hip, holding a bottle of wine in one hand and a bouquet of flowers in the other. Astrid and Birdie hadn't been hiding all these years, but it felt good to do better than not hide. Everything seemed more unseemly the longer it was kept out of the light, and there was nothing unseemly about Birdie—she was hardworking and kind and funny and beautiful.

"Bird," Astrid said.

Elliot was tapping his foot next to Wendy on the bench, bobbing his head like he was listening to music that no one else could hear. They were all in such close quarters, like rush-hour commuters, only with nowhere to go. He clenched his teeth, a habit he'd developed as an angry teenager. Why had he been so angry? Why hadn't his mother helped? It was so easy to look backward and see the way through the maze, and so much harder when the way out was still in front of you.

"About what you said," Elliot said to Astrid, still bobbing in place. "I've been thinking. About what you said when you came over. I do remember. Jack. And what you said. I'm just not, you know. It wasn't anything. I mean it wasn't anything serious, it was just . . ." Elliot got a funny look on his face. "It's embarrassing to talk about it with your mother, you know, but whatever. I think it meant more to Jack than it did to me, if you know what I mean. But that's not what you have to apologize for."

Now Astrid was paying attention. "Okay?"

Elliot nodded, clearly chewing on something inside. "You told Dad that I wasn't smart enough to

be a lawyer. Or good enough. You guys were outside laughing, talking about me being an idiot."

Astrid put her fingers to her lips. "I said what?
When was this? I don't think I said that."

"You definitely said it. I don't know, it was the
summer I started working at Valley. And you and
Dad were outside, and I was in the kitchen, and I
heard you. Dad **laughed**. But he felt bad about it,
I could tell. But you weren't laughing. **That's** what
I want an apology for, not for when some kid tried
to kiss me when I was fourteen or whatever."

"Shit," Porter said.

"Damn," Nicky said.

"Yeah, and so I'm sorry if I'm a little bit para-
lyzed, you know, when it comes to making decisions, or to having the career that I want, but it's
kind of hard when you know even your parents
think you're a total idiot."

Astrid shook her head, her mouth hanging
open. "No, oh no, honey!" she said. "I said that?"
She reached over Cecelia and Nicky and put
her hand on Elliot's wrist. "Oh, god. And poor
Barbara. I was so ashamed—not of you, but of
how I reacted—that I avoided her for so long that
I forgot why! Until she got hit by the bus, I hadn't
actually **thought** about why I didn't like her in
years! I love you," she said. She wished she could
have a printout of all the mistakes she'd made as
a parent, the big ones and the small ones, just to

see how many of them she could guess (her temper was always shortest at bathtime) and how many she couldn't. She wondered how much her secrets had led to Porter's secrets, what pain she could have saved along the way.

"Also," Elliot said, raising a finger between them like a pause button, "the reason that I'm telling you is that I just want to do the right thing. For you, for Dad, for Clapham. I don't want to be the asshole that turns the town into something else, you know? I want you to be wrong." Wendy clutched his arm. She loved him—Astrid hated that she'd ever thought of her as anything other than perfect, if Wendy looked at her son that way. That was all anyone could ever need, really.

"I was wrong," Astrid said. She didn't remember the day he mentioned, but they'd had a hundred conversations like that, about their children. About each of them. That's what happened in marriages, and with children—you talked about the good things and the bad things and one was usually up and another was down. That's how it was with her and Russell—she was the bad cop and he was the good one. But it was all just a way of sorting out all the things that made up life. It was too much, otherwise, too enormous a feat to wrap your head around. Sometimes Astrid thought that they'd had a third baby because the first two seemed a bit cracked, and they wanted a fresh start. A fresh start at parenting. But the children should never know. They should always have perfect confidence in themselves and their adults. The words came easily now. "You've never disappointed me," Astrid said. "And it's not up to me, Elliot. Your life? Your choices? They don't belong to me. Neither does this town—not any more than it belongs to any of you." She looked into her son's eyes and thought about the moment he was born, about how he came out of her body and Russell had cried and that they had both looked at this brand-new baby, who was as beautiful a thing as they'd ever seen, and how the nurse had passed Elliot—still bloody, still screaming—to Russell, who handed him to Astrid. She hadn't ever really been naked before that moment, Astrid thought—that was the very bottom layer of her person, giving birth to a child and then holding that child against her body; inside, then outside. What kind of parents had they been? The poor children expected love without context, but context always existed—Astrid had not liked breastfeeding, Elliot had been fussy, he was born in winter and so they were all trapped indoors, unlike Porter and Nicky, who were lucky and had birthdays in April and June. Who ever did something right the first try? Astrid knew that she had failed, maybe not in the ways that she thought she had, but in so many ways she had never even noticed. This was the job of a parent: to fuck up, over and over again. This was the job of a child: to grow up anyway.

Elliot stood in front of her, holding his elbows.

"Your father was so proud of you," Astrid said. "He would be so proud of you. Do you know that he couldn't sleep after you were born, and so he took the night shifts? He would sit in the rocking chair in your bedroom and watch you sleep. Sometimes I would come in in the morning and he'd be asleep in the chair and you'd be awake, and babbling, like you were the one who'd been watching over him." She reached out and held on to his wrist. "Without you, we wouldn't have been parents. We would have just been two people, spinning in their own orbits. You were what made us a family. I love you."

Elliot didn't want to cry and so he didn't. "Whatever. Okay. I love you too." That was as good a reaction as she could expect. There they were, both standing on the same ever-shifting ground.

Birdie had made her way closer and was now standing just over Elliot's shoulder. "Hi," she said, peeking over, as if his body were a hedge. "Hi," Astrid said back.

Elliot walked around Astrid, toward the back of the salon, where he stood still for a few seconds before turning to his brother and putting his arm around his shoulder. The twins were at the sink in the back, spraying each other. There would be water to clean up later, but no one hurried to stop them. Astrid heard Nicky and Elliot begin to talk about the 1994 Knicks, and who'd been a more important part of the team, John Starks or Patrick Ewing, and Astrid put her hands on Birdie's cheeks and kissed her on the lips and thought, **I want to marry you,** and then she opened her mouth and said, into Birdie's ear, "I want to marry you." If she hadn't learned anything else, she had learned this—say it. Say it now, while you have the chance.

Chapter 42

Barbara Goes Wild

Barbara always bought orange juice with no pulp, because that's what Bob preferred. He had narrowly spaced teeth, and if she bought the extra-pulpy kind, which she liked because it tasted the most like orange juice and the least like water, then it would get caught in his teeth like a lobster in a trap, unable to get loose without manual assistance. And so Barbara bought orange juice meant for picky children, and she didn't complain. She had time during the day, to do what she liked, and so she could compromise when it came to things that weren't important.

When Bob retired and was home all day, Barbara realized it wasn't just the juice. He needed help, always. Help making lunch, help figuring out whether he wanted to go for a walk, help deciding on the route and whether to wear a jacket. Bob followed her to the bathroom and would keep talking to her through the door as she did her business. Some of her friends had warned her about this phenomenon, that husbands needed hobbies, but Bob didn't want a hobby unless it was attached to Barbara, and so Barbara decided to get herself a hobby instead, somewhere Bob couldn't follow.

"What do you mean, braces?" Bob asked. "For your teeth?"

"Yes, for my teeth," Barbara said. "What other kinds of braces are there?"

There were other kinds, though, she knew, because she had done research. There were so many kinds that she'd never heard of! There were the metal kind, of course, but then there were plastic ones, and ceramic ones, and braces that ran along the inside of your teeth, and invisible ones, like condoms, that fit over your teeth! The brightly colored rubber bands were available for anyone who desired more self-expression. There were so many choices, and so many visits necessary. Barbara was excited.

A new orthodontia practice had opened across the river in Kingston, which would take Barbara twice as long to get to as Dr. Piesman, who affixed metal brackets to every adolescent's teeth in Clapham. That was part of the point, the time it would take to drive there and back. Barbara had searched online and found a dentist with a nice photo, a young man with a white coat and a (of course) gleaming smile. Barbara wanted a smile like that—her teeth had started to drift decades ago, slow as glaciers, but now they had solidly collided with each other and overlapped at odd angles, everything the color of pale yellow corn on the cob. It was time.

River Valley Orthodontics was on the first floor of a newly renovated building in downtown Kingston. The waiting room was neat, as it had not yet been destroyed by teenagers putting their dirty sneakers on the seats of chairs. Barbara gave her name at the desk and then waited for her name to be called. When the dental hygienist led Barbara into the exam room and she put her purse on a chair in the corner, Barbara was happier than she would have been at a day spa, a place in which she always felt too old and too soft. But taking care of your teeth wasn't vanity. Teeth were important.

The hygienist attached a paper bib around Barbara's neck and adjusted the chair so that Barbara was lying parallel to the floor.

"Would you like to watch something?" the hygienist asked through her mask. She was arranging tools on a little steel tray, and they clinked as she set them all in a straight row.

"Watch something? Oh, no, thank you," Barbara said. She wasn't one of those people who needed to be stimulated all the time, with a smartphone and a TV screen and a podcast in her eardrum. She liked to be where she was.

"Are you sure? We have Netflix." The hygienist swiveled a small rectangle until it hung directly over Barbara's face. She clicked a button and the screen lit up.

"No, no, thank you," Barbara said again, now self-conscious about her choice. The menu screen stayed illuminated, and so she stared at the colorful little boxes, each one promising a half hour of jolly entertainment. The hygienist patted her on the arm and told her that the dentist would be in shortly.

Barbara hadn't had braces as a child—her teeth had been straight enough, and it wasn't so common then, not like it was when she was a crossing guard and half the middle schoolers had mouths full of metal. When she was twelve, in 1962, her only worry had been how to make her hair curl like Shirley Jones in **The Music Man**. It never did, and eventually she stopped trying. Her sister, Carol, had the curls in the family, and the attention from the boys, and the worry from their parents. Her sister was the pretty one, and Barbara, two years younger, was the family dog, dutiful and always hungry for scraps.

After high school, Barbara had taken courses at Norwalk Community College, some business administration classes, with thoughts of becoming a secretary. Carol wanted to be an actress and had moved to Los Angeles, where she was living with a man whom she wasn't married to, a source of great pain for their parents. Barbara met Bob in the small cafeteria—he was studying engineering— and they had an easy time together. Barbara couldn't remember a single conversation they'd had in that period, just that Bob looked at her like she were the movie star, like she was important, and desirable, and before long they were engaged and then married. Her parents were thrilled, and the wedding—in the backyard in high summer, with two dozen guests, mostly friends of her mother's—was short and sweet. Barbara had worn pearls, and Carol had scowled throughout, irritated at their parents for not inviting her boyfriend, just because he was (as it turned out) married to someone else. It was 1972, and free love still hadn't reached Connecticut.

Of course she and Bob planned to have children. That was what you did. The only woman Barbara knew who had chosen not to have children was her maiden aunt Dora, a nurse who lived happily with a roommate in Rhode Island, and who brought her roommate home for holidays with several pies and cakes that they'd baked and no one thought anything of it except that it was rather sad that two very nice women had never found men to marry them. Barbara wanted to have enough children to spread the responsibility and pressure evenly, the way a baseball team all felt it was their duty to get a hit, not just whoever was swinging the bat at any given moment.

And they had tried. Barbara remembered tossing her diaphragm in the garbage dramatically after the wedding, though she went back later that night to rescue it. She and Bob made love over and over that week, almost every night, so excited to finally live together. They had had sex before the wedding, but not often—it had been too hard to find the space and time to be alone. But now, in their own apartment, they could have sex whenever they liked, and so they did. Barbara drew the curtains, as if anyone could peek into their second-floor windows, and when they got home from work, after a perfunctory dinner, they would leap into bed and play with each other's bodies like the shiniest toys on their birthdays.

When a year passed and Barbara still hadn't gotten pregnant, she went to her doctor, who asked lots of questions about her menstrual cycle and took what felt like pints of blood from the crook of her arm. The next year, there was a miscarriage, and the year after that, two more. Barbara's doctor told her that she could expect more of the same, and that she should look into adoption, if parenthood was what she was after. She and Bob talked about it for years, until Barbara was thirty, and finally Bob said, "You know, Barb, I just don't think I want someone else's baby," and then that was that. It was a good thing to know about yourself, Barbara thought. Better to know that and not do it than to feel conflicted and go ahead with it. Better for the long term, anyway. She didn't feel that way—she could have loved any baby put in her arms, she knew it like she knew her own name— but it wasn't only up to her, was it.

The door creaked and Barbara turned. The young dentist whose picture she'd seen on the website walked in and sat down on the stool next to her.

"Hi there," he said. "I'm Dr. Dan. You can call me Dr. Weiss, if you like, but most of my patients call me Dr. Dan." He shook Barbara's hand, which was a little bit clammy from resting on her forearm as it had been. She hoped he didn't notice.

"Hello," Barbara said. She smiled. He was even more handsome in person, not yet thirty, she guessed, with hair that looked freshly trimmed and only the slightest hint of razor burn on his cheeks where he had no doubt shaved that morning.

"Can I take a look?" he said, and pointed toward her mouth.

Barbara rolled her eyes with embarrassment. "Of course," she said, and opened wide.

"Now bite down? And let me see you smile?" Dr. Dan bit and then smiled, for reference. The walls of the office were painted a pale orange, like a Californian sunset. Barbara knew certain colors were supposed to make people feel certain ways—that people fought more in red rooms, that sort of thing. Maybe orange was supposed to put you at ease? Dr. Dan probably knew. Barbara demonstrated the movement of her jaw. "I see," Dr. Dan said. "May I?" He waited for Barbara's nod, then gently reached his gloved hands into her mouth, one on each side of her teeth. It was so funny, going to the doctor, who was, in most cases, a stranger, and feeling totally free to let them touch whatever part of your body you'd agreed to by making the appointment. He slid his fingertips alongside Barbara's teeth, slipping from one to the next, like a bicycle ride over gentle, rolling hills. She closed her eyes as he lowered his hands to her bottom teeth and bumped along those too. No one touched her anymore. At night, Bob snuggled close, hugging her torso like a koala bear, but five minutes later he'd roll away and start to snore. She couldn't remember the last time he had reached underneath her clothes. And who else? Barbara tried to make a mental list of people who physically touched her and couldn't think of a single one, except a woman for whom she'd held open the door at the bank, who had patted Barbara's shoulder like you would a Labrador after it dropped a saliva-coated tennis ball at your feet. This was different. This was attentive. Barbara pushed everything else out of her head and concentrated on the feeling of Dr. Dan's young, strong hands in her mouth.

"Okay," he said. Dr. Dan slowly slid his hands

out and then pulled off his gloves. "This is going to be no problem. Let's get you fitted with a mold. I think six months with brackets would do just what you need. Maybe a year. And we could do natural, instead of silver, so that they're tooth-colored, and less noticeable. A lot of adults like that."

Barbara nodded. "Oh, that'd be great." She wanted him to put his hands back in her mouth. There were those women in Japan, weren't there, who were paid not to sleep with men, but just to sit and talk with them? That was what she wanted. Not sex, necessarily, or even the future promise of sex. She wanted a companion who didn't need anything from her. She wanted someone to buy the juice she liked, without her asking, and kiss her on the cheek when he delivered it. Surely that sort of thing existed. It was America, wasn't it, where everything was possible? But it wasn't the sort of thing she could look up on her computer, because what if Bob saw? Couldn't people see what you'd looked for? Not that Bob knew how.

"And how often would I need to come in?" Barbara hoped she didn't sound too eager.

Dr. Dan shrugged. "Every six weeks would be great. Smile for me again?" Barbara smiled. "Oh yeah," Dr. Dan said. "Every six weeks should do it. I think this will be great. And plus, we'll get to spend so much time together!" He laughed. No one wanted to spend time with their dentist. No one but Barbara. She laughed at his joke and then laughed longer at her own. Dr. Dan looked pleased. "Okay then! Cassidy will take some x-rays and get everything set up so that we can get the impressions we need. Sound good? I'll be back."

Barbara swallowed. "Yes, thank you." She watched Dr. Dan swivel his stool toward the door and then leap up gracefully, Gene Kelly in a lab coat. She snuggled back into the chair and stared up at the screen. Who would look at that when they could look at Dr. Dan? When the appointment was over, Barbara booked her follow-up in five weeks, fibbing and saying she was going to be traveling, and wanted to fit it in before she went away, though she wasn't actually going anywhere at all.

Bob was waiting by the door when Barbara got home. "How was it?" he asked. The cats jogged down the front steps to greet her and rubbed their bodies against her bare legs. She supposed they had adopted, after all, and Bob hadn't really noticed. If they'd had children, she might not have been so angry at him. She'd thought of the children she'd crossed back and forth across the street all those thousands of times as her children, but they weren't, not really. They went home to their own mothers, who knew best. Barbara had just been an onlooker, a bystander. That wasn't the same. If they'd had children, Bob would be inside, talking to one of them on the telephone, bothering them about their daily lives the way he bothered her. Bob would have been a great father; that stung. But now, so many decades later, he was the child and she was the parent and she only had the one life, didn't she? "Did you stop on the way home and get orange juice?" Bob asked. "We only have the thick kind."

"No," Barbara said. She was still young enough to make decisions. Barbara walked past Bob, nearly tripped over a sleeping cat—oh, she would miss those cats at night—and walked straight up the stairs into her bedroom and packed a small overnight bag. She'd figure out the details. For now, this was enough.

"Where are you going, Barb?" Bob asked, his eyes wide. He watched her walk back down the stairs, back through the door, and back toward her car.

"I'm going to my mother's for a bit, Bob," Barbara said. "I'll be in touch. The juice you like is in the milk aisle, just so you know, at the store. On the right. Just past the milk."

Bob opened his mouth but no words came out. Barbara put her bag in the back seat, shut the door with a **thunk,** and then drove toward Heron Meadows. It was temporary. Everything was temporary. It was an illusion to believe otherwise. But nevertheless, it did feel good.

Epilogue

onths later, when Birdie and Astrid were planning their honeymoon, Astrid looked up Alaskan cruises and finally found just the right one: **This summer, come along as we explore America's icy frontier! This six-day cruise is round-trip out of Seattle and then sails right up the Pacific Coast, stopping in Ketchikan, Juneau, and Skagway before its final stop in beautiful Vancouver, Canada! The days are long, and from our decks you'll be able to see bald eagles, whales, bears, and sea lions. All this, plus glaciers and 1,200 lesbians! Now that's what we call a cruise.** Astrid booked it on the spot.

The baby—Porter's baby—Eleanor Hope Strick,

who Astrid had decided she was going to call Hopie—was six months old. She was tiny and well behaved, with a bald head and perfect circles for eyes, like a cartoon. Astrid had hemmed and hawed about going away, leaving them all alone, but Porter had insisted that she'd be fine—Nicky and Juliette had offered to come and stay to help—and so the newlyweds rolled their pulley suitcases to the airport and flew across the country to set sail.

The boat was enormous, much larger than Astrid had expected, though she'd seen photographs on the website. A hotel on water! And not the kind of hotel that Astrid was used to staying in, but a behemoth of a hotel, with a casino and a theater and three swimming pools and five different restaurants. She couldn't tell if the idea was to enjoy the boat or enjoy the world outside the boat—maybe it depended on the person. They were in a sea of women waiting to board, everyone excited and anxious and hauling their luggage, some kissing, some bickering with their wives or girlfriends or friends, some jostling with strangers about their spot in line, just like any airport departure gate where men had been willed out of existence. There were more young women than Astrid had expected—women in their forties, with a few maybe even still clinging to their thirties. She'd imagined it would be all old ladies like her and

Birdie, a sea of gray hairs, like the water aerobics class at the Rhinebeck YMCA.

"Here we go," Astrid said. She was a reluctant traveler. They'd gone to Disney World once, when the kids were ten, seven, and five, and Astrid had briefly lost Nicky while Russell took the bigger kids on Space Mountain, and the horror of it had lingered for the rest of their trip. She snapped at the children whenever they wandered out of her line of sight; she shouted when Elliot accidentally sent a pat of cold butter flying across the hotel restaurant. After that the Stricks never went anywhere they couldn't get to in their station wagon. And where would she have gone alone? Now it had been so long that she'd forgotten the point of travel in the first place. The boat looked too big, and for a moment, Astrid worried that it would sink immediately after they were all aboard, like a giant bath toy plunged to the seafloor.

Their room was on the Verandah Deck, the sixth floor out of ten. Uniformed staff lined the halls. "I feel like we're on **Downton Abbey**," Birdie said, bowing.

"Or the **Titanic**," Astrid whispered as she opened the door to their room, which looked like any other hotel room, only with furniture that was all bolted to the floor, and none of the stupid

knickknacks that always drove Astrid crazy—
decorative ceramic sea stars, a bowl of inedible
fruit. Maybe cruises were for practical people.
All along the deck outside their room, there were
heavy chairs and bins, everything cemented to the
ground so that it didn't fly off into the ocean and
knock a dolphin unconscious (Astrid assumed).
There were two life preservers in the closet, ready
for the muster drill they'd been warned about—
before the ship set sail, everyone had to practice
getting to their rescue stations, where they would
be counted and, theoretically, saved from a watery
death. It seemed an ominous start to a voyage, but
those were the rules.

On her first honeymoon, Astrid and Russell
had taken the train to Montreal. It was April,
and colder by far than they'd expected, and they
went home with their suitcases stuffed full of extra
layers, purchased in Canadian department stores
as needed. What else did she remember? They'd
played gin rummy in the hotel lobby, betting each
other peanuts, though the bartender kept refill-
ing both their bowls, so it didn't matter much
one way or the other. They'd made love every
day. Astrid thought about mayflies, who lived for
only a day, and tortoises, who lived for a hundred
years—neither creature had remotely the range of
experience a person could have. How funny, how
ridiculous, for Astrid still to be the same person

that she'd been in that hotel lobby, sitting across from Russell Strick.

The wedding had been small: the children, the grandchildren, a few friends. Nicky was already ordained from the internet (he'd married half a dozen pairs of his friends), and he performed the service, swearing to both of them that it was in all ways legal and legitimate. Porter cried, Cecelia cried, Wendy cried. They stood in a circle in the gazebo at nine o'clock on a Saturday morning. Nicky read a Mary Oliver poem and Birdie slid a ring onto Astrid's finger and Astrid slid a ring onto Birdie's finger and then there they were, in the middle of town, brides. Afterward, they all went to Spiro's for pancakes.

The ship had warned that internet service was spotty when they were at sea, and so Astrid made sure to find the business center. She wanted to check in at home before they were too far, just in case. She and Birdie sat in heavy chairs and dialed into a FaceTime with Porter. Astrid clapped her hands over her mouth when the screen went from showing their own faces to showing Eleanor Hope, her gummy mouth snacking on her mother's index finger.

"How is it?" Porter asked, only the lower half of her face in the frame.

"Great!" Birdie said.

"Great!" Astrid said. She squeezed Birdie's thigh. "She's gotten bigger since yesterday, don't you think?"

"Mom, have **fun,** please. Birdie, please make her have fun. Eleanor has not done anything exciting, I promise." Onscreen, the baby sucked and sucked, drenching Porter's finger.

"Well, no," said another voice in the background. The screen swiveled and Nicky's face swooped down to fill the frame. He was grinning, his open mouth so large on the computer screen that Astrid could see his fillings. "Eleanor rolled over, and then she rolled back! It was epic."

Astrid moaned. "Oh, no, I knew we were going to miss something."

Elliot appeared over his brother's shoulder. "It really was epic."

Porter took the phone back. "Shut up, guys. Mom, it's fine. Birdie, you guys have fun. Go adopt a seal, save a glacier, please, something." She pointed the camera back toward the baby, whose enormous brown eyes blinked at them.

Astrid rubbed Birdie's back. "Yes. Yes, we will."

Birdie blew a kiss. "Love you, Eleanor!"

There was so much that Astrid hadn't considered: getting married again, having someone to coparent, copilot, cograndparent! What a thing to do, to skip having children and go straight to being a grandparent. Birdie was magnificent at it: Of all the adults, she was the best at dancing Eleanor to sleep. Maybe it was her arms, strong from decades of steady scissor-holding, maybe it was that Astrid had used up her powers on her own children, maybe it was just that Eleanor and Birdie were fast friends. Astrid hadn't thought of herself as one of those people who just wanted to be married, but now that she was, she was so delighted, all over again. The word **wife,** which had once felt oppressive, diminutive, belittling— she thought of all the times she'd been introduced simply as Russell's wife, with no additional quali- fying details, nothing so brash as a name—now the word **wife** meant something else. It wasn't Russell's fault, it was the world's! Now that it was a double—your wife, my wife—the word felt twice its original size. This was how it was supposed to feel. It wasn't just that she belonged to someone else, it was that she belonged.

"Mom, it's fine," Porter said. "We are all fine. Honestly. We are all adults here. Except for Eleanor. She's just a baby. But we'll be fine. We love you. Have fun."

"Okay," Astrid said, and then Porter and Eleanor's round cheeks vanished into thin air too quickly, and she and Birdie were left staring at their own reflections. Sometimes Astrid thought about everything in her life that could have been different—all the men and women she could have married, having her children or not having any children at all, moving to Paris, she and Russell dying in bed together at a hundred years old. She thought about how every decision of hers had rippled into her children's lives, even this one, when she was still their mother every day but not actually in charge of their lives, not making decisions on their behalf. People said that everyone was born alone and everyone would die alone, but they were wrong. When someone was born, they brought so many people with them, generations of people zipped into the marrow of their tiny bones. She reached under the bolted-down desk and took Birdie's hand and it felt just the way it had felt on their first date. Astrid had still been young then, though she hadn't known it. Was it like that until you died, always realizing how young you'd been before, how foolish and full of possibility? Astrid hoped so. Outside, sunlight sparkled off the surface of the water, as if the ocean wanted to show the sky exactly how astonishing it was. Every day was a new day. She would call Cecelia later, and Wendy and the boys, her whole family. She'd call them until they were sick to death with love, just like she was. Astrid looked at their reflections on the blank screen, at herself and her wife, and felt so, so happy.

ACKNOWLEDGMENTS

My life changed enormously over the writing of this book, and so please forgive my lengthy acknowledgments. I was pregnant while writing my last two books (with two separate children—I am neither a speed machine nor an elephant), but while writing **All Adults Here,** I birthed a bookstore, with the help of my husband.

People sometimes have the misconception that working in a bookstore means sitting perched on a stool, reading in absolute silence for hours on end. Would that it were so! Books Are Magic is an elaborate beast full of boxes and orders and systems and eccentricities and, yes, thousands and thousands of books, as well as a staff of fifteen, and in the last two years, we've hosted more than six hundred events. The first person I need to thank is my husband, Michael Fusco-Straub, for caring for our bookstore, and for the people inside it, all day long, every single day, which made it possible for me to finish writing this book. The bookstore has made our lives both much richer and much harder, and I am grateful to my husband for keeping everything running beautifully in my absence. It is an astonishing amount of work, from changing lightbulbs to paying the bills and everything in between, and oh my stars, he is so good at it all.

Thank you also to the entire staff of Books Are Magic, without whom it would be a far less magical place. I value your brilliance, your energy, and your care. Thank you for bringing your whole selves to the bookstore, and for helping us to be a space where people want to spend time. Thank you to Eddie Joyce and Martine Beamon for believing in our potential so early on, and for being such wonderful partners.

Thank you to Alex Sagol and everyone at Cantine, where I spent many hours working on this book, and thank you to Audrey Gelman and the entire staff of the Wing Dumbo, where I spent many, many, **many** hours working on this book. The ability to sit somewhere comfortable that is not your own house, full as it is with laundry and toys to be put away, and to be fed and plied with endless pots of tea is an incredible gift, and I am grateful.

Thank you to my friends and family who were called upon for their various areas of expertise:

Laura Royal, Tyler Ford, John Fireman, Meg Wolitzer, and Adam Koehler.

Thank you to Julian Foster, my mother, and my sons' teachers for taking such good care of my children.

Thank you to Claudia Ballard, my agent and friend.

Thank you to Team Riverhead, and in particular to my thoughtful and emotionally astute editor, Sarah McGrath, who made this book better over and over again, and thank you to my hardworking sister-wives Claire McGinnis and Lydia Hirt, and to Geoff Kloske, Kate Stark, and Jynne Martin, for steering the ship in such a good direction. (It's a big steering wheel.) Thank you to Jessica Leeke and Gaby Young, my sister-wives across the pond at Michael Joseph.

When I was finishing this book, there were two things I encountered that led me to understand what I needed to do: the apology episode of Jenna Wortham and Wesley Morris's always brilliant podcast **Still Processing** and Mary Oliver's poetry, which crashed over me in a wave following her death. I recommend both things heartily.

EMMA STRAUB is the **New York Times**–bestselling author of three other novels, **The Vacationers, Modern Lovers,** and **Laura Lamont's Life in Pictures,** as well as the short story collection **Other People We Married.** Her books have been published in twenty countries. She and her husband own Books Are Magic, an independent bookstore in Brooklyn, New York.

EMMASTRAUB.NET